DANNY FISHER never got an even break.

He loved the house in Brooklyn where he had lived when he was small. But his family lost it and moved to a shabby East Side tenement. He might have been a sensational boxing champ. But he took a bribe and then forgot to lose. Persecuted for his religion, disowned by his father, hunted by crooked gamblers, Danny Fisher stood almost alone against the world.

Two girls believed in him, one a prostitute, and the other a girl he loved. With their faith and his toughness...and while there was still breath left in his scarred body, Danny would never quit!

Few novelists know the seamy side of New York life as well as Harold Robbins, or tell about it in so realistic a way, as readers of his novels *79 Park Avenue* and *Never Love a Stranger* can testify.

A STONE FOR DANNY FISHER
was originally published by Alfred A. Knopf, Inc.

HAROLD ROBBINS

A Stone for Danny Fisher

PUBLISHED BY POCKET BOOKS NEW YORK

A STONE FOR DANNY FISHER

Alfred A. Knopf edition published March, 1952

Pocket Book edition published March, 1953

37th printing........October, 1970

This *Pocket Book* edition includes every word
contained in the original, higher-priced edition. It is printed
from brand-new plates made from completely reset, clear, easy-to-read
type. *Pocket Book* editions are published by Pocket Books, a division
of Simon & Schuster, Inc., 630 Fifth Avenue, New York, N.Y. 10020.
Trademarks registered in the United States and other countries.

L

What man is there of you,

whom if his son ask bread,

will he give him a stone?

—MATTHEW vii, 9

CONTENTS

A STONE FOR DANNY FISHER

A Stone for Danny Fisher

Chapter One

THERE are many ways to get to Mount Zion Cemetery. You can go by automobile, through the many beautiful parkways of Long Island, or by subway, bus or trolley. There are many ways to get to Mount Zion Cemetery, but during this week there is no way that is not crushed and crowded with people.

"Why should this be so?" you ask, for in the full flush of life there is something frightening about going to a cemetery—except at certain times. But this week, the week before the High Holy Days, is one of these times. For this is the week that Lord God Jehovah calls His angels about Him and opens before them the Book of Life. And your name is inscribed on one of these pages. Written on that page will be your fate for the coming year.

For these six days the book will remain open and you will have the opportunity to prove that you are deserving of His kindness. During these six days you devote yourself to acts of charity and devotion. One of these acts is the annual visit to the dead.

And to make sure that your visit to the departed will be noted and the proper credit given, you will pick up a small stone from the earth beneath your feet and place it on the monument so that the Recording Angel will see it when he comes through the cemetery each night.

You meet at the time appointed under an archway of white stone. The words MOUNT ZION CEMETERY are etched into the stone over your head. There are six of you. You look awkwardly at one another and words come stiffly to your lips. You are all here. As if by secret agreement, without a word, you all begin to move at once and pass beneath the archway.

1

On your right is the caretaker's building; on your left, the record office. In this office, listed by plot number and burial society, are the present addresses of many people who have walked this earth with you and many who have walked this earth before your time. You do not stop to think of this, for to you, all except me belong to yesterday.

You walk up a long road searching for a certain path. At last you see its white numbers on a black disk. You turn up the path, your eyes reading the names of the burial societies over each plot section. The name you have been looking for is now visible to you, polished black lettering on gray stone. You enter the plot.

A small old man with a white tobacco-stained mustache and beard hurries forward to meet you. He smiles tentatively, while his fingers toy with a small badge on his lapel. It is the prayer-reader for the burial society. He will say your prayers in Hebrew for you, for such has been the custom for many years.

You murmur a name. He nods his head in birdlike acquiescence; he knows the grave you seek. He turns, and you follow him, stepping carefully over other graves, for space is at a premium here. He stops and points an old, shaking hand. You nod your head, it is the grave you seek, and he steps back.

An airplane drones overhead, going to a landing at a nearby airport, but you do not look up. You are reading the words on the monument. Peace and quiet come over you. The tensions of the day fall from your body. You raise your eyes and nod slightly to the prayer-reader.

He steps forward again and stands in front of you. He asks your names, so that he may include them in his prayer. One by one you answer him.

My mother.

My father.

My sister.

My sister's husband.

My wife.

My son.

His prayer is a singsong, unintelligible gibberish of words that echoes monotonously among the graves. But you are not listening to him. You are filled with memories of me, and to each of you I am a different person.

At last the prayer is done, the prayer-reader paid and gone to seek his duty elsewhere. You look around on the ground beneath you for some small stone. Carefully you hold it in your hand and, like the others, one at a time, step forward toward the monument.

Though the cold and snow of winter and the sun and rain of summer have been close to me since last you were here together, your thoughts are again as they were then. I am strong in each of your memories, except one.

To my mother I am a frightened child, huddling close to her bosom, seeking safety in her arms.

To my father I am a difficult son, whose love was hard to meet, yet strong as mine for him.

To my sister I am the bright young brother, whose daring was a cause of love and fear.

To my sister's husband I am the friend who shared the common hope of glory.

To my wife I am the lover, who, beside her in the night, worshiped with her at the shrine of passion and joined her in a child.

To my son—to my son I know not what I am, for he knew me not.

There are five stones lying on my grave and still, my son, you stand there wondering. To all the others I am real, but not to you. Then why must you stand here and mourn someone you never knew?

In your heart there is the tiny hard core of a child's resentment. For I have failed you. You have never made those boasts that children are wont to make: "My daddy is the strongest," or the smartest, or the kindest, or the most loving. You have listened in bitter silence, with a growing frustration, while others have said these things to you.

Do not resent nor condemn me, my son. Withhold your judgment, if you can, and hear the story of your father. I was human, hence fallible and weak. And though in my lifetime I made many mistakes and failed many people, I would not willingly fail you. Listen to me then, I beg you, listen to me, O my son, and learn of your father.

Come back with me to the beginning, to the very beginning. For we who have been of one flesh, of one blood, and of one heart are now come together in one memory.

Moving Day

JUNE 1, 1925

I GO back to the beginning of memory, and it is my eighth birthday. I am sitting in the cab of a moving-van, scanning the street-corner signs anxiously. As the big van neared one corner, it slowed down. "Is this the block?" the driver asked the colored man sitting next to me.

The big Negro turned to me. "Is this the block, boy?" he asked, his teeth, large and white, showing in his face.

I was so excited I could hardly speak. "This is it," I squeaked. I squirmed to look at the street. This was it. I recognized the houses, each looking like the others, with a slim young tree in front of each. It looked just as it did the day I went with Mamma and Papa, the day they bought the house for me, for my birthday.

Everybody had been smiling then, even the real-estate man who sold Papa the house. But Papa hadn't been fooling. He meant it. He told the real-estate man that the house had to be ready by June 1 because that was my birthday, and it was my birthday present.

And it was ready on the first just like Papa had wanted, because here it was June 1 and it was my eighth birthday and we were moving in.

Slowly the truck turned up the block. I could hear the soft biting of the tires into the gravel on the street as the van left the pavement. My new street wasn't even paved yet. It was covered with grayish-white gravel. Stones rattled as the tires picked them up and threw them against the mudguards.

I jumped up in the cab of the truck. "There it is!" I shouted, pointing. "That's my house! The last one on the block! The only one that stands by itself!"

4

The truck began to roll to a stop in front of the house. I could see our car standing in the driveway. Mamma and my sister, Miriam, who was two years older than I, had gone on before us to take the loaf of bread and box of salt into the house and to have things ready. Mamma had wanted me to come with her, but I had wanted to ride on the truck, and the head driver had said I might.

I tried to open the door of the cab before the truck had stopped, but the colored man kept his hand on it. "Wait a minute, boy," he said, smiling. "You'll be here a long time."

When the truck stopped, he released the door. Clambering down from the cab, I slipped on the running board in my hurry and sprawled in the street. I heard a muttered curse behind me and then felt strong hands pick me up and put me on my feet.

The Negro's deep voice asked in my ear: "Are you hurt, boy?"

I shook my head. I don't suppose I could have spoken even if I'd wanted to; I was too busy looking at my house.

It was brown-red brick halfway up and then brown shingles up to the edge of the roof. The roof was covered with black shingles, and there was a little porch, sort of, in front of the house, like a stoop. It was the most beautiful house I had ever seen. I drew a deep proud breath and looked down the street to see if anybody was watching. There was no one there We were the first people on the whole block to move in.

The colored man was standing beside me. "Sho is a pretty house," he said. "You a mighty lucky boy to own a fine house like that."

I smiled at him gratefully because when I had told him how Papa had given it to me for my birthday, he had scoffed like everyone else Then I was running up the steps and knocking at the door. "Mamma, Mamma!" I hollered. "It's me. I'm here!"

The door opened and Mamma was standing there, a rag tied around her head. I pushed past her into the house and came to a stop in the middle of the room. Everything in the house smelled new. The paint on the walls, the wood on the stairs, everything was new.

I heard Mamma ask the driver what took him so long. I missed his reply because I was looking up the staircase, but Mamma came back into the room saying something about their stretching the job because they get paid by the hour.

I grabbed at her arm. "Mamma, which room is mine?" I asked. For the first time I was going to have a room of my own. Before this we had lived in an apartment and I had shared a room with my sister. Then one morning just before Papa decided to buy me a house, Mamma came into our room as I was sitting up in bed watching Mimi get dressed. Mamma looked at me and later that day at breakfast told us that we were going to get a house and from now on I would have a room of my own.

Now she shook her hand free of mine. "It's the first one at the side of the stairs, Danny," she answered excitedly. "And keep out of the way. I have a lot to do!"

I bolted up the stairs, the heels of my shoes making loud clumping sounds. At the top of the stairs I hesitated a moment while I look around. Mamma and Papa had the big room in front, then came Miriam's room, then mine. I opened the door to my room and walked in softly.

It was a small room about ten feet wide and fourteen feet long. It had two windows in it and through them I could see the two windows of the house across the driveway from us. I turned and closed the door behind me. I crossed the room and put my face against the windowpane and tried to look out, but I couldn't see very far, so I opened the window.

I looked out on the driveway that ran between the houses. Right underneath me was the top of the new Paige, the car Papa had just bought, and up the driveway behind the house was a garage. Behind the garage was nothing but fields. This was a new section in Flatbush. All these lots had once been dumps, but the city had filled them in. Around the corner from us they were building more houses that looked like ours, and I could see them when I hung out the window far enough.

I came back into the middle of the room. Slowly I turned in a circle, studying each wall. "My room, this is my room," I kept saying to myself over and over.

I could feel a lump come into my throat, a funny sort of feeling. Like the time I stood next to Grandpa's coffin, holding Papa's hand and looking down at the still white face with the little black yamalka on the head, so startling against the plain white sheet. Papa's voice had been very soft. "Look at him, Danny," he said to me, but it was more as if he were speaking to himself. "This is the end to which all men come, this is the last time we can look at his face." Then Papa bent and kissed the still face in the coffin and I did too. Grandpa's lips were icy cold and they didn't move when mine touched them. Some of the chill of them ran through me.

A man was standing beside the coffin with a pair of scissors. Papa opened his jacket, and the man snipped off a piece of his tie. The man looked at me questioningly. Papa nodded his head and spoke in Yiddish. "He is of his blood," he said. The man snipped off a piece of my tie and I could feel a lump rise in my throat. It was a new tie and this was the first time I had ever worn it. Now I would never be able to wear it again. I looked up at Papa. He was looking back at the coffin and his lips were moving. I strained my ears to hear what he was saying but I couldn't. He let my hand fall from his and I ran to Mamma with the lump still in my throat.

That was the way I felt now.

Suddenly I threw myself on the floor and pressed my cheek against it. The floor felt cool to my face, and the smell of the new shellac came up through my nose and made my eyes smart. I closed my eyes and lay there a few minutes. Then I turned and pressed my lips to the cool floor. "I love you, house," I whispered. "You're the most beautiful house in the whole world, and you're mine and I love you."

"Danny, what are you doing there on the floor?"

I scrambled to my feet quickly and faced the door. It was Miriam. She had a handkerchief tied around her head like Mamma. "Nothin'," I answered awkwardly.

She looked at me queerly. I could see she hadn't been able to figure out what I had been doing. "Mamma says for you to come downstairs and get out of the way," she said bossily. "The men are ready to bring the furniture upstairs."

I followed her down the staircase. Already the newness of the house was beginning to wear off. I could see places on the steps where our feet had rubbed off the paint. The furniture was already in the living-room, and the rug, which had been rolled up on a bamboo stick, was standing in the corner ready to be put down when the men were through.

Mamma was standing in the middle of the room. There were smudges of dirt on her face. "Is there anything you want me to do, Mamma?" I asked.

I heard Mimi's derisive snort behind me. She didn't like boys and didn't think they were good for anything. It made me mad. "Is there, Mamma?" I repeated.

Mamma smiled at me. When she smiled at me her face softened. I liked her to smile at me. She put her hand on my head and playfully tugged at my hair. "No, Blondie," she answered. "Why don't you run outside and play for a while? I'll call you when I need you."

I smiled back at her. I knew she was feeling good when she called me Blondie. I also knew it made Mimi mad. I was the only one in the whole family with blond hair; all the others were dark. Papa used to tease Mamma about it sometimes and it always made her angry, I don't know why.

I made a face at Mimi and went outside. The men had unloaded the truck and there was a lot of furniture on the street. I stood there watching them for a while. It was a warm day and the Negro had taken off his shirt and I could see the muscles rippling under his black skin. The sweat was pouring down his face because he was doing most of the work while the other man was always talking and telling him what to do.

After a while I got tired of watching them and looked up the block toward the corner, wondering what the neighborhood was like. The open fields on the next block in back of my house, which I had seen from my window, made me curious. In the old neighborhood there had never been an empty lot, only the big ugly apartment houses.

Through the open door of my house I saw that Mamma was busy, and when I called to ask her if I could walk up the block, she didn't answer. I stepped off the stoop and headed for the corner, feeling pleased and proud, I had such a nice house and it was such a nice day. I hoped all my birthdays would be as nice.

I could hear a dog's frightened yips almost as soon as I had turned the corner. I looked in the direction of the sound, but couldn't tell where it came from. I walked toward it.

The neighborhood was just being developed—Hyde Park they called it, in the East Flatbush section of Brooklyn. I walked down the street of half-finished houses, their naked white wooden frames gleaming in the bright midafternoon sun. I crossed the next street and the buildings fell behind me. Here was nothing but open fields. The dog's frightened barks were slightly louder now, but I still couldn't tell where they came from. It was strange how far sounds could carry out here in the open. Where we used to live before, down by Papa's drugstore, you couldn't hear a noise even if it was just around the corner. The field in the next block hadn't been filled in yet and was nothing but a deep empty pit running from corner to corner. As soon as they filled in these pits, I guessed, they would start building here too.

Now I could tell where the dog's yips were coming from: the block after next. I could see two boys standing at the edge of the pit there, looking down. The dog must have fallen into the hole. I quickened my step and in a few moments was standing beside the boys. A little brown dog was yelping as he tried to scramble up the sides of the pit. He could manage to get only part way; then he would slip and fall back to the bottom. That was when he would yip the loudest, as he rolled over and over on his way down. Then the two boys would laugh. I don't know why. I didn't think it was funny.

"Is he your dog?" I asked.

They both turned and looked at me. They didn't answer.

I repeated the question.

The bigger of the two boys asked: "Who wants to know?" Something in the tone of his voice frightened me. He wasn't friendly at all.

"I'm only asking," I said.

He came toward me, swaggering a little. He was bigger than I. "And I said: 'Who wants to know?' " His voice was even rougher now.

I took a step backward. I wished I hadn't left the new house. Mamma had only told me to keep out of the way until the moving-men had finished bringing the furniture into the house. "Is he your dog?" I asked, trying to smile and wishing my voice wouldn't quaver.

The big boy put his face very close to mine. I looked him steadily in the eye. "No," he answered.

"Oh," I said, and turned to look at the little dog again. He was still trying to scramble up the side of the pit.

The boy's voice was in my ear. "Where you from?" he asked. "I never seen you before."

I turned back to him. "East Forty-eighth Street. We just moved in today. In the new houses. We're the first people on the whole block."

His face was dark and glowering. "What's your name?" he asked.

"Danny Fisher," I replied. "What's yours?"

"Paul," he said. "And this is my brother, Eddie."

We fell silent for a minute watching the dog. He made it about halfway up before he fell back.

Paul laughed. "That's funny," he said. "That dopey mutt ain't got enough sense to get outta there."

"I don't think it's so funny," I said. "Maybe the poor dog'll never get out."

"So what?" Paul snorted. "It serves him right for goin' down there in the first place."

I didn't say anything. We stood there on the edge of the pit looking down at the dog. I heard a movement on the other side of me and turned. It was Eddie. He was smaller than me. I smiled at him, and he smiled back.

Paul walked around me and stood next to him. There was something in his manner that made both of us stop smiling. Eddie looked sort of ashamed. I wonder why.

"What school yuh goin' to?" Paul asked.

"I don't know," I answered. "That one over near Utica on Avenue D, I guess."

"What class you in?"

"Four A."

"How old are yuh?"

"Eight," I answered proudly. "Today's my birthday. That's why we moved. Papa bought me the house for a birthday present."

Paul sniffed scornfully. I could see that I hadn't impressed him. "You're a smart kid, huh? You're in my class an' I'm nine."

"Well, I skipped 3 B," I explained half-apologetically.

His eyes became cold and wary. "You gonna go to Sacred Heart?"

I was puzzled. "What's that?" I asked.

"Sacred Heart Church," he answered. "Near Troy."

"No," I said, shaking my head.

"Holy Cross?" he asked. "The big church that owns the cemetery?"

"What cemetery?" I asked. I was beginning to feel strange. I didn't want to answer his question. I wondered what was so important about it that he should keep asking.

He pointed across Clarendon Road. About a block past it I could see the black iron picket fence of the cemetery. I turned back to him. "No," I said.

He was silent for a moment while he thought it over. "Don't you believe in God?" he finally asked.

"Sure I do," I replied. "But I don't go to church."

He looked at me skeptically. "If you don't go to church, then you don't believe in God," he said emphatically.

"I do so," I insisted. I could feel angry tears start coming to my eyes. He had no right to say that. I stood up as straight as I could. "I'm a Jew," I said, my voice shrill, "and I go to shul."

The two brothers looked at each other, a sudden knowing look in their eyes. Their faces settled into dull unfriendly masks. Paul took a threatening step toward me. Instinctively I stepped back. My heart was pounding. I wondered what I had said to make them mad.

Paul stuck his face in mine. "Why did you kill Christ?" he snarled at me.

I was really scared at the savagery in his voice. "I didn't kill Him," I quavered. "I never even knew Him."

"You did!" Eddie's voice was higher than his brother's but it was just as savage. "My father told us! He said the Jews killed Him, they nailed Him to the cross. He told us the kikes would move into all the new houses in the neighborhood."

I tried to pacify them. "Maybe some Jews I don't know killed Him," I said placatingly, "but my mother always said that He was a king of the Jews."

"They killed Him just the same," Paul insisted.

I thought for a second. The dog started to yelp again, but I was afraid to turn and look. I tried to change the subject. "We oughtta try to get that dog outta there."

They didn't answer. I could see they were still mad. I tried to think of something that would satisfy them. "Maybe they killed Him because He was a bad king," I suggested.

Their faces grew white. I got frightened and turned to run away, but I wasn't fast enough. Paul caught me and held my arms pinned to my side. I tried to wriggle loose but couldn't. I began to cry.

Paul's face suddenly broke into a contemptuous smile. He let go of my arms and stepped back. "So you wanna get the dog outta there?" he asked.

I tried to stifle my sobs. With one hand I wiped at my eye. "Y-yes," I said.

He took a deep breath, still smiling. "Okay, Jew-baby, go get him!" He rushed at me suddenly, his arms straight out in front of him.

In a panic I tried to get out of his way, but his hands hit my chest, and all the wind went out of me. And then I was falling, rolling over and over, down the sides of the pit. I tried to grab at something to keep myself from slipping, but there wasn't anything. I hit the bottom and for a minute lay there trying to catch my breath.

I heard a whining happy sound and felt a warm tongue licking my face. I sat up. The little brown dog, which was only a puppy, was licking my face, his little tail wagging, and happy little noises deep in his throat.

I got to my feet and looked up. I felt ashamed now because I had cried, but somehow the dog seemed so happy to see me that I wasn't afraid any more.

Paul and Eddie were looking down at me. I shook my fist at them. "You dirty bastards!" I shouted. It was the worst name I knew.

I saw them bend down and pick something up from the ground. A second later a shower of stones and pebbles came pouring down on us. The dog yelped as one hit him. I covered my head with my arms until the shower stopped, but none hit me. Then I looked up again.

"I'll get you for this," I shouted.

They laughed derisively. "Jew son of a bitch," Paul shouted.

I picked up a stone and threw it up at them, but it fell short and another shower of rocks and pebbles came down on me. This time I didn't cover my face quickly enough and one stone cut my cheek. I tossed another at them but it, too, fell short. They bent down to pick up more stones.

I turned and ran out into the center of the pit, where their rocks couldn't reach me. The dog ran beside me. In the middle of the pit I sat down on a big rock. The dog came over to me and I scratched his head. I wiped my face on my sleeve and looked up at the two brothers again.

They were shouting and waving their fists at me, but I couldn't hear what they were saying. The dog was sitting on my foot, wagging his tail and looking into my face. I bent down and put my cheek against his face. "It's all right, doggy," I whispered. "When they go away, we'll get outta here."

Then I straightened up and thumbed my nose at them. They got sore and began to throw more rocks at me, but I only laughed at them. They couldn't touch me from where they were.

The sun had started to go down in the west when they finally went away. I sat there on the rock and waited awhile. I waited almost half an hour before I made up my mind that they had really gone. By that time it was almost dark.

I walked back to the side of the pit and looked up. It was pretty high and steep, but I didn't think I'd have much trouble getting to the top. There were plenty of rocks and bushes I could hold on to. I grabbed hold of a big rock and started up slowly, climbing on my hands and knees to keep from slipping back. I had got maybe five feet up when I heard a whining sound below me. I looked back.

The little dog was sitting in the pit watching me with bright shining eyes. When he saw I had turned to look at him, he gave a sharp, happy yip. "Well, come on," I said to him. "What are you waiting for?" He leaped against the side of the pit and began crawling up toward me. He, too, was moving on his belly. Almost a foot from me, he began to slide back. I grabbed at him, caught him by the scruff of the neck, and pulled him next to me. His tail was wagging happily. "Come on," I said. "We gotta get outta here."

I started upward again and moved a few feet, but when I looked to see how the dog was doing, he wasn't there. He was crouching where I had left him, his eyes on me, his tail drooping. I called him. His tail started wagging, but he didn't move. "What's the matter?" I asked. "You afraid?" He just wagged his tail. He wasn't going to move, so I started to climb again.

I had gone another few feet when he began to cry in high-pitched whining sounds. I stopped and looked down. Immediately his whining ceased and his tail started wagging. "All right," I said, "I'll come down and help you."

Carefully I slid back to where he was and grabbed him again by the scruff of the neck. Holding onto him with one hand, I started inching up again. It took almost fifteen minutes to get halfway up, pulling him up to me after every step. There I stopped to catch my breath. My hands and face were covered with dirt and my shirt and trousers were scuffed and torn. The dog and I clung there to the side of the pit, afraid to move for fear of slipping back.

After a few minutes we started up again. We were almost at the top when a stone gave way under my foot and I slipped. Frantically I let go of the dog and clutched at the dirt to keep myself from sliding down. I had lost only a few feet when I could feel my fingers catch and take hold in the earth. The dog began to yip. When I turned to see, he was gone.

I looked back into the pit. He was just picking himself up. He looked up at me and gave a short bark, but when I turned away from him and started on, he began to whine again. I tried not to listen to his soft, piteous little cries, coming from deep in his throat. He was running back and forth, stopping almost every second to cry up at me, and he seemed to be limping. I called to him. He stopped and looked up at me, his head cocked to one side.

"Come on, boy," I called.

He sprang to the side of the pit and tried to scramble toward me, but fell back. I called again, and again he tried and fell. Finally he sat down and held one paw toward me and barked.

I sat down and slid back to the bottom. He ran into my arms wagging his tail. His paw made a bloody imprint on my shirt as I picked him up to look at it. Its soft puppy pads had been cut and scraped on the rocks.

"All right, doggy," I said softly, "we'll get out of here together. I won't leave you."

He seemed to understand my words, for his tail wagged in happy circles as his soft moist tongue washed my face. I put him down and walked toward the other side of the pit to find an easier place to climb out. He ran along beside me, his eyes looking up at my face. I hoped Mamma would let me keep him.

It was almost dark now. We started climbing again, but it was no good. Less than halfway up I slipped and went to the bottom once more. I was very tired, and hungry too. We couldn't make it. Until the moon came up, there was no use trying any more.

I sat down on a rock in the middle of the pit and tried to figure out what to do now. Mamma would be angry because I hadn't come home in time for supper. It had turned cool. I began to shiver and tried to button the collar of my shirt, but the button had been torn off.

A gray-black shape ran past me in the darkness. The dog let out a growl and snapped after it. Suddenly I was afraid; there were rats in this pit. I put my arms around the dog and began to cry. We would never get out of here. Another rat ran past us in the dark. With a frightened scream I ran to the side of the pit and tried to scramble up. Again and again I tried to climb out, but each time I fell back.

At last I lay on the ground, too exhausted to move. I was wet and uncomfortable. I caught my breath and began to yell. "Mamma! Mamma!" My voice echoed hollowly back across the pit to me. I kept shouting until my voice was hoarse and a mere squeak in my throat. There was no answer.

The moon had come up now and its white light threw a deep shadow from every rock. The night was alive with strange sounds and peculiar movements. As I began to get to my feet, a rat came hurtling through the air against my chest. I fell back screaming in terror. The dog jumped after the rat and caught it in midair. With an angry toss of his head, he broke the rat's neck and flung it away from him.

I stood up and placed my back against the wall of the pit, too cold and frightened to do anything but stare out into it. The dog stood in front of me, the hackles standing out sharply as he barked. The echoes sounded as if a hundred dogs were waking up the night.

I don't know how long we stood there like that. My eyes kept closing and I tried to keep them open, but I couldn't. At last I sank wearily to the ground.

Now I didn't know whether Mamma would be angry with me. It wasn't my fault. If I hadn't been a Jew, Paul and Eddie wouldn't have pushed me into the pit. When I got out I would ask Mamma if we please couldn't be something else. Then, maybe, they wouldn't be mad at me any more. But deep inside me I somehow knew even that wouldn't do any good. Even if Mamma was willing, Papa wouldn't change. I knew that about him. Once his mind was made up, he never changed. That must be why he had remained a Jew all these years. No, it wouldn't do any good.

Mamma would be very angry with me. Too bad, I remembered thinking as I began to doze, too bad this had to happen after the nice way the day had started out.

The dog's barks were louder now, and somewhere mixed up in their harsh echo I could hear someone calling my name. I tried to open my eyes but couldn't, I was so tired.

The voice grew louder, more insistent. "Danny! Danny Fisher!"

My eyes were open now and the eerie white light of the moon threw crazy shadows in the pit. A man's voice called my name again. I struggled to my feet and tried to answer, but my voice was gone. It was only a weak, husky whisper. The dog began to bark furiously again. I heard voices at the top of the pit, and the dog's barks became more shrill and excited.

The gleam of a flashlight came pouring into the pit and moved around searching for me. I knew they couldn't hear me calling, so I ran after the ray of light, trying to show myself in it. The dog ran at my heels, still barking.

Then the light was on me and I stood still. I put my hands over my eyes; the light was hurting them. A man's voice shouted: "There he is!"

Another voice came from the darkness above me: "Danny! Danny!" It was Papa's voice. "Are you all right?"

Then I heard a scrambling, sliding sound of a man coming down the side of the pit toward me. I ran to him, crying, and felt myself caught up in his arms. He was shaking. I could feel his kisses on my face. "Danny, are you all right?" he was asking.

I pressed my face against him. My face was sore and scratched, but the feel of the rough wool of his suit was good. "I'm all right, Papa," I said between sobs, "but Mamma will be sore. I peed in my pants."

Something that sounded like a laugh came from his throat. "Mamma won't be angry," he reassured me. Raising his face toward the top of the pit, he shouted: "He's okay. Throw down a rope and we'll get him out."

"Don't forget the dog, Papa," I said. "We got to take him out too."

Papa bent and scratched the dog's head. "Sure, we'll take

him out," he told me. "If it wasn't for his barking, we wouldn't have known where you were." He turned suddenly and looked at me. "Is he the reason you're down here?"

I shook my head. "No," I answered. "Paul and Eddie threw me down here because I'm a Jew."

Papa stared at me strangely. The rope fell at our feet and he bent to pick it up. I could hardly hear the words he was muttering under his breath: "The neighborhood is new, but the people are the same."

I didn't know what he meant. He fastened the rope around his middle and picked me up under one arm and the dog under the other. The rope tightened and we began to move up the side of the pit.

"You're not mad, are you, Papa?"

"No, Danny, I'm not mad."

I was silent for a moment as we inched further up the side. "Then is it okay if I keep the dog, Papa?" I asked. "He's such a nice little dog." The dog must have known I was talking about him; his tail thumped against my father's side. "We'll call him Rexie Fisher," I added.

Papa looked down at the little pup and then at me. He began to laugh. "You mean you'll call *her* Rexie Fisher. It isn't a him, it's a her."

The room was dark, but I was warm and cozy from my bath as I lay in my bed. There were new sounds in the night, new sounds coming in the window from a new neighborhood. New sounds to live with.

My eyes were wide with the wonder of them, but I wasn't afraid. There was nothing to be afraid of. I was in my own house, in my own room. Suddenly my eyes began to close. I half turned in my bed, and my hand brushed against the wall. It was rough from the freshly stippled paint.

"I love you, house," I murmured, already half asleep.

Under my bed the dog moved, and I put my hand down alongside it. I felt her cold nose in the palm of my hand. My fingers scratched the top of her head. Her fur was damp and cool to my touch. Mamma had made Papa give Rexie a bath before she would let me take her up to my room. Her tongue was licking my fingers. "I love you too, Rexie," I whispered.

A sense of warmth and comfort and belonging began to steal

through me. Slowly I could feel the last trace of tautness slip from my body, and the nothing that is sleep came over me.

I was home. And the first day of my life that I remembered faded into yesterday, and all the days of my life became tomorrow.

All the Days of My Life

THE FIRST BOOK

Chapter One

THE SUN pressed warmly against my closed lids. Vaguely annoyed, I threw an arm over my eyes and moved restlessly on the pillow. For a few minutes I was comfortable; then the light seemed to creep under my arm and search me out. I stopped trying to hide from it and sat up in bed, rubbing my eyes. I was awake.

I stretched. I yawned. I pushed my hair back from my eyes and looked sleepily toward the window. It was a bright, clear morning. I wished I could have gone on sleeping, but my windows faced east and the first morning sun always hit me in the face.

I looked lazily around the room. My clothes lay rumpled on a chair. The half-strung tennis racket I never got around to fix was leaning against the side of the dresser. The old alarm clock on the dresser next to my comb and brush showed it was a quarter past seven. My purple and white Erasmus Hall High School pennant hung drooping across the mirror.

I looked down at the side of the bed for my slippers. They weren't there. I grinned to myself. I knew where they were. Rexie usually pulled them under the bed and made a pillow out of them for her head. I reached down and gave her a scratch. She lifted her head and lazily wagged her tail. I gave her another scratch and took the slippers away from her. Then I got out of bed and stepped into them. Rexie had closed her eyes and gone back to sleep.

I could hear a faint sound coming from my parents' room as I walked over to the open window. That reminded me. Today was the big day: my Bar Mitzvah day. I began to feel an excited nervousness in me. I hoped I wouldn't forget any of the

19

elaborate Hebrew ritual I had specially learned for the occasion.

I stood by the open window and breathed deeply. Slowly I counted to myself: "In—two—three—four; out—two—three—four." After a few moments of this I began to feel the nervousness go away. I would be all right, I wouldn't forget anything. Still facing the window, I pulled my pajama top over my head and threw it on the bed behind me. Bar Mitzvah day or not, I had to get my setting-up exercises in or I would never weigh enough to go out for the football team in the fall.

I stretched out on the floor and did ten push-ups, then I stood up and began to do knee-bends. I looked down at myself. The thin stringy muscles on my body stood out sharply. I could count my ribs. I scanned my chest carefully to see if any real hairs had come out in the night, but it was still the same small golden fuzz. Sometimes I wished that my hair was black like Paul's instead of blond. Then they would show up more plainly.

I finished the knee-bends and picked up the pair of Indian clubs from the corner of the room. Back in front of the window I began to swing them. I heard the click of a light-switch through the open window and a flood of light poured into the windows of the room across the driveway from mine. Almost instantly I dropped to my knees and cautiously peered over the windowsill.

That was Marjorie Ann Conlon's room. She was Mimi's closest girl friend. Sometimes her shade was up and I could get a good look. I was glad her house faced west, for that made it necessary for her to turn the light on every morning.

Carefully I peeked over the windowsill and held my breath. The shades were up. That was the third time this week she had forgotten to pull them down. The last time I had watched her I thought she had known I was looking, so I had to be extra careful. She was a funny kind of a girl, always teasing me and staring at me when I spoke to her. In the last few weeks we'd had several hot arguments about almost nothing and I didn't want to invite her to my Bar Mitzvah party, but Mimi insisted on it.

I saw the closet door in her room move slightly and she came out from behind it. All she had on was her panties. She stopped in the middle of the room for a moment, looking for something. Finally she found it and leaned toward the window to pick it up. I felt a damp sweat break out on my forehead. I could see her real good.

Paul said she had the nicest figure in the neighborhood. I didn't agree with him. Mimi's was much nicer. Besides, Mimi wasn't all out of proportion around the breasts the way Marjorie Ann was.

Paul had suggested that we get the girls down cellar and find out. I got mad at that and grabbed him by the collar and told him I'd beat hell out of him if he ever did that. Paul only laughed and pushed my hand away. The only reason I didn't have the nerve, he said, was that I was afraid Mimi would snitch on us.

Marjorie Ann was facing the window now, seeming to be looking out at me. I lowered my head even more. She was smiling to herself as she hooked on her brassiere, and I began to feel uncomfortable. It was a very knowing smile. I wondered if she knew I was watching. There seemed to be a peculiar awareness in the way she moved around the room.

She had the brassiere half on when a frown crossed her face. She shrugged her shoulders and it slipped down on her arms. She cupped her breasts in her hands for a moment and moved nearer to the window, seeming to be examining them in the light.

My heart began to hammer excitedly. Paul was right. She really had them. She looked up again, the proud smile back on her face, and went back into the room. Carefully she slipped into the brassiere and hooked it behind her.

Outside in the hall there was a noise. I could hear Mimi's voice. Quickly I turned and dove back into bed. I didn't want Mimi to catch me peeking. I stole a quick glance out the window and saw the light go out in Marjorie Ann's room. I sighed. That proved it. I had been right: she knew I was watching her. I heard footsteps coming toward my door, and I closed my eyes and pretended I was asleep.

Mimi's voice came from the doorway. "Danny, are you up?"

"I am now," I answered, sitting up in bed and rubbing my eyes. "What do yuh want?"

Her eyes swept across my bare chest and shoulders. A suspicious light came into them. "Where's your pajama top?" she asked. Then her eyes fell on it lying at the foot of the bed. "You were out of bed already?"

I stared at her. "Yeah."

"What were you doing?" she asked suspiciously. Her eyes wandered over to Marjorie Ann's windows across the driveway.

I made my eyes big and innocent. "My exercises," I said. "Then I hopped back in bed for a snooze."

I could see my answer didn't satisfy her, but she didn't say anything. She bent over the foot of the bed and picked up my pajama top from where it lay, half on the floor. Her breasts were pushed hard against the thin rayon pajamas she wore. I couldn't keep my eyes from them.

Mimi noticed where I was looking and her face flushed. Angrily she threw the pajama top back on my bed and walked toward the door. "Mamma told me to wake you up and remind you to shower," she flung back over her shoulder. "She doesn't want you to be dirty for your Bar Mitzvah."

I jumped out of bed as soon as the door closed behind her, and dropped my pajama pants. I felt warm and tingling, as I always felt after I had watched Marjorie Ann. I looked down at myself. I was in good shape all right. I was five foot four and weighed close to one hundred and fourteen pounds. Six more pounds and I'd be okay for the football team. I knew how to handle the tingling too, I wasn't worried about that. "Cold showers," the P.T. teacher in school had said. "Cold showers, boys." And a cold shower was just what I was going to have.

I slipped into my bathrobe and looked out into the hall. It was empty. The bathroom door was open, so I started toward it. Mimi's door was open too, and she was standing there making her bed. I thumbed my nose at her as I passed, and my robe slipped open. I snatched it close around me. Damn! Now she would know how I felt when she came into my room. Maybe I'd better make peace with her or she might snitch. You could never figure her out. I went back to her door still holding the robe around me.

"Mimi."

She looked at me. "What do you want?" Her voice was cold.

I looked down at my slippers. "Yuh want to use the toilet first?"

"Why?" she asked suspiciously.

I could hear Mamma and Papa talking downstairs. I kept

my voice as low as possible. "I'm—uh—goin' to shower an' maybe you're in a hurry."

"I'm in no hurry," she answered, her voice still cold and formal.

I could see she was sore. "Mimi," I said again.

"What?" She was staring at me.

My eyes fell from her gaze. "Nothin'," I answered. I started to turn and then looked up at her suddenly.

She had been watching my hands where they clutched the robe. This time she lowered her eyes. "You boys are disgusting," she muttered. "You're getting more like your friend Paul every day. He's always looking."

"I wasn't looking," I said defensively.

"You were too," she said accusingly. "I bet you were spying on Marjorie Ann too."

My face flushed. "I was not!" I said, waving my hands emphatically. The robe fell open again. I saw Mimi's eyes fall and I hurriedly snatched it close. "I notice you don't mind lookin', Miss Hoity Toity!"

She paid no attention to me. "I'm going to tell Mamma what you were doing," she said.

I crossed the room to her quickly and grabbed her hands. "You will not!"

"You're hurting me!" Her eyes fell from my face. She was staring at me.

"You will not!" I repeated harshly, gripping her wrists tighter.

She looked up into my face, her brown eyes wide and frightened, yet with a curiosity deep within them. She drew a deep breath. "Okay," she said, "I won't tell Mamma, but I'm going to tell Marge she was right. She said you were peeping on her. I'm going to tell her to keep her shades down!"

I let go of her wrists. A vague triumph coursed through me. I had been right, Marge had known all along that I was watching. "If Marge leaves her shades up," I said, contempt creeping into my voice, "she knows what she's doing."

I left Mimi standing beside the bed and went into the bathroom. Papa's shaving brush was still on the sink drying out. I put it back in the medicine chest and closed the door. Then I threw my bathrobe on the toilet seat and got under the shower.

The water was ice-cold, but I gritted my teeth. After a while my teeth began to chatter, but I still stood there. It was good for me. I knew what I was doing. When I finally came out of the shower and looked in the mirror, my lips were blue with cold.

Chapter Two

I FINISHED buttoning my shirt and looked in the mirror. I picked up the comb and ran it through my hair again. Mamma would be pleased. My skin was clean and shining, even my hair seemed lighter in color.

I bent down and looked under the bed. "Wake up, Rexie," I told her. "Time to go out." She jumped to her feet, wagging her tail. I bent over and scratched her head. She licked my hand. "How are you this morning, girl?" I asked, giving her a quick hug. Her tail began to go around in circles and she rubbed against my trousers.

I walked out of the room and down the stairs. I could hear Mamma's voice coming from the kitchen. She sounded all excited over something. She was saying: "You know your sister-in-law, Bessie. She'll be looking for something to talk about. She thinks she's the only one that could ever make a Bar Mitzvah. Her Joel—"

Papa interrupted her. "Now, Mary," he said soothingly, "keep calm. Everything'll go all right. After all, you were the one that decided to have the reception at home."

I heaved a sigh of relief. At least they weren't talking about me. Mimi hadn't said anything. This argument had been going on for six months—ever since the subject of my Bar Mitzvah had come up.

Papa had wanted to hire a small hall for the reception, but Mamma would have none of it. "We can't spare the money," she had said. "You know how bad business is, and you're having a hard enough time meeting the payments on your loan as it is. And the Corn Exchange Bank won't wait for its three thousand dollars." Papa had given in to her. He had to; he had no other choice. Business hadn't got any better. If anything, judging from what he had let drop around the house, it had got worse. In the past few months he had become very nervous and irritable.

I pushed open the door and walked into the kitchen, Rexie close on my heels. "Good morning," I said to both of them. "What do you want at the store?" I asked Mamma.

She scarcely looked at me. "The usual, Danny," she replied.

"Can I get some jelly doughnuts, Ma?"

She smiled at me. "All right, Danny." She took a dollar from a glass tumbler on the shelf over the sink and gave it to me. "After all, it's your Bar Mitzvah day."

I took the dollar and started out the kitchen door. I heard Mamma's voice behind me: "Don't forget to count your change, Danny."

"I won't, Ma," I called back over my shoulder, opening the door to let Rexie out. The dog loped down the driveway ahead of me, running for the gutter.

I heard voices on the Conlon stoop as I came out of the driveway. Out of the corner of my eye I saw Mimi and Marjorie Ann, their heads very close together. I walked past them as if I hadn't seen them, but I had to stop for Rexie in front of the stoop. Marge was looking at me and began to giggle. I could feel my face turn red.

"I'll be at your party this afternoon," she called.

I was angry with myself for blushing. "Don't do me any favors," I told her insultingly. "You don't have to come for my sake."

Her laugh was taunting. "Why, Danny, how you talk!" she said sarcastically. "You know you wouldn't feel right if you didn't see me! Besides, you'll be a man when you come back from your Bar Mitzvah. It'll be fun to see how you act then!"

Rexie began to run happily down the street. I followed her without answering.

The light in the synagogue was dim and gray as it came through the small windows high on the walls. I looked around nervously. I was standing on the small platform looking down on the room in front of the Torah. The three old men on the platform with me all wore little black yamalkas. Mine was of white silk.

The faces below the platform looked up at me expectantly. I

recognized most of them. They were my relatives. At the back of the synagogue there was a small table covered with cakes and bottles of whisky and wine, gleaming in the dimness.

Rev Herzog, my teacher, took down the Torah and opened it. He motioned me toward the edge of the railing, then turned toward the congregation and spoke in Yiddish.

"In these troubled days," he said, in a thin and wavering voice, "it is good for a man to find a boy who is not ashamed to be a Jew. It is also good for a man to teach such a boy. It is an honor for a man to prepare such a boy for Bar Mitzvah and to welcome him into the state of Jewish manhood." He turned to me solemnly. "I have with me such a boy." He turned back to the congregation and continued to speak.

I tried to keep a straight face. The old hypocrite! He used to yell at me all the time he was giving me the lessons. I was no good, would never be any good; I would never make my Bar Mitzvah because I was too stupid.

I caught a glimpse of my sister's face watching him. There was a rapt, intent look on her face. She smiled up at me swiftly, a gleam of pride in her eyes, and I smiled back at her.

Rev Herzog's voice was fading away and he turned toward me. Slowly I moved to the center of the platform and placed my hands on the Torah. Nervously I cleared my throat. I could see Mamma and Papa smiling up at me expectantly. For a moment my mind went blank and a panic went through me. I had forgotten the elaborate ritual I had spent so many months memorizing.

I heard Rev Herzog's hoarse whisper in my ear: *"Borochu ess—"*

Gratefully I picked up the cue. *"Borochu ess Adonai. . . ."* I was all right now and the rest of the words came easily. Mamma was smiling proudly at the people around her.

I began to feel the solemnity of the prayer. I wished I had paid more attention to what the words I was reciting so glibly in Hebrew meant. Vaguely I remembered that I was asking God's assistance to become an honorable man and to help me lead a good Jewish life. A deep sense of responsibility came over me. One day you were a boy, the next a man. In this ritual I accepted that responsibility. I swore before a group of relatives and friends that I would always discharge my obligations as a good Jew.

I had never thought much about that before. Deep inside me

I knew I had never wanted to be a Jew. I remembered the first time I had thought about it: the time Paul and his kid brother, Eddie, had pushed me into the pit at Clarendon and Troy, the day I found Rexie. The pit was filled in now and there were houses on the spot, but I could never pass the place without remembering. I remembered asking Mamma the next day if we couldn't be something other than Jews. Whatever her answer had been, it wasn't important now. I was consecrating myself to be a Jew.

The last phrases of the prayer passed my lips and, looking down at the congregation, I had a feeling of triumph. Mamma was crying, and Papa was blowing his nose into a large white handkerchief. I smiled at them.

Rev Herzog was draping the tallith on my shoulders, the white silk tallith with the blue star of David emblazoned on it that Mamma had bought for me. He spoke a few words and it was over.

I ran down the steps. Mamma threw her arms around me and kissed me, saying my name over and over. I began to feel embarrassed, I wished she would let me go. I was supposed to be a man now, but she was acting as if I was still a kid.

Papa clapped me on the shoulder. "Good boy, Danny." He was smiling. He turned to Rev Herzog, who had come down the steps behind me. "He was good, Rev, wasn't he?" he asked.

Rev Herzog nodded his head briefly without answering and pushed past Papa, heading for the refreshment table. The other men on the platform followed him quickly.

Papa caught at my arm and led me toward the table. He was pleased, I could see. Ceremoniously he poured a little whisky into a paper cup and offered it to me.

"Harry!" Mamma's voice was protesting.

He smiled happily at her. "Come now, Mary," he said jovially, "the boy's a man now!"

I nodded my head. Papa was right. I took the cup from him.

"*L'chaim!*" Papa said.

"*L'chaim,*" I replied.

Papa tipped his head back and threw the whisky down his throat. I did the same thing. It burned like fire on the way down to my stomach. I began to choke and cough.

"See what you've done, Harry," Mamma said reproachfully.

I looked at Papa through the tears in my eyes. He was laughing. Another paroxysm of coughing overtook me, and Mamma pulled my head close to her bosom.

Chapter Three

THE HOUSE was overflowing with people. I had to put Rexie up in my bedroom and close the door. Crowds always made her nervous. I pushed my way through the living-room on my way to the cellar stairs. Mamma had fixed up a play-room for the kids down there.

My Uncle David called me. He was standing in a corner of the room, talking to Papa. I walked over to him, and he held out his hand. *"Mazeltov,* Danny!"

"Thanks, Uncle David." I smiled automatically.

Taking my hand, he turned to Papa. "It seems like only yesterday I was at his B'riss, Harry," he said.

Papa nodded his head in agreement.

I flushed impatiently. I knew just what he was going to say, I had heard the same thing twenty times already today. And he didn't disappoint me.

"Time flies, doesn't it?" Uncle David's head was nodding too. "And now you're a big boy." He reached into his pocket and took out a coin. "Here, Danny, for you."

I turned the gold coin over in my fingers—a ten-dollar gold piece. "Thanks, Uncle David," I said.

He grinned at me. "A big boy," he said. He turned to Papa. "Soon he'll be able to give you a hand in the store like my Joel does for me."

Papa shook his head in disagreement. "No store for my Danny," he answered firmly. "My Danny's going to be a professional man. He's going to be a lawyer or a doctor maybe, and if things are right I'll open a fine office for him some day."

I looked at Papa in surprise. This was the first time I had

heard about it. I never thought very much about what I was going to be. I never cared very much.

A knowing look came into Uncle David's face. "Of course, Harry, of course," he said soothingly. "But you know how times are. Not good. And you're having enough of a struggle as it is. Now, if your Danny came into the store for the summer like my Joel does for me, what harm can it do? None at all. And you save five dollars a week for a boy. Five dollars is five dollars." He looked at me. "And Danny's a fine boy. I'm sure he would want to help out like my Joel does. Wouldn't you, Danny?"

I nodded my head. Nobody was going to say that my cousin, Joel, was better than I. "Sure, Uncle David," I said quickly.

Papa looked at me. There was a troubled shadow in his eyes. His lips trembled slightly. "There's time enough to talk about that, Danny," he said slowly. "Vacation time's a month away yet. Meanwhile, you run downstairs. The children must be looking for you."

I headed for the stairway, slipping the coin into my pocket. Behind me I could hear Uncle David's voice repeating that it was a good idea and would do me no harm.

On the stairway I stopped and looked into the playroom. Mamma had hung streamers on the walls and ceiling and it looked very gay and partylike, but the kids were very quiet. Upstairs the grownups were all talking loudly, each trying to outshout the others, all talking at once as if they would never have the chance to talk to one another again, and their voices echoed hollowly down here. All the boys were on one side of the room, the girls on the other. Their voices were muted and self-conscious. It wasn't like upstairs at all.

As I walked over to the boys' side of the room, my cousin, Joel, came forward to meet me. He was about a year and half older than me and his face was covered with pimples. I'd heard stories about that. I hoped I wouldn't get them.

"Hello, Joel," I said awkwardly. "Having a good time?"

He nodded politely, his eyes on the girl across the room. "Sure," he answered quickly—too quickly.

I followed his gaze. He was looking at Marjorie Ann. She saw me looking at her and whispered something to my sister, who began to giggle. I walked over to her, Joel at my side.

"What's funny?" I asked belligerently. I had the idea they were laughing at me.

Mimi shook her head silently and giggled again. Marge smiled tauntingly. "We were waiting for you to come down and liven up the party," she said.

I forced a smile on my face and looked around. All the kids were looking at me solemnly. She was right, the party was dying. The grownups were having a good time, but the kids didn't know what to do.

"Hey, what are we so quiet about?" I yelled, holding up my hands. "Let's play games."

"What games?" Mimi's voice was challenging.

I looked at her dumbly. I hadn't thought about that. I looked around the room helplessly.

"How about starting with post office?" Marge suggested.

I made a wry face. That was just the kind of game I didn't want to play. Sissy stuff.

"What do you want to play?" she snapped sarcastically, seeing my expression. "Touch tackle?"

I started to speak, but Joel cut me off. "That's okay," he said eagerly, "I'm willing."

I turned to him with a look of disgust on my face. I knew why he had pimples all right: girls. I would have given him an argument, but all the other kids went for the suggestion big.

When we were sitting in the semicircle on the floor. I looked sullenly down at my crossed legs, wishing I had been able to think of another game. Joel had called Marge into the small furnace room that acted as the post office and I was sure that she would send for me when it was her turn.

I was right. The furnace-room door opened and Joel was standing in front of me. He made a jerking motion with his thumb at the closed door behind him. I could feel my face flush as I got to my feet. "What a gal!" he whispered as I passed him.

I looked down at Mimi. She was watching me with a speculative look on her face. I could feel my cheeks burning.

I hesitated a moment before the furnace-room door, then opened it and stepped inside. I leaned against the closed door behind me, trying to see through the dimness in the room. Its only light came from a tiny window in the corner.

"I'm over here, Danny." Marge's voice came from the other side of the furnace.

I was still holding the doorknob. I could feel a pulse begin to race in my temples. "What—what do you want?" I stammered hoarsely. I was suddenly afraid of her. "What did you call me for?"

She was whispering. "What do you think I called you for?" There was a taunting quality in her voice. "I wanted to see if you really were a man."

I couldn't see her. She was standing behind the furnace. "Why don't you leave me alone?" I asked bitterly, not moving from the door.

Her voice was flat. "If you want to get this over with, you'd better come here." I could hear her almost silent laugh. "I won't hurt you, Danny boy."

I walked around the furnace. She was leaning against it, smiling. Her teeth shone brightly in the dim light. Her hands were behind her. I didn't speak.

Her eyes were laughing. "You were watching me through the window this morning," she shot at me suddenly.

I stood there stiffly. "I was not!"

"You were too!" she snapped. "I saw you, and Mimi said you were."

I stared at her. I'd get even with Mimi for this. "If you were so sure," I said angrily, "then why didn't you pull down the shades?"

She took a step toward me. "Maybe I didn't want to," she said teasingly.

I looked down into her face. I didn't understand it. "But—"

Her fingers on my lips silenced me. There was a strained, tense expression on her face. "Maybe I wanted you to look." She paused for a second, watching my face. "Didn't you like what you saw?"

I didn't know what to say.

She began to laugh softly. "You did," she whispered. "I could see you did. Your cousin, Joel, thinks I'm terrific, and he hasn't even seen half as much of me as you."

She was standing very close to me. She put her arms around my neck and pulled me toward her. I moved woodenly. I felt her breath against my mouth, then her lips. I closed my eyes. This was like no kiss I had ever known before. Not like my mother's, not like my sister's, nor like anyone's I ever kissed.

She pulled her face away from mine. I could feel the rush of her breath still against my mouth. "Give me your hand," she demanded quickly.

Stupidly I held out my hand. My head was reeling and the

room seemed vague and distant. Suddenly a shock seemed to run through my fingers like an electric current. She had put my hand down the front of her dress and I could feel her breast, her nipple hard. Frightened, I jerked my hand away.

She began to laugh softly, her eyes shining up at me. "I like you, Danny," she whispered. She went to the door and turned back to look at me. The mockery was back on her face again. "Who shall I send in now, Danny?" she asked. "Your sister?"

Chapter Four

I WALKED through the parlor, Rexie at my heels. "Danny, come here a minute." Papa's voice came from the couch where he was sitting next to Mamma.

Mamma looked tired. She had just finished cleaning up after everyone had gone. The house seemed curiously quiet now.

"Yes, Papa." I stood in front of them.

"You had a good Bar Mitzvah, Danny?" Papa said, half questioningly.

"Very good, Papa," I answered. "Thanks."

He waved his hand slightly. "Don't thank me," he said. "Thank your Mamma. She did all the work."

I smiled at her.

She smiled wearily up at me, and her hand patted the cushion beside her. I sat down. Her hand reached up and rumpled my hair. "My little Blondele," she said wistfully. "All grown up now. Soon you'll be getting married."

Papa began to laugh. "Not so soon yet, Mary. He's still young."

Mamma looked at him. "Soon enough," she said. "Look how quick the thirteen years went."

Papa chuckled. He took a cigar out of his pocket and lit it, a thoughtful expression settling on his face. "David made the suggestion that Danny come to work in the store this summer."

Mamma started forward in her seat. "But, Harry, he's still a baby yet!"

Papa laughed aloud. "Today he's getting married, but this summer he's too young to work." He turned toward me. "How do you feel about it, Danny?"

I looked at him. "I'll do anything you want, Papa," I answered.

He shook his head. "That's not what I meant. I asked what do you want to do. What do you want to be?"

I hesitated a moment. "I really don't know," I confessed. "I never thought about it."

"Time you should start thinking about it, Danny," he said seriously. "You're a smart boy. A year in high school already and you're just thirteen. But all that smartness is no good unless you know where you're going. Like a ship without a rudder."

"I'll come into the store this summer, Papa," I said quickly. "After all, if it will help you, that's what I want. I know business is not so hot these days."

"It's bad enough, but not so bad that I want you to do something you don't want," he said, looking at his cigar. "Your mamma and me, we have great hopes for you. That you would be a doctor or a lawyer and go to college. Maybe if you come into the store you won't go to college. That's what happened to me. I never finished school. I don't want it to happen to you."

I looked at him, then at Mamma. She was watching me, sadness in her eyes. They were afraid that what had happened to him would happen to me. Still, business was bad and Papa needed my help. I smiled at them. "Going to work in the store for the summer doesn't mean anything, Papa," I said. "In the fall I go back to school again."

He turned to Mamma. For a long moment they looked at each other. Then Mamma nodded her head slightly and he turned back to me. "All right, Danny," he said heavily. "Let it be that way for a while. We'll see."

The boys were shouting as the volley ball shuttled back and forth across the net. There were four games going in the school gymnasium. Out of the corner of my eye I could see Mr. Gottkin walking toward us. I pulled my eyes back to the ball. I wanted to look good for him. He coached the football team.

The ball was coming toward me, high over my head, but I leapt and stabbed at it. It caught the top of the net, rolled over the other side, and fell to the floor. I looked around proudly, feeling pretty good. That made the eighth point I had scored out of the fourteen for my side. Mr. Gottkin couldn't help noticing that.

He wasn't even looking my way. He was talking to a boy on the next court. The ball came back into play again. I missed what seemed like a couple of easy shots, but each time they were recovered. When the play seemed to be going over to the other side of the court, I stole another glance at the teacher.

From behind me I could hear Paul's sudden shout: "Danny! Your ball!"

I spun around quickly. The ball was floating easily across the net toward me. I set myself for it and jumped. A dark figure on the other side of the net flashed up before me and hit the ball toward the floor. Automatically my hands went up to cover my face, but I wasn't fast enough. I went A.O.E. on the floor.

I scrambled to my feet angrily, one side of my face red and stinging where the ball had hit me. The dark boy on the other side of the net was grinning at me.

"Yuh fouled it!' I shot at him.

The smile left his face. "What's the matter, Danny? he sneered. "You the only hero allowed in the game?"

I started under the net for him, but a hand gripped my shoulder firmly and stopped me.

"Get on with the game, Fisher," Mr. Gottkin said quietly. "No roughhousing."

I ducked back under the net to my side. I was angrier now than before. All Gottkin would remember was that I had got sore. "I'll get hunk," I whispered to the boy.

His lips formed a soundless raspberry accompanied by a gesture of derision.

My chance came on the very next play. The ball floated over my head and the boy shot up for it. I beat him to it and hit it savagely downward with both hands. It struck him squarely in the mouth and he rolled over on the floor. I hooted loudly at him.

He came off the floor and, charging under the net, tackled me around the legs. We rolled over and over on the floor pummeling each other. His voice was hot and angry in my ear: "Yuh son of a bitch!"

Gottkin pulled us apart. "I tol' yuh, no roughhousing."

I looked down at the floor sullenly and didn't answer.

"Who started this?" Gottkin's voice was harsh.

I looked at the other boy and he glowered at me, but neither of us answered.

The P.T. teacher didn't wait for an answer. "Get on with the game," he said in a disgusted voice. "And no roughhousing." He turned away from us.

Automatically we started for each other as his back turned. I caught the dark boy around the middle and we were on the floor again before Mr. Gottkin pulled us apart.

His arms held us at each side of him. There was a weary, speculative look on his face. "You guys insist on fightin'?" he stated rather than asked.

Neither of us answered.

"Well," he continued, "if you're gonna fight, you'll fight my way." Still holding us, he called over his shoulder to the substitute teacher who was his assistant: "Get out the gloves."

The sub came up with the gloves, and Gottkin gave a pair to each of us. "Put 'em on," he said almost genially. He turned to the boys in the gym who had started to crowd around. "Better lock the doors, boys," he said. "We can't have anyone walking in on us."

They laughed excitedly while I fumbled with the unfamiliar gloves. I knew what they were laughing at. If the principal came in, there would be hell to pay.

The boxing gloves felt clumsy on my hands. I'd never had a pair on before. Paul silently began to tie the laces for me. I looked over at the other boy. The first flush of anger had died away in me. I didn't have anything against this kid. I didn't even know his name. The only class we were in together was this one. He looked like he was beginning to feel the same way. I walked up to him. "This is stupid," I said.

Mr. Gottkin replied before the boy could open his mouth. "Goin' yella, Fisher?" he sneered. There was a peculiar excitement in his eyes.

I could feel the heat flaming in my cheeks. "No, but—"

Gottkin cut me off. "Then get back there an' do what I tell yuh. Come out fightin'. When one of you is knocked down, the other will not hit him until I give the okay. Understand?"

I nodded. The boy wet his lips and also nodded his head.

I could see Gottkin felt good again. "All right, boys," he said, "go to it."

I felt someone shoving me forward. The dark boy was coming toward me. I raised my hands and tried to hold them the way I had seen some fighters in the movies do. Warily I circled around the boy. He was just as cautious as I was, watching me carefully. For almost a minute we didn't come within two feet of each other.

"I thought you guys wanted to fight," Gottkin said. I stole a glance at him. His eyes were still burning with excitement.

A light exploded in my own eyes. I could hear the boys begin to yell. Another light flashed. Then a sharp stinging pain in my right ear, then on my mouth. I could feel myself falling. There was a grinding buzzing sound in my head. I shook it angrily to clear it and opened my eyes. I was on my hands and knees. I looked up.

The boy was dancing in front of me. He was laughing.

The louse had hit me when I wasn't looking. I got to my feet, anger surging in me. I saw Gottkin tap him on the shoulder, then he was all over me. Desperately I pushed in close and grabbed at his arms and held on.

My throat was raw, I could feel my breath burning in it. I shook my head. I couldn't think with that buzzing around in there. I shook my head again. Suddenly the noise stopped and the breath was easier in my throat.

I felt Gottkin pull us apart. His voice was husky in my ears. "Break it up, boys."

My legs were steady now. I held my hands up and waited for the other boy to come after me.

He came charging in, arms flailing. I moved aside and he surged past me. I almost smiled to myself. This was easy: you just had to keep your head on your shoulders.

He turned around and came after me again. This time I waited for him. I could see his fists were high. I drove my right hand into his belly. His hands came down and he doubled up. His knees began to buckle and I stepped back. I looked questioningly at Mr. Gottkin.

He pushed me back toward the boy roughly. I hit the boy twice and he straightened up, a dazed look on his face.

I was standing flatfooted now. I could feel a surge of power flowing through my body into my arms. I brought my right up almost from the floor, and it caught him flush on the chin. The shock of the punch ran through my arm. He spun around once and then fell forward, flat on his face.

I stepped back and looked at Mr. Gottkin. He was standing there with a flushed look, staring down at the boy. His tongue was running nervously over his lips, his hands were clenched, and the back of his shirt was covered with sweat as if he had done the fighting.

A sudden silence fell over the gymnasium. I turned back to the boy, who lay there quietly, not even moving. Slowly Mr. Gottkin knelt beside him.

He rolled the boy over on his back and slapped at his face. The teacher was pale now. He looked up at the sub. "Get me the smelling-salts!" he cried hoarsely.

His hands were trembling violently as he waved the bottle back and forth under the boy's nose. "Come on, kid." He seemed to be pleading. "Snap out of it." There were beads of sweat on his face.

I stared down at them. Why didn't the kid get up? I shouldn't have let them bulldoze me into a fight.

"Maybe we better get a doctor," the sub whispered anxiously to Mr. Gottkin.

Gottkin's voice was low, but I could hear him as I bent down. "Not if yuh like this job!"

"But what if the kid dies?"

The sub's query went unanswered as color began to flood back into the boy's face. He tried to sit up, but Gottkin held him back on the floor.

"Take it easy, kid," Gottkin said almost gently. "You'll be okay in a minute."

He picked the boy up in his arms and looked around. "You fellas keep your mouths shut about this. Understand?" His voice was menacing. Silently they gave their assent. His eyes swept past them and came to me. "You, Fisher," he said harshly, "come with me. The rest of you get back to your games."

He strode into his office, still carrying the boy, and I followed. He put the kid down on a leather-covered dressing-table as I closed the door behind us. "Get me that water pitcher over there," he called over his shoulder.

Silently I handed it to him and he upended it over the boy's face. The boy sat up sputtering.

"How're yuh feeling, kid?" Gottkin asked.

The boy forced a grin to his face. He looked at me shyly. "As if a mule kicked me," he replied.

Gottkin began to laugh in relief. Then his glance fell on me and the smile disappeared. "Why didn't yuh tell me yuh knew how to fight, Fisher?" he snarled. "I got a mind to—"

"I never fought with gloves before, Mr. Gottkin," I said quickly. "Honest."

He looked at me dubiously, but he must have believed me, for he turned back to the boy. "Okay if we forget the whole thing?" he asked him.

The boy looked at me and smiled again. He nodded his head. "I don't even want to remember it," he said earnestly.

Gottkin looked back at me for a second, a speculative look in his eyes. "Then, shake hands, you two, an' get outta here."

We shook hands and started out the door. As I closed it I could see Mr. Gottkin opening a drawer in his desk and taking something out of it. He began to raise it toward his mouth.

Just then the sub pushed past me on his way into the office. "Give me some of that," he said as the door shut. "I never want to go through another minute like that again."

Gottkin's voice boomed through the closed door. "That Fisher kid's a natural fighter. Did you see—?"

I looked up self-consciously. My former opponent was waiting for me. Awkwardly I took his arm and together we walked back to the volley-ball game.

Chapter Five

I STOOD impatiently on the corner of Bedford and Church Avenues behind the school waiting for Paul. The clock in the drugstore window across the street showed a quarter after three. I'd give him five more minutes, then I'd start for home without him.

I was still tingling with a new excitement. The news of my fight in the gym had run through the school like wildfire. All the boys were treating me with a new respect and the girls were looking at me with a curiously restrained awareness. Several times I had overheard groups of people talking about me.

A Ford roadster pulled to the curb in front of me and honked its horn. I looked up at it.

"Hey, Fisher, come over here." Mr. Gottkin was leaning out of the car.

Slowly I walked toward him. What did he want now?

He opened the door. "Hop in," he invited. "I'll drive yuh home."

I looked at the clock quickly and made up my mind. Paul would have to walk home alone. I got into the car silently.

"Which way do you go?" Mr. Gottkin asked in a friendly voice as he pulled the car away from the curb.

"Over to Clarendon."

We rode a few blocks in silence. I watched him out of the corner of my eye. He must have had a reason for picking me up. I wondered when he was going to talk. Suddenly he slowed the car and pulled toward the curb.

A young woman was walking there. Gottkin leaned out of the car and shouted after her. "Hey, Ceil!"

She stopped to look back at us and I recognized her: Miss Schindler, the art teacher. Her class was one of the most popular in school. The girls couldn't understand why all the boys suddenly signed for art in the third term, but I could. Next term I would be in her class.

She had dark brown hair, dark eyes, and a soft tan skin. She had been to Paris to study, and the boys said she never wore a brassiere. I had heard them talking about how she looked when she bent over their desks.

"Oh, it's you, Sam," she said, smiling and walking back toward the car.

"Hop in, Ceil," he urged her, "I'll take you home." He turned to me. "Shove over, kid," he told me. "Make room for her."

I moved closer to him, and Miss Schindler sat down beside me and closed the door. There was just room enough for the three of us on the seat. I could feel the press of her thigh against me. I stole a look at her out of the corner of my eyes. The boys were right. I shifted uncomfortably.

Gottkin's voice was louder than usual. "Where you been keepin' yourself, baby?"

Her voice was low. "Around, Sam," she answered evasively, looking at me.

Gottkin caught her look. "You know Miss Schindler, Fisher?" he asked.

I shook my head. "No."

"This is Danny Fisher," he said to her.

She turned to me, curiosity in her eyes. "You're the boy who had the fight in school today?" she said half-questioningly.

"You know about it?" Gottkin sounded surprised.

"It's all over the school, Sam," she replied in a peculiar tone of voice. "Your boy here is the most famous man in the place today."

I fought back an impulse to smile proudly.

"You can't keep anything quiet in that place," Gottkin grumbled. "If the old man gets wind of it, I'm sunk."

Miss Schindler looked at him. "That's what I always told you, Sam," she said in the same peculiar tone of voice. "Teachers can't lead their own lives."

I looked up at her quickly, puzzled.

She caught my glance and her face flushed. "I heard it was quite a fight," she said.

I didn't answer. I had the idea she wasn't really interested in the fight.

Gottkin answered for me. "It was. Fisher got off the floor and knocked the other kid for a loop. Yuh never seen nothin' like it."

There was a shadow in her dark eyes. "You can't forget what you were once," she said bitterly, "can you, Sam?"

He didn't answer.

She spoke again, her voice unchanged. "You can let me out here, Sam. This is my corner."

Silently he stopped the car. She got out and leaned over the running board to us. "Nice to meet you, Danny"—she smiled pleasantly—"and try not to get in any more fights. So long, Sam." She turned and walked away. She had a nice walk too.

I turned back to the P.T. teacher. He was staring after her thoughtfully, his lips tight across his teeth. He put the car into gear. "If you got a few minutes to spare, kid," he said, "I'd like you to come over to my place. I got somethin' I want to show you."

"Okay, Mr. Gottkin," I replied, my curiosity returning in full force.

I followed him through the basement entrance of a small two-family house. Gottkin pointed at a door. "Go in there, kid," he told me. "I'll be with yuh in a minute."

I watched him run up the steps to the upper floor, then turned and went into the room he had indicated. I could hear faint voices upstairs as I opened the door. I stopped in the doorway and gaped at the room. It was fixed up as a small but complete gym—parallel bars, punching bag, horse, chinning bar, weights. On a small leather couch against the wall were several pairs of boxing gloves. Photographs were scattered all around the walls of the room. I went over to look at them. They were pictures of Mr. Gottkin, but he looked different. He wore trunks and boxing gloves and on his face a menacing scowl. I hadn't known he was a fighter.

A telephone on a small table near the couch began to ring. I looked at it hesitantly. It rang again. I didn't know whether to answer it or not. When it rang once more, I picked up the receiver. As I was just about to speak, I heard Mr. Gottkin's voice answer. There must have been an extension upstairs.

I listened. I had never used an extension before and I was afraid to hang up for fear I'd disconnect the call. A woman's voice was talking now. "Sam," she was saying, "you're a damn fool for picking me up with that kid in the car."

I recognized that voice too. I kept on listening.

Gottkin's voice had a pleading sound in it. "But, baby," he said, "I couldn't stand it any more. I gotta see yuh. I'm goin' crazy, I tell yuh."

Miss Schindler's voice was hard. "I said we were through and I meant it. I was crazy to start up with you anyway. If Jeff ever found out, we'd all be washed up."

"Baby, he'd never find out. He's too busy with his classes. He don't even know what day it is. I don't know how you ever came to marry that lunkhead anyway."

"He's not as crazy as you are, Sam. Jeff Rosen will be principal some day. He'll get further than you," she said defensively. "You'll wind up getting thrown out."

Gottkin sounded more sure of himself now. "But, baby, he pays you no mind. With night school an' all, he's got no time to keep a real woman like you happy."

"Sam!" she said, protesting weakly.

His voice was strong on the phone. "Remember what you said the last time, Ceil? How it was with us? There was never anything like it. Remember, you said so yourself? I remember. I get hard just rememberin'. Come on over, baby, I want you."

"I can't, Sam," Her voice was pleading now. "I said—"

"I don't care what you said, Ceil," he interrupted. "Come on over. I'll leave the downstairs open and you can duck right in."

There was a moment's pause, then her voice came heavily through the receiver: "Do you love me, Sam?"

"Like mad, baby." Gottkin's voice was roughly tender. "Like mad. Yuh comin' over?"

I could almost hear her hesitation, then her voice came through softly. "I'll be there in half an hour, Sam."

"I'll be waitin', baby." Gottkin sounded like he was smiling.

"I love you, Sam," I heard her say, and then the phone clicked dead in my hand. They had hung up. I put the receiver back on the hook. Outside on the stairs I heard footsteps and turned back to the pictures on the wall.

The door opened behind me and I turned around. "Mr. Gottkin," I said, "I didn't know you were a fighter."

His face was flushed. He glanced at the telephone quickly, then back at me. "Yeah," he answered. "I wanted to show yuh my stuff, an' if yuh was interested, I'd give yuh some lessons. I think yuh got the makin's of a great fighter, kid."

"Gee, Mr. Gottkin, I'd like that," I said quickly. "You want to start now?"

"I'd like to, kid"—he sounded embarrassed—"but some unexpected business just came up an' I can't. I'll let you know in class tomorrow when we can start."

"Aw, gee, Mr. Gottkin," I said disappointedly.

He put his hand on my shoulder and steered me toward the door. "I'm sorry, kid, but it's business. You understand?"

I smiled at him from the doorway. "Sure, Mr. Gottkin, I understand. Tomorrow'll be okay."

"Yeah, kid. Tomorrow." Mr. Gottkin quickly closed the door.

I ducked quickly across the street and up a driveway. I sat down where I could watch his door and waited. About fifteen minutes passed before she came walking down the street.

She was walking quickly, not looking around until she reached his door. Then she glanced up and down the street and ducked into the door, closing it behind her.

I sat there another few minutes before I got up. Mr. Gottkin would be surprised if he knew just how much I understood. What a day this had been! First the fight in school, now this. And Miss Schindler was married to Mr. Rosen in the math department, too. There was a new feeling of power in me. One word from me and they were all through.

There was a fire hydrant in my path. I leapfrogged over it easily. Boy, was I glad Paul had been late!

Chapter Six

MY ARMS were tired. The sweat was running down my forehead into my eyes, which were beginning to burn. I brushed at them with the back of my boxing glove and turned, facing the teacher.

His voice was harsh and he, too, was covered with sweat. "Keep your left up, Danny. And snap it. Sharp! Don't swing it like a balley dancer. Snap, from the shoulders. Fast! See, like this." He turned toward the punching bag and snapped his left at it. His hand moved so quickly it seemed like a blur. The bag rocked crazily against the board. He turned back to me. "Now, snap it at me—fast!"

I put my hands up again and moved warily around him. This had been going on for two weeks now and I had learned enough to be careful with him. He was a rough teacher and if I made a mistake I usually paid for it—with a poke in the jaw.

He circled with me, his gloves moving slightly I feinted with my right hand. For a split second I noticed his eyes following it, and I snapped my left into his face just as I had been told.

His head jerked back with the punch, and when it came forward again, there was a red bruise marking his cheekbone. He straightened up and dropped his hands.

"Okay, kid," he said ruefully, "that's enough for the day. You learn fast."

I let my breath out gratefully. I was tired. I pulled at the laces on the gloves with my teeth.

"School's over next week, Danny." Mr. Gottkin was looking at me thoughtfully.

I managed to get one glove off. "I know," I answered.

"Goin' to camp for the summer?" he asked.

I shook my head. "Nope. I'm gonna help my dad out in the store."

"I got a job for the summer as a sports director at a hotel in the Catskills," he said. "I can get you a busboy's job if you want. I'd like to keep these lessons up."

"Me too, Mr. Gottkin"—I looked down at the gloves hesitantly—"but I don't know whether Pop'll let me."

He sat down on the couch. His eyes swept over me. "How old are yuh, Danny?"

"Thirteen," I answered. "Made my Bar Mitzvah this month."

He looked surprised. "That all?" he said in a disappointed voice. "I thought you were older. You look older. You're bigger than most fifteen-year-old kids."

"I'll ask Papa though," I said quickly. "Maybe he'll let me go with you."

Gottkin smiled. "Yeah, kid. Do that. Maybe he will."

I slipped Rexie a scrap of meat under the table and looked over at Papa. He seemed in a good mood. He had just belched and opened his belt. He was stirring sugar into his glass of tea.

"Papa," I said hesitantly.

He looked at me. "Yes?"

"My gym teacher's got a job in the country at a hotel," I said hurriedly, "and he says he can get me on as a busboy if I want to go."

Papa continued to stir his tea while I watched him. "You told Mamma about this yet?" he asked.

Mamma came in from the kitchen just then. She looked at me. "Told me what?"

I repeated what I had told Papa.

"And what did you tell him?" she asked me.

"I told him I was going to help Papa out in the store, but he said to ask anyway."

She looked at Papa for a moment, then turned back to me. "You can't go," she said with finality. She picked up some dishes and started back to the kitchen.

I was disappointed even though she had answered what I had expected. I looked down at the table.

Papa called her back. "Mary," he said softly, "such a bad idea, it's not."

She turned to him. "It was decided already that he's going into the store this summer and that's where he is going. I'm not going to let him go away for the whole summer by himself. He's still a baby yet."

Papa sipped at his tea slowly. "Such a baby he can't be if he's coming into the store. You know the neighborhood. Besides, a summer in the country will do him good." He turned back to me. "Is it a good hotel?"

"I don't know, Papa," I said hopefully. "I didn't ask him."

"Get for me all the facts, Danny," he said, "and then your Mamma and me, we'll decide."

I was sitting on the stoop when they came out of the house. Papa stopped in front of me.

"We're going to the Utica to the movies with Mr. and Mrs. Conlon," he said. "Now, remember to go to bed by nine o'clock."

"I will, Papa," I promised. I didn't want to do anything that might queer my chances of going to the country with Mr. Gottkin.

Papa walked across the driveway and rang the Conlons' bell. Mimi came out on the stoop with her coat on.

I looked at her questioningly. "You going too?" I asked. I really didn't care much. We hadn't been on such good terms since the Bar Mitzvah party. She had wanted me to tell her what Marge and I did in the furnace room and I had told her to find out from her friend if she wanted to know so much.

"Marge and I are going," she said importantly. "Papa said I could." She walked down the steps haughtily.

The Conlons came out on their stoop. Marge wasn't with them.

Mimi asked: "Isn't Marjorie Ann coming, Mrs. Conlon?"

"No, Mimi," Mrs. Conlon answered. "She was tired, so she's going to bed early."

"Maybe you better stay home too, Mimi," Mamma said doubtfully.

"But you said I could go." Mimi's voice was pleading.

"Let her come, Mary," Papa said. "We promised her. We'll be home by eleven."

I watched them all get into Papa's Paige. The car pulled away. I looked into the living-room at the clock on the fire-place. It was a quarter to eight. I felt like a cigarette. I got up and went to a hall closet, where I found a crumpled pack of Luckies in one of Papa's jackets. Then I went back out on the stoop and sat down and lit the cigarette.

The street was quiet. I could hear the breeze rustling the leaves on the young trees. I leaned my head against the cool bricks and closed my eyes. I liked the feel of them against my cheek. I liked everything about my house.

"Is that you, Danny?" It was Marge's voice.

I opened my eyes. She was standing on her stoop. "Yeah," I answered.

"You're smoking!" she said incredulously.

"So?" I dragged on the cigarette defiantly. "I thought your mother said you went to bed."

She came over to my stoop and stood at the bottom of the steps. Her face shone white in the light of the street lamps. "I didn't feel like going," she said.

I took a last drag on the butt and threw it away, stood up and stretched. "I guess I'll turn in," I said.

"Do you have to?" she asked.

I looked down at her. There was an intent expression on her face. "Nope," I said shortly, "but I might as well. There's noth-in' doin' around here."

"We can sit out and talk," she said quickly.

The way she said that made me curious. "About what?" I asked.

"Things," she answered vaguely. "There's lots of things we can talk about."

A peculiar excitement began to fill me. I sat down on the steps again. "Okay," I said, deliberately casual. "So we'll talk."

She sat down on the steps beneath me. She was wearing a smock that tied on the side. As she turned to look up at me, it parted slightly and I could see the shadow fall between her breasts. She smiled.

"What are you smiling at?" I asked, instantly defiant.

She tossed her head. "You know why I stayed home?" she countered.

"No."

"Because I knew Mimi was going."

"I thought you liked Mimi," I said with surprise.

"I do," she said earnestly, "but I knew if Mimi went you'd be home, so I didn't go." She looked up at me mysteriously.

The excitement was surging in me again. I didn't know what to say, so I kept quiet. I felt her hand touch my knee and I jumped. "Don't do that!" I snapped, pulling my leg away.

Her eyes were round and innocent. "Don't you like it?" she asked.

"No," answered. "It gives me the shivers."

She laughed softly. "Then you do like it. That's what it's supposed to do." Her next question took me by surprise. "Then why do you always watch me through your window?"

I could feel my face flush in the darkness. "I told you before, I wasn't!"

She laughed again, excitedly. "I watch you," she said almost in a whisper. "Almost every morning. When you do your exercises. And you haven't any clothes on. That's why I leave my shades up—so you could see me."

I lit another cigarette. My fingers were trembling. In the glow of the match I could see her laughing at me. I threw it away. "So I looked," I said defiantly. "What're you gonna do about it?"

"Nothing," she said, still smiling. "I like you to look at me."

I didn't like the way she stared at me. "I'm going in now," I said, getting to my feet.

She stood up, laughing. "You're afraid to stay out here with me!" she challenged.

"I am not," I retorted hotly. "I promised my father I would go to bed early."

Her hand made a quick movement and caught mine. I pulled away from her. "Cut it!" I snapped.

"Now I know you're afraid!" she taunted. "Otherwise you'd stay out yet. It's still early."

I couldn't go now, so I sat down again. "Okay," I said, "I'll stay out until nine."

"You're funny, Danny," she said in a puzzled voice. "You're not like the other boys."

I dragged at the cigarette. "How?" I asked.

"You never try to feel me or anything."

I looked down at the butt in my hand. "Why should I?"

"All the other boys do," she said matter-of-factly, "even my brother, Fred." She began to laugh. "You know what?" she asked.

I shook my head silently. I didn't trust my voice any more.

"He even tried to do more, but I wouldn't let him. I told him I'd tell Pa. Pa would kill him if he knew."

I didn't speak. I dragged on the cigarette. The smoke burned into my lungs. I coughed and threw it away. It would raise hell with my condition. I glanced up at her. She was staring at me. "What're you lookin' at?" I asked.

She didn't answer.

"I'm going to get a drink of water," I said quickly. I hurried into the house and through the darkened rooms into the kitchen. I turned on the water, filled a tumbler, and drank it thirstily.

"Aren't you going to give me any?" she said over my shoulder.

I turned around. She was standing behind me. I hadn't heard her follow me. "Sure," I said. I filled the glass again.

She held it in her hands for a moment, then put it back on the sink untouched. She put her hands on my face. They were cold from the tumbler.

I stood there woodenly, my body stiff and unmoving. Then her mouth was against mine. She was bending me back, across the sink. I tried to push her away, but I was off balance.

I gripped her shoulders tightly and heard her gasp in pain. I squeezed harder and she cried out again. I straightened up. She was standing in front of me, her eyes swimming in pain. I laughed. I was stronger than she. I squeezed her shoulders again.

She grimaced and her hands caught wildly at mine. Her lips were against my ear. "Don't fight with me, Danny. I like you. And I can tell you like me!"

I pushed her away violently. She half stumbled back a few steps, then stood looking at me. Her eyes were glowing, almost luminously, like a cat's eyes in the dark, and her chest was heaving from exertion. I knew it then as I watched her: she was right.

The noise of a car turning up the block came to our ears. My voice was a frightened sound in the night. "They're coming back! You better get out of here!"

She laughed and took a step toward me. Alarmed by a fear I didn't understand, I bolted for the stairway and stood nervously on the steps, listening to her voice float up to me out of the dark.

She was so sure, so wise. She knew so much more than I that as I answered her I knew it would do no good. Nothing could stop what was happening to me.

Then she was gone, the house was quiet, and I climbed slowly up the stairs to my room.

Chapter Seven

I LAY there on the bed, staring out into the dark. I couldn't sleep. The sound of her laughter, sure and knowing, still echoed in my ears. I felt soiled and dirty. I would never be able to look at anybody now, everyone was sure to know what had happened.

"Never again," I had said to her.

She had laughed that funny knowing laugh of hers. "That's what you say, Danny. But you'll never stop now."

"Not me." But I knew I was lying. "Not me. I feel too dirty."

Her laughter followed me up the stairs. She sounded sure of herself. "You can't stop, Danny. You're a man now and you'll never stop."

I had stood at the head of the stairs, wanting to shout down to her that she was wrong; but there was no use. She was already gone. I went into my room and undressed and threw myself on the bed in the dark.

My body was weak and there was an aching in my legs. I tried to close my eyes, but sleep escaped me. I felt drained and empty.

I could hear the light click on in her room. Automatically I glanced toward it. She was there, looking toward my windows and smiling. She took off her smock slowly and her naked body glistened in the electric light. Her voice was a husky half-whisper as it came through the open window. "Danny, are you awake?"

I shut my eyes and turned away from the window. I wouldn't look. I wouldn't answer.

"Don't try to fool me, Danny. I know you're up." Her voice had grown harsh, with a tone of command. "Look at me, Danny!"

I couldn't stand the sound of her voice hammering at me any longer. Angrily I went to the window and leaned against the windowsill, my body trembling. "Leave me alone," I begged her. "Please leave me alone. I told you never again."

She laughed at me. "Look at me, Danny," she said softly. "Don't you like to look at me?" She arched herself proudly, her hands stretching high, her head bending all the way back.

I stood there staring at her speechlessly. I didn't want to look at her, but I couldn't turn away.

She straightened up and laughed. "Danny!"

"What?" I asked in an agonized voice.

"Turn on your light, Danny. I want to see you!"

For a moment I didn't understand her; then her words sank into the depths of my mind. My breath caught sharply in my throat and I was suddenly aware of myself. I had been betrayed. My own body betrayed me.

"No!" I cried out. Shame and fear tore through me. I moved away from the window. "Leave me alone, I tell you, leave me alone!"

"Turn on the light, Danny." Her voice was soft and persuading. "For me, Danny, please."

"No!" I screamed at her in a blazing moment of rebellion.

I hesitated a moment, my hand half reaching for the light-switch. She was right, I would never escape her. I was lost.

"No!" I screamed at her in a blazing moment of rebellion. I hated everything that was happening to me—all the things I would become, my growing manhood and its manner of expression.

"I won't!" I shouted, and ran out, slamming the door on my room and all that I could see from it.

I ran down to the bathroom and stripped off my pajamas. I stared down at my traitorous body. Angrily I slapped at myself. Pain brought with it some sense of satisfaction. This was right. I would make it pay for what it did to me. I hit myself again. The pain tore through me and I bent over.

I held onto the sink with one hand and turned the water on in the shower. The sound of the water drumming against the bottom of the tub was soothing. For a moment I stood there, then stepped under the spray.

The cold water striking my heated body sent a rapid chill through me. I braced myself against the needle spray. Then suddenly I slumped to the floor of the tub and began to cry.

In the morning when I woke up it was as if nothing had happened. As if last night had been part of a dream, a nightmare, that sleep had washed away.

I brushed my teeth and combed my hair, and while I dressed I hummed a song. In surprise I looked at myself in the mirror. With a sense of wonder I realized there was nothing wrong with me. Everything they had told me would happen to me was a lie. My eyes were blue and clear, my skin was shining and smooth, the soreness had gone from my lips.

I left the room smiling. No one would know what had happened. Mimi was in the hall, going to the bathroom. "Good morning," I sang out.

She looked at me and smiled. "Good morning," she replied. "You were sleeping so soundly last night you didn't even hear us come in."

"I know." I grinned at her. I guessed our private war was over. Rexie followed me down the stairs.

"Morning, Ma," I called, going into the kitchen. "Rolls today?"

Mamma smiled tolerantly at me. "Don't ask foolish questions, Danny."

"Okay, Ma." I took the money from the tumbler at the sink and started for the door. "C'mon, Rexie."

Wagging her tail, she followed me out of the house. She ran past me in the alleyway and out into the street, where she squatted down in the gutter. I looked at her smiling. It was a beautiful morning, it would be a wonderful day. The sun was shining and the air was fresh and crisp.

Rexie started off down the block and I followed her. Last night was a bad dream, that's what it was, it never really happened. I took a deep breath. I could feel my chest bursting against my shirt as my lungs filled.

"Danny!"

Her soft, quiet voice stopped me in my tracks. Slowly I

turned and looked up at her stoop. She was standing there, her eyes wise and smiling. "Why did you run away last night?" she asked, almost reproachfully.

A bitter taste rose into my mouth. It was true. It wasn't a dream, then; I couldn't escape. I began to hate her. I spat on the sidewalk. "You bitch!"

She was still smiling as she came off the stoop toward me. Her body reflected the sureness she felt. Her walk reminded me of the way she'd looked last night in front of her window. She was close to me, her lips smiling up into my face. "You like me, Danny, so don't fight," she said cajolingly. "I like you."

I stared at her coldly. "I hate your guts," I said.

She stared back at me. The smile left her face, and an expression of excitement came into it. "You think you mean it, but you don't," she said, lifting her hands and making a curious gesture. "You'll get over it. You'll come back for more of this."

I stared at her fingers as she slid her forefinger around in the palm of her other hand. I looked up at her face again and she was smiling. I knew what she meant. She was right. I would come back.

I turned quickly and ran down the block, calling Rexie. But I wasn't really running after the dog; I was running away from her. And I knew I could never run fast enough to keep from growing up.

Chapter Eight

I COULDN'T wait for the last class to end. Mr. Gottkin had given me all the information that Papa had asked for, and I had decided to run down to the store and tell him. Papa would like that; he always was glad when I came down there. I remember when I was smaller Papa used to send me into the stores of all the other merchants on the block in order to show me off. I used to get a kick out of it too, they all made such a fuss over me.

I caught the trolley at Church and Flatbush, went downtown, and transferred to the crosstown trolley that ran out along Sands Street near the Navy Yard. The trolley let me off two blocks from the store.

I hoped Papa would let me go to the country with Mr. Gottkin. I wanted to go more than ever now. It was the only way I could get away from Marjorie Ann. I was afraid of her, of how she made me feel. I would be okay if I could stay away the whole summer.

The sound of a bugle came to my ear. I looked across the street to the Navy Yard. It was four o'clock and they were changing the guard. I decided to watch them—a few minutes more wouldn't make any difference.

I WASN'T THERE WHEN—

Papa lifted the lid of the cash register and looked in. The dial showed nine dollars and forty cents. He shook his head and looked at the big clock on the wall. Four o'clock already. In normal times the register would show ten times as much. He didn't know how he could keep up his loan payments if things continued like this.

He heard the sound of a truck pulling to a stop in front of the store and looked out. It was the Towns & James truck. They were jobbers he had dealt with for as many years as he had been in business. The truckman came into the store with a small package under his arm.

"Hello, Tom," Papa said, smiling.

"Hi ya, doc," the man answered. "Got a package for yuh. Twelve O six."

Papa took a pencil out of his pocket. "All right," he said, "I'll sign for it."

The truckman shook his head. "Sorry, doc. C.O.D."

"C.O.D.?" Papa asked, a sudden hurt coming into his eyes. "But I've done business with them for almost twenty years and I always paid my bills."

The driver shrugged his shoulders sympathetically. "I know, doc," he said gently, "but I can't help it. Them's orders. It's stamped on the bill."

Papa rang up no sale on the register and counted out the money slowly on the counter. The driver picked it up and left the package on the counter. Papa was ashamed to look at him. His credit had always been a great source of pride.

A woman came into the store and Papa put a smile on his face. "Yes, ma'am?"

She put a dime down on the counter. "Kin I have two nickels, doc? I wanna use the phone."

Silently he picked up the dime and pushed two nickels toward her. He watched her go into the phone booth. The package was still on the counter where the truckman had left it. Papa didn't feel like unpacking it yet. He didn't want to touch it.

I turned the corner in front of the speakeasy and looked across the street. The blue and gray lettering on the store windows reached out to me:

FISHER'S PHARMACY
FARMICIA ITALIANA NORSK APOTHEKE
EX-LAX

I ran past the open door of the speakeasy. From inside, the sound of loud angry voices came to me, but I didn't stop. There were always arguments going on in there.

I stood in the doorway of the store. Papa was behind the counter, a small dark man in a light tan store jacket. He seemed to be studying a package on the counter in front of him. I walked in.

"Hello, Papa." My words seemed to echo in the empty store. The musty familiar smell of drugs came to my nose. I would always remember that smell whenever I saw a drugstore. When I was little I used to smell it on the clothes Papa wore home from work.

"Danny!" Papa's voice sounded pleased. He came around the counter. "What are you doing down here?"

"I got that information on the country hotel from Mr. Gottkin," I explained, looking into his face.

Papa smiled wearily. He seemed very tired. "I should have known you'd have a reason," he said ruefully.

"I was comin' down anyway," I said quickly.

Papa looked at me knowingly. I wasn't fooling him. He

pushed his hand fondly across my head. "Okay," he said gently. "Come into the back room and we'll talk it over."

I started to follow him to the back of the store. I had just passed the counter when a scream came from the doorway. I spun around, startled.

"Doc!" the man screamed again.

I felt Papa's hands on my shoulders and he pushed me behind him. Papa's face was white.

The man in the doorway was covered with blood. There was a long, ragged gash on the side of his face running down to his neck. The flesh hung open and the white of the jawbone showed beneath the welling blood. He took several hesitant steps into the store, the blood spattering at his feet. His hands found the counter and he gripped it desperately, turning a pain-ridden face toward us. "They cut me, doc."

His grip weakened and he began to slide to the floor. He sank to his knees in front of the counter, still gripping the edge over his head, his face still turned toward us. He looked like a man at prayer. "Help me, doc." His voice was a weak, husky whisper. "Don't let me die."

Then his grip broke and he sprawled out on the floor at our feet. I could see the slow welling of blood in the wound. I looked up at Papa. His face was white and his lips were moving silently. He looked sick. There were cold beads of sweat on his forehead.

"Papa!" I cried.

He stared down at me with empty, anguished eyes.

"Papa, aren't you going to help him?" I couldn't believe that he would let the man die there.

Papa's lips tightened grimly. He dropped to one knee at the man's side. The man had fainted, his mouth hung open loosely. Papa looked up at me. "Go to the phone, Danny," he said calmly, "and call for an ambulance."

I ran to the telephone. When I came back the store was filled with people crowded around the man on the floor, and I had to push my way through them.

Papa was pleading with them: "Stand back. Give him air."

They paid no attention, but another voice took up his plea— a cop's voice. "You hoid the doc," it rasped with accustomed authority. "Now do what he sez!"

The ambulance came too late. The man was already dead.

He had died there on the floor because he and another man had quarreled over a glass of beer. I didn't know a glass of beer could be that important, but this one was. It was worth a man's life.

I finished wiping the last trace of blood from the counter. Papa was watching me from the back of the store. This was exciting. I turned to him. "Gee, Papa," I said, filled with admiration, "you were brave, helping the man like that. I couldn't do it. I would have got sick."

Papa looked at me curiously. "I was sick, Danny," he said quietly, "but there was nothing else I could do."

I smiled at him. "I changed my mind, Papa," I said. "I don't want to go away this summer after all. Do things like this happen often?"

"No," Papa said. He took a pack of cigarettes from the counter behind him, took one out, and lit it. "You're going away," he said.

"But, Papa—" There was real disappointment in my voice.

"You heard me, Danny," he said firmly. "You're going away."

I straightened up slowly. Something was wrong, something seemed to be missing. "Did you take the package on the counter, Papa?" I asked.

Papa looked curiously at the counter. A shadow came into his eyes then went away quickly. He took a deep breath, and his lips twisted into a wry grin. "I didn't take it," he said.

I was puzzled. "You think somebody clipped it, Papa?"

The weary lines etched themselves into his face as he answered. "It doesn't matter really, Danny. It wasn't anything important. I didn't want it anyway."

Chapter Nine

I SAT quietly on the stoop, my hand idly scratching Rexie's head. It was my last night at home. Tomorrow morning Mr.

Gottkin would pick me up in his Ford and we would go off to the country. I felt sad. It would be the first time I had been away from home for any length of time.

The night hung quietly around us. The house was dark. Only the kitchen was lit up, where Mamma and Papa were still talking. I leaned over the dog. "Now you be a good girl while I'm away," I whispered to her. She wagged her tail slowly. She understood everything I said to her, she was the smartest dog I ever saw.

"The summer isn't very long anyway," I said. "Before you know it, it'll be fall an' I'll be back."

She nuzzled her cold nose into my hand, and I rubbed her under her chin. She liked that.

I heard the Conlons' door open and looked up. Marjorie Ann came out on the stoop. I got to my feet quickly, called Rexie, and started down the block. I didn't want to talk to her.

"Danny!" I could hear Marjorie Ann's footsteps running after me. I turned back. She caught up to me all out of breath.

"You're going away tomorrow?"

"Yeah." I nodded my head.

"Mind if I walk a little way with you?" she asked in a small, humble voice.

I looked at her in surprise. This didn't seem like her at all. "It's a free country," I said, starting off again.

She fell into step alongside me. "Pass everything, Danny?" she asked sociably.

"Uh-huh," I said proudly. "Eighty-five average."

"That's good," she said flatteringly. "I almost flunked math."

"Math is easy," I said.

"Not for me," she replied brightly.

We turned the corner silently, our footsteps echoing hollowly on the sidewalk. We walked another block before she spoke again.

"Still mad at me, Danny?"

I looked at her out of the corner of my eye. There was a hurt expression on her face. I didn't answer.

We walked almost another block. Then I heard her sniff. I stopped and turned to her. If there was anything I hated it was a girl bawling. "Now what?" I asked harshly.

Her eyes shone with tears. "I didn't want you to go away mad, Danny," she sniffed. "I like you."

I snorted derisively. "You have a funny way of showing it. Always teasing me and making me do things I don't want to."

She was really bawling now. "I—I was only trying to do what you'd like, Danny."

I started on again. "Well, I don't like it," I said shortly. "It makes me nervous."

"If I promise to stop, Danny, will you still be mad at me?" Her hand caught at mine.

I looked down at her. "Not if you really promise to stop," I said.

"Then I promise," she said quickly, a smile breaking through her tears.

I returned her smile. "Then I'm not mad any more," I said. Suddenly I realized I had never really been mad at her. It was myself that I had been angry with. I had liked what she had done to me.

We walked along, her hand still holding mine. Rexie ran into some open lots, and we waited for her to come out.

Marjorie Ann looked up into my face. "Can I be your girl, Danny?"

"Holy cow!" The exclamation burst from me involuntarily. Instantly the tears spilled over into her eyes again. She turned and began to run away from me, sobbing.

I stood there for a moment gawking after her. Then I ran and caught her by the arm. "Marjorie Ann!"

She turned to face me, her body still shaking with her tears. "Stop bawlin'," I said. "You can be my girl if you want."

"Oh, Danny!" She threw her arms around my neck and tried to kiss me.

I dodged her. "Aw, cut it, Marge. You promised."

"Just a kiss, Danny," she said quickly. "That's all right if I'm your girl."

I stared at her. There was no arguing with her logic. Besides, I wanted to kiss her. "Okay," I said grudgingly, "but that's all!"

She pulled my face down to her and kissed me. I could feel her warm lips moving under mine. I pulled her closer to me and she hid her face against my shoulder. I could hardly hear her voice. "I'll do anything you want, now I'm your girl, Danny!" She pressed my hand against her breast. "Anything you want," she repeated. "I won't tease you any more."

Her eyes were shining earnestly. She didn't seem like the

same girl I had known all this time. There was a warmth in her that I had never seen before.

I kissed her again, slowly. I could feel her pressing closely against me, and a fever rising in my blood. A pulse began to pound in my temples. Quickly I pushed her away.

"Then let's go home, Marjorie Ann," I said gravely. "This is all I want."

Papa called me as I started up the stairs. I came back to him. "Yes, Papa?"

There was an embarrassed look on his face. He looked at Mamma, but she was reading the evening paper and didn't even look up. He fixed his eyes somewhere on the floor and cleared his throat. "You're going away for the first time, Danny," he said awkwardly.

"Yes, Papa."

He was looking up at the ceiling now, carefully avoiding my eyes. "You're a big boy, Danny, and there's certain things your mother and I feel we ought to tell you."

I grinned. "About girls, Papa?" I asked.

He looked down at me in surprise. Mamma had put down her paper and was watching me.

I smiled at them. "You're a little late, Papa. They teach those things in school nowadays."

"They do?" he asked incredulously.

I nodded my head, still grinning. "If there's anything you want to know, Papa, don't be shy. Just ask me."

A smile of relief came to his lips. "See. Mary," he said, "I told you we didn't have to say anything to him."

Mamma looked at me doubtfully.

I smiled at her reassuringly. "You don't have to worry, Mamma," I reassured her. "I can take care of myself."

I went up the stairs still smiling. They just didn't know who they were talking to. I was an expert on girls. Hadn't I just proved that this evening?

Chapter Ten

"DOES she lay, Danny?" I glanced at the boy disgustedly. His face was flushed as his eyes followed the girl onto the porch.

I reached down and locked the concession counter before I answered him. If I had heard the question once, I had heard it a thousand times since I'd come up here. This was my third summer at the Mont-Fern Hotel and Country Club.

"They all do," I replied casually. "What the hell do you think they come up here for, fresh air and sunshine?"

The other boys around the counter all joined in the laughter, but he was still watching her. "Man," he said in an awed voice, "there's something about some dames in slacks!"

"Who looked at the slacks?" I asked carelessly. "I'm strictly a blouse man myself." I started to lock up the concession while they were still laughing. These waiters and busboys never spent a dime. They were up here for the few bucks and the tail. They weren't even good at their work, but the hotel didn't care. All they wanted them for was to keep the guests happy, and the guests were mostly dames, so everybody was happy with the arrangement.

The boys drifted out on the porch and I watched them go. Most of them were older than me, but I thought of them as kids. I felt old. Maybe it was my size—I was five eleven—or maybe it was just because I was a veteran of three summers. I picked up the daily receipts report and began to make it out. Sam liked to have his reports in order.

I remembered my first summer up here. I was real green then. That was right after my Bar Mitzvah. I was just a punk kid sucking after Gottkin, hoping it would get me on the football team in the fall. What a lot of crap that was!

Gottkin never came back to school. The first night up here he cleaned out the concessionaire in a crap game. The next day he was in business. Before the first week had passed, he knew he

60

wasn't going back. "This is for me," I remember him saying. "Let some other shmoe wet-nurse a bunch of kids."

I helped him instead of working for the hotel, and he did all right. Hit the Miami Beach route in the winter, and the next summer he took over the concession at the next hotel along the road as well as this one. This summer he had five working. A couple of boys in each place and all he did was come around once a day and pick up the dough. No more Ford for him, he drove a Pierce roadster with the top down now.

But that first summer had been rough. I guess the green stuck out of my ears. I was the butt of every joke the boys could think of, and all the girls teased hell out of me. Sam finally had to tell them to lay off. He was afraid I would lose my temper and belt one of them.

I didn't want to go back the next summer, but when Sam came over to the house and told me that he had picked up the second spot and I would run this one, I had gone with him. We needed the money. Papa's business was really up the creek. I picked up five hundred dollars for my end of the summer.

I remember Mamma's face when I put the dough on the kitchen table and told her to keep it. There were tears in her eyes; she turned to Papa, trying to hide them from me. Her lips were quivering, but I could hear what she said: "My Blondie." That's all.

Papa came close to tears himself. Each day in the store had become more frustrating than the one before. The money would go a long way. But his lips had tightened with stubborn pride. "Put it in the bank, Danny," he had said. "You'll need the money to go to college."

I had smiled. He wasn't kidding me, I knew better. "We can use the dough now," I had said with undeniable logic. "I got two more years before college stares me in the face. We can worry about it then."

Papa had looked at me for what seemed like a very long time. Then he reached out a trembling hand and picked up the money. "All right, Danny," he had said, "but we'll remember it. When things get better, you'll get it back."

But even as he spoke we all knew the money was gone. Business wasn't getting any better, it was getting worse. It went the same way everything else did, down the drain.

But that was last summer and I had already kissed the dough good-by. This summer Sam had promised me an extra hundred if I beat last year's take. I finished the report and summed up the season's business thus far. All I needed was a break during these last few weeks of the season and I was set. I looked at my watch. There was just time enough for me to grab a swim before lunch.

I finished locking up the concession and went out on the porch. The new broad and the boy with big eyes were playing table tennis. The girl had style all right, but her backhand could stand a little work.

I walked up behind her and took the racket out of her hand. "Loose, baby, loose," I said confidently. "Watch me. You're too stiff."

Big Eyes glared at me viciously and slammed the ball at me. Easily I returned it. He smashed it back at me. Again I returned it. I was good and I knew it. The next time I cut a little english onto the ball and it veered away sharply from his frantic stab.

I smiled at the girl. "See, baby, it's easy."

"The way you do it," she snowed me, smiling back, "but not for me."

"Sure it is," I said casually. "I'll show yuh."

I put the racket in her hand and stood behind her. I reached out and held her hands from the back. Slowly I brought her right arm across her left side almost shoulder high. She pressed back against me as our arms crossed together. She couldn't help it, I had her tied up. I could feel her breasts taut against my forearm. I smiled knowingly at Big Eyes. He was flaming with anger, but he didn't dare open his yap. I was too big for him.

I socked it into her and looked down smiling. "Isn't it easy?" I asked conversationally.

Her face was turning red. I could see the color coming up from her throat. Unobtrusively she tried to shake my grip. She could just as easy have tried to fly. She couldn't. I was too strong for her. She didn't dare say anything because all the fellows were watching us and she'd be marked lousy. "I—I guess so," she finally answered.

I grinned and let her go. That was one ping-pong lesson she wouldn't forget in a hurry. The fellows wouldn't forget it either. I saw them watching me, envy in their eyes. Dollars weren't the standard up here, dames were. None of them would

ever suspect now that all I ever got out of my summers here
was dough.

"Just keep practicin', baby," I said, and sauntered off the
porch feeling pretty satisfied with myself.

I cut across the ballfield toward the casino. Sam and I shared
a one-room bungalow behind it. The first year we had been up
here we had slept in a room over the casino and had never been
able to get any rest. This year Sam had taken the bungalow and
we used it as a combination stock room and sleeping-quarters.
Sam even had a telephone put in so he could keep in touch with
the other concessions.

I unlocked the door of the bungalow, went in, and looked
around me disgustedly. The place was a mess. Cartons and
boxes were all over the room. It seemed I never could get time
to straighten it out.

From a line over the bed I took a faded pair of gabardine
swim trunks and slipped into them. Stepping carefully over the
boxes, I made my way to the door and out. I promised myself I
would straighten up the room this afternoon. I locked the door
carefully and walked to the pool.

The pool was the way I liked it—deserted. I liked room to
swim in. That's why I came down in the morning; the guests
rarely showed up until after lunch. I looked at the old sign over
the entrance to the pool as I walked under it. I got a kick out of
that sign. It used to be a bright red color at the beginning of the
summer, when it was newly painted, but now it was faded and
only a gentle whisper.

> BEWARE OF ATHLETE'S FOOT
> ALL BATHERS MUST STEP IN
> FOOT BATH BEFORE ENTERING
> POOL—by ord. Bd. Health

I obeyed its order religiously. One thing I didn't want was
athlete's foot. I stood there almost two minutes before I walked
out on the rim of the pool, my feet leaving wet tracks on the
cement walk.

I looked down at the porch to see if anyone was watching
me. Big Eyes and the dame were still at the tennis table. Nobody was looking. I felt oddly disappointed.

I cut into the water smoothly and swam briskly down to the
far end of the pool. The water was cold this morning and I'd

have to keep on swimming if I didn't want to chill. Good enough. I could practice up on my crawl stroke while there was nobody around. Sometimes I would lose my count and inhale when I should exhale and I'd get a noseful of water. Then I'd come up sputtering and choking and feeling like a fool.

I settled into the stroke, counting grimly. I had been swimming for about fifteen minutes when I heard a man's voice calling me. Startled, I lost my count and got a mouthful of water. I looked up angrily.

It was one of the bellhops. "There's a dame down at the desk lookin' for your boss."

I swam over to the side of the pool and looked up at him. "You know he ain't here," I said heatedly, "so why bother me? Tell her to blow."

"I tol' her," the bellhop said quickly, " 'nen she asked for you."

Who could be asking for me? "She say who she is?" I asked.

The bellhop shrugged his shoulders. "How'n hell would I know? I didn't ask. I was too busy lookin' at this babe. I'd see 'er 'f I were you. She's really got it." He rolled his eyes expressively and smacked his lips.

I grinned and climbed out of the pool. The water ran down off me and formed small puddles around my feet. I reached for a towel and began to dry myself. "What are you waitin' for, then?" I asked. "Send her up here."

He looked at me lewdly. "Okay, Danny." He laughed as he turned away. "But 'f I were you I'd make sure muh jock is on good an' tight before she got here."

As I finished drying myself and sat down on a bench to slip into my sandals, a shadow fell across my feet. I looked up.

"Hello, Danny." Miss Schindler was standing there smiling at me.

I jumped to my feet, suddenly self-conscious. With surprise I realized I was a good head taller than she was. "Muh—Miss Schindler," I stammered.

She looked up into my face, still smiling. "You've grown, Danny. I wouldn't have recognized you.'"

I stared down at her. I was funny how she made me think of home. It was almost like another world up here. Suddenly I remembered that I had to answer Mamma's letter. It had been lying on the table back in the bungalow for almost a week.

Chapter Eleven

"SAM isn't here right now," I replied in answer to her question. "He's checking the other concessions. He'll be back tonight."

A curious look of relief came over her face. "I was just in the neighborhood," she said quickly, "and I thought I'd drop by." She stood there awkwardly in the bright sunlight and squinted up into my face.

I kept it blank and unknowing. Close neighborhood. Ninety miles from the city. "Sure," I said. I had an idea. "Where are you staying? I can have him call you when he gets back."

"Oh, no, he can't do that!" she answered. Too quickly, I thought. Her husband must be around somewhere; she wouldn't want him to know. She must have guessed what was going through my mind. "You see, I'm traveling around and I don't know where I'll be stopping tonight."

"How about here?" I suggested brightly. "It's a nice place and I can get you a discount."

She shook her head.

"Sam will feel bad if I tell him you left without waiting," I said.

Her eyes were shrewd as she looked at me. "No," she said definitely. "I'd better not."

I was disappointed. Suddenly I realized that I wanted her to stay. In a way she was a touch of home and I was glad to see her. The telephone in the bungalow began to ring. I grabbed my towel and started to run toward it.

"Wait a minute," I called back over my shoulder. "That's probably Sam calling. I'll tell him you're here."

I pushed open the door and grabbed at the phone. "Hello. Sam?"

"Yeah." His voice was husky through the receiver. "How's it goin'?"

"Okay, Sam," I answered. Excitement crept into my voice. "Miss Schindler's up here to see you."

Sam's voice grew huskier. "What's she doin' up there?"

"She said she was just passing through an' she thought she'd drop in an' see you."

"Tell her I can't get back till late tonight," he said quickly. "Get her a good room an' keep her there till I get back."

"But, Sam," I protested, "I already asked her. She don't want to stay."

His voice grew confidential. "Listen, kid, I'm dependin' on you. If you ever had a yen for a babe like I got for her, you'd know what I mean. Get her anythin' she wants, but keep her there. I'll be back before one in the mornin'."

The phone went dead in my hand. I looked at it bewilderedly. What did he expect me to do? Kidnap her? Slowly I put the receiver down and turned to the door. Sam had spoken as if I knew what to do, as he would to another man, not a kid. I began to feel a glow of pride as I started for the door, but before I reached it she stood framed in the doorway.

She peered into the bungalow curiously. "May I come in?" she asked.

I stood still in the center of the room. "Sure, Miss Schindler." I pushed some boxes from the floor in front of her so she could pass. "I was supposed to straighten up, but I haven't had time," I explained.

She closed the door behind her and I straightened up to face her. My face was flushed.

"Was it Sam?" she asked.

My eyes met her gaze. I nodded silently.

"What did he say?"

"He said for me to get you a room an' anything you want an' to keep you here until he comes," I said boldly.

Her voice grew challenging and suspicious. "He seems pretty sure of himself, doesn't he?"

I could feel the flush grow deeper and my eyes fell away from her piercing look. I didn't answer.

She sounded angry now. I had been too wise. Somehow she realized that I knew. "What will you tell him if I don't stay?" she snapped.

I turned away from her and fiddled with a few of the boxes. I still didn't answer.

Her hand gripped my shoulder and turned me around. Her

face was flushed now. "What will you tell him?" she repeated heatedly.

I looked deep into her eyes. To hell with her. There was nothing she could do to me. I wasn't in school now. "Nothing," I said mockingly. I took her hand from my shoulder.

She looked at my hand gripping her wrist, then slowly around the room. I could see she was making up her mind. Her eyes came back to me. "All right," she said suddenly, "I'll stay. Clean up this room for me."

I was startled. "But Sam said for me to get you a room—"

Her voice grew stubborn. "I said I'll stay here."

"But it's all messed up," I protested. "You'll be much more comfortable up in the hotel."

She turned toward the door and opened it. "Sam said you were to do anything I wanted if I stayed. I'm staying here." She stepped over the threshold and looked back at me. "I'm going down to get my car. You can clean up the room while I'm gone."

I watched her close the door. She had me and she knew it. I wondered why she was so angry. I couldn't have let on that much. I walked over to the window and looked out after her.

She disappeared below the swimming-pool. I could understand how Sam felt. She sold more with her walk than most of the broads up here did in a bathing suit.

I turned back from the window and looked disgustedly around the room. Mamma's last letter gleamed whitely at me from the table. I hadn't answered it yet, in more than a week. Now I wouldn't have time.

I WASN'T THERE WHEN—

Mamma tied the smock around her as she walked down the stairs. The air was still and quiet and she knew it would be another hot day. She was tired before the day began. She was always tired lately. She hadn't been sleeping well.

Papa had brought home a tonic for her. She had taken it every morning for a week, but it hadn't helped. Of course she had told him that it had helped her—it made him feel good. A man had to feel useful, and he felt bad enough over the way business was going.

She felt sorry for Papa. Last night in his sleep he had cried.

His voice in the dark woke her up and she lay there quietly, listening to the soft, mumbled words coming from his heart. He seemed so bewildered that tears had come to her eyes.

She hadn't been able to fall asleep afterwards. The night seemed to last forever. Now she was tired again and nothing would help. The muggy heat of the morning didn't make it any easier. These last few weeks of August were generally the worst. She felt she could not take much more of this heat and wished the summer was over already.

She walked through the kitchen and opened the icebox door and looked in. It was almost empty. She had always taken great pride in keeping a well-stocked icebox. She had always said that she liked to keep enough in the house so that she didn't have to run out shopping every day. Now something about its bleakness was another ache in her body. The small piece of ice, shrunk from the day before; the almost empty carton of eggs; the half a quarter pound of butter. Even the milk bottle with the small drop of milk in it seemed to hurt her.

She closed the icebox door slowly. The three eggs would do for breakfast. Suddenly she was glad I wasn't home. She decided to look in the mailbox to see if my letter had arrived.

The sound of the milk wagon came to her. She began to feel better; she would be able to get eggs and butter from him as well as milk. And at least he would put in on the bill so she could use the few dollars she had in the tumbler over the sink for a soup chicken. She hurried to the front door to catch him before he went away.

The milkman was kneeling in front of the storage box when she opened the door. He slowly rose to his feet with a peculiarly guilty expression on his face. "Mornin', Missus Fisher," he said in a strained, embarrassed voice.

"Good morning, Borden, it's a good thing I caught you," Mamma replied. The words were spilling from her lips breathlessly from her slight exertion. "I need some eggs and butter this morning.'"

The milkman shifted awkwardly on his feet. "Gee, Missus Fisher, I'm sorry but—" His voice trailed off into nothingness.

Disappointment etched her face. "You mean you're all out?"

He shook his head silently. His hand gestured toward the storage box on the stoop in front of her.

Mamma was bewildered. "I—I don't understand," she said hesitantly, her eyes following his pointing fingers. Then she did understand. There was a yellow note in the box. Only the note, no milk.

She picked up the note slowly and began to read it. They were stopping her service. She owed them three weeks' bills. The eyes she raised to the milkman were filled with horror. Her face was white and sick-looking.

"I'm sorry, Misus Fisher," he murmured sympathetically.

A spray of water began to fall across the lawn in front of the house. She was suddenly aware of Mr. Conlon, who had been watering his garden. He was watching them.

He saw her glance. "Good morning, Mrs. Fisher," his voice boomed out.

"Good morning," she replied automatically. She would have to do something. She was sure that he had seen and heard everything. She looked down at the bill again: four dollars and eighty-two cents. There was just five dollars in the tumbler over the sink.

She forced her voice up into her throat and tried to smile. Her lips were almost white and the smile was more like a grimace on a stone statue. "I was just going to pay you," she said to the milkman in a purposely steady voice. "Wait a minute."

She closed the door quickly behind her. For a second she leaned against it weakly; the bill fluttered to the floor from her trembling fingers. She didn't try to pick it up; she was afraid she would faint if she did. Instead she hurried back into the kitchen and took the money from the tumbler over the sink.

She counted the bills slowly, reluctantly, as if with each recounting some miracle would make them double. There were only five dollars. She felt cold. A shiver ran nervously through her as she turned and went back to the door.

The milkman was standing on the stoop where she had left him, but now he had milk, butter, and eggs in a little wire basket on his arm. She handed him the money silently, and he put it in his pocket and counted out the eighteen cents change into her hand.

"Here's your order, Missus Fisher," he said understandingly, not quite meeting her eyes.

She wanted to tell him to keep it, but didn't dare. Shame coursed inside her as she took the basket from his hands. She didn't speak.

He cleared his throat. "It's not my fault, Missus Fisher. It's the credit man down at the office. You understand?"

She nodded her head. She understood all right. He turned and ran down the steps as she watched him. Mr. Conlon's voice boomed out at her.

"It's gonna be a scorcher today, Mrs. Fisher." He was smiling.

She looked at him absently. Her mind was far away. "Yes, it is, Mr. Conlon," she replied gently, and, closing the door behind her, went back into the kitchen.

She put the milk, butter, and eggs into the icebox thoughtfully. The box still looked empty. She felt she should be crying, but her eyes were dry. There was a noise on the stairs. She closed the icebox door quickly. The family was coming down for breakfast.

A few minutes later the milk and butter and eggs were out on the table and they were eating. As she watched them, a slight warmth came into her body.

Mimi was excited. There had been an ad in the papers last night. A&S, one of the downtown Brooklyn department stores, wanted some part time girls to act as clerks and she was going down there. Papa ate his breakfast silently. His face was drawn and weary, showing the lines that appear when sleep is not restful.

Then the kitchen was empty and Mamma was alone. Slowly she finished washing the dishes. Then she noticed the milk and butter and eggs still on the table. She picked them up and balanced them on her arm. With her free hand she opened the icebox door and put them in. Nothing remained of the little piece of ice; it had melted. She closed the door.

She heard footsteps on the stoop. It must be the mailman, she thought. She ran to the front door and opened it. The mailman had already gone on to the next house. She opened the mailbox quickly, took out a few letters, and turned them over in her hand. Nothing from me. Only bills. She went back into the kitchen slowly, opening them as she walked. Gas, telephone, electricity—all overdue.

She dropped them on the table, holding one more unopened letter in her hand. She didn't recognize its marking. She opened it. It was a notice from the bank that the mortgage payment on the house was overdue.

Heavily she sank into a chair beside the table. Jarred by the vibration, the icebox door swung slowly open. She sat there staring into the open box. She ought to get up and close the door. Whatever cold was left in it would escape, but somehow it didn't matter. She didn't have the strength to get up and close the door. Nothing mattered any more. There wasn't even the strength in her to cry. Her body felt terribly weak. She stared into the almost empty icebox until it seemed to grow larger and larger and she was lost in its half-empty, half-cold world.

Chapter Twelve

I WAS busy yakking with a broad just after I had closed the concession when I saw Miss Schindler come into the casino. I watched her out of the corner of my eye as she stood in the doorway looking around.

I had seen her only once before that evening, when I had run over to the bungalow to pick up a few cartons of cigarettes that I needed for the concession. It was one of those nights you feel you can almost reach out and touch the stars that hang so brightly over your head—one of those nights you never see in the city. She had been sitting on the front step of the cottage, and the faintly off-beat sound of music came from the casino. She had looked at me and for a moment I thought she was going to speak, but evidently she changed her mind. She didn't say a word—just watched me in sulky silence as I picked up the cartons and left. I didn't speak to her.

I looked down at my watch. Eleven thirty. The night must have dragged, back there in the bungalow. I had been wondering all evening whether she would come down.

Her gaze settled on me and she started to walk toward me. I shook the girl with me quickly. "The boss's wife is coming, baby," I lied. "I gotta report."

I left the girl with an angry expression on her face, but I didn't care. I met Miss Schindler before she got halfway across the room. "Hello," I said, smiling at her. "I been wonderin' how long you would take to get down here."

She smiled back at me. It was a real smile and I knew she had got over her mad. "Hello, Danny," she said. Her eyes met mine. "I'm sorry for the way I acted this afternoon."

I checked her eyes. She meant what she said. I relaxed suddenly and felt very warm and friendly toward her. "That's all right, Miss Schindler," I replied gently. "You were upset."

Her hand reached out toward mine. "I was lonely back there in the bungalow."

"I know how you feel," I said slowly, looking down at her hand where she touched my arm. "Sometimes I feel the same way up here. In the city you don't notice it, but up here in the country the sky is so big you feel kinda small."

We stood there in awkward silence for a moment, then I heard the band go into a rumba. I smiled at her. "D'ya wanna dance, Miss Schindler?"

She nodded her head and I led her to the dance floor. She came into my arms and we picked up the rhythm of the music. She was light on her feet and easy to dance with.

"You dance very well, Danny." She smiled up at me. "Do you do everything else as well?"

"I'm afraid not, Miss Schindler." I shook my head ruefully. I knew I was a good dancer, though; after three summers up here I had to be. "But Sam says I got a good sense of rhythm. He says that's why I'm a good boxer."

"You still want to be a fighter?" she asked curiously.

"I never wanted to be one," I replied, "but Sam says I'm naturally good at it an' that I can make a lotta dough when I'm old enough."

"And money is that important?"

I could feel the sure movement of her hip under my hand as I led her through an intricate dip. "You tell me, Miss Schindler," I parried. "Isn't it?"

She had no answer for that. Nobody had an answer when you talked money. She looked up at me. "We don't have to be so formal up here, Danny," she said with a smile. "My name is Ceil."

"I know," I said quietly.

Then we were dancing and I was humming the music half under my breath. Siboney—tum tum, ti tum—tum tum, ti tum—Siboney. There was something about rumba music. If you really like it, you can lose all sense of time when you're dancing. I liked it and I could tell that she did too. It was the way the music brought us close together. It was as if we had danced together many times before.

Abruptly the orchestra switched into *Auld Lang Syne* and we were mildly surprised. We stood awkwardly smiling at each other.

"That's all for the night, Ceil," I said. "It must be twelve o'clock."

She checked her watch. "Exactly."

"Thanks for the dance, Miss Schindler."

She laughed. I was surprised to hear her laugh. It was the first time since she came up here. "I told you—Ceil." She smiled.

I laughed too. "I enjoyed the dance, Ceil," I said quickly, "but now I gotta scrounge up a room for myself or I'll be sleeping on the porch."

Her voice was filled with dismay. "Did I put you out of your room?"

I smiled down at her. "It's okay, Ceil, you didn't know."

"I'm really sorry, Danny," she said contritely. "Will you be able to get a place?"

I grinned. "I won't have any trouble." I turned to leave her. "Good night. Ceil."

Her hand caught at my arm. "I'd like a drink, Danny," she said quickly. "Can you get me one?"

There was a nervous look on her face—like you get when you're waiting for someone and you don't know whether they're going to show. I felt sorry for her. "I got some cold three-point-two stashed away for Sam that I can let you have," I said. Three-point-two beer had just been legalized the spring before.

She shuddered delicately. "Not beer. Anything else?"

"Sam's got a bottle of Old Overholt in the cottage. I can get you some seltzer and some ice cubes."

She smiled. "That will be fine."

I unlocked the small refrigerator behind the concession counter, I took out a bottle of seltzer and a tray of ice cubes, and locked the refrigerator again.

The casino was almost empty when I came back to her. "Here you are," I smiled. "I'll carry it up to the bungalow for you and show you where the liquor is."

She followed me into the night. As we left the casino some-one turned out the lights, and the grounds were plunged into darkness. I felt her hesitate beside me. "Hold onto my arm," I suggested. "I know my way around here."

I expected her to rest her hand on my arm, but instead she slipped her arm under mine and walked very close to me. I was so conscious of her that several times I almost stumbled. I could feel my face warm and flushed when I turned on the light just inside the cottage door.

I stood there looking at her. There was laughter deep in her eyes. She had me all mixed up. I didn't know what to say.

"I'm still thirsty, Danny," she said pointedly.

Turning to the bureau in hurried confusion, I pulled open a drawer and took out a bottle.

She was on her third or maybe fourth drink and we were sitting on the cottage steps when the telephone began to ring. She had been laughing at me, trying to tease me into taking a drink.

I jumped to my feet, went inside, and picked up the receiver. She followed me but not so quickly. By now the whisky had hit her and she was slightly rocky, but she was next to me at the telephone when I answered it.

Sam's voice crackled through the receiver and roared through the darkened room. "Danny?"

"Yeah, Sam."

"I can't get up there tonight like I said."

"But, Sam—" I started to protest.

The sound of a woman's laughter echoed in the phone. Ceil drew in her breath sharply beside me. Her face seemed very white in the darkness.

Sam seemed to be choosing his words very carefully. "Tell this guy that's waitin' for me that I got jammed up an' that I'll be up tomorrow after lunch to close the deal, y' unnerstan'?"

"Yeah, Sam." I understood all right. "But—"

"Okay then, kid," Sam shouted into the phone. "I'll see yuh tomorrow."

The phone went dead and I hung up. I turned to her. "Sam got jammed up on a deal," I said clumsily. "He can't get up here tonight."

She was staring at me, weaving a little. But she wasn't rocky enough not to know the score. "Don't lie to me, Danny!" Her voice was husky with rage. "I heard him!"

I looked at her. There was a hurt expression on her face.

That was the second time that evening I'd felt sorry for her. I started for the door. "I guess I'd better be going, Ceil."

I felt her hand clutch at my arm and I turned in surprise. I saw her other hand swinging and I ducked. I wasn't fast enough. The side of my face was stinging from her slap and then she was swinging wildly at me with both hands.

In the dark I grabbed her wrists and held them. "What the hell are you trying to do?" I gasped.

She was trying to pull her hands free, but I was too strong for her. Her voice was husky and bitter as she spilled the words out over me. "You think it's funny, don't you?" she shouted. Her voice echoed out into the night.

I tried to hold her with one hand and cover her mouth with the other. Her teeth sank into my fingers and I pulled my hand away with a cry of pain.

She laughed wildly. "That hurt, didn't it? Now you know how I feel! Now maybe it won't be so funny!'"

"Ceil!" I whispered urgently, my heart pounding. "Please be quiet. I'll get thrown out of here!" The night watchman didn't give a damn what went on up here as long as you didn't make any noise.

But I didn't have to worry, for now she was leaning against me weakly and sobbing. I stood there quietly, not daring to move for fear I'd start her off again.

Her voice was muffled against my chest between her sobs. "No good, no good. You're all alike. No good."

I smoothed her hair. It was soft under my fingers. "Poor Ceil," I said softly. I was really sorry for her.

She looked up at me. Her eyes couldn't seem to focus in the darkness. She weaved slightly as I held her. "Yes," she agreed with me. The rage had mixed with the liquor and had made her more rocky. "Poor Ceil. Only Danny knows how she feels."

Her eyes narrowed speculatively. "Danny knows why Ceil came here?"

I didn't answer. I didn't know what to say to her.

Her arms went around my neck, she turned her face up to me. "Danny feels sorry for Ceil," she whispered. "Kiss Ceil."

I stood there woodenly, afraid to move. I wasn't looking for any more trouble.

She tightened her arms around my neck and pulled my face down to her. I could feel her teeth sinking into my lower lip and I started in pain. Her voice whispered to me: "Danny knows why Ceil came here and he wouldn't let her go away without, would he?"

I stared down through the darkness at her face. Her eyes were closed and her lips were soft across her mouth. I began to laugh suddenly. This was for me.

My arms tightened around her and I kissed her. Again and again. The press of her teeth was strong against my lips. She seemed to wilt in my arms and go limp. I picked her up and carried her toward the bed. Her teeth were biting into my neck as I put her on it.

I stood there looking down at her, my fingers impatiently loosening my clothes. Then I leaned over her, my grip firm on her bodice. Her arms reached up to me in the darkness. I could hear the ripping, tearing sound of her dress as I sank toward her.

Her voice was a roaring whisper in my ear; and mine, a muted echo first, then rose slowly to meet her in a screaming crescendo.

"Danny!"

"Oh God, Miss Schindler! Ceil!"

The night was quiet and I was listening to her soft breath against my shoulder. I touched her eyes gently, they were closed; her cheeks, they were wet, she had been crying; her lips, they were bruised and slightly swollen and moved under my fingers. I leaned forward to kiss her.

Her face turned under mine, her lips moved. "No more, Danny. No more, please."

I smiled to myself and sat up in the bed. I stretched and felt my body tingling and warm. I left the bed and walked to the door and opened it. The night air was cool and soothing on me.

I went down the steps and onto the grass, flexing my toes into the ground and feeling the strength of earth seeping up into me. I raised my hands to the night sky, trying to touch the shining stars. I jumped high in the air after them and fell, rolling over and over on the ground, laughter bubbling deep in my throat.

This was the joy of discovery. This was what I had been created for, this was why I was here in this world. I scooped up a handful of earth and rubbed it in my palms. It trickled through my fingers to the ground. This was my earth, my world. I was part of it and it was part of me.

I turned and went back into the cottage and stretched out beside her naked body. In a moment I was sound asleep.

Chapter Thirteen

THE HAND shook my shoulder violently and I sat up in bed, rubbing my eyes sleepily. Sam's voice roared in my ears. "Where is she?"

My eyes flew open. The bed beside me was empty. The faint gray of morning had come into the bungalow. Sam's bloodshot eyes stared angrily at me. "Where is she?" he roared again.

I stared at him bewildered. I didn't know what to say. My heart began to pound frightenedly. The bungalow was empty except for us, but I was too scared to think of lying.

His arms gripped my shoulders and dragged me out of bed. "Don't try to lie to me, Danny!" he said fiercely, his clenched fist waving in my face. "I know she was here. The clerk told me she didn't take a room, she was staying down here. You been sleepin' with my girl!"

I opened my mouth to answer, but there was no need for me to speak. Ceil's voice came from the doorway.

"Who's your girl, Sam?"

We both turned and looked toward her in surprise. Frantically I grabbed at the bedsheet and wrapped it around me as Sam loosened his grip. She was in a bathing suit and dripping wet from the pool. Her feet made wet tracks across the floor as she walked toward us. She stopped in front of Sam and looked up into his face.

"Who's your girl, Sam?" she repeated quietly.

It was his turn to be bewildered. "You came up here lookin' for me," he said confusedly.

Her eyes widened. "That's what I thought, Sam," she said in the same low voice, "but I found out different." She took a step away from him and looked back. "But you don't know why I really came up here, do you, Sam?"

He shook his head and looked at me. I was already slipping into my trousers. He turned back to her.

Her voice was low and bitter and she didn't look at either of us. "I came up here to tell you that I believed all your promises. That I would divorce Jeff and go with you."

Sam took a step toward her. She held out her hand and pushed him back. She was looking up into his eyes.

"No, Sam," she said quickly. "That was yesterday. Today it's another story. I was standing right next to the phone when you spoke to Danny last night and heard everything you said." Her lips twisted in a bitter smile. "That was the first time anything made sense to me. About you. About myself. It wasn't that I wanted you, or that you wanted me. It was just that we were alike. We wanted. Period. Who it was didn't matter."

She picked up a cigarette from the table and lit it. "Now if you both will get the hell out of here, I want to get dressed."

I turned in the doorway. I didn't understand half of what she said, but somehow I felt grateful toward her. She didn't look at me, just dragged at her cigarette.

Sam and I walked in awkward silence toward the hotel, our shoes crunching in the crisp morning grass. His head was down and he seemed thoughtful.

"I'm sorry, Sam," I said.

He didn't look at me.

"I couldn't help it. She was wild," I continued.

"Shut up, Danny!" His voice was rough.

Our footsteps clumped on the wooden steps of the hotel porch and we walked over to the concession counter. I went around behind it and picked up the report sheet. "I'll leave as soon as I square the report for you," I said stiffly.

He was staring at me thoughtfully. "What for?" he asked.

I was surprised. "You know what for," I replied.

He smiled, and suddenly his hand reached out and rumpled my hair. "Take it easy, Champ. Nobody said nothin' about your leavin'."

"But, Sam—"

"But hell!" He laughed aloud. "I couldn't expect you to stay a kid forever. Besides, maybe you did me a favor at that!"

I went home the day after Labor Day with six hundred

dollars. I put the money on the kitchen table, feeling almost like a stranger. The summer had changed all of us.

I had grown even more. I towered head and shoulders over Mamma and Papa. They seemed to have shrunk in some indefinable manner. Both were thinner than in the spring. Papa's usually round cheeks were hollow and his eyes had strange blue circles under them. Mamma's hair was almost all gray. This time they made no pretense about the money. The need was too urgent.

We spoke of many things at that first supper together, but some things were left unsaid. It was better so. No need to talk about what we already knew. It was visible in our faces, in the way we spoke and acted.

After supper I went out and sat on the stoop. Rexie came and stretched out beside me. I scratched her ear. "Yuh miss me, girl?" I asked softly. She wagged her tail and laid her head in my lap. She'd missed me all right. She was glad I was home.

I looked out at the street. It, too, had changed that summer. It had been paved and its asphalt gave the street a brighter, newer look.

Mimi came out and sat down on the step beside me. For a long while we sat there without speaking. Fat Freddie Conlon came out of his house and, seeing me, called a greeting. I waved my hand and watched him walk down the block.

At last Mimi spoke. "Marjorie Ann got engaged this summer." She was watching me closely.

"Yeah," I said casually. I felt nothing about her. She belonged to my kid days.

"To a cop," Mimi continued. "She's getting married when he graduates in January. He's much older than she is. He's in his thirties."

I turned to look at her. "Why bother me about it?" I asked directly.

Her face reddened. "I was just bringing you up to date on what went on around here this summer," she said defensively.

I looked away from her and down the street again. "So what?" I asked quietly. At least this hadn't changed much. I'd been back only a few hours and was fighting with Mimi already.

Her voice hardened and took on a nasty edge. "I thought you liked Marjorie Ann."

I almost smiled to myself. "What made you think that?"

She looked down at Rexie, lying between us and scratched the dog's head. "I thought you were always sweet on her. She told me—"

"What did she tell you?" I cut in.

Our eyes locked in silent battle. Hers fell before mine. I still watched her, my eyes wide and unblinking.

"She—she told me you did things with her," she stammered.

"What things?" I asked insistently.

"Things you shouldn't," she said, studying her nail polish. "After you went away last June she told me she was afraid she was going to have a baby."

I smiled suddenly. "She's crazy!" I exploded. "I never even touched her."

Relief flooded into Mimi's eyes. "Honest, Danny?"

I was still smiling. I remembered what had happened up in the country. Marjorie Ann was a nut. No girl ever got knocked up by a finger. I looked at her. "Honest, Mimi," I said quietly. "You know I wouldn't lie to you."

She was smiling back at me. "I never believed her really, Danny. She makes up so many stories." Her hand touched mine lightly. "I'm glad she's going to get married and go away now. I don't like her any more."

We looked silently down the street. It was growing dark and the street lamps came on with a sudden yellow radiance.

"The days are getting shorter again," I said.

She didn't answer and I turned to her. She looked like a kid sitting there in the glow of the street lamp, her black hair cascading down to her shoulder. Though she was two years older than I, I felt much older. Maybe it was the features of her face. Her bones were small and her mouth was unmarked. I wondered if she had ever been kissed. Really kissed, I mean. Then I put the thought quickly out of my mind. Not my sister, she wasn't that kind of a girl.

"Papa and Mamma look tired," I said, changing the subject. "It must have been hot down here in the city."

"It's not only that, Danny," she answered. "Things haven't been going too good. Business is bad and we're behind on all our bills. Just the week before last the milk company almost cut us off. It was a good thing I got some part time work at A&S; otherwise things might have been worse."

My eyes widened. I had known things were bad but I hadn't

realized they were that bad. "I didn't know," I said. "Mamma never said anything in her letters."

She looked at me seriously. "You know Mamma. She wouldn't write anything like that."

I didn't know what to say. I reached into my pocket and took out a pack of butts. I put one in my mouth and was about to light it when she interrupted me.

"Me too, Danny," she said.

I held the pack toward her. "I didn't know you smoked," I said in surprise.

"I didn't know you did," she countered. She looked up at the house. "And we both better be careful Mamma don't see us or we'll both catch it."

We laughed together and held the cigarettes concealed in the cupped palms of our hands.

"I'm glad I'm graduating this summer," Mimi said. "Then maybe I'll be able to get a job and really help out."

"Things are really that rough, eh?" I said thoughtfully.

"Yes," she answered simply. "Mamma is even talking about having to give up the house. We can't keep up the mortgage payments."

"We can't do that!" I was really startled now. Not my house. I just couldn't believe that.

Mimi shrugged her shoulders expressively. "Whether we can or we can't's got nothing to do with it. We're running out of money."

I was quiet for a moment. I wasn't a kid any more and I never really believed that this was my house as Papa had once said, but I didn't want to move out of it. Somehow the thought of this house with other people living in it, another family eating in the kitchen, some other person sleeping in my room, bothered me. I liked it here, I didn't want to have to move away.

"Maybe I ought to quit school and get a job," I said carefully.

"Danny, you couldn't!" Her voice was protesting. "You gotta finish school. Mamma and Papa got their hearts set on it."

I didn't speak.

"Don't worry, Danny," she said consolingly, placing her hand on my shoulder. "Everything'll work out okay. I just know it will."

I looked at her hopefully. "You really think so?"

She smiled at me. "Sure I do." She got to her feet and threw her cigarette into the gutter. "I"d better get in and help with the dishes or Mamma'll be after me."

I hoped she was right. She had to be. We just couldn't move from here. There was no other place to live as far as I was concerned.

Chapter Fourteen

MY NAME is Danny Fisher. I'm fifteen years and four months old. I'm in the sixth term at Erasmus Hall High School and I attend the morning session. It is one o'clock in the afternoon and school is over for the day. I am standing on the corner of Flatbush and Church Avenues watching the pupils stream by on their way home.

They say there are more than three thousand pupils in the school, and at this moment it seems as if all of them are walking past this corner. They are laughing. Some boys are kidding some girls. There is envy in my glance as I watch them. Nothing bothers them.

They have nothing on their minds until tomorrow when they must return to class. Not like me. I got a house I want to keep more than anything else in the world. So I have to go to work. I look at a clock in the window. It is already a few minutes past one. I hurry, for I have to be at work by half past the hour.

I walk down Flatbush Avenue. It is late October and the first chill of winter settles about me. I tighten my lumberjacket. I stop for a minute in front of a movie house and read the lobby cards. It looks like a good show, and as I stand there some of the kids from school go in to see it. I'd like to catch the show too, but I can't spare the time. I start walking again.

I am past the heavy shopping district. The stores here are smaller and seem to cater more to the neighborhood shopper than they did farther up the avenue near the school. My pace quickens. There isn't much here to catch my eye and slow me up.

I have been walking almost a half-hour when I get to the six corners, where Flatbush and Nostrand come together. It is the terminal station of the Flatbush division of the IRT subway.

There are many food stores on this corner: A&P; Bohack's; Roulston's; Daniel Reeves; Fair-Mart. It is this last that I enter. I walk through a long, narrow store.

A man behind the counter looks up and yells at me. "Snap it up, Danny. We got a flock of orders waiting."

I break into a run and go into the back of the store. I place my schoolbooks on a shelf, take down an apron, and wrap it around me while running back to the front of the store. The orders are on the floor near the door and I begin to carry them out to the hand wagon.

One of the clerks comes out and checks the bills with me. He gives me the exact change for the C.O.D.'s and I start off. The wagon and I weave in and out of the streets and traffic all afternoon until the sun sets and it is six o'clock. Then I take a heavy broom and begin to sweep down the store.

At seven o'clock I take off my apron and fold it neatly back on the shelf so that it will be ready for tomorrow. I pick up my schoolbooks and walk to the front of the store and the manager lets me out, locking the door carefully behind me. I hurry up Nostrand Avenue to Newkirk. A bus is waiting at the subway exit there and I board it. I stand, for the bus is crowded with people coming home from work.

I get off on my corner and walk up the block. My feet hurt and my neck and shoulder muscles are sore from lifting the heavy cartons, but I forget the pain when Rexie comes running down the street to greet me. She is wagging her tail happily in her excitement and I laugh and scratch her head. I go into my house still smiling, warm from the joy of her greeting.

I spill a handful of change on the kitchen table. Slowly I tot up the nickels and dimes. Eighty-five cents. Tips were good today. I put twenty-five cents in my pocket and spill the rest of the change into the tumbler over the sink.

Mamma has been watching me. Now she speaks. "Go upstairs and wash, Danny. Supper is waiting."

Papa has been sitting at the table. He reaches out a hand and sort of pats my shoulder as I walk by. He doesn't speak and neither do I. We both know how we feel. I am content.

For every day there is the little stream of change, and on Saturdays after I've worked a full day, from seven in the morning until eleven at night, the manager hands me my week's pay. Three and a half dollars. Good weeks it can come to as much as ten dollars altogether with the tips.

It is a good thing that school work comes easy to me, because most nights I fall asleep over my homework and have to finish it in a study period the next day. I sink into bed and sleep the sleep of the exhausted, but when I wake the next morning I am new and strong again. I have the indefatigability of youth on my side.

There are times when I watch the boys in the street playing touch tackle and I feel like joining their game. Sometimes I get my hands on a football that one of the boys has failed to catch. I pick it up and my fingers instinctively caress the soft, smooth pigskin. I remember how much I wanted to be on the team at school. Then I throw the ball back. I watch it spiral lazily in the air until it falls into the receiver's hands. Then I turn away.

I have no time for play. I am somber and thoughtful. I am engaged in a much greater game. I am working to keep my home secure.

But there are forces at work of which I know nothing. The cold unemotional mechanics of finance and credit, the machinery of business and economics, which hold a careful level on every life in every stratum of society and are only words in a textbook to me. And there are the people who watch this machine.

They are people very much like Papa and Mamma, Mimi and me. They are victims as well as administrators. They are as much subject to the rule of the level as the people to whom they apply it. When the level is far enough out of balance, they make a note on a slip of paper. This note is then given to other people. If these agree with the first watchers, other slips of paper are filled out and forwarded, and then all the rules of the level are taken away. For what they do disturbs the balance so much that it is impossible to get a straight ruling from the level ever again.

Then we become a statistic.

Statistics are very cold things. They are levels of another

sort administered by actuaries. From them many things are determined. All sorts of reasons are drawn from them as the source of our failure to maintain an even level on our economics. But none of these things sum up my emotions, my feelings, upon learning of the failure. Either mine or that of my family. It is only the balance they are interested in, not the way we feel.

And surely not the way I felt that night shortly before the end of October when I came home from work and found Mamma crying.

Chapter Fifteen

I WASN'T THERE WHEN—

Mamma looked up at the clock. In a few minutes it would be time for lunch. She wondered where the morning had gone. She had awakened with such a strong presentiment of evil and bad luck hovering over her that she forced herself to keep busy every moment.

She had cleaned and dusted every corner of the house, had even gone down into the cellar and sifted through the ashes to save the half-burned lumps of coal that fell through when the grate was shaken out. But in spite of all her preoccupation the feeling hung about her. It was always there in the back of her mind.

She hurried into the kitchen and put some water into a pot on the stove and turned the light on underneath it. She heard a rustling on the floor. Rexie had got up from underneath the kitchen table and gone to the door, where she stood wagging her tail and looking back at Mamma.

"You want to go out?" Mamma said to the dog as she opened the kitchen door.

The dog ran out barking happily and she turned back to the

stove. She put an egg into the water, which was just beginning to boil.

After she had eaten she cleaned off the table and put the dishes into the sink. She was tired. She stood looking into the sink at them. She was too tired even to wash them.

Suddenly she could feel her heart pounding so heavily that it seemed to vibrate all through her body. She was frightened. She had heard many times how heart attacks come upon people without warning. She went into the parlor and sat down on the couch, leaning back against the pillows. The palms of her hands were wet with perspiration. She closed her eyes and rested.

Slowly the beating of her heart quieted. Her breathing was easier and her fear disappeared. "I'm just tired," she said aloud. The words echoed in the empty room. She would take a hot bath; it would relax her and do her good. It was all nerves anyway, she decided. She undressed in the bathroom while the tub was filling, folded her clothes neatly and hung them on the towel rack, and looked into the mirror.

Her hand reached up wonderingly and touched her hair. There was a great deal of gray in it, and the black seemed faded and dull. It seemed only yesterday that it had been alive and lustrous. And her face had tired little lines etched into it, the skin was not soft and smooth as she remembered it. It seemed almost as if someone else, not she, was looking at her from the mirror.

She unhooked her brassiere. Her breasts, free of the mechanical support, tumbled from it and sagged shapelessly against her chest. She studied herself in the mirror. She had always been proud of her breasts. She remembered how well shaped they had always been, how firm and strong and bursting with life while she had been nursing the children. Papa used to love to watch her. He would sit admiringly and after a while would say laughingly to the child: "Hey there, little momser, haven't you had enough? Can't you leave something for Papa?" She used to blush and laugh and tell him to go away and not be such a pig, but she was always proud. Now look at her. There was no joy in them for him any more. Who could be attracted to such things as these?

She turned away from the mirror toward the tub. It didn't make much difference now. Neither of them had any appetite left. The struggle of the past few years had taken it from them.

The memory of pleasure was dim in her mind. It was best left for youth and those without care.

She sank into the tub carefully. Slowly the warmth of the water seeped through her. She felt light and buoyant. The gentle swishing of the water seemed to drive away her fears and once more she felt comfortable and secure. She leaned back against the tub, loving the feel of the water as it crept up to her shoulders. She rested her head against the tiles over the tub. She was drowsy and her eyelids felt heavy.

"I'm getting to be a silly old woman," she thought as she closed her eyes. She dozed.

Her heart was pounding again. She tried to move her arms, but they felt heavy and lifeless. She must get up, she thought desperately, she must. With an effort she raised her head and opened her eyes. She looked about her with a startled look.

The ringing of the telephone came to her ears. Suddenly she was wide awake. She remembered having come upstairs to take a bath. She must have been dozing for quite a while, she realized; the water was almost cold. The telephone downstairs was ringing with an urgency she could not ignore. She got out of the tub quickly, hurriedly dried her feet on the bathmat and, throwing a towel around her wet body, ran downstairs to answer it.

As soon as she picked up the phone and heard Papa's voice she knew something was wrong. Somehow she had been expecting it all day.

"Mary," he cried, his voice shaking, "the bank's got a judgment out against me and they're gonna serve it tomorrow!"

She tried to be calm. "Did you talk to them?" she asked, her voice reflecting his fears.

"I did everything," he answered resignedly. "I begged them, I pleaded with them to give me more time, but they told me they couldn't do any more."

"Did you talk to your brother, David?" Mamma asked. "Maybe he can spare you some money."

"I spoke to him too," he answered. He paused for a moment and a sound of finality came into his voice. "We're finished—through."

"Harry, what are we going to do?" A vision of the family walking through the street in rags flashed before her. She fought her hysteria.

David is coming with his car tonight," Papa replied. "We're

gonna try to empty the store as much as we can. We'll hide the stuff in his place until I can find a way to open up somewhere else."

"But if you're caught, you'll go to jail," she cried.

"So I'll go to jail," he answered, his voice flat and dull. "Things can't be much worse." Somehow in telling what had happened he had lost all capacity for emotion. "They attached the house too." He lapsed into Yiddish, as he didn't do very often. *"Alles iss forloren,"* he said, "everything is lost."

That was the night I came home and found Mamma crying at the kitchen table, and Mimi, with tears in her eyes too, holding her hand.

That was the night I left without supper and went down to Papa's store and helped move hastily packed cartons of merchandise out to Uncle David's car.

That was the night when I stood in the darkened street at two o'clock in the morning and my father, crying bitterly all the while, looked at the store windows and murmured: "Twenty-five years, twenty-five years."

That was the night I watched my mother and father fall sobbing into each other's arms and learned that they too had feelings they could not control. For the first time I saw fear and despair and hopelessness plainly in their faces.

I went quietly to my room and undressed, crept into bed and lay there looking up into the dark. The muted sounds of their voices came from downstairs. I could not fall asleep and watched the morning creep into my room, and there was nothing I could do. Nothing.

That was the night when for the first time I admitted to myself that it was not my house, that it really belonged to someone else, and there was no heart left in me for tears.

Moving Day

DECEMBER 1, 1932

IT WAS WRONG. Everything was wrong, nothing was right. I knew it the minute I went into the BMT subway station at Church Avenue instead of walking home. When I got up that morning, there was a dull choked feeling in my gut as if someone had poked me in the solar plexus and it had been getting worse all day. Now I could feel its ache spreading all through me. I was going home from school, but I wasn't going home any more.

There was an express in the station when I got down the steps and automatically I ran for it. I got aboard just as the door was closing. There weren't any seats, so I leaned against the door on the other side. This door opened only once on the way, at Atlantic Avenue, so at least I could stand there with as little disturbance as possible.

It was cold in the train and I pulled the collar of my sheepskin jacket up around my neck. It had snowed a few days before, but the streets were pretty well cleaned up by now. Some snow still lay on the tracks as the train pulled into Prospect Park. The tunnel closed around us, choking off the day. I took a deep breath trying to get rid of the sick feeling inside me. It didn't help. If anything, it only made it worse.

That morning the barrels and boxes around the already strange, empty-looking rooms had reminded me: today was moving day. I had left my room without a backward glance, Rexie close upon my heels. I wanted to forget all about it— forget I was ever kid enough to believe that it was really my house. I was old enough now to know that was the kind of a story you told to children.

Suddenly day swept back into the train. I looked out the window: we were on Manhattan Bridge. The next stop was mine, Canal Street. I had to change there for the Broadway-Brooklyn train. The train went back into the tunnel and in a moment the doors were opening. I had to wait a few minutes for the other train, but it was only a quarter to four when I came up on the street at the corner of Essex and Delancey.

It was like a different world. The streets were crowded with people moving restlessly, talking in many languages. There were street peddlers with pushcarts, hawkers shouting, standing on the corner with their little stands, ready to collapse them and run when the cops told them to move on. It was cold, but many were without overcoats and hats, women with only shawls thrown around their shoulders. And all about me I could hear the low, muted voice of poverty. There was little laughter on the street except from children, and even they were restrained in their joy.

I walked down Delancey Street, past the cheap stores with their gaudy sales, past the movie house with its big sign still advertising the early-bird matinee, admission ten cents. I turned left at Clinton Street and walked the two blocks to Stanton with my head down. I didn't want to look around me, and all the time the tight feeling in the pit of my stomach seemed to grow larger until I could feel it choking in my throat.

I looked up suddenly. This was it: an old gray house with faded narrow windows reaching five stories into the sky. A small stoop led up to its entrance, and on each side of the stoop was a store. One was a tailor shop, its windows dark and covered with dust; the other was empty.

Slowly, reluctantly, I climbed the steps. At the top I stood and looked down into the street. This was where we were going to live. A woman came out of the house and pushed past me on her way down the steps. I could smell the garlic on her breath. I watched her cross the street to a pushcart, where she stopped and began to haggle with the man standing there.

I turned and went into the house. The hall was dark and I stumbled over something on the floor. With a muttered curse I bent to straighten it up. It was a paper bag filled with garbage. I dropped it quickly where I found it and began to climb the stairs.

Three flights up, and at every landing, I saw the small paper bags standing in front of the door, waiting for the superintendent to collect them. The heavy odor of cooking hung in the stale cold air of the hallways. I knew which apartment was ours by the barrels standing in the hall beside the door. I knocked.

Mamma opened the door. We stood there for a moment looking at each other and then, not speaking, I walked into the apartment. My father was sitting at the table. I could hear Mimi's voice coming from somewhere in the front.

I was standing in the kitchen and the walls were covered with a strangely colored flat white paint that fought unsuccessfully to hide the layers of dirt beneath it. The bright yellow curtains Mamma had already put on the small window beside the table gave the room a forced air of gaiety. She looked at me anxiously. I didn't know what to say. Just then Rexie came running to me from another room, wagging her tail, and I knelt to pet her.

"It's very nice," I said, not looking up.

There was silence for a moment, and from the corner of my eyes I could see Mamma and Papa looking at each other. Then my mother spoke. "It's not so bad, Danny. It will do for a little while until your father gets back on his feet. Come, I'll show you the rest of the apartment."

I followed her through the rooms. There wasn't much to see, I don't suppose there ever is in a small four-room apartment. My room was about half the size of my old room, and theirs wasn't much larger. Mimi was going to sleep on the couch in the parlor.

I didn't say anything as I looked at them. The rooms were all covered with the same discouraged-looking white paint. What could I say? The rent was cheap and that was the main thing: twenty-eight dollars a month with steam heat and hot water.

We went back into the kitchen, Rexie still following at my heels. My father hadn't said a word. He just sat there at the table smoking his cigarette, his eyes watching me.

I scratched the dog's ear. "Was Rexie any trouble?" I asked him.

He shook his head. "She was no bother," he said almost formally. His voice sounded different, not like his at all, as if he weren't sure of himself any more.

"You better take her out, Danny," my mother said. "She hasn't gone all day. I think she's a little upset."

I was glad to have something to do. I went to the door and called her.

"Take her leash, Danny, it's a strange neighborhood and she might get lost," my father said, holding it toward me.

"Yeah, that's right," I said. Rexie and I went out into the dark hallway and I started down the stairs.

About halfway down the first flight I realized she hadn't come with me. She was standing at the head of the stairs, looking down at me. I called: "Come on, girl." She didn't budge. I called again. She crouched down on the floor and looked at me, wagging her tail nervously. I went back up the stairs and snapped the leash onto her harness. "Come on, now," I said to her, "don't be such a baby."

When I started down the stairs again, she followed me cautiously. At each landing I had to urge her down the next flight. At last we were out on the stoop, where she stood looking out into the street. Suddenly she tried to dart back into the hallway. The leash pulled her up short and she crouched down. I knelt beside her and took her head in my hands. I could feel her body trembling. I picked her up and carried her down the stoop. In the street she didn't seem so afraid, but as we started off toward Clinton Street, she kept looking around apprehensively. The noise of the traffic seemed to frighten her.

Down the block there seemed to be less traffic, so I decided to walk her that way. In front of a candy store I waited for the light to change. A big truck came rattling past, and she began to pull anxiously on her leash. I could hear the rasping sounds in her chest as the leash tightened on her throat. Her tail was down between her legs. She was really frightened now. As I knelt down again to comfort her, I heard a raucous laugh behind me and looked back over my shoulder.

Three boys, somewhere around my age, were standing in front of the candy store. One of them was laughing at the dog's fright. They saw me looking at them.

"What's a matter, pal?" the boy who was laughing said sneeringly. "Your mutt yella?"

"No more than you, pal," I replied sarcastically, still trying to soothe her.

The other two boys fell quiet at my answer. They seemed to look at the boy I was talking to expectantly. He looked at them knowingly for a second and then swaggered over to me. I knew the setup too well. He would have to make good his words. I smiled grimly to myself. He had a surprise coming. I began to feel a little better; the opportunity for violence seemed to ease the pain in my belly.

He stood over me. From beside the dog, I looked up at him, my hands still busy with her. "Wat'cha say, pal?" he said very slowly.

I smiled thinly. "You heard me the first time, pal," I replied, mimicking his tone of voice. I started to get to my feet.

I saw his foot coming, but I couldn't move fast enough. His shoe caught me flush on the mouth and I spilled over backward in the gutter. The leash flew from my grasp. I rolled over desperately to grab it, but it sped out of my reach. I shook my head dizzily, trying to clear it; then I heard the scream.

I scrambled to my feet anxiously, the fight forgotten. Rexie was running out in the middle of the street among the traffic, darting back and forth crazily.

"Rexie!" I screamed at her.

She turned in her tracks and started back for me. I heard her high-pitched yip as she disappeared beneath the wheels of a small delivery truck, turning the corner, racing to make the light. I ran toward her. She cried once more, but more weakly. She was lying on her side in the gutter, her chest heaving, her beautiful brown fur covered with blood and dirt. I fell to my knees in the gutter beside her.

"Rexie!" I cried, my voice choked. As I picked her up, a soft moan escaped her, almost a sigh. Her eyes were soft and filled with pain. Her tongue crept out from between her lips and licked at my hands gently, leaving a smear of blood.

I was holding her against me now, her body trembling violently. Suddenly she gasped and was still. Her paws fell limply against my jacket. The light had gone from her eyes. "Rexie," I said pleadingly. I couldn't believe it. She had been so alive, so beautiful. "Rexie, girl."

A man pushed his way through the crowd of people that had gathered around. His face was pale. "Jesus, kid, I didn't even see her."

I stared at him for a moment without seeing him. All I could remember about him was that his face was pale—nothing else. I started toward the house still carrying Rexie. People moved away from in front of me silently. I couldn't cry. My eyes were burning, but I couldn't cry. I was at the stoop, now in the dark hallway on the strange stairway with the heavy odors, now in front of our door. I kicked it open.

Mamma rose from her chair with a half scream. "Danny! What happened?"

I looked at her dumbly. For a moment I couldn't speak. Papa and Mimi had come running into the room when they heard her. Now they were all facing me, staring at me.

"She's dead," I said at last. I didn't recognize my own voice. I was hoarse and gruff. "She got run over."

On the floor in front of me was an empty cardboard carton. I knelt and placed her in it gently. Slowly I closed the flaps down over her and stood up.

Mimi's eyes were filled with tears. "H-how did it happen?"

I envied her tears. I wished that I could cry; maybe I would feel better. The bitterness rose in my throat. "It happened," I said flatly. "What difference does it make now how?"

I washed the blood from my hands at the sink and dried them on a dish towel. Then I picked up the carton and started to open the door.

My father's voice stopped me. "Where are you going?"

"To bury her," I answered dully. "I can't keep her here."

His hand was on my shoulder, his eyes looking into mine. "I'm sorry, Danny," he said, his voice filled with sympathy. His eyes were dark with understanding, but it didn't matter—nothing mattered any more.

I wearily brushed his hand from my shoulder. "You should be," I said bitterly, accusingly. "It's all your fault. If we hadn't lost the house and had to move, this would never have happened."

I saw the flash of pain in his eyes as his hands fell to his side. I went out into the hall and shut the door behind me. It was his fault. He didn't have to lose the house.

I boarded the Utica-Reid trolley in the plaza beneath the bridge and held the carton on my lap all through the long ride over the bridge, through Williamsburg, and at last into Flatbush. I got off the trolley at Clarendon Road, and the box was heavy in my hands as I walked through the familiar streets. In my mind I could see her running after me. I could see the beautiful reddish-brown fur and feel its soft silkiness as I scratched behind her ears. I could feel her cool, moist tongue licking my ears when I knelt to greet her.

It was dark when I reached the house. I stood in the street looking into it. Its windows were wide and gaping and empty. We had only moved out that morning, but already it had assumed a forlorn, deserted look. I looked up and down the street to see if anyone had seen me. The street was empty.

Some lights were on in the Conlons' house as I quietly walked up the driveway, but no one heard me. I went into the back yard and put the carton down. It was only right. This was where she had lived, this was where she should rest. Where she had been happy.

I looked around me. I would need a shovel to scoop out the ground for her. I wondered if there was still one in the cellar, the one we used for the furnace. I started for the house. Then I stopped and went back for her. She never liked being left alone.

I still had my key in my pocket and I opened the door. I carried the box inside and put it on the kitchen steps. The house was dark but I didn't need any light. I knew every inch of it.

I went down into the cellar. The shovel was up against the coalbin just where it always had been. I picked it up and went back up the stairs. I was going to take her outside with me while I dug her grave, but I changed my mind and left her on the kitchen steps. She had always been shy of the shovel.

I dug as silently as I could; I didn't want anyone to hear me. The cold night air began to beat against my face, but I didn't care. I was sweating beneath my sheepskin jacket. When the hole was big enough for her, I went back into the house, picked up the box, and carried it outside. There I placed it gently in the ground. As I stood up and reached for the shovel, a thought came to me: what if she wasn't dead? What if she was still alive?

I knelt down and lifted the lid of the carton, placed my face close to the box, and listened. I heard nothing. I still didn't trust myself. I put my hand in the box and felt her muzzle. The warmth had already gone from her body. Slowly I closed the carton and got to my feet.

The tears came to my eyes as I spilled the dirt over her. Do you say prayers for dogs? I didn't know, but I said a prayer for her. It passed my lips soundlessly in the night and at last the earth lay evenly on her. I smoothed the ground with my feet. The moon had risen and its cold winter light cast eerie shadows in the yard. She liked the cold weather, it made her brisk and frisky and want to run. I hoped she would like the weather wherever she was.

I don't know how long I stood there, the shovel in my hand,

but I was chilled through when I turned away. The tears were streaming silently down my cheeks, but I wasn't crying.

I went back into the house and without thinking went up to my room. I put the shovel against the wall and went over to where my bed used to be. By the bright moonlight that came in the window I could see the markings on the floor where Rexie used to sleep under my bed. I lay on the floor and cried. The bitter salt of my tears rolled into my mouth as my body responded to my grief. At last I was spent and rose to my feet dully. Without looking back I left the room and walked down the stairs and out of the house.

Fat Freddie Conlon was coming home as I walked out of the driveway. He looked at me in surprise. "Danny! What are you doing here?" he asked. "Did you leave something behind?"

I pushed past him without answering, leaving him standing in the street behind me. Yes, I had left something behind all right. More than I had expected.

The clock in the window of the jewelry store near the corner of Clinton and Delancey Streets read nine o'clock when I turned down the block. I was moving as if in a dream. People were pressing around me and there was noise and confusion, but I didn't see it or hear it. My body seemed to be throbbing with a dull aching pain and the side of my face was sore where I had been kicked.

I was on the steps of the house when suddenly I seemed to waken. I could hear the noises of the traffic, the voices of people. I looked around me as if I were seeing it for the first time. The light from the candy store on the corner seemed to beckon to me. A group of boys were still hanging out in front of it. I went down the steps again and started for the corner.

There I stopped and looked at the gang in front of the store. He wasn't there. After watching them quietly for a few minutes I was just about to turn away when I saw him. He was inside the store, sitting at the counter drinking an egg cream.

I walked slowly into the store. His back was toward the door and he didn't see me. I tapped him gently on the shoulder. He turned. A look of recognition spread quickly on his face.

"Outside." I gestured with my hand.

He looked at me, then at the other boys in the store. I didn't give him any time to think. My hand prodded at his shoulder again, this time roughly. "Outside," I said, my voice harsh and flat.

He pushed his drink away from him and stood up. "Save this for me, Moishe," he said to the counterman in a cocky voice, "I'll be back for it in a minute."

I picked up the glass and emptied it in the sink behind the counter. Its chocolate flowed into the dirty water. "Forget it, Moishe," I said in the same flat voice. "He won't be drinking this.'"

I turned my back on him and walked out into the street. His footsteps sounded behind me on the concrete floor. At the curb I stopped and turned. "Put up your hands," I said almost casually.

He looked at me for a moment, then stepped very close to me. His lips bared over his teeth in a half snarl. "Tough, eh? Think yer tough, huh?" he sneered.

That crazy feeling I'd had in my gut all day began to explode in me. "Yeah, tough enou—" I started to answer when I suddenly remembered.

I moved back quickly, but not quickly enough. His knee caught me in the groin and his fist lashed across my face. I fell forward on my hands and knees. I saw his shoe coming at my face and tried to roll away from it. The toe of his boot caught me behind the ear and I went flat on the ground.

The noise of the traffic seemed to be coming from far away, there was strange dizziness in my head. I shook myself and got to my knees again.

He was laughing at me. "Tough, huh?"

I grabbed a hydrant near me and pulled myself up. I shook my head again. It was clearing rapidly and I could taste the warm blood running down inside my mouth.

He was still laughing, still taunting. "Think yer tough now, Shmuk?"

I watched him cautiously, still clinging to the hydrant. Let him keep talking, he was doing me a favor. He was giving me time. I could feel the strength coming back into my legs.

He came toward me again, slowly, deliberately, taking his time. He was full of confidence.

Still stalling for time, I moved around the hydrant. All I needed was a few more seconds. For once I was glad Sam had taught me to gauge my strength and how to save it.

He stopped and sneered again. "Yella, too?" he taunted. "Jus' like yer dog!"

I let go of the hydrant. I was all right now. I stepped in front of it.

He came at me swinging, leading with his right. He didn't know it, but that was his second mistake, and par for the course. His first was in giving me time.

My left brushed aside his right lead, my right hand tore into his belly just below his belt. He started to bend forward, his hands going down to his crotch, and I caught him with a left uppercut on the side of the jaw. He half turned sideways and started to go down. I hit him eight times on the face and jaw before he hit the sidewalk.

There he sprawled at my feet. I bent over him. He must have been as strong as a horse, he was trying to get up. I kicked him in the side of his head and he went out flat.

For a few seconds I watched him; then I turned and started away. For the first time I became aware of the crowd of people that had gathered around us. I sensed rather than heard a sudden movement behind me.

Quickly I whirled. He was on his feet after me. Something shining in his upheld hand slashed down at me as I jumped aside. I could feel it ripping down my sleeve. Switch knife. He carried past me with the momentum of his swing and I rabbit-punched the back of his head.

The crowd parted in front of him as he staggered against the side of the building. I followed him quickly. I couldn't give him a chance to turn around.

I gripped his knife hand and pulled it back toward me. He screamed. I pulled again and the knife fell clattering to the sidewalk. I kicked it away and turned him around. His face was contorted with pain and fear. His eyes bugged out in their sockets. Holding his head against the brick of the building, I began to pound his face with my free fist.

A wild violence was running through me, a savage joy. For the first time in my life I liked fighting. My first punch flattened his nose against his face. I could feel the bone crunching beneath my fist. He screamed again.

I laughed wildly and hit him in the mouth. When he gasped for breath I could see a hole where some teeth had been. I was happy. I had never been so happy before. Blood was running down the side of his face. I wanted to turn it all into blood, I didn't want him to have a face at all. A red haze settled over my eyes and I was laughing and hitting him and yelling for joy.

Then I felt hands tearing at me, pulling me away from him. I fought them to let me go. There was sudden sharp pain at the back of my head and I felt curiously weak. I let him go and he fell forward to the ground at my feet. Arms pinioned my hands to my sides. I looked up to see who was holding me. As the red haze began to lift, I saw the dark-blue uniforms of the cops.

They took me to the station house just off Williamsburg Bridge and threw me into a cell. A man came in to see me, a doctor, who put some adhesive tape on my arm where I had been cut. Then he left me.

I sat there almost four hours before anyone came near my cell again. I was tired, but I couldn't sleep. My eyes were heavy, but they wouldn't close. All I could do was think. All I could see in front of my eyes was a little reddish-brown puppy trying to scramble up the side of a pit after me.

The cell door clanked. A cop stood there. "Your father's come to get you, son," he said gently.

I stood and picked up my coat from the bunk behind me. It was almost as if I had done this many times before, but I was past all feeling. Slowly I followed him down the gray-painted corridor and up the stairs. He opened a door and motioned me through it. My father and a man were sitting there in the room.

Papa jumped to his feet. "I've come to take you home, Danny," he said.

I stared at him dully for a moment. Home? To that place? It would never be home to me.

The man beside my father stood up and looked at me. "Lucky for you, kid, we found out what happened. That boy you beat up will be in the hospital for weeks. But he's no good and maybe you did us a favor. Go along now and don't give us any more trouble."

I didn't answer him but started out the door. My father's voice behind me was thanking the man for what he had done. I walked through the station house and out into the street, where my father caught up to me and fell into step beside me. At Delancey Street we waited for the traffic light.

"Your mother and I were frightened, Danny. We didn't know what happened to you." His voice was husky, but he was trying to speak easily. His usually ruddy face was pale in the glow of the street lamp. It seemed to me that I had heard those words before. Another time, another place. I didn't answer.

The light changed and we crossed the street. On the other side he tried to speak again. "Why did you do it, Danny?" There was anguish on his face. Something had happened that he did not understand. "It's not like you to do something like that."

Maybe it wasn't before, but it was different now. I was in a different world and maybe I was a different Danny Fisher. I didn't know. Again I didn't answer.

He tried to speak once more and then fell silent. We walked two blocks and turned up our street. At the corner we hesitated for a moment and caught each other's eye and then looked quickly away.

Up the block the street was empty now and dirty and filled with garbage left by the day. Our footsteps clattered on the sidewalk.

It had begun to snow. I pulled the collar of my jacket up around my neck. From the corner of my eye I could see my father walking beside me. It was then I first caught a glimpse of what would be: my father and I were strangers as we walked silently through the night.

Chapter One

PAPA looked at his watch as we came out of the dark hallway into the street. He thrust it quickly back in his pocket and glanced at me awkwardly. "Quarter to three," he muttered. "I gotta hurry or I'll be late."

I looked at him without interest. Five months of living down here and it seemed as if years had separated us. Since the very first day we moved, nothing had gone right. Now Papa had a job, in a drugstore on Delancey Street. Twenty-three a week.

"Walking my way?" Papa asked.

I nodded silently. Might as well. I was going to meet the gang on the corner near the five and dime. My step quickened to match his as he hurried off.

The memory of those five months was fresh in our minds. The days I came home from school and found him sitting in the kitchen of the dingy apartment, staring at the walls, an expression of hopelessness and despair painted on his face. I had tried to feel sorry for him but I couldn't. He had brought it on himself. If only he had been a little smarter.

Still there was something about his expression the night he had come a few days ago and told us about the job he had just snagged. It reached out and caught me in the gut. Twenty-three bucks a week for a registered pharmacist with twenty-five years' experience. It wasn't right. It was barely eating-dough.

We turned the corner at Delancey and were in front of the store where Papa worked. He stopped and looked at me hesitantly. I could see he wanted to ask me what I was going to do the rest of the afternoon, but he was too proud. I didn't offer to tell him.

"Tell Mamma I'll be home by two thirty," he said at last.

I nodded.

He opened his mouth as if to say more, then closed it as if he had changed his mind. Instead he shook his head slightly and, squaring his shoulders, walked into the store. The clock in the window showed exactly three as he walked in.

I had some time to kill so I leaned against the store window and watched the people walking by. A voice from inside the store came to my ears and I turned and looked in.

A man was coming out from behind the drug counter, taking off his jacket. "Christ, Fisher," he was saying in that quiet kind of voice that carries twenty yards in front and not one inch behind, "am I glad to get out of here! The boss is got his tail up and he's been eatin' my ass off all day."

Papa took the jacket from him silently and looked up at the wall clock to check his time. An expression of relief crossed his face.

A small, pompous man with an irascible face came out of the back room. He peered up through the store, his thick glasses shining in the light. "That you, Fisher?" he queried in a thin, irritating voice. He didn't wait for an answer. "Snap it up," he continued, "I got a couple of Rx's waiting for you."

There was a sound of fear and meekness in Papa's voice. I had never heard it before. "Yes, Mr. Gold," Papa answered. He hurried toward the back of the store. His hat and jacket were already in his hand as he turned toward the little man with an apologetic look. "I didn't mean to keep you waiting, Mr. Gold."

The little man looked at him contemptuously. "You could get here early, you know. It wouldn't hurt."

"I'm sorry, Mr. Gold," Papa said abjectly.

"Well, don't stand there like a fool, Fisher," Mr. Gold said, thrusting two slips of paper into Papa's hand. "Put on your jacket and get to work!" He turned his back and walked away.

Papa stared after him for a moment, with no expression on his face at all. Then he looked at the prescriptions in his hand and walked slowly to the prescription counter. He put his hat and jacket on a chair and slipped into the store jacket quickly.

He placed the prescriptions on the counter, smoothed them with his hand, and studied them again for a moment. Then he took a bottle and a measure from the shelf. I could almost hear the thin rattling sound the bottle made against the glass measure as he poured some liquid into it with trembling hands.

Suddenly he looked up and saw me staring at him. Embarrassment came into his eyes and a quick shame crossed his face. I let my eyes go vague and blank as if I hadn't seen him and turned away casually.

The gang was already waiting when I got there. Quietly we moved away from the corner. We didn't want to drag any eyes. I didn't waste any time with them.

"You know what to do," I said in a low careful voice. "We drift in easylike. Two at a time. Quiet. When we're all in there, I'll give the signal an' Spit and Solly will start the fight in the back of the store. When everybody's lookin' that way, the rest of you get busy. An' remember these things. Don't grab no crap, only stuff we can sell. Don't hang around to see how the other guy made out. As soon as you made your snatch, blow. Don't wait for nothin'. Get out fast! You all know where we're meetin' afterwards. Kill an hour before you show up."

I looked around at them. Their faces were serious. "Understan'?" There weren't any replies. I grinned. "Okay then. I'm goin' in now. Keep an eye on me an' don't do nothin' till I give the signal."

The gang scattered and I walked away quickly. I turned the corner and went into the five and ten. It was crowded with people. Good, it would make things easier.

I pushed my way through the aisle along the soda fountain to the end of the counter. There I climbed up on a seat and waited for the girl to come up and serve me. In the mirror behind the counter I could see Spit and Solly walking past me.

The counter girl stood in front of me. "What'll you have?"

"What you got, baby?" I countered. I was stalling for time. Things weren't ready yet.

She looked at me tiredly, pushing some stray hairs back from her forehead. "It's all on the signs," she replied in a flat, bored voice. "You can read."

I pretended to read the signs pasted on the mirror behind her. Two of the other boys were coming in. "A double-dip chocolate ice-cream soda," I said. "The dime special."

The girl walked down the counter and tossed the soda together with a careless expert skill. So much syrup, so much carbonated water, then the ice cream—two scoops, with the top of the scoop toward the customer so that he couldn't see it was really half empty—then some more carbonated water. I looked around the store.

The boys were all set up and ready to go. I waited for the soda, wishing she would snap it up. All at once I wanted to get this over with. It had been a bright idea when we were talking about it, but now I was jumpy. She came back down the aisle and put the soda on the counter in front of me.

I pushed a dime toward her and she rang it on the register.

The boys were watching me from the corners of their eyes. I put the straws into the soda, stirred it, and began to suck on the straws. The taste of the soda was sweet in my mouth when the noise of the fight broke out behind me.

I was grinning to myself as I turned toward the sound. Solly was just falling into a display case filled with canned goods. The crash roared through the store and people began running toward it. The boys were working smoothly. The counter girl spoke and I jumped, startled. She was looking past me curiously.

"What's goin' on there?"

"I dunno. A fight, I guess."

"Looks like a setup to me," she said.

I felt my pulse quicken nervously. "What do you mean?" I asked.

"Those boys ain't hurtin' each other," she said flatly. "I bet they got friends cleanin' out the joint. It's an old gimmick." Her eyes were roving through the store. "Look over there, see?"

She had spotted one of the boys stuffing his pockets at the cosmetic counter. Just then the boy turned and looked at me. He began to smile, but I shook my head quickly and he started out the door.

I turned back to the counter. The girl was staring at me, her eyes wide. "You're in on it," she whispered.

I reached across the counter quickly and grabbed her arm, smiling coldly. "What're you gonna do about it?" I asked quietly.

She stared at me for a moment, then smiled back. "Nothin'," she answered. "It's none of my business. Barbara Hutton can afford it."

I let go of her hand and looked back at the store. All the boys had gone and Solly was just being pushed out of the door by a couple of men. Relief came over my face. Still smiling, I turned back to the soda and took a spoonful of ice cream. I could taste the chocolate melting there.

"You make a mean soda," I said.

She smiled again. She had thick black hair, and her eyes were a soft dark brown. Her lipstick was a startling red against her pale thin face. "You're pretty smooth, all right," she whispered.

I felt a glow spread through me. I could see I had scored with this kid. "What's your name, baby?" I asked.

"Nellie," she answered.

"Mine's Danny," I told her. "Live in the neighborhood?"

"Over on Eldridge Street."

"What time you get through?"

"Nine o'clock, when the store closes," she replied.

I stood up proudly. I was very sure of myself. "I'll pick you up on the corner," I said. "Maybe we'll get some chinks." I didn't wait for her answer but sauntered down to where the men were busy putting up the display that Solly had fallen into. I watched them for a few minutes, then walked back to the counter.

The girl was still watching me. I grinned at her. "See you at nine, Nellie."

She flashed me a quick smile. "I'll be on the corner, Danny."

I half waved my hand to her and walked toward the entrance. I could feel her eyes following me. As I passed the drug counter, I picked up a comb and idly ran it through my hair. Then I went out the door, dropping the comb into my shirt pocket.

Chapter Two

THE PEDDLER looked up at me wisely. "Where'd you get this stuff?" he asked.

"Yuh wanna buy it," I countered sarcastically, "or yuh want its pedigree?"

He looked down at the small carton. His hand picked up a jar of Mum and he tossed it nervously from one hand to the other as he spoke. "I don't want the cops should bother me," he said.

I reached for the carton meaningfully. "Then somebody else will buy it."

He grabbed at my hand quickly. "Wait a minute. I didn't say I didn't want the stuff."

I let go of the carton. "Then don't ask so many questions. Fifteen dollars and it's all yours."

He parted his lips over yellowed teeth. "Ten."

"Fourteen," I said quickly. The ritual had begun. You bargained for everything on the East Side. It was expected.

"Eleven."

I shook my head.

"Twelve." He was studying my face.

"Nope," I replied.

He drew a sharp breath. "Twelve fifty," he almost whispered. "That's the top."

I looked at his face for a moment, then I put out my hand. "Pay me," I said.

He reached into his pocket, took out a dirty old change purse, and snapped it open, revealing a small roll of bills. Carefully he counted the money into my hand.

I counted it again, shoved the money into my pocket, and turned to walk away, but the peddler called me back.

"When you got some more stuff," he said greedily, "bring it to me. I'll treat you right."

I was looking at him, but I couldn't see him. I couldn't see the whole thing for dust. Twelve fifty cut seven ways was less than two bucks apiece. It wasn't worth the effort. "Sure," I answered, turning away. "I'll remember." But he wouldn't see me again. There was no percentage in it.

I looked at my watch as I crossed Rivington Street. It was almost six o'clock. I didn't have to pick up the gang at the candy store before seven. I decided to stop by the house and pick up Papa's supper. Every day Mamma sent his supper down to the store. It would save her a trip.

The halls smelled. Disgustedly I noticed the paper bags of garbage stuck in front of the doors. The lousy super had been drunk again and forgotten to collect the garbage that morning. Much as I had seen of it, I couldn't get used to it.

I stumbled on a loose stair and cursed under my breath. I hated it here. I wished we had enough dough to get out. Some day I would get enough dough together and we would buy our house back and leave this stinking neighborhood.

I opened our door and walked in. Mamma was bending over the stove. She looked up at me wearily.

"Papa said he would be home by two thirty," I told her.

She nodded her head.

"I thought I'd bring him his supper," I volunteered.

She looked at me in some surprise. It was the first time since he'd had the job that I'd offered. "You want your supper first?" she asked.

I shook my head. "I'm not hungry," I lied. "A guy treated me to a couple of hot dogs at Katz's."

"Some soup you'll have, maybe?" she persisted.

"No, Mamma," I answered. "I'm full." I could see from the pot there was barely enough to go around as it was.

She was too tired to argue and took down a white enamel dinner pail from the closet and began to fill it. When she had finished she carefully wrapped it in a paper bag and gave it to me. I started out the door.

"Come home early tonight, Danny," she called after me as the door closed.

"Sure, Ma," I called back as I started down the stairs.

I stopped in front of the store and looked in. There were a few customers inside and a clerk was waiting on them. Papa must be in the back room. I walked into the store and waited at the counter.

The high-pitched sound of a man's shouting came from the back room. Involuntarily I listened, remembering it from earlier in the day.

"You stupid ass," the thin nasty voice was shouting, "I don't know why I hired you anyway. That's the trouble with all you guys who been in business for yourselves. You think you know everything, you don't listen to anybody!"

The voice faded away and the low-pitched murmur of Papa's voice took its place. I couldn't make out the words, so I looked back through the glass partition separating the back room from the store. Papa was standing there talking to Mr. Gold. Mr. Gold was glaring up at him, his face ruddy with rage. He began to shout again even before Papa had finished speaking.

"I don't want no excuses, no alibis! I felt sorry for you when you came in here crying how you needed a job, but, God-dammit, you'll either do the work the way I want it done or out on your ass you'll go! You hear me, Fisher? My way or out! That's all!"

I could hear Papa distinctly now. "I'm sorry, Mr. Gold," he was saying. There was a beaten, servile quality in his voice that made me sick to my stomach. "It won't happen again, Mr. Gold. I promise."

A wild impulse was running through me. I could kill the little son of a bitch who spoke to my father like that, who made him crawl like he did. No man had the right to do that to another. Papa had turned to the little man. I saw his back through the glass partition, his shoulders drooping heavily, his head inclined respectfully.

The clerk's voice interrupted my thoughts. "Anything I can do for you, sir?"

I turned to him bewilderedly. The sickish feeling had replaced my rage. I shook my head and started for the door angrily. Then I remembered the dinner pail I had in my hand and went back to the counter and put it down. "This is Doc Fisher's supper," I told the clerk, and ran out the door, Mr. Gold's high-pitched voice following me out into the street.

"A buck and a half apiece?" Spit's voice was querulous.

I looked at him coldly. My voice was flat. "You kin do better, you fence it."

Saliva ran in tiny beads from the corner of Spit's mouth as it always did when he was excited. "Okay, Danny, okay," he said hastily. "I ain't arguin'."

I finished distributing the money, then looked up at them. I had held out two bucks on them, but that was my due. I had figured out the job.

"What we gonna do next, Danny?" Spit asked, looking at me expectantly.

"I dunno," I answered, taking out a cigarette. "But no more uh this. There ain't enough in it." I lit the cigarette. "Don't worry, I'll think of somethin'." I looked at my watch. It was almost seven o'clock. "I'm gonna take a shot at the crap game in the garage," I said. "Anybody wanna come with me?"

"Not for me," Spit drooled quickly. "I got a dame lined up. At least I'll get somethin' outta my dough that way."

The gang broke up and I walked alone around the corner. Spit had reminded me. I had a date at nine with that girl behind the soda fountain. She seemed like a bright kid. That was okay with me, I liked them bright. I couldn't stand the stupid ones. They only knew one thing when you wanted them to polish doorbells with their behinds. No. The bright ones could be talked into it—sometimes.

I was almost at the garage now. I felt better as I came near the entrance. The three and a half bucks I had in my pocket was as good as nothing. If I was lucky I could afford to buy the dame some chinks.

A thin-faced Italian kid was standing in the garage entrance acting as lookout. I walked past him. The kid put out a hand to stop me. "Where ya goin'?" he asked.

I brushed his hand off me without anger. "Easy, luksh," I smiled. "I'm just gonna try my luck."

The Italian boy smiled back at me in recognition. "Okay, Danny," he said, turning back to the entrance.

I walked through the darkened garage toward a light in the back. In a space hidden by the automobiles surrounding it, a group of men and boys were standing in a small semicircle. Their voices were low and quiet, punctuated only by the metallic clicking of the dice. Several of them looked at me as I came up, but their gaze returned quickly to the floor as they recognized me. Their attention was riveted on the dice as they rolled along the floor and bounced back from the wall.

I stood there quietly for a few minutes trying to get the feel of the game. I didn't believe in bucking the dice, I tried to nose out who was hot and then follow that player. There was a small swarthy guy who seemed to be doing all right. I watched him for a while. He had picked up two bets before I made up my mind. The next time he bet against the dice I went along with him. I threw a buck down on the floor. "Against," I said. The bookie covered it.

The shooter made the point and I lost my bet. I followed the swarthy man again. This time I won. Again I bet and won. I began to feel excitement stirring in me. I bet again and won. I had seven bucks now, I began to feel lucky.

The man who had been shooting looked up. "I'm through," he said disgustedly, standing up and dusting off his trousers.

The book looked around. "Who wants them?" he asked.

There were no takers. Nobody wanted the dice. The book was used to that. There was something in the small gambler's lexicon that said pro dice were jinxed. Still, he had to keep the game going. He looked at me. "Take 'em, Danny," he gestured. "First buck for free."

I moved forward reluctantly and picked up the dice. I had no choice. I was last in the game and that was regulation. I couldn't refuse. I began to rattle the dice in my hand.

Suddenly a feeling of sureness came over me. I felt my heart begin to hammer excitedly. I couldn't miss. I was hot. I threw two bucks down on the floor. Another dollar floated down beside it, that was the book's stake. I blew hotly into the palms of my hands as more money floated down on the floor. I snapped the dice out. They bounced crazily against the wall and came to a stop.

A natural! I picked up the dice again and began to shake them. This time I talked the whole thing over with them. Dice talk no outsider could understand. I could feel them warm up in my hand and I knew that they understood me if nobody else did. I rode the six bucks.

Four was the point. I picked them up again and continued to whisper to them. When they were nice and cozy I spun them out and made my point.

I picked up nine bucks and let the rest ride. I could feel the perspiration breaking out on my face as the dice rattled in my hand. I had the fever.

It was almost a quarter to nine when I came to and looked at my watch. I turned in the dice and checked out of the game. I was better than twenty fish ahead. My shirt clung damply to my back as I walked out of the garage.

The kid at the door grinned at me. "Clean already, Danny?" he jeered.

I grinned back at him and tossed him a half a buck. "Buy yourself a shtickel fleish, luksh," I told him. "You'll find it more fun than your fist."

Chapter Three

I STOOD on the curb in front of the five and ten and watched the girls coming out. I lit a cigarette. It was ten after nine. She was certainly taking her time. Maybe she was giving me a stand-up. I'd give her five more minutes and then to hell with her.

"Hello, Danny," she said quietly. She was standing beside me. I had watched her come out the door, but hadn't recognized her, she looked so much younger in her own clothes than in her uniform.

"Hi, Nellie." My eyes widened. She was just a kid. At the most she was no older than me. "Yuh hungry?" I asked after a moment's hesitation.

She nodded quietly. She seemed a little embarrassed, not as sure of herself as she had been behind the counter of the store.

I took her arm and steered her toward the corner, looking at her from the corner of my eyes. Her hair was jet-black, and bluish tones seemed to flicker in it as the lights from the store windows struck it. Her eyes were wide and looked straight ahead as she walked. She wore lipstick but of a softer shade than she had worn during the day.

"You look younger," I exclaimed in a sort of surprise.

She turned her face toward me. "A lot of girls make up to look older in the store. Otherwise they might not hold their jobs." A shy warmth came into her eyes. "You look older than you did in the store."

I smiled back at her. That made me feel good. We were in front of the restaurant, its faded yellow and blue sign blinking at us:

CHOW MEIN 30¢ CHOP SUEY

"Let's eat," I said, opening the door and letting her walk in before me.

111

A tired-looking, wizened old Chinese showed us to a table. He dropped two menus on the table before us and shuffled slowly back to the door. The restaurant was almost empty; only two other tables were occupied. I glanced down at the menu perfunctorily, I already knew what I wanted. Then I looked across the the table at her.

She met my glance. "Chow mein for me." She smiled.

"And fried rice. We'll mix it," I added quickly. I didn't want her to get any wrong ideas. I wasn't made out of dough.

A young Chinese waiter, as tired-looking as the old man who had seated us, placed a pot of tea on the table and languidly waited for our order. I gave it to him quickly and he went away. Then I turned back to the girl. As my eyes caught her gaze, she lowered her glance. A faint flush began to creep into her face and a strained air suddenly came between us.

"What's the matter?" I asked.

She raised her eyes to meet mine. "I shouldn't be here," she replied nervously. "I don't even know who you are. My father—"

"Your old man wouldn't like it?" I interrupted, smiling confidently. I felt more sure of myself now. "How old are you anyway?"

Her eyes met mine levelly. "Sev—no, sixteen," she answered hesitantly.

"Been working there long?" I asked.

"Almost a year," she said. "They think I'm older."

"Your old man rough on you?" I asked. A sympathy I couldn't restrain had crept into my voice, and it seemed to lessen the strangeness between us.

"He's all right, I guess. You know those old-fashioned Italians. It's always in the old country this, the old country that." She looked into my eyes candidly. "I'm supposed to come right home after work. I'm old enough to lie about my age to get a job and bring home money, but I'm not old enough to go out with boys. If he knew I was out with you, he'd give me hell."

I looked at her speculatively, wondering why the long build-up. "Then why did you come?" I asked.

She smiled. "Maybe I'm getting tired of living in the old country. Maybe it's time he learned this is a new place. We do things differently here."

"Is that the only reason?" I asked, still watching her closely.

Her face began to blush under my scrutiny. "No, it isn't," she confessed, shaking her head slightly. "I wanted to come with you. I wanted to see what you were like."

"Do you like what you see?"

She nodded silently, her face still flushing. "Do you?" she asked in a shy little voice.

I reached across the table and took her hand. This was going to be a pushover. "I sure do, Nellie," I said confidently. "I sure do."

She stopped on the street corner under the light. "You better leave me here, Danny," she said, looking up at me. "My father might be waitin' on the steps for me."

"That's a good brush," I said coldly.

A shadow came into her eyes. "Danny, it's not." Her voice was earnest. "Really, it's not. You don't know my old man."

I couldn't help it, she sold me. "Sure," I said lightly, "I know it's an old gag, but I'm a sucker for it. I half believe yuh."

Her hand caught mine. "You must believe me, Danny," she said quickly. "I wouldn't fool you. Honest, I wouldn't."

I still held onto her hand tightly. "What'll yuh tell him you're comin' in so late for?"

"I'll tell him we got stuck in the store. He knows sometimes we have to stay."

"Will he be mad?"

"No," she replied. "He don't care if it's that. He don't care how late I work."

I let go of her hand and stepped back into the doorway of a store, away from the street lamp. "C'mere," I said.

She watched me for a second, then took a hesitant step toward me. Her voice was suddenly nervous. "What for?"

I looked at her steadily. "You know what for," I said quietly. "C'mere."

She took another half step and then stopped. A strange hurt came into her face. "No, Danny. I'm not that kind."

I made my voice bitter and cutting. "Then it is the brush." I took a cigarette from my pocket and put it between my lips. "Okay, baby. Beat it. You had your fun."

I struck a match and held it to my cigarette. When I looked up she was still watching me. There was a peculiar tenseness in the way she stood there, like a doe about to run. The street light behind her threw blue sparkling lights into her hair.

I blew a cloud of smoke toward her. "What're you waitin' for? Go on home. Your ol' man's waitin'."

She took another step toward me. "Danny, that ain't the way I want it. I don't want you to be mad at me."

I was getting sore. If I got the brush, I got the brush, that's all. I never expected to bat a thousand. But why was she making such a big deal out of the whole thing? My voice mimicked her: "Danny, that ain't the way I want it!" I laughed bitterly. "What the hell d'yuh think I took you out for?" I snapped harshly. "To get the brush on the corner? I can get plenty of dames. I didn't have to bother with you."

There were tears in her eyes. "I thought you liked me, Danny," she said in a small voice. "I liked you."

I reached out quickly and grabbed her arm and pulled her toward me in the dimly lit doorway. I dropped the cigarette to the ground and put my arms around her.

I could feel the stiffness in her body as she looked up at me, her eyes wide and frightened. But she stood still, very still. "Danny!"

I kissed her swiftly, feeling her lips crush beneath mine, her hard teeth behind them. Her lips were cold. I kissed her again. They were a little warmer now and parted slightly. I felt them move and kissed her again. They were warm now and pressed back against me.

I looked down at her, smiling slightly. "Is that so bad, Nellie?"

She hid her face against my shoulder. "You'll think I'm no good," she cried.

I was puzzled. This wasn't what I had expected at all. My confusion spilled over into my voice. "What you play up to me this afternoon for? Yuh should know the score by now. You been aroun' long enough."

She looked up at me and in the dark her eyes were soft and wide but no longer afraid. "I liked you, Danny, that's why. That's why I didn't go home when you told me."

I looked at her for a moment; then I sought her lips again. I could feel the tension seep from her body and she loosened up as she kissed me back. This kiss was for real. I held her close to me. "But yuh acted so wise," I whispered. "About the fight an' all that. You knew that Spit and Solly were fakin'. How'd yuh know somethin' like that if yuh never been aroun'?"

"My oldest brother, Giuseppe, was a pug," she answered, not

stirring in my arms. "He taught me to tell when they were fakin' it."

Our eyes met in the dark and held. "You're not givin' me the business?" The last remaining trace of skepticism was in my voice.

"No, Danny." Her voice was level.

I kissed her again. It was different this time. There was a new looseness, a comfortable understanding in the kiss. The fierce urgency had gone.

"I like you," I said, laughing suddenly. "You're funny but you're nice."

She smiled up at me. "Not mad any more?"

I shook my head. "No, baby."

This time she held her face up to me and waited for my lips. I looked down at her, not moving. Her eyes were closed. "Danny," she whispered shyly, "kiss me, Danny."

I felt the change in her lips. They were suddenly open to me and she was pressing desperately against me. My arms tightened around her. I dropped my hand along her spine, molding her to me.

Her eyes were still closed. We were drifting in a hazy cloud. The corner was gone, the street lamp was gone, the doorway was gone. Everything had vanished except the pressure of our lips. I closed my eyes as my hands sought the warmth of her body.

Her whisper was almost a scream in my ears. "Danny! Danny, stop!" Her hands were grabbing excitedly at mine, pushing them away from her.

I caught her wrists and held them. Her body was trembling frightenedly. "Easy, baby, easy," I said gently. "I ain't gonna hurt you."

The panic left her as suddenly as it had come and she hid her face against my shoulder. "Oh, Danny, I never felt like this before."

I put my hand under her chin and lifted her face toward me. Tears were standing in her eyes. "Me neither," I said earnestly. And I meant it too.

Her eyes grew large and round with wonder. "Danny, do you—" her voice hesitated. "Do you think maybe we're in love?"

I was puzzled. I didn't know. I tried to smile. "Maybe we are, Nellie. Maybe we are."

Almost as I spoke, an embarrassment seemed to spring up between us and we moved apart. She looked down and began to rearrange her clothing. By the time she had finished I was smoking a cigarette. Her hand reached toward me and I took it. We stood there silently, hand in hand, until the cigarette burned down.

Then I threw it away and it fell into the gutter, spilling small sparks, and we turned and looked at each other. I smiled. "Hi, Nellie."

"Hello, Danny," she whispered back shyly.

We stared at each other for a moment and then began to laugh. With our laughter, the embarrassment seemed to fall away. I bent and kissed her quickly, our handclasp tightening and loosening as our lips met and quit.

"Hope your father won't be mad," I said.

"He won't be," she smiled. "I'll tell him I was working."

We walked out of the doorway to the corner under the street light. Her face was flushed and bright, her eyes shining with a brand-new warmth, and her teeth were white and sparkling under her red lips as she smiled at me.

"Did I tell you you were pretty?" I asked jestingly.

"No," she answered.

"I guess I didn't have time," I grinned, "so I'll tell you now. You're very pretty. Like a movie star."

"Oh, Danny!" Her hand clung to mine very tightly.

"I guess yuh gotta go," I said seriously.

She nodded.

"Well—good night then," I said, letting go of her hand.

"Will I see you again, Danny?" Her voice was very small.

"Sure thing." I grinned quickly. "I'll drop around to the store tomorrow."

Her face brightened. "I'll make you a special soda. Three full scoops of ice cream!"

"Three scoops!" I exclaimed. "You couldn't keep me away then!"

She was smiling again. "Good night, Danny."

"Good night, baby."

She started across the street, then turned back to me. There was an anxious look on her face. "You won't bring your friends, will you? They might get caught."

"Yuh worried about them, Nellie?" I laughed.

"I don't give a damn about them," she said fiercely. "It's you I'm worried about."

I felt a glow kiting through me. She was a good kid. "I won't bring them."

The serious look was still on her face. "Do you have to run around with them and do things like that, Danny? You might get caught. Can't you get a job?"

"No," I answered stiffly. "My folks won't let me quit school."

Her hand reached for mine and squeezed it understandingly. There was deep concern in her eyes. "Be careful, Danny," she said softly.

I smiled down at her. "I will," I promised.

She stepped up on the curb and kissed me quickly. "Good night, Danny."

"Night, baby."

I watched her run across the street and turn into a doorway. She stopped there for a moment and waved at me. I waved back. Then she disappeared into the hallway.

I turned and started down the street. I felt good. I felt so good I almost forgot how much I hated living down here until I crossed Delancey Street in front of Papa's store and saw Mr. Gold again.

Chapter Four

HE WAS standing in front of the store stuffing a small canvas and leather pouch into his pocket. I knew what it was right away. It was a pouch used to make a night deposit in the bank.

Automatically I ducked into a doorway and watched him. A glance at my watch told me it was a few minutes to twelve. He glanced once more in the store window, then started down Delancey Street toward Essex. I followed him slowly, lagging half a block behind.

At first I didn't know why I did it, but as I moved along behind him, the reason came to me. He turned up Essex and began to walk quickly. I crossed to the opposite side of the street and kept pace with him, the idea taking quick shape in my mind.

He walked to the bank on the corner of Avenue A and First Street. There he took the little pouch from his pocket and dropped it in the night depository. Then he turned and started up Avenue A.

I lingered behind on the corner, watching him go. I had no further interest in where he was going. I lit a cigarette and began to think.

When I had first moved down here, it had seemed like another world. And it was. It was a different world from any I had ever known. Down here there was only one rule: you either fought or went hungry. And there were no holds barred.

The kids knew that even better than the adults. There were brought up to scrounge for themselves as early as they could. They were tough, bitter, and cynical beyond anything I had ever imagined. There was only one thing that kept me from being killed. I could fight better than they could and in many ways think faster.

It had taken a little time, though. For a while they looked at me crosseyed. They couldn't figure me. After the fight I had the day Rexie was run over they had shown a certain respect for me. It wasn't until I had taken to hanging out in the candy store on the corner that I began to know them.

From that point on, it became my show. The boy I had beaten up was the leader of the gang. Now they shifted around without purpose. Spit and Solly had tried to take over, but they couldn't command respect from the others. The only language they could understand was physical superiority.

Then one day Spit came over to me while I was having an egg cream. Covering me with a fine spray of saliva, he invited me to join the gang. I listened to him cautiously, but after a while I came in with them. I was too lonely down here, I had to identify myself with somebody. It might as well be with the Stanton Street Boys.

But the main concern remained dough. Lack of money was the miasma that hung over the lower East Side like a plague. You could see it everywhere you turned, in the dirty streets, in the placarded store windows, in the ill-kept tenements. You could hear it everywhere, in the crying hawk of the street peddlers on Rivington, in the careful haggling over pennies in the shops.

If you had a buck in your pocket you were a king; if you didn't, you looked for someone who did and would pay your freight. But kings did not live on the East Side any more unless they were the kind who could drag enough pennies from the general poverty to make life comfortable for themselves.

There were plenty of those—bookies, shylocks, and petty criminals. They were the smart ones, the heroes. They were the envied, the strong who managed to survive. They were our examples, our men of distinction.

They were the people we wanted to be. Not shnooks like our fathers, who had fallen by the wayside because of an inability to cope with the times. Our fathers were the people of the lower East Side. And there were enough of them as it was. We weren't going to be like them if we could help it. We were smarter than they were. We were going to be kings. And when I was king I would buy back my house in Brooklyn and move away from this rotten place.

I strolled back toward my house. Spit had asked me what we were going to do next. I hadn't known then. All I knew was that the five-and-dime job wasn't worth the effort. But I knew now. I could knock over two birds with this caper. I decided to drop in at the candy store before I went upstairs to talk it over with Spit and Solly.

I stirred restlessly in the bed. I was too steamed up to fall asleep. A horn honked loudly in the street outside my window. I got out of bed silently and sat down near the window. I lit a cigarette and stared out.

A D.S. truck was parked down there. The faint metallic sounds of the garbage cans clanging against its sides as the men emptied them came up to me. I remembered the expression on Spit's face when I first explained the job to the boys.

He had been afraid. But Solly was hot for it, and that won him over. Just the three of us could handle it. But first Gold's routine would have to be checked; that was important.

One of us would have to follow him for several nights in a row as he left the store and make sure of all his stops and habits. Then on the right night we'd jump him.

There was a couple of hundred bucks in it, I had told them.

All we had to do was coldcock the geezer and snatch the
dough. It was a cinch. I hadn't told them anything about my
father working in the store. It was none of their business.

The sound of a girl's voice coming in the open window made
me think of Nellie. She was a strange kid for a luksh. Usually
they were loud and tough and you could tell they were Italian
as soon as they opened their mouths, but she was different. She
was soft-spoken and gentle and nice.

She had liked me, too. I knew that. It was funny how
things happened. You took out a dame for one reason and
suddenly you find out that things weren't what they seemed.
That the dame was level and that you really liked her. Then you
didn't want to do anything that might make her dislike you.

That was a strange thing. I had never felt like that about any
dame before. I remembered what she had said: "Maybe we're
in love." Maybe we were. I couldn't explain any other way how
I felt. There had never been any other dame I was content just
to hold and talk to and be near. Maybe she was right in what
she said.

The girl's voice floated in the window again. I craned my
neck into the street in order to see her. The street was empty.
Again I heard the girl's voice. There was something familiar
about it, I knew that voice, but it sounded strange coming in
my window.

The girl was talking again. This time I traced the sound to
the roof over my head. I looked up. I could see the glow of a
cigarette over the parapet. Then I recognized the voice. It was
Mimi's. I wondered what she was doing up on the roof at this
hour. It was after one o'clock. Then I remembered she had said
something about a date with that guy in her office she had a
crush on—a George somebody. I had twitted her about going
out with a jerk who worked in an office and she had been
angry. "He's better than those candy-store bums you hang out
with," she had retorted.

I decided to go up there and see what Miss High-and-Mighty
was doing. All I knew was that if you went up on the roof down
in this neighborhood at night, you weren't going to look at the
stars. I slipped into my trousers and silently left my room.

The roof door was open and I quietly stepped outside. I hid
in the shadow of the door and looked toward the front of the
roof. She was there all right. So was the guy. They were in a
hell of a clinch. I watched them.

They separated and in the moonlight I could see Mimi's face. I caught my breath sharply. She didn't look like no goody-goody now. The guy was talking, his voice low. I couldn't make out his words, but he seemed to be pleading. Mimi shook her head and he went off again in another torrent of words.

She shook her head again and began to speak. "No, George, forget about marriage. I like you very much but I'm tired of worrying about money and we'll only have the same thing. I don't want that."

I grinned to myself. Mimi was no dope. A buck was a buck. Still, it seemed funny to think about her getting married. It made me realize that she was all grown up now, she wasn't a kid any more.

The fellow pulled her to him again. He said something to her and kissed her. I watched them, still grinning. For all her high-and-mighty ways, she knew the score when it came to necking. It didn't look like this was the first time she had been up on a roof. I turned silently and went back down the stairs to my room.

About fifteen minutes later I heard the door open and I went out into the hall. She was closing the door silently and she jumped when she turned around and saw me.

"What are you doing up, Danny?" she asked in surprise.

I didn't answer, just stood there grinning at her.

She stared at me angrily. "What are you grinning at?"

"Your lipstick is smeared," I told her, my grin becoming broader and more knowing.

Her hand flew to her mouth. "You stayed up to spy on me!"

"Uh-uh." I shook my head. "You and your boy friend were making so much noise up on the roof over my head I couldn't sleep."

"You got a dirty mind!" she flung at me.

"Have I?" I asked, still smiling. I pointed at her dress.

She looked down, her eyes widening in surprise. The whole front of her dress was covered with lipstick stains. She looked up at me, her face reddening.

"Take some advice from your kid brother, baby," I said. "Next time you go in for any heavy lovin', wipe your lipstick off first. It don't clean out an' it saves wear an' tear on your clothes."

She bit her lip furiously. She was too angry to think of a retort.

I grinned again and went back to my room. "Good night, Mimi," I said over my shoulder. "Remember what I said."

Chapter Five

PAPA came in for breakfast just as we were beginning to eat. I looked up at him. There were lines on his face that hadn't come from weariness alone. Lines of pain and discouragement that came from eating humble pie were etched sharply into his once round cheeks.

A twinge of sympathy for him ran through me. The fierce pride I had in my being was hurt by the slow disintegration of his own. I stood up. "Here, Papa," I said quickly, "sit here by the window." It was the comfortable place in the kitchen.

Slowly he slumped into the chair. He looked over at me gratefully. "Thanks for bringing me over my supper, Danny," he said wearily. "I was busy and I didn't see you come in."

I nodded my head. "The clerk told me," I said, sparing his feelings. I knew he wouldn't want me to admit I had heard Gold hollering at him.

Mamma came over to the table and put a bowl of cereal in front of him. "Why didn't you sleep later, Harry?" she asked concernedly.

He looked up at her. "Who can sleep when the daylight comes? I can't get used to it."

"You should rest, though," Mamma said. "You work hard."

He picked up the spoon and began to eat without answering, but he had no appetite and soon he pushed the plate away from him. "Just give me coffee, Mary," he said in a tired voice.

Mamma put a cup of coffee in front of him. "Were you busy yesterday?" she asked.

"Mr. Gold kept me busy," he said without looking up. Then he looked at me, realizing what he had said. I could see he was wondering what I knew.

I kept my face impassive. As far as he was concerned, I knew nothing, had seen nothing, and had heard nothing. "What kind of a guy is this Gold like?" I asked, looking down at my plate.

I could feel Papa's gaze on me. "Why do you ask?"

I didn't look up. "Just curious, I guess," I answered. I couldn't tell him the real reason.

Papa thought for a moment. When he spoke, his words were very carefully chosen. He surprised me with his understatement. "He's all right, only very nervous. Got a lot of things to do, a lot of things on his mind."

I put another spoonful of cereal in my mouth. "Yuh like workin' for him, Papa?" I asked as casually as I could manage.

Our eyes met and his fell to his coffee cup. "It's a job," he answered evasively.

"How come he's manager?" I asked.

"The man before him got sick and had to quit. He had my job as the only other registered man, so naturally he was promoted."

I looked at him interestedly. That was an angle. "If he quit would you get the job, Pop?"

Papa laughed self-consciously. "I don't know, but I guess I might. The supervisor likes me."

"Who's that?"

"He's the boss of a group of stores. He comes from the main office."

"He's boss over Mr. Gold too?" I continued.

Papa nodded. "Over everybody." He looked at me with a curious smile. "So many questions, Danny," he chided. "You thinking of going to work in a drugstore for the summer?"

"Maybe," I said evasively.

"You're not going to work for Mr. Gottkin in the country?" he asked.

"I don't know," I said, shrugging my shoulders. "I haven't heard from him yet." I was disappointed about that too. I had expected that Sam would drop me a line by now, but I guess that business last year with Miss Schindler had burned him more than he let me know.

"Why don't you write him?" Mamma asked.

I turned to her. "Where?" I don't even know where he is. He's always traveling. For all I know, he may have given up the business entirely." I couldn't tell them the reason why I wouldn't write him.

Just then Mimi came rushing in. "I've just got time for coffee, Mamma," she said. "I'll be late for work."

Mamma shook her head. "I don't know what's the matter with you, staying up so late you can't get up in the morning."

"I do," I said grinning, remembering last night. "Mimi's got a feller."

Papa looked at her with interest. "A nice boy, Miriam?" he asked.

I answered before she had a chance. "A schmoe," I said quickly. "A jerk from her office."

"He is not!" she retorted angrily. "He's really a very nice boy, Papa. He goes to college at night."

"Yeah," I teased her, "Tin Beach U."

She turned on me furiously. "Keep your mouth shut!" she snapped. "At least he's got more sense than to hang around a candy store all day and night like you do. He's going to make something out of himself, not be a street-corner bum."

Mamma put out a placating hand. "Don't say things like that to your brother. It's not nice."

Mimi turned angrily to her. Rage was shaking her voice. "Why not?" she queried, almost shouting. "Who is he? God? Who does he think he is that everybody has to be afraid to tell him what they think? Ever since we moved here, it's been Danny this and Danny that. When he changed school it was terrible, but I changed school in the last term and nobody said anything. Does he try to get a job after school or do some work? He knows how bad we need money but he doesn't lift a finger to help and nobody says nothing to him. Everybody's afraid to hurt his feelings. All he does is hang out in a candy store all day and night with a bunch of bums and comes home to eat and sleep like a king. He's a bum, nothing but a bum, and it's about time somebody told it to him!"

"Mimi, shut up!" Papa was on his feet, his face pale. He looked at me guiltily.

She was staring at him, her eyes filled with angry tears; then she turned toward me. I stared at her coldly. For a moment she looked at me, then turned and ran, crying, from the kitchen.

Papa sat down heavily and looked at me. Mamma was watching me too. They were waiting for me to speak, but I had nothing to say. At last Papa spoke in a heavy voice. "Altogether wrong she's not, Danny," he said gently.

I didn't answer. My lips were grimly shut.

"Those fellers down at the candy store, they're no good," he continued.

I pushed my plate away from me and stood up. "I didn't pick this neighborhood. It wasn't my fault we moved down here. What d'ya want me to do, become a hermit because Mimi doesn't approve of my friends?"

Papa shook his head. "No, but other friends you can't find?"

I stared at him. It was no use. He would never understand. There was nothing to say. The estrangement I had felt between us the first day we moved down here grew stronger. And it was too late to go back. "There are no other friends to find," I said flatly.

"Then there's something you can do," he persisted. "There must be."

I shook my head with finality. "It's not anything I can do, Papa," I told him coldly. "Only you can do it."

"What's that?" he asked.

Mamma came toward me. "Yes, what's that?" she echoed.

"Get back my house," I said slowly. "You lost it. You get it back. Then maybe we can start all over."

I watched the pain grow and grow in their eyes until I couldn't stand it any longer. Then I walked out of the apartment.

She spotted me instantly, almost as soon as I came through the door. I sauntered down the counter to where she stood. I could see her look hurriedly in the mirror behind her and pat her hair. I climbed up on a stool and she turned around smiling.

"Hello, Danny," she whispered shyly. I could see a blush running up her neck into her face.

I smiled back at her. She was a nice kid. "Hi, Nellie," I whispered quietly. "Was your father mad?"

She shook her head. "He believed me," she whispered. She looked up suddenly. In the mirror I could see the manager walking toward us. "A chocolate soda," she said quickly in a businesslike tone. "Yes, sir."

She turned and took a glass from the shelf behind her. I smiled at her in the mirror. The manager passed us without a glance. She sighed in relief and went about making the soda.

She came back down the counter and placed the soda in

front of me. "Your hair is so blond it's almost white," she whispered. "I dreamed about you last night."

I looked at her quizzically. The kid had it bad. But I felt flattered. "A good dream?" I asked, slipping the straws into the soda.

She nodded, excitement lurking in her eyes. "Did you think about me?"

"A little," I admitted.

"I want you to think about me," she said quickly.

I stared at her. Her face was warm and attractive. She had less makeup on today than yesterday. Today she looked younger. She began to blush under my gaze.

"Will you meet me tonight?" she asked eagerly.

I nodded. "Same place."

I could see the manager coming back toward us again. "That will be ten cents, please," she said in her business voice.

My dime rang on the counter and she picked it up. She pressed down the register keys and the bell rang as the drawer opened. She dropped in the dime and closed it. The manager had gone again. She came back to me. "Nine o'clock," she whispered.

I nodded my head again and she turned away in answer to another customer. I finished my soda quickly and left the store.

The three of us walked down Delancey Street. Solly slouched along listening to Spit and me.

I pulled them to a stop in front of the drugstore. "This is the place," I said.

Spit's voice was surprised. "This is the joint where your old man works," he said.

It was my turn to be surprised. I didn't think he knew. But I should have known better, there were no secrets down here. "So?" I asked belligerently.

"What if he gets wise?" Spit asked excitedly.

"What's he got to get wise to?" I retorted. "They'll never think of me."

"But this is the McCoy," Spit said; "this ain't no penny-ante rap. If the cops getcha, yuh go in the can an' they throw away the key."

"Yuh like workin' the five and dime for peanuts," I asked sarcastically, "or yuh lookin' for some real dough?"

Solly finally spoke. "Danny's right. To hell with the cheap seats. This looks okay to me."

I gave him a grateful glance. We walked on to the corner before we stopped again. There I turned to face Spit. "Quit crappin' around. Yuh in or out?" I asked flatly.

Spit looked from one to another. We watched him steadily. His face flushed. "Okay," he said quickly, "I'm in."

I could feel my face relax into a smile. I slapped Spit on the shoulder heartily. "Good boy," I said softly. "I knew I could count on yuh. Now listen again, this is the way we'll work it."

We stood on the corner and figured the job. Around us swirled the hungry lower East Side. A cop stood a few feet away, but he paid no attention to us. Nor us to him. He had no reason to bother us. Kids always stood on street corners down here and always would. He couldn't go around chasing all of them. If he did, he wouldn't have time to do anything else.

Chapter Six

IT WAS drizzling and we huddled together in the doorway across the street from Nellie's house. Somehow we began to think of it as if we owned it, and whenever someone else came near it we would resent them as if they were trespassers. My lips were sweet with the taste of her, but now we stood quietly, my arms around her, looking out into the wet, dark streets. Her voice seemed to float in the night. "Next week will be June, Danny."

I nodded my head and looked down at her. "Yeah," I said.

Her eyes were almost shy as she looked up at me. "I know you almost three weeks now, but it seems like I knew you all my life."

I smiled at her. I felt the same way. I felt good when she was around. It was like being home again. "Like me, Nellie?" I fished.

Her eyes were shining now. "Like you?" she whispered softly. "I'm crazy about you. I love you, Danny. I love you so much I'm afraid."

I pressed my lips to her. "I love you too," I whispered back.

She gave a soft cry deep in her throat and her arms pulled me close to her. "Oh, Danny," she cried, "I wish we were old enough to get married!"

I couldn't help it, at first it seemed so funny. My lips began to twitch with a smile.

She pulled her face away from me. "You're laughing at me!"

I shook my head, smothering the smile. "I'm not, doll. Really. I was just thinking what your old man would say if he knew."

She pulled my face down to her again. "Who gives a damn what he would say, once we got married!" she whispered wildly.

I kissed her again and held her tight. I could feel her shiver in my grasp.

"Hold me, Danny," she cried breathlessly. "Hold me. I love you to hold me. I love the feel of your hands on me. I don't care if they say it is a sin!"

I looked at her in surprise. "A sin?" I questioned. "Who says so?"

Her hands held mine against her bosom as her wide dark eyes looked up at me. "I really don't care, Danny," she said earnestly. "Even if Father Kelly says so. I'll do whatever penance I have to just so long as you don't stop loving me."

I was puzzled. "What's Father Kelly got to do with it?" It was the first time I had thought about the difference in our religions.

She looked at me trustingly. "I'm not supposed to say it, but each week after confession he gives me a lecture about you."

"You tell him about us?" I asked curiously. "What does he say?"

She rested her head against my shoulder. "He says that it's wrong and I should stop," she answered in a low voice, "and that it's even worse with you."

"Why with me?" I asked, beginning to get a little angry.

"Because you're not even Catholic. He says we'll never be able to get married. No church would accept us. He says I shouldn't bother with you, that I should find some nice Catholic boy."

"The bastard!" I said bitterly. I looked across the street toward her house. What difference did it make to him what she did? I looked back at her. "What if he tells your father?" I asked worriedly.

She looked surprised at my question. "He would never do that!" she replied quickly in a shocked voice. "A priest would never tell. What you tell him is for God's ears alone. He is just the communicant for your confession. I thought you knew that."

"I didn't know," I admitted. I was still curious about her relationship with the priest. "What does he make you do when you tell him about us?"

"I have to say prayers and do penance before the Virgin Mother. After that I'm all right."

"He doesn't punish you?" I asked.

She seemed bewildered. "You don't understand, Danny," she replied. "He just tries to make you realize that you've done wrong and feel sorry for it. When you feel sorry for it, then you're punished enough."

I began to smile. This was nothing. "Are you sorry?" I asked.

She looked up at me guiltily. "No, I'm not sorry at all," she said in a wondering voice. "Maybe that's what seems so wrong about the whole thing. I guess I'll never be forgiven then."

I pulled her to me laughing. "Don't worry about it then, baby," I reassured her. "Nothing can be wrong as long as we love each other." I was just about to kiss her when I heard footsteps coming toward us in the street. We separated hastily. A man walked by without a sideward glance.

I looked at my watch. "Jesus! It's after eleven! You better get goin' or your old man will raise the roof!"

She smiled at me. "I don't want to go, Danny. I want to stay here with you forever!"

I grinned back at her. I didn't want her to go either, but tonight I had something else to do. We had finally decided that tonight we'd pull that job. Spit and Solly would be waiting for me at the store at half past eleven. "Go on," I said with a forced lightness. "I got to get home even if you don't."

She leaned toward me. "All right, Danny." She kissed me. "Tomorrow night?"

I grinned at her. "Tomorrow night."

She walked across the street. I watched her get to her house and stop in the doorway to wave at me. I waved back and she disappeared inside.

I looked at my watch again. It was twenty-five after eleven. I would have to snap it up if I wanted to get there in time. I broke into a half run and then slowed down suddenly. Too many people notice a guy running through the streets at this time of night.

Solly was standing on the corner across the street from the store. "Where's Spit?" I asked, a little out of breath.

Solly gestured with his hand. "Over there." Spit was standing on the other corner, grinning at me.

Across the street Mr. Gold was standing in the middle of the store talking to Papa. Papa was listening to him with a downcast expression on his face. The son of a bitch was probably giving the old man hell again, I thought bitterly. I turned back to Solly. "I hope the old man don't go with him again tonight or we'll have to put it off until next week."

That was what had held us back this long. Some nights Papa used to walk Mr. Gold as far as the bank. Twice before we had been primed to do the job, but each time we'd had to call it off.

Solly's eyes were blank. "We'll see," he replied succinctly.

I looked at him. Solly was okay, he didn't talk very much but I could depend on him. I turned back to the store and we quietly took up our wait.

Mr. Gold was still talking to my father. Gold's hands were flying as he talked. They were always moving, first pointing one way, then another. He seemed generally disgusted. Papa stood there patiently listening, an attitude of resignation in the droop of his shoulders. He was getting it, all right. I could tell. My lips tightened bitterly. Mr. Gold wouldn't feel much like talking after we got through with him tonight.

Solly's hand touched my arm. "He's gettin' ready to go!"

I craned my neck to see what Gold was doing. He had walked away from Papa and was looking at the register. He pointed at the register, his lips moving rapidly. Slowly Papa walked over and looked in, nodding his head. Gold came out in front of the counter and started for the door, leaving Papa at the register, a tired look on his face.

I turned quickly to Solly. "Yuh remember what I tol' yuh,

now?" There was just the slightest trace of excitement in my voice.

Solly nodded. "I remember."

"Okay," I said hurriedly. "Gimme the sap." I held out my hand and Solly swiftly passed it to me. I slipped it into my pocket and started across the street.

"Let's get goin', boy," I said as I picked Spit up on the other corner. We turned up the street, walking in an opposite direction to Gold's path, reached the next corner, and turned to look back.

Mr. Gold was just turning up Essex Street. Solly, right behind him, seemed to be coming home from a late movie. I knew that he saw us watching him because he made a tiny gesture with his hand: thumb and index finger circled. Okay.

I sent it back to him and in a moment we were moving quickly up Ludlow Street which runs parallel to Essex. We were walking rapidly, our breath coming hard with excitement.

I looked at Spit. "Got everything straight?"

"Yeah, Danny. I got it." Spit's face was wet clear down to his chin. He wiped it on his sleeve as we continued to move along.

I nodded my head and we hurried on. There was no time to lose. We covered three blocks before we came to the open lot just before Houston Street. I looked at Spit. This was it. The lot went clear through to Essex. I was beginning to feel frightened. Vaguely I wished I had never started this thing. Then I remembered how Mr. Gold had spoken to my father.

"This is for me," I said. My voice seemed to ring loudly in my ears.

Spit grinned. "Good luck."

I gave Spit a shove with my hand and tried to smile. I don't know how it came off, but he turned and continued on toward the corner. I watched him fade around it, then ducked into the shadows of the lot.

I was standing in the dark, my back against a building. My heart was beating so loudly it could be heard half a block away. I held my breath trying to quiet its noise. That only seemed to make it worse. I reached into my pocket, took out the sap, and slapped it softly in my hand to get the feel of it. It made a shallow dull thump. My hands felt wet and I wiped them on my trousers to dry them.

I was beginning to worry. What if something went wrong? Why weren't they there? I wished I dared to stick my head out from beside the building to see if they were coming but I couldn't take any chances. I drew a deep breath. Stop worrying, I told myself angrily. Nothing could go wrong. I had the whole thing too well worked out.

It was simple. Too easy to go wrong. Solly would be walking up the street behind Mr. Gold. He could see anyone coming toward them. Spit would be walking down the street, facing them. He would be able to see anyone coming up behind them. If there was the slightest chance of anyone spotting us, they would start whistling and I would let Mr. Gold walk by. It was that simple. Nothing could go wrong. I leaned back against the building, watching the far corner for the first sign from Spit that was to tip me off that they were coming.

The seconds seemed to drag by. I was beginning to get nervous again. I wished I could light a cigarette. I strained my eyes through the dark. There were footsteps coming down the sidewalk toward me.

It was Spit, shuffling along in that funny walk he had. Suddenly my nervousness was gone and calm settled down over me. There was no backing out now. I let the sap hang loosely in my hand and waited, poised on the balls of my feet, ready to move at the signal.

I began to count slowly to myself, like I was trying to set up a rhythm for the punching bag. "One—two—three—four—one two—"

Spit lifted his hand to his cheek. I began to move swiftly toward the edge of the building. Mr. Gold came into view just across the building line and I slipped out silently behind him.

In the dark the falling sap was a swift blur. There was a dull, sickening sound and then Solly caught the falling man and was hauling him into the shadows of the lot.

Mr. Gold lay silently on the ground and we looked down at him. Spit's voice was frightened; his words made a fine spray over my face. "Maybe yuh croaked him!"

I could feel my heart leap in sudden fright. I dropped to one knee and slipped a hand inside Mr. Gold's vest. With a sense of relief I felt his heart beating. I took my hand from beneath his vest and ran my fingers lightly over his head. No dent, no blood. I was in luck. No concussion or broken head.

Solly's voice snapped from over my head. "Quit the crappin'!" he said flatly. "Get the dough. We ain't got all night!"

His words dispelled my fear. Solly was right. We hadn't done this so I could play doctor. I ran my fingers through his pockets quickly and found the money pouch just as Spit dropped to one knee beside me. Spit was fumbling with Mr. Gold's wrist.

"What're yuh doin'?" I barked.

"Grabbin' his watch. It's a beaut!"

I slapped his hand away. I was myself again. I could think now that I was no longer afraid. "Jerk! Leave it! Yuh want the cops should finger you the first time yuh show with it?"

Spit got to his feet grumbling. Again I slipped my hand inside Gold's vest. His heart was beating stronger now. I withdrew my hand and started to my feet. "Okay," I whispered, "let's blow!"

Before I could start moving, a hand suddenly gripped at my ankle. Mr. Gold's voice rang out like a clarion in the quiet lot. "Help! Police!"

Spit and Solly started running. I looked down wildly. Mr. Gold was holding my ankle with both hands, yelling at the top of his lungs, his eyes tightly shut.

I looked around frantically. Spit and Solly were almost out of sight across Essex Street. My heart was really banging now. I tried to move but couldn't. Fear had paralyzed my legs. I looked across the empty lot. Someone had come out of Katz's delicatessen and was running toward us.

I had to get out of here. I kicked violently at Gold's hand and felt the toe of my shoe strike his arm. Something seemed to snap under my foot and the man groaned, then screamed in pain and I was free and running.

The street behind me was suddenly alive with noise, but by that time I was around the corner on Stanton Street. An instinct made me stop running and I stood on the corner, hesitating a second. Quickly I made up my mind. I had to find out whether he had seen me. I cut up the block. There was a crowd in the lot now.

I pushed my way through them. The cops were there already, yelling for everybody to stand back. Mr. Gold was sitting up on the ground, holding his arm and rocking to and fro in pain.

"What happened?" I asked one of the spectators.

The man answered without turning his head to me. He was too busy watching Mr. Gold. "That guy there got mugged."

I pushed my way closer to Mr. Gold. A cop was kneeling beside him. I could see his lips move but I couldn't hear what he was saying. I was almost on top of them now and I could hear Mr. Gold's voice. His words chased the fear in me.

"How could I see who it was?" Mr. Gold was yelling, his voice shrill with pain. "I was unconscious, I told you." He moaned again. "Oy, get me a doctor. The son of a bitch broke my arm!"

Slowly I let myself drift back through the crowd. When I was near its fringe the cops began to chase us. "Go on, now," they were saying, "break it up."

The crowd began to disperse and I went with them. I took them at their word and headed for home. I slipped into the house quietly and it wasn't until I took my trousers off that I remembered I still had the money pouch with me.

I ducked into the bathroom and locked the door. Then I opened the pouch by cutting through it with my penknife and counted the dough. A fortune! One hundred and thirty-five bucks!

I shoved the money into my pocket and looked around the room. I had to get rid of the pouch. There was a small window over the toilet that opened on an airshaft that was never cleaned. I climbed up on the toilet seat and dropped the pouch out the window. I heard it clink against the sides of the building as it went down, and I went back to my room and got into bed.

I closed my eyes and tried to fall asleep, but thoughts kept chasing crazily through my mind. What if the cops were only playing dumb? What if Mr. Gold remembered once his pain had gone? He had plenty of time to get a good look at me. My pajamas were becoming clammy with perspiration and clinging to my skin. I squeezed my eyes tightly shut in the dark and desperately tried to fall asleep. There was no use. My nerves were jumping at every little sound in the night. A door slammed and I bolted upright in the bed. They were coming after me.

I jumped out of bed quickly and into my trousers and went to the door, straining my ears to hear the voices just beyond it. It was only my mother and father. Papa had just come home.

I slipped out of my trousers and got back into bed again. I sank back against the pillow with a sigh of relief. I was being a fool. Nobody could suspect me. Slowly my nervousness began to leave me, but still I couldn't sleep.

The night seemed a thousand hours long. At last I turned on my side and stuffed the corner of the pillow into my mouth to keep from screaming. I began to pray silently. I had never consciously prayed before. I begged God not to let them catch me. I swore I would never do it again.

But the gray light of morning had come into the room before my eyes closed in sheer exhaustion. And then I didn't really sleep. For echoing in my mind was the sickening sound of the snapping bone as I had kicked and Mr. Gold's sharp piercing scream was ringing in my ears.

Chapter Seven

SOMEONE was shaking me. I tried to move away from the hands that were holding me. I put up my arms to fend them off. Why couldn't they leave me alone? I was so tired.

A voice was yelling in my ear. It repeated the same words over and over: "Wake up, Danny! Wake up!"

I rolled over on my side. "I'm tired," I mumbled, burying my face in the pillow. "Go away."

I heard footsteps leave the room and I dozed tensely. I was waiting for the signal. There it was, Spit's hand was going up to his face. I was moving quickly now. Mr. Gold had just come past the edge of the building. My hand went up. The weight of the sap was heavy in it. It started falling. Just then Mr. Gold turned around.

His white frightened face was staring at me. "I know you!" he screamed. "You're Danny Fisher!" Just then the sap came down and hit him on the side of the head and he was falling.

"No!" I groaned. "Never again!" I tried to claw my way into the pillow. A hand fell on my shoulder and I jumped around in bed, my eyes open and staring.

"Danny!" Mamma's voice was startled.

I sat up in bed quickly, my eyes adjusting to the realities of the room. I was breathing heavily, as if I had been running.

Mamma was staring at my face. It felt white and clammy with sweat. "Danny, what's the matter? Don't you feel good?"

I looked at her for a moment; then I slowly sank back against the pillow. I was very tired. It was only a dream, but it had seemed so real. "I'm all right, Ma," I said slowly.

A look of concern crossed her face. She placed a cool hand on my hot forehead and pressed me back against the pillow. "Go back to sleep, Danny," she said gently. "You were crying in your sleep all night."

The sun was bright in the street outside when I opened my eyes again. I stretched lazily, pushing my feet all the way down against the foot of the bed.

"Feeling better, Blondie?"

My head snapped round. Mamma was sitting next to the bed. I sat up. "Yeah," I said shamefacedly. "I wonder what was the matter with me."

I was glad Mamma didn't insist on an answer to my question. All she did was hold a glass of tea toward me. "Here," she said quietly. "Drink this tea."

I looked at the kitchen clock as I walked into the room. It was after two o'clock. "Where's Papa?" I asked.

"He had to go down to the store early," Mamma answered without turning from the stove. "Something happened to Mr. Gold."

"Yeah," I said noncommittally, crossing to the door. I opened it.

The sound made her turn around. "Where are you going?" she asked anxiously. "You're not going out feeling like you do?"

"I gotta," I answered. "I promised some fellas I would meet them." Spit and Solly would be wondering about me.

"So you'll meet them some other time. It's not so important. Go back to bed and lie down."

"I can't, Mamma," I said quickly. "Besides, a little fresh air will do me good!" I slammed the door quickly and ran down the stairs.

I caught Solly's eye as I walked past the candy store, gave

him the come-on, and continued down the block. A few doors away I ducked into a building and waited in the hallway. I didn't have to wait long. The money was in my hand when they came in. "Here y'are," I said, shoving it at them.

Solly put the money quickly into his pocket without counting it, but Spit thumbed through the bills. He looked up at me suspiciously.

"Only thirty bucks?" he asked.

I met his gaze. "Yer lucky to get that," I snapped. "I oughtta give you crap the way you powdered."

Spit's eyes fell. "I thought it would be more'n that."

I clenched my fist. "Why didn't yuh stay an' count it?" I half snarled at him.

His eyes came up suddenly and he looked at me through half-closed lids. I could see he didn't believe me, but he was afraid to say anything. I stared back at him and his eyes fell again. "Okay, Danny," he said, placating me with a fine spray. "I ain't beefin'." He turned and slipped silently out the doorway.

I turned to Solly. He had been watching us. "Anything on your mind?" I asked nastily.

Solly's lips spread in a slow smile. "No, Danny. I ain't got no complaints."

I smiled back at him and placed my hand on his shoulder, gently pushing him toward the doorway. "Go on, then, beat it," I said gently. "I don't want to stay in here all day."

We got off the trolley car and Nellie took my arm. She looked up at my face. "Where we going?" she asked curiously.

"You'll see." I smiled, not wanting to tell her yet.

It had been like that all night. I had picked her up at the store after closing. "C'mon," I had told her. "I wanna show you something."

Willingly she had come down into the plaza with me and we had boarded the Utica-Reid trolley. All through the ride we had been silent, looking out the window, our hands clasped tightly together. I had wanted to tell her where we were going but I was afraid to. I was afraid she might laugh at me. But now I could tell her because we were there. We were standing on a dark empty corner, almost ten o'clock at night, in a neighbor-

hood of Brooklyn she had never even known about. I raised my
hand and pointed across the street. "See it?" I asked.

She peered across the street, then turned back to me, a
bewildered expression on her face. "See what?" she asked.
"There's nothing there but an empty house."

I smiled at her. "That's it." I nodded happily. "Beautiful, isn't
it?"

She turned back to look at it. "There's nobody living in it,"
she said in a disappointed voice.

I turned back to the house. "That's what we came out to
see," I said to her. For a moment I had almost forgotten she
was there. I stared at the house intently. I didn't imagine there
would be much trouble in getting the house back when Papa
got Mr. Gold's job.

Her voice interrupted my thoughts. "It that what we came
out to see in the middle of the night, Danny?" she asked. "An
empty house?"

"It's not an empty house," I told her. "It's my house. I used
to live there. Maybe soon we'll be able to move back."

A sudden light came into her eyes. She glanced quickly at the
house, then back at me. Her mouth softened gently. "It is a
beautiful house, Danny," she said in an understanding voice.

My hand tightened on her arm. "Papa gave it to me for my
birthday when I was eight years old," I explained to her. "On
the very first day we moved in I fell into a pit and found a little
dog and they had to get the cops out to find me." I took a deep
breath. The air was sweet and fresh out here. "She died when
we moved. She was run over on Stanton Street. I brought her
back here and buried her. This was the only home we had ever
known an' I loved that little dog more'n anything. That's why I
brought her back. It's the only place she—we could be
happy."

Her eyes were shining and tender in the night. "And now you
will move back here," she whispered softly, pressing her face
against my shoulder. "Oh, Danny, I'm so happy for you!"

I looked down at her. A warm feeling came into me. I knew
she would understand, once she knew about it. I raised her
fingers and pressed them to my lips. "Okay, Nellie. Now we
can go back." Somehow I didn't mind going back now. I
knew it wouldn't be for long.

I stood in the doorway, my eyes blinking in the bright kitchen light. Mamma and Papa were staring at me as I stepped into the room. "You're home early," I said to my father, smiling. Maybe he had the good news already.

Papa's face was tense and angry. "But you're late," he snapped. "Where were you?"

I closed the door behind me and looked at him. He wasn't acting the way I had expected. Maybe something had gone wrong; maybe Gold had recognized me. "Around," I said cautiously. Better to say nothing yet.

Papa's anger raged through his self-control. "Around?" he shouted suddenly. "What kind of an answer is that? Your mother has been worrying herself sick over you all night. You don't come home, you don't say nothing, you're just 'around'! Where were you? Answer me!"

I tightened my lips stubbornly. Something had gone wrong. "I told Mamma I was all right, she didn't have to worry."

"Why didn't you come home for supper, then?" Papa screamed. "Your mother didn't know what happened to you. You could have dropped dead in the street and we wouldn't have known about it. She got herself sick worrying over you!"

"I'm sorry," I said sullenly. "I didn't think she would worry."

"Don't be sorry!" Papa shouted at me. "Just answer me! Where were you?"

I looked at him for a moment. There was no use in saying anything to him now. He was purple with rage. I turned and started from the room without a word.

Suddenly Papa's hand was on my shoulder, spinning me back toward him. My eyes widened in surprise. Papa was holding his leather belt in his hand and waving it threateningly at me.

"Don't go without answering me!" he shouted. "I got enough of your high-and-mighty ways! Ever since we moved down here, you think you can come and go as you please with nobody to answer to. Well, I've had enough of it! You'll come down to earth if I have to beat you down to it! Answer me!"

I pressed my lips firmly together. Papa had never hit me in anger in his life. I couldn't believe he would do it now. Not when I was bigger than he was and stood there looking silently down at him.

He shook me roughly. "Where were you?"

I didn't answer.

The belt came whistling through the air. It caught me on the side of the face. Lights flashed in front of my eyes and I could hear my mother screaming. I shook my head and opened my eyes.

Mamma was grabbing at his arm, begging him to stop. He pushed her away, shouting: "I've had enough, I tell you, enough! A man can only take so much, but from his own son he'll get the proper respect!" He spun toward me and the belt came flying through the air.

I threw up my arms to ward it off, but the belt tore its way past them to my face. The buckle caught me on the forehead and I felt myself slipping dizzily to the floor.

I looked up at my father through a sea of pain. I didn't have to let him hit me. I could take the belt away from him any time I wanted. Yet I didn't. I didn't even make a move to escape the next blow. The belt came down again and I gritted my teeth against the pain.

Mamma threw her arms around his sides. "Stop, Harry! You'll kill him!" she screamed.

He shook his arm and she fell back helplessly into a chair. His eyes, staring down at me, were rimmed with red and puffed as if he had been crying. The belt rose and fell, rose and fell until it seemed as if I had lived forever in this curious world of pain. I closed my eyes.

His voice came floating down to me. "Now will you answer me?"

I looked up at him. Papa seemed to have three heads and they were all going around in circles, first past and then through each other. I shook my head trying to clear it. Papa was raising three hands. There were three belts flying down at me. I shut my eyes quickly against them.

"I was out at the house!"

The blow I expected didn't come and I opened my eyes. The three belts hung suspended in the air over my head. Papa's voice was coming from a long way off: "What house?"

It was then I first realized that I had answered him. I let out a slow sigh. My voice was barely a squeak, I didn't know it at all. "Our house," I answered. "I went out to see if anyone was living there yet. I thought with Mr. Gold out, Papa would be managing the store and we would be able to move back there!"

There was a silence in the room that seemed to drag interminably. The only sound was the rasping of my breath in my ears and then Mamma was on the floor beside me, cradling my head against her bosom.

I opened my eyes again and looked at Papa. He had sunk exhaustedly into a chair and was staring at me with wide, frightened eyes. He seemed to grow old and shrunken before me. His lips moved, almost silently. I could hardly hear him.

"Where did you get that idea?" he was saying. "Last night Gold told me they were closing the store at the end of the month. They were losing money and I'll be out of a job on the 1st."

I couldn't believe it. I just couldn't. The tears began to run silently from my eyes and down my cheeks. Then gradually I began to understand. That's what Gold had been doing, when he called Papa over to the cash register last night. That's why Papa had looked so beaten.

Everything was clear to me now. Papa's anger, Mamma's worried look this morning, her preoccupation at the stove. For a moment I was very young again and I turned my head back to the comfort of her bosom.

It was for nothing. The whole damn thing was for nothing.

How long could I go on living a kid's life, dreaming a kid's dream? It was about time I stopped. There was no way on God's earth for me to get the house back.

Chapter Eight

I ROLLED easily away from a tired right-hand punch and shot back sharply with my left. I felt it tear through the boy's guard and I knew I had him. I cocked my right just as the bell rang ending the round.

I let my hands drop to my sides quickly and swaggered back to my corner. I dropped down on the stool and grinned at the man who clambered into the ring with the towel and pail of water. I opened my mouth and let some of the water trickle into it from the sponge on my face.

"How you feelin'?" he asked anxiously.

I grinned again. "Okay, Gi'sep," I said confidently. "I'll take him in this round. He shot his load."

Giuseppe Petito shushed me. "Save yer breat', Danny." He ran the sponge across my neck and shoulders. "Be careful," he warned me. "The guy's still got a wicked right. Don't take no chances. I promised Nellie I wouldn' let yuh get hoit. She'd have me head if I did."

I brushed my glove fondly across Giuseppe's head. I liked this guy. "I guess you're safe this time," I grinned.

Giuseppe smiled back at me. "Make sure I am," he retorted. "She may be your girl but she's my sister an' you don' know her like I do. I still catch hell from her for gettin' you into this."

I was just about to answer when the bell sounded. I bounced to my feet as Giuseppe slipped out of the ring. I walked quickly to the center of the ring and touched gloves with my opponent. The referee struck up the gloves and I side-stepped a sudden left jab.

I held my hands high and loose in front of me, circling the boy carefully, waiting for an opportunity to start punching. I dropped my left slightly, trying to feint him into a right-hand lead. The kid didn't bite and I dropped back.

I started circling him again. The crowd began to boo and stamp their feet in unison. I could feel the vibration in the taut canvas floor of the ring. What did they want us to do for a ten-dollar gold watch? Kill each other? I looked anxiously back to my corner.

A sixth sense made me duck. From the corner of my eye I had caught a glimpse of a right hand coming toward my chin. It whistled over my shoulder and I came up inside the kid's guard.

I brought my right hand up in an uppercut carried by the momentum of my body. It landed flush on the boy's chin. His eyes glazed suddenly and he stumbled toward me, trying to grope his way into a clinch.

The crowd was roaring now. I stepped away from him quickly and shot my left. It tore into the kid's unprotected face and he stumbled forward and fell flat on his face. I turned and walked confidently back to my corner. Nobody had to tell me the fight was over.

Giuseppe was already in the ring, throwing a towel around

my shoulders. "Cripes!" he grinned. "I wisht you was eighteen already!"

I laughed and went back to the center of the ring. The referee came toward me and held up my hand. He whispered out of the side of his mouth: "Yer gettin' too good for this racket, Fisher."

I laughed again and swaggered back to my corner.

Giuseppe stuck his head into the dressing-room. "Yuh dressed yet, kid?" he asked.

"Tyin' my shoes, Zep," I called back.

"Snap it up, Danny," Zep said. "The house boss wants to see yuh in his office."

I straightened up and followed him out into the corridor. The noise of the crowd came faintly to our ears. "What's he want, Zep?" I asked. Generally when Skopas wanted to see one of the simon-pures it meant no good. Everybody knew Skopas fronted for the fight mob even though he was officially the arena manager.

Zep shrugged his shoulders. "I dunno. Maybe he wants to give yuh a medal or somethin'." But I could tell from his tone of voice that he was worried.

I looked at him quizzically. My voice was light and caustic, I didn't want him to think I was worried too. "I don't care what he gives me so long as I can hock it for ten bucks."

We stopped in front of a door marked: *"Private."* Giuseppe opened it. "In yuh go, kid," he said.

I entered the room curiously. I had never been in here before. This was only for the big-time boys, the boys who worked for dough, not us punks who fought for watches. I was disappointed to find it only a small room with dirty gray painted walls and photographs of fighters hanging on them. I had expected something grander.

There were several men in the room and they were all smoking cigars and talking. When I came in they stopped talking and turned to look at me. Their eyes were shrewd and appraising.

I glanced at them briefly and then, ignoring their gaze, looked at the man sitting behind the small littered desk. "You sent for me, Mr. Skopas?"

He looked up at me. His eyes were gray and expressionless and his bald head gleamed in the light of the single overhead bulb. "You Danny Fisher?" His voice was just as expressionless as his eyes.

I nodded.

Skopas smiled mirthlessly at me, showing irregular yellowed teeth. "My boys been tellin' me you got the makin's. I hear you got a big collection of watches."

I smiled back at him. He didn't sound as if he was going to make trouble. "I would have," I said, "if I could afford to keep them."

Giuseppe nudged me nervously. "He means he gives 'em all to his ol' man, Mr. Skopas," he injected quickly. His eyes flashed warnings at me about the other men in the room. I knew what he meant right away. One of them might be an A.A. inspector.

Skopas turned to Giuseppe. "Who are you?" he asked, fish-eyed.

It was my turn to butt in. "He's my manager, Mr. Skopas. He used to fight under the name of Peppy Petito."

Skopas's eyes widened slightly. "I remember. A fancy boy with a glass jaw." His voice took on a chill. "So that's what you do now—work the punks."

Giuseppe shifted uncomfortably. "No, Mr. Skopas, I—"

Skopas's voice cut in on him. "Blow, Petito," he said coldly. "I got business with your friend."

Giuseppe looked down at him and then at me. His face was pale under his swarthy complexion. He hesitated a moment and then, with a miserable look in his eyes, started for the door.

I put my hand on his arm and stopped him. "Hold it, Zep." I turned back to Skopas. "Yuh got Zep wrong, Mr. Skopas," I said quickly. "Zep's my girl's brother. He's only lookin' out for me because I asked him. If he goes, I'm goin' with him."

The expression on Skopas's face changed swiftly. He smiled. "Why didn't yuh say so in the first place? That makes it different." He took a cigar from his pocket and proffered it to Giuseppe. "Here, Petito, have a cigar, an' no hard feelin's."

Zep took the cigar and put it in his pocket. The sick look had gone from his eyes and he was smiling.

I stared down at Skopas. "Yuh sent for me," I said flatly. "What about?"

Skopas's face went blank. "You been doin' pretty good aroun' this club, so I wanted you should know it."

"Gee, thanks," I snapped sarcastically. "What about this 'business' I heard yuh mention a minute ago?"

For a second a light blazed in his eyes and then it was gone and they were cold and empty as before. He continued speaking as if I hadn't interrupted him. "The boys uptown are always on the lookout for promisin' new talent so I tol' them about you. I wanted you to know they was watchin' your last few fights an' they liked what they saw." He paused importantly, put a fresh cigar in his mouth, and chewed on it for a moment before he began speaking again. "We think you're too good for this racket, kid, an' from now on we're takin' you over. You're through fightin' for watches." He struck a match and held it up to his cigar.

I waited until the match burned down before I spoke. "What do I fight for now?" I asked impassively. There was no use in asking for who. I already knew that.

"Glory, kid," Skopas replied, "glory. We decided you're goin' into the Gloves to build yerself a rep."

"Great!" I exploded. "And what do I do for dough? At least I get ten bucks for the watch."

Skopas's smile was as cold as his eyes. He blew a cloud of smoke toward me. "We ain't pikers, kid. Yuh get a hunnert a month until yer old enough to turn pro, then we split outta yer earnin's."

"I knock down more'n ten watches a month on this beat," I retorted heatedly. I felt Giuseppe's hand restrainingly on my arm. Angrily I shook it off. This wasn't what I was looking for. "What if I don't buy this deal?" I asked.

"Then yuh get nothin'," Skopas said flatly. "But you look like a bright kid. You know better'n to buck the boys. We even got a guy down here who's goin' to manage yuh when yuh move over to the pros."

I sneered. "You're too sure of yourselves. What makes you guys think I want to be a fighter anyway?"

Skopas's eyes were wise. "You need the dough, kid," he said surely. "That's why you'll be a fighter. That's why you took up the gold-watch beat."

He was right about that. I did need the dough. Papa was still out of work and this was the only buck I could be sure of outside of knocking somebody over the head. And my experience with Mr. Gold had taught me that I didn't have the stomach for that business. But now I'd had enough of this. It was okay to pick up a few bucks here and there, but I didn't buy it for a living. I'd seen too many guys walking around with their punches showing. That wasn't for me.

I turned to Zep. "Come on, let's go," I said succinctly. I looked back at the desk. "So long, Mr. Skopas. Thanks for nothing. It's been nice knowing you."

I flung the door open and stalked out. A man standing in the doorway put out a hand to stop me. I pushed his hand away without looking up and started to step around him. A familiar voice beat at my ears: "Hey, Danny Fisher, ain't yuh gonna stop an' say hello to your new manager?"

I looked up suddenly, a grin leaping to my face. My hand flew out, grabbing the man's arm. "Sam!" I ejaculated. "Sam Gottkin! I should've known!"

Skopas's voice came over my shoulder. It had a slightly apologetic note in it. "The kid ain't buyin', Mr. Gottkin."

Sam's eyes were looking questioningly at me. I made up my mind quickly. I turned to Skopas, a smile on my face. "If it's okay with you, Mr. Skopas," I said, "you can tell your friends uptown they got themselves a new boy!"

Chapter Nine

"C'MON, Danny," Sam said a few minutes later. "I'll get you somethin' to eat."

I grinned at him. "Sure, Sam," I said. "Just a minute." I walked over to Skopas's desk and looked down at him. The tension had gone from the room; even Skopas was smiling. The other men were watching me carefully. They knew if I had been tapped by boys uptown I was a real comer.

"Mr. Skopas," I said with a smile, "I'm sorry I blew up. Thanks for what you did."

He smiled at me. "It's okay, kid."

I held out my hand. "But don't forget my watch."

He laughed loudly and turned to the men in the room. "The

kid's okay," he announced. "He'll go far. If I had five grand I would have gone for him myself."

The surprise showed on my face, for the men laughed aloud. I looked at Sam and he nodded his head. I turned back to Skopas, wondering. Sam must be doing all right if he could afford to shell out five grand for me.

Skopas fished two bills from his pocket and placed them in my hand. "I ain't got any watches on me, kid, so this time we'll cut out the middleman."

I put the money in my pocket. "Okay, Mr. Skopas," I said. I walked back to Sam with a new respect. "Let's go."

I looked down at my plate regretfully. One thing about Gluckstern's special Rumanian broilings. If you could eat all of it you were a hero. I put down my fork. "I'm bustin'," I admitted. I turned to Giuseppe. "How you doin'?"

Giuseppe grinned with a mouthful of steak. "Okay, Danny."

I looked across the table at Sam. He had quit too. He was watching me, a curious look on his face. "I see you couldn't make it either," I said.

"Too much," he said. "I gotta watch my weight now."

He was right about that. He had put on a little weight since I saw him last. "How come yuh never answered the letter I sent yuh last year?" he asked suddenly.

I looked at him in surprise. "I never got it," I said simply.

"I was lookin' for yuh," he said. "I even went out to your old house to see yuh, but nobody had your address." He lit a cigarette. "I had a job for yuh."

"Last summer?" I asked.

He nodded.

I fished a cigarette out of the pack Sam had left on the table. "I could'a used one too," I said. "Things were pretty rough."

"Did yuh graduate school yet?"

I shook my head. "This June," I replied. I looked at Sam curiously. "How'd you happen to find me?" I asked. "Last I heard you had gone to Florida."

"I did go," Sam answered. "Did good too. But I didn't forget about you. I always said some day I'd make a champ outta you, so I put out the word to some friends to keep an eye peeled for yuh. I figured sooner or later you'd turn up. A guy who fights as good as you don't stay out altogether." He reached across the table and plucked the cigarette from my mouth with a smile. "You ain't usin' these any more if you're workin' for me."

"I like working for you," I said, watching him squash out the butt. "But I don't know if I like the idea of being a fighter."

"Then what were you doin' in those penny-ante clubs fightin' for watches?" he asked pointedly.

I nodded toward Giuseppe. "I needed the dough and he knew where I could pick up maybe three, four watches a week for three-round amateurs. It looked like easy dough, so I did it. But I never meant to turn pro—it was only till I got out of school."

"Then what were you gonna do?" Sam asked. "Set the world on fire? Get a job for ten bucks a week? If you're lucky, that is?"

I flushed. "I didn't think about that," I admitted.

Sam smiled. "I thought so," he said confidently. "But from now on, I'm gonna do your thinkin'."

Zep left us on the corner. He started off but I called him back. "Wait a minute, Zep, you forgot somethin'." I held a bill toward him. "Tell Nellie it's for the account."

Zep put the dough in his pocket. "I'll tell her, Danny."

"Tell her I'll pick her up at the store tomorrow night," I called after him as he walked away. I turned back to Sam. "Nice guy," I said.

Sam looked at me. "A luksh?" he said questioningly.

I stared back at him coldly. "So what?"

Sam raised his hands protestingly. "It don't mean nothin' to me, kid," he said quickly, "but what do your folks say to your goin' with an Italian girl?"

I watched him steadily. "They don't like it, but hell, her folks don't like the idea of me either. They say 'kike' like we say 'wop.' It's nobody's business but Nellie's and mine anyway."

"Sure, kid," Sam said placatingly. "Don't get sore."

"I'm not sore," I said quietly. But I was. This went on all the time at home.

Sam took my arm. "Come on over to the car an' I'll give yuh the lowdown on this business."

I studied him as he leaned his back against the car. He was doing okay, I could see that. His face was round and he had developed a little pot. Good living did that.

He took out a cigar and bit the end off it, stuck it in his

mouth, and chewed on it reflectively. "Now," he said in a low voice, "I want yuh to listen carefully to me an' remember what I say. Because from now on until you turn pro we can't be seein' too much of each other. But I'll be in touch with you, unnerstan'?"

I nodded. I understood. The rules covering amateur fighters were pretty strict.

Sam held a match to his cigar. It flickered briefly, giving his face a round moon-shape quality. "Tomorrow you go down to the East Side Boys Club. Ask for Moe Spritzer, and when you see him, tell him your name an' that I sent you. He'll know what to do. He has an entry in the Gloves already made out in your name, all you gotta do is sign it. From now on until you move over, he'll be your trainer. You'll do everything he says, unnerstan'?"

"I understand." In spite of myself I was impressed. Sam had thought of everything.

"Each month you keep in line, Moe'll give you a hundred bucks. If you kick off, you're through. Behave yourself, kid, and you got the world by the tail. I'll drop into the club every now and then to see how you work out. When I do, pay no attention to me. If I want to talk to you, I'll arrange it."

He opened the door of his car and got behind the wheel. "Yuh got any questions, Danny?"

I shook my head and then changed my mind. I had one question: "What if I don't show up good in the Gloves, Sam? What then?"

Sam looked at me for a moment before he answered. His voice was calm and low. "Then I'm out the five grand I shelled out to get yuh, kid. The boys were just about to move in on yuh when I bought 'em off." His eyes were suddenly bright and hard in the glowing light of the cigar. "Yuh're gonna be what I couldn't, Danny. I put a lot of hard-earned dough on you an' I don't expect to lose it."

He turned on the ignition key and started the motor. His voice rose slightly above its hum. "You're not a kid any more, Danny. You're in a rough business. I won't expect you to ever do what you can't, but don't cross me once you start. I won't like it."

The car started smoothly from the curb and I could feel my heart pounding in excitement. Sam wasn't fooling, he meant what he said. A hand fell on my shoulder and I turned around startled. Zep was standing next to me.

"You heard him?" I asked. I had known he wouldn't go too far away.

Zep nodded.

"What do you think?"

His dark eyes met mine, and his lips parted in a smile. "He's riding a lot of dough on you, but he ain't taking any chances an' he knows it. You're gonna be champ some day, kid, I know it already. The fix is in even now."

I turned and looked after the car. Its rear light was just turning the corner. I was still doubtful. "You think I ought to take it, Gi'sep?" I asked.

His voice rang in my ear with excitement. "Would yuh turn down a million bucks, Danny?"

Chapter Ten

I LOOKED at my face in the mirror. Outside of the small bruise high on my cheekbone I didn't show any signs of the fight last night. I grinned at my reflection. I was lucky.

I finished combing my hair and left the bathroom. As I approached the kitchen, I could hear Papa's voice. I went into the room smiling. "Good morning," I said.

Papa's voice stopped in the middle of what he had been saying, his face turned toward me. He didn't answer.

"Sit down, Danny," Mamma said quickly, "and eat your breakfast."

I slipped easily into the chair. Papa had been watching me. Each day had brought more lines to his face, lines of worry and hopelessness. His eyes seemed veiled with a curtain of despair that vanished only in the heat of his temper and anger. It seemed to me that Papa's temper was displayed more and more frequently as time went on, as if he found some sort of relief from his worries in giving way to it.

I put my hand in my pocket, took out a ten-dollar bill, and tossed it on the table. "I made a few bucks last night," I said casually.

Papa looked at the money, then up at me. His eyes began to glitter. I knew the look: it was a sign he was working up his temper. I bent my head over my plate and began to shovel the oatmeal into my mouth rapidly. I wanted to avoid the scene I knew would follow.

For a moment Papa was quiet, then his voice, strangely husky, rasped at my ears: "Where'd you get it? Fighting?"

I nodded without looking up from the plate. I continued to spoon the cereal quickly into my mouth.

"Danny, you didn't?" Mamma's voice was anxious, and her face had set in worried lines.

"I had to, Ma," I said quickly. "We need the dough. Where else we gonna get it?"

Mamma looked at my father. There was a faint white pallor showing beneath his skin. It gave him a sick, unhealthy look. She turned back to me. "But we told you we didn't want you to do it," she protested weakly. "You might get hurt. We'd manage to get along somehow."

My eyes were on her face. "How?" I asked matter-of-factly. "There are no jobs anywhere. We'd have to go on relief."

Mamma's face was set. "That might be better than you taking chances of getting yourself killed."

"But, Ma," I said, "I'm not taking any chances. I've gone through thirty of these things already and the worst that happened was that I got a scratch over my eye that healed in a day. I'm careful and the dough is handy."

She turned hopelessly to Papa. There was no use arguing with me. I had all the logic on my side.

Papa's face was completely white now, his fingers trembled against the coffee cup in his hand. He was staring at me but he didn't talk directly to me, he spoke to Mamma. "It's his girl," he said in a flat nasty voice, "that shiksa. She gets him to do it. She doesn't care if he gets himself killed as long as he has a buck to take her out and show her a good time."

"It is not!" I flared hotly. Somewhere in the back of my mind I had known this was coming the moment I saw him this morning. "She doesn't want it any more than you do! I'm doin' it because it's the only way to make a buck that I know!"

Papa ignored me. His bright feverish eyes were the only

thing in his face that seemed alive. His voice was freezing with contempt. "A shiksocha whore!" he continued, his eyes fixed on me. "How much do you have to give her for the nights you spend with her in hallways and on street corners? A Jewish girl is not good enough for you? No, a Jewish girl won't do the things she does. A Jewish girl won't let a boy fight to get money for her, let a son become a stranger to his own parents. How much do you pay her, Danny, for the things she gives to her own kind for nothing?"

I felt a chill hatred replace the heat of anger in me. I rose slowly to my feet and looked down at him. My voice was shaking. "Don't talk like that, Papa, don't ever say things like that about her again. Not where I can hear them."

I could see Nellie's white frightened face dancing in front of my eyes, the way she had looked when I first told her I was going to pick up some dough fighting. "She's a good girl," I went on, barely able to speak, "as good as any of our own and better than most. Don't let out on her your own failures. It's your fault we are where we are, not hers."

I leaned over the table glaring into his eyes. For a moment he stared back at me, then his gaze dropped and he raised the coffee cup to his lips.

Mamma put her hand on my arm. "Sit down and finish your breakfast. It's getting cold."

Slowly I dropped back into my chair. I wasn't hungry any more. I was tired and my eyes burned. Chill and drained of feeling, I reached for my coffee and drank it quickly, its hotness running through me, warming my body.

Mamma sat down next to me. For a while there was a smoldering tense silence in the kitchen. Her voice cracked into it. "Don't be angry with your father, Danny," she said softly, "he only talks for your own good. He's worried about you."

There was a curious hurt in me as I looked at her. "But she's a good girl, Mamma," I said, bitterness in my voice. "He shouldn't talk like that."

"But, Danny, she's still a shiksa." Mamma was trying to show understanding.

I didn't answer. What good would it do? They would never understand. I knew a lot of Jewish girls who were nothing but tramps. What made them any better than Nellie?

"Maybe Papa will get a job and you can stop this fighting," Mamma added hopefully.

Suddenly I felt old, very old. Those words were lollipops for children, I had heard them before. They might as well know it now. "It's too late, Mamma," I said wearily. "I can't stop."

"What—what do you mean?" Her voice was trembling.

I got to my feet. "I'm through fighting in the dumps. The boys uptown think I'm good. I made a deal with them." I stared at my father. "I'm going into the Gloves and start building a rep. They're gonna give me a hundred a month, and when I'm old enough I turn pro."

Mamma looked at me with a stricken face. "But—"

I felt sorry for her but there was nothing I could do about it; we had to eat. "No buts, Mamma," I interrupted her. "I made the deal and it's too late to back out now. A hundred a month is as much as Papa would get on a job. We can live on that."

The tears sprang into her eyes and she turned helplessly to Papa. "Harry, what are we going to do now?" she cried. "He's only a baby. What if he gets hurt?"

Papa was staring at me, a muscle in his cheek twitching. He drew a deep breath. "Let him," he answered without taking his eyes from my face. "I hope he does get hurt, it would serve him right!"

"Harry!" Mamma was shocked. "He's our son!"

His eyes narrowed slightly, still burning into mine. "More like the son of the devil, he is," he said in a low, bitter voice, "than a son of ours."

Chapter Eleven

I CAME out of the dark hallway, my eyes blinking at the bright sunlight, and stood for a moment letting the warm spring air roll over me. The house still hadn't shaken the chill and damp of winter, and before you knew it, it would turn into a smoldering oven.

I felt good. Four months had passed since I had thrown in with Sam. Good months, too. I'd come through the Gloves eliminations and now had only one more fight to go and I would be ready for the finals in the Garden—if I won. But I had no doubts about winning.

I filled my lungs with the fresh air. My collar cut into my neck and I opened it. Spritzer was a bug for conditioning. Sam was, too. They made me toe the mark, but they were right. Condition was half the fight.

If Papa would only realize that it was just another way to make a living, everything would be perfect. But he didn't, he kept harping on me, blaming the whole thing on Nellie and saying only bums were fighters. Now we hardly spoke to each other any more. He wouldn't give an inch. He was too stubborn, like just now when I left the house.

Papa had been reading a paper spread across the kitchen table as I walked through the room. He didn't look up.

"I'll be a little late tonight, Ma," I had said.

She had asked anxiously: "Another fight?"

I nodded. "The semifinal, Ma. Out at the Grove in Brooklyn." My voice was proud. "And after this the finals at the Garden and then no more till next year."

"You'll be careful, Danny?" she asked doubtfully.

I had smiled confidently. "Don't worry, Ma, I'll be all right."

Papa had raised his head from the newspaper at my words and spoken to Mamma as if I weren't in the room at all. "Don't worry, Mary, he'll be all right. Listen to what the paper has to say about him." He began to read from the paper in a low sarcastic voice:

"Danny Fisher, the sensational East Side flash with dynamite in each fist, is expected to take another step toward the championship in his division when he meets Joey Passo in the Gloves semifinals at the Grove tonight. Fisher, called by many 'the Stanton Street Spoiler,' because of his record of fourteen straight kayos, is being closely watched by the whole fighting world. There is a strong rumor that he is set to turn pro as soon as he is of age.

"A slim, quiet-speaking blond boy, Fisher, in the ring, turns into a cold merciless killer, going to work on his opponent without feeling or compassion, like a machine. This writer believes without a doubt that Fisher is the most ruthlessly promising amateur he has ever seen. If you fight fans will show up at the Grove tonight, we can safely promise you won't be disappointed. You will see blood, gore, and sudden death, for when Fisher goes to work with either hand, friend, it's nothing short of 'murder'!"

Papa let the paper rattle back to the table in front of him and looked up at Mamma. "Good words to read about your own son—'killer, murder, sudden death.' Words to make a man proud of his child."

Mamma looked at me hesitantly. I could see she was upset. "Danny, is it true what the man said?"

I tried to reassure her. I felt embarrassed. "Naw, Ma, you know how it is. After all, his paper sponsors the Gloves an' they try to build it up so's to sell more tickets."

She wasn't convinced. "You'll be careful anyway, Danny," she insisted.

Papa laughed shortly. "Don't worry, Mary," he said sarcastically. "Nothing will happen to him. He won't get hurt. The devil looks after his own." He turned to me. "Go on, Killer," he taunted. "For a dollar you can murder all your friends."

Those were his first direct words to me in weeks. I had taken enough side insults from him and kept my mouth shut; now I was through taking them. "I'll kill 'em for the dollar, Pop," I said through tight lips, "so you can sit here in the kitchen on your fat ass an' live off it!"

I had slammed out of the house and down the stairs, but now in the sunlight and warm air I began to feel better. I checked my watch. I had promised Spritzer I would be at the gym by four o'clock. There was just twenty minutes left to make it. I scaled down the steps and headed for the corner.

As I turned the corner, a voice called to me. Spit was standing in a doorway, waving. "Hey, Danny, c'mere a minute."

"I can't, Spit, I'm late," I called back, hurrying on.

Spit came running after me and grabbed at my arm excitedly. "Danny, my boss wants to meet'cha."

I looked at him. "Who, Fields?"

"Yeah, yeah, Mr. Fields." Spit's head bobbed up and down. "I tol' him I knew yuh an' he says get him."

The doorway from which Spit had come was a store entrance. On the plate glass of the window were the words: FIELDS CHECK CASHING SERVICE. "Okay," I said. You don't slough off a guy like Maxie Fields down here. Not if you like being happy. Fields was the big man in the neighborhood. Politics, gambling, shylocking—the works. He was top dog.

I remembered how envious some of the gang had been when
Spit had told us that his uncle, who was a numbers runner, had
talked Fields into giving him a job as an errand boy. He had
shown us his working papers proudly and bragged that he
wouldn't have to go to school any more; that some day he, like
Fields, would be a big man in the neighborhood while the rest
of us would be knocking our brains out trying to make a living.
I didn't see much of him after he got the job, but when I did, I
couldn't see where he was doing so great. Like now, he was still
wearing the same sloppy clothes he always wore, the saliva-
stained shirt, shiny trousers, and dirty scuffed shoes.

I followed Spit into the store and through a small room with
cages in it like a bank. A man behind a cage looked at us
without curiosity as we walked through a door in the back. We
passed through a horse room, where a few men were standing,
idly studying the big blackboard. They paid no attention to us
as we went through another doorway, behind which was a
stairway. I followed Spit up to the first landing, where he
stopped in front of a door and knocked softly.

"Come in," a voice roared.

Spit opened the door and walked in. I stopped dead in my
tracks, blinking my eyes. I had heard about this but I'd never
really believed it. This room was out of the moving pictures, it
didn't belong in a partly condemned old dump like this.

A big man with a red face, a fat stomach, and the largest
shoes I ever saw came toward us. Nobody had to tell me: this
was Maxie Fields. He didn't look at me. "I thought I told yuh
not to bother me, Spit," he roared angrily.

"But, Mr. Fields," Spit stammered, "yuh tol' me to bring
Danny Fisher here as soon as I saw him." He turned to me.
"This is him."

Field's rage disappeared as quickly as it had come. "You
Danny Fisher?"

I nodded.

"I'm Maxie Fields," he said, holding out his hand.

He had a good warm grip—too warm. I didn't like him.

He turned to Spit. "Okay, kid, beat it."

Spit's smile disappeared. "Yes, Mr. Fields," he said hurriedly, and the door closed behind him.

"I wanted to meet yuh," Fields said, walking back to the
center of the room. "I heard a lot about yuh." He sat down
heavily in a chair. "Care for a drink?" he asked casually.

"No, thanks," I replied. Maybe this guy wasn't so bad after all. At least he wasn't treating me like a punk. "I got a fight tonight," I added quickly.

Fields's eyes sparkled. "I seen yuh last week. Yer good. Sam's a lucky guy."

I was surprised. "You know him?"

"I know everybody an' everything," he replied, smiling. "Nothin' goes on down here that I don't know about. There ain't no secrets kept from Maxie Fields."

I had heard that. Now I believed it.

He waved his hand at me. "Sit down, Danny. I want to talk to you."

I stayed on my feet. "I gotta run, Mr. Fields. I'm late at the gym."

"I said sit down." His voice was friendly, but an undertone of command had come into it.

I sat down.

After watching me for a moment, he turned his head and yelled into the next room: "Ronnie! Bring me a drink!" he turned back to me. "Sure you won't have any?"

I shook my head and smiled. No use getting him sore at me. Just then a young woman came into the room carrying a drink. I blinked my eyes again. This dame was out of place down here too. Like the apartment, she belonged uptown.

She walked over to Fields's chair. "Here, Maxie." She looked at me curiously.

He almost drained the glass with one draught, then he put it down and wiped his mouth on his shirtsleeve. "Christ, I was thirsty," he announced.

I said nothing, I was watching the girl standing next to his chair. He laughed. His hand went out and he patted the girl on the behind. "Beat it, Ronnie," he said jovially. "Yer distractin' my friend here an' I wanna talk to him."

She turned silently and left the room. I could feel my face flush, but I couldn't take my eyes off her until the door had closed behind her. Then I looked at Fields.

He was smiling. "Yuh got good taste, kid," he said heartily, "but yuh gotta be able to afford it. That kind of stuff sets you back twenty bucks an hour."

My eyes widened. I didn't know chippies could come that high. "Even when she's serving drinks?" I asked.

His laughter roared in the room. When he stopped laughing he said: "Yer okay, Danny. I like yuh."

"Thanks, Mr. Fields."

He took another swallow of his drink. "Yuh gonna win tonight, kid?" he asked.

"I think so, Mr. Fields," I answered, wondering what he wanted.

"I think yer gonna win, too," he said. "An' so do a lot of people. Yuh know a lot of people down here think yer gonna take the championship."

I smiled. Maybe my father didn't think I was much, but a lot of other people did. "I hope they're not wrong," I said modestly.

"I don't think they will be. The boys downstairs tell me they took about four grand in bets on you from the neighborhood. That's a lot of dough even for me to shell out, but you look like a right guy an' I don't mind it now that I met you." It was a long speech for him and he finished out of breath. He picked up his glass and emptied it.

"I didn't think you bet the simon-pures," I said.

"We bet anything. That's our business. Nothing too big, nothing too small, Fields takes 'em all." He finished in a semi-chant, laughing.

I began to feel bewildered. What did he want me up here for? I wondered what he was getting at. I sat there silently.

Fields's laughter stopped suddenly. He leaned forward and slapped my knee. "Yer okay, kid, an' I like yuh." He turned his head. "Ronnie!" he shouted. "Bring me another drink."

The girl came back into the room carrying the drink. I watched her. She put the drink down and started from the room.

"Don't go, baby." Fields called her back.

She turned around in the center of the room and looked at us.

Fields's face leered at me. "Yuh like that, huh, kid?"

I could feel my face flame.

He grinned. "Well, I like yuh, kid, an' tell yuh what. You win tonight 'n' then come back here. It'll be waitin' for yuh an' the treat's on me. How yuh like that?"

I gulped. I tried to speak, but the words couldn't get past the lump in my throat. There was nothing wrong with it that I could see, but somehow I knew it wasn't for me. Nellie had changed a lot of things.

Fields was watching me closely. "Don't be bashful, kid," he grinned. "She ain't."

I found my voice. "No, thanks, Mr. Fields," I stammered. "I got a girl. Besides I'm in training."

His voice was persuasive. "Don't be a fool, kid. It won't kill yuh." He turned to the girl. "Take yer dress off, Ronnie. Show the kid what he's passin' up."

"But, Max!" the girl protested.

His voice went cold and harsh. "You heard me!"

The girl shrugged her shoulders. She reached behind her and unfastened a button, and the dress slipped to the floor. Fields got out of his chair and walked over to her. His hand reached out and settled on her breast. He made a sudden motion and her brassiere came off in his hand.

He turned back to me. "Take a good look at that, kid. The sweetest meat in town. What d'yuh say?"

I was on my feet, edging toward the door. Something about this guy scared me. "No thanks, Mr. Fields." My hand found the doorknob behind me. "I gotta be goin'. I'm late down at the gym."

Fields grinned at me. "Okay, kid, if that's the way yuh want it. But remember, the offer holds any time."

"Thanks, Mr. Fields." I looked at the girl. She was standing there, her face a mask. Suddenly I was sorry for her. Twenty bucks an hour was a lot of dough, but it couldn't buy you pride. It was still spelled the same way, cheap or expensive. I smiled awkwardly at her. "Good-by, miss."

Her face flushed suddenly and she turned away from me. I stepped outside the door and began to close it. "Good-by, Mr. Fields," I said.

He didn't answer.

I shut the door quickly and ran down the steps. The man was a gopher. He was real gone. I was glad to get out in the street. Even the dirty streets seemed clean after being inside that room with him. But I had the feeling as I headed toward the gym that I hadn't seen the last of him yet.

Chapter Twelve

I CAME back to my corner moving stiffly, my back and sides a red welted sheet of pain. Slowly I slumped back on the stool. I leaned forward, my mouth open, taking great gulps of air.

Zep was on his knees in front of me, pressing a damp towel to my forehead. Mr. Spritzer was massaging my side, his hands moving in a slow circular motion.

Zep peered into my face. "Yuh all right, Danny?"

I nodded painfully. I didn't want to speak, I had to save my breath. Something had gone wrong. This was supposed to be a cinch for me. I couldn't understand it. According to the papers, I should have taken him by the second round, but here it was going into the third and I hadn't been able to land one solid punch.

"He okay, Mr. Spritzer?" Zep's voice was anxious.

Spritzer's voice was dry. It cut through the fog that was beginning to gather in my head. "He's okay. He's been reading the papers too much, that's all."

My head snapped up. I knew what he meant. He was right, too; I had been too sure of myself. I had begun to believe everything I had read about myself. Across the ring, Passo was sitting in his corner, breathing easily and confidently, the lights shining brightly on his ebony skin.

The bell sounded and I sprang to my feet, moving toward the center of the ring. Passo was coming toward me confidently, a sort of smile on his face. I knew the look. I had worn it many times when I knew I had the fight won. Seething anger began to surge through me. The wrong face was wearing that look tonight. I shot my right viciously.

A fountain of pain geysered through my side. I had missed and Passo caught me with a left to the kidneys. I dropped my hands to cover my side. A flashbulb exploded in my face.

I shook my head to clear it. There was blackness in front of my eyes as if I had just come from staring at the sun. A hollow sound came floating toward me. "Five!" I turned my head and looked in the direction of the sound.

The referee's arm was going up again, his mouth shaping another word. I looked down and a dull surprise came through me. What was I doing on my hands and knees? I hadn't fallen. I stared at the gleaming white canvas.

"Six!" A shock tore through me. He was counting me out! He couldn't do that. I scrambled to my feet awkwardly.

The referee seized my hands and wiped my gloves off on his shirt. I could hear the crowd roaring as he stepped back. It sounded different, somehow. Tonight they weren't yelling for me, they were yelling for Passo. There were yelling for him to finish me off.

I fell into a clinch. Passo's body was wet with perspiration. I gasped gratefully for the moment's respite. The referee pushed us apart.

Again a pain shot through my side, then on the other side. Passo's dark face was dancing in front of my eyes. He was smiling. He was coming toward me. His gloves were flashing at me, tearing at me. I had to get away from them, they were cutting me to ribbons. I looked desperately toward my corner.

Zep's eyes, wide and frightened, stared at me. I turned my head quickly back to Passo. He was swinging. The punch was coming at me, the kayo punch. I could see it. It was coming with a tantalizing slowness. A crazy fear tore through me. I had to stop it. I swung wildly, desperately at his uncovered jaw.

Suddenly Passo was falling. I stumbled toward him. The referee turned me around and pushed me toward my corner. Tears of pain were streaming down my face. I had to get out of there, I couldn't stand any more.

Zep was coming through the ropes, grinning. I looked bewilderedly at him. What was he grinning about? It was over and I had lost. Relief came over me, I was glad it was finished. Nothing else mattered.

I lay on the dressing table, my head cradled in my arms, feeling Spritzer's hands moving soothingly on my back. I could feel the pain subsiding slowly and a sense of comfort coming over me. I was tired. I closed my eyes.

I heard Zep put down the bottle of rubbing alcohol, and his

voice drifted toward me. "He gonna be all right, Mr. Spritzer?"

Spritzer's hands were still kneading my back. "He'll be okay. He's tough an' young an' he's got guts."

I didn't move. At least he wasn't sore because I'd lost. There was a knock on the door and Zep opened it. I heard a heavy footstep in the room.

"Is he okay, Moe?" Sam's voice was worried.

The trainer's voice was flat. "He's okay, Sam. Nothing to worry about."

"So what the hell happened then?" Sam's voice was harsh with anger. "He looked lousy out there tonight. He took a hell of a beating."

Spritzer's voice was patient. "Take it easy, Sam. The kid was just beginning to believe his own clippings, that's all. He went out there thinkin' all he had to do was look at Passo an' it was all over."

"But you're supposed to keep him on edge." Sam's voice was still harsh.

"There's some things even I can't do," Spritzer answered. "I been expectin' this before, but from now on he'll be all right. He learned his lesson."

I heard Sam's footsteps coming over to me and felt his hand rest lightly on my head. He ruffled my hair gently. I kept my eyes closed. I began to feel good; he wasn't angry with me.

The last trace of harshness disappeared from his voice; there was a note of pride in it now. "You see that last wallop he hit the nigger, Moe? It was murder!"

"It almost was," Spritzer replied soberly. "That boy's jaw is broke in two places."

I spun around on the table and sat up. They were all staring at me. "That true?" I asked.

Zep nodded his head. "I just got the word a few minutes ago, Danny."

"Then I—I won?" I still couldn't believe it.

Sam smiled. "Yeah, kid, you won."

I sank slowly back on the table, but there was no triumph in me. All I could think about was what my father said: "Go on, Killer, for a dollar you can murder all your friends."

We stood on the corner of Delancey and Clinton Streets. It

was a few minutes after midnight. The lights still shone brightly in the store windows and people still thronged the sidewalks.

"Kin yuh get home okay, Danny?" Zep asked.

"Sure I can," I laughed. Most of the pain had gone, leaving just an aching soreness in my back and sides. "Don't be an old woman."

Spritzer looked at me closely. "Sure, kid?"

I turned to him. "I wouldn't be sayin' I could, Mr. Spritzer, if I couldn't. I'm okay now."

"Okay if you say so," he said quickly, "but do what I tell you. Get a good night's rest and stay in bed as much of tomorrow as you can. Don't bother comin' down to the gym until the day after."

"I'll do it, Mr. Spritzer," I promised. I turned back to Zep. "Tell Nellie I'll come over tomorrow night."

"Okay, Danny, I'll tell her."

I left them on the corner and walked down Clinton Street heading for home. I took a deep breath. It had been a close one. Mr. Spritzer had been right, though. I had been reading the papers too much. I wouldn't after this. I turned my corner and walked toward home.

A figure came out of the shadows next to my door. "Danny!" Spit was standing there.

"What d'yuh want?" I asked impatiently. I wanted to get to bed.

"Mr. Fields wants to see yuh," he answered.

"Tell him I'm bushed," I said quickly, pushing past him. "I'll see him some other time."

Spit's hand caught my arm. "Yuh better come, Danny," he said. "Fields is no guy to give the brush. He might take a notion to make it tough for yuh." Spit's eyes were blinking rapidly, as they always did when he was excited. "You'd better come," he repeated.

I thought for a moment. Spit was right. You don't screw around when Maxie Fields sends for you. I had to go, but I would only spend a few minutes and then get out. "Okay," I said gruffly.

I followed Spit back around the corner. At the doorway next to Fields's store Spit took a key out of his pocket and opened the door. I followed him into the hallway.

He turned to me and held out the key. "Go on upstairs," he said. "You know the door."

I looked at the key, then at him. "Ain't yuh comin' along?"

He shook his head. "No. He said he wanted to see yuh alone. Don't ring, the key'll let yuh in." He pressed the key quickly into my hand and vanished out into the street.

I stared after him and then looked down at the key in my hand. It twinkled brightly in the hall light. I took a deep breath and slowly began to climb the stairs.

Chapter Thirteen

THE KEY worked smoothly in the lock and the door swung open with hardly a sound. I stood in the doorway looking into the room. It was empty. For a second I hesitated. Something seemed to be wrong and suddenly I knew what it was: the lights were on.

I was used to turning off the lights when I walked out of a room—Edison had enough money. But all the lights in this room were on though nobody was there.

I stepped in, leaving the door open behind me. "Mr. Fields!" I called. "I'm here, Danny Fisher. You wanted to see me?"

The door on the other side of the room opened and the girl I had seen earlier in the day came out. "Close the door, Danny," she said quietly. "You'll wake the neighbors."

Automatically I shut the door. "Where's Mr. Fields?" I asked. "Spit said he wanted to see me."

There was a doubting look in her eyes. "Is that why you came?" she asked, her disbelief echoing in her voice.

I stared back at her. Then my face flushed as I remembered Fields's invitation. "That's why," I answered gruffly. "Where is he? I want to see him and get home to bed. I'm dead tired."

A quick smile came over her face. "You sound like you mean it."

"Of course I mean it," I said coldly. "Now take me to him. I want to get this over with."

"All right," she said. "Follow me."

She led me through a small kitchen, past an open bathroom door, and into a bedroom. She flicked on a light and gestured toward a bed. "There he is—the great Maxie Fields in all his glory. The son of a bitch!" There was a raw grating hatred in her voice.

I stared down at the bed. Fields was stretched across it, fast asleep. His shirt was open to the waist, exposing the heavy mass of black hair on his chest to the light. He was breathing heavily, one arm thrown across his face. There was a strong reek of liquor in the room.

I looked at the girl. "He's out?" I asked questioningly.

"He's out," she confirmed bitterly. "The fat pig!"

I stepped back out of the bedroom and held the key toward her. "Give him this and tell him I couldn't wait. I'll see him some other time."

As I started back through the apartment, she called me. "Wait a minute," she said quickly. "Don't go. He said for me to keep you here until he wakes up."

"Christ!" I exploded. "He's out for the night! I can't wait."

She nodded. "I know, but wait a little while anyway to make it look good. If you go right now, he'll know I didn't keep you and he'll be angry."

"How'll he know?" I asked. "He's dead to the world."

"He'll know," she said quietly. She walked over to a window and lifted a slat of the venetian blind. "C'mere, look."

I looked out the window but I didn't see anything. "What?" I asked.

"Over there in the doorway of the store across the street."

There was a faint shadow there and a cigarette was glowing. Just then an automobile turned the corner, its headlights piercing the darkness of the doorway, and I saw Spit standing there.

I dropped the blind and turned to her. "So he's watchin'," I said. "So what?"

"He'll tell Fields how long you stayed."

"What if he does?" I asked impatiently. "He's out anyway. I can't stay until he wakes up." I started for the door again.

She caught my arm, a sudden fear painted on her face. "Kid, give me a break," she pleaded, a note of desperation in her voice. "Stick around a little while. Make it look good. You don't know that guy inside. He'll make it rough for me if he finds out I didn't keep you at least for a little while."

Her eyes were wide and frightened and her hand was trembling on my arm. I remembered how sorry I had been for her when I had seen her last. "Okay," I said, "I'll stay."

Her hand dropped quickly from my arm. "Thanks, Danny," she said with relief.

I sat down on the couch and leaned back against the cushions wearily. A throbbing ache came back into my body. "Christ, I'm tired," I said.

She came to the couch and looked down at me sympathetically. "I know, Danny," she said softly. "I saw the fight. Maybe I could get you some coffee?"

I looked up at her curiously "No, thanks," I said. "You saw it?"

She nodded "Maxie took me out there."

There was a twinge of pain in my back and I shifted uncomfortably. "What's his angle?" I asked wearily.

She didn't answer my question. "You're tired," she said. "Why don't you stretch out and make yourself comfortable?"

It was a good idea. My body sank into the soft down cushions and I closed my eyes for a moment. This was even softer than my bed. Living was good when you had the dough. I heard the light-switch click and opened my eyes. She had turned off the ceiling light; now only a corner lamp was glowing. She was just sitting down in a chair opposite me, holding a drink in her hand.

"You didn't answer my question," I said.

She lifted her glass and drank. "I can't," she replied. "I don't know."

"He must have said something," I insisted. I raised myself on one elbow. My back suddenly twinged and a groan escaped my lips.

She was on her knees beside the couch, her arm around my shoulder. "You poor kid," she said softly. "You're hurt."

I sat up, moving away from her arm. "My back is sore," I admitted, trying to smile. "I caught a lot of punches."

Her hand slipped down to my back, rubbing it gently. She looked at her watch. "Lie down again," she said gently. "It's half past twelve; another half-hour and you can go. I'll rub your back."

I stretched out, feeling her hands moving on me. Their touch was light and soothing. "Thanks," I said. "That feels good."

She was still on her knees, her face close to mine. She smiled suddenly. "I'm glad," she answered. She leaned forward quickly and kissed me.

I was surprised, and stiffened awkwardly. She withdrew her lips at once. "That's my way of saying thanks," she explained. "You're a good kid, Danny."

I stared at her. I was all mixed up. "Yuh shouldn' a done that," I said. "I got a girl. Besides, it's what he wants me to do an' I don't like doin' anythin' unless I want to."

"You don't want to?"

"I didn't say that," I said stubbornly. "I only said it's what he wants and I don't know the angle."

Her eyes were wide. "What if I say this is between us? That he'll never know."

I searched her eyes. "I wouldn't believe yuh."

Her voice was level. "Would you believe me if I told you I hated his guts?"

"He's payin' for your time," I said flatly. "For that kind of dough I don't believe nothin'."

She was silent for a moment, then she looked at the floor. "Would you believe me if I told you what he wants from you?"

I didn't answer. I watched her face impassively, waiting for her to speak.

"He wants you to throw the next fight. He stands to lose a lot of money if you win." Her voice was low.

I nodded my head. I had guessed something like that. "He ought to know better," I said.

Her hand caught at my arm. "You don't know him," she whispered bitterly. "He's bad and he's mean. He won't stop at anything. You should have seen him at the fight while you were taking a beating. He was laughing and happy as could be. It was a lot of fun for him until you knocked that boy out. If you had lost, he wouldn't have bothered getting you up here tonight."

I laughed shortly. "I won, an' now there's nothin' he can do."

Her fingers were gripping tightly into my arm. "You're just a kid, Danny, and you don't know him. He'll stop at nothing. If he can't buy you one way or another he'll have his boys take care of you. Then you won't be able to fight."

I stared at her, my lips tightening. "Where do you fit in?" I asked.

She didn't answer, she didn't have to. She was no different from anyone else. Nobody had a chance against the guy with the buck. It was the old story, I thought bitterly. Now I had all the answers. To go along with Sam and become a fighter was my only way out, the only chance to escape being a nebuch like everybody else, a nobody, one of the many who walked the streets of the city anonymously, who are never missed. It was my only chance to make a buck.

Slowly I sat up. She slipped into the seat beside me, her eyes alive with sympathy. She knew what I was thinking. "Now do you believe me?" she asked. "We're both in the same boat."

I got to my feet, nodding silently, and went to the window. I raised the blind and peeked out. Spit was still in the doorway, his cigarette glowing.

"Is he still there?"

"Yeah," I said in a dull voice.

She looked at her watch. "Another fifteen minutes and you can go. You might as well sit down until then."

I slumped into a chair, facing her, and felt the tiredness all through me.

"What are you going to do, Danny?" she asked.

"Nothin'." I shrugged my shoulders. "What can I do?"

She came over to me and sat down on the arm of my chair. Her hand stroked my forehead. I closed my eyes wearily.

"Poor Danny," she said gently. "There's nothing you can do, nothing anybody can do." Her voice grew suddenly bitter. "He's got you like he's got me, like he's got everybody around him. Like a blood-sucking monster that lives off everything a-round it." There were tears running from her open eyes.

"You're crying," I said in surprise.

"So I'm crying." She stared back at me defiantly. "You know a law that stops a whore from crying, or don't you think he'd like that either?"

"I'm sorry," I said quickly. It wasn't her fault. We were both lost, neither of us could escape. There was no use in kidding ourselves. We couldn't win.

I put my hand on her shoulder and pulled her down to me. I kissed her. Her lips were soft and I could feel her teeth behind them. Now she lay across my lap, looking up at me. Her eyes were wide and wondering. "Danny," she said softly, "you said you had a girl."

"I have." I laughed grimly. "But you're here." I kissed her again. "What's your name?" I asked suddenly.

"Ronnie," she answered. "But that's not my real name. My name is Sarah, Sarah Dorfman. I want you to know it."

"What difference does it make?" I laughed bitterly. "Maybe my name is not my own. Nothing else belongs to me. The only thing important is that if I have to do what he says, I might as well take everything he's willing to give me."

Her arms went up around my neck and pulled me down to her. I felt her lips moving against my ear. "What I have to give you, Danny, is something he could never buy—no matter how much he is willing to pay."

Her lips were against mine. I dropped my hands to her body, and her flesh was warm for me. I could hear her crying softly.

Then the tension had gone, dissolved in a caldron of heat, and we were silent, our breath rushing in each other's ears. She was staring at me. I could see she understood.

"You're going to take his money?" she asked, a sound of disappointment in her voice.

I stared back at her. "I don't know," I said bitterly. "I don't know what I'm gonna do."

Chapter Fourteen

I CLOSED the door behind me and stepped out on the sidewalk. The night air was cool on my face. It was fresh and sweet and for a few short hours would stay that way—until the street started waking up. Then it would grow heavy and dirty again so that you couldn't stand the taste of it in your lungs.

The glow of a cigarette in a doorway across the street caught my eye. I crossed the street quickly, anger swelling inside me. Spit was still in the doorway, a pile of cigarette butts scattered around him. His startled face stared at me.

"Gimme a butt, will yuh, Spit?" My voice was cold and echoed flatly in the empty street.

"Sure, Danny," Spit's voice was nervous, but his hand held a cigarette toward me.

I put it in my mouth. "Light."

"Sure, Danny." Spit's hand held a trembling match. It flickered and burst into flame, casting a dancing shadow over his face.

I drew the smoke deep into my lungs. It felt good, it had been such a long time. Mr. Spritzer insisted on it, but it didn't make any difference now.

"Did yuh see him, Danny?" Spit's voice was anxious.

I stared at him. There was a wise and knowing look on his face. Even he had known what Fields wanted. I could feel the anger growing stronger inside me. The whole world knew what Fields wanted. It also knew what I would do. Nobody expected anything different. I was just another shnook. I didn't stand a chance.

"No," I answered, a sudden tension in my voice. "He was out cold. Drunk."

"You were up there wit' the dame alla time?" Spit's voice was curious, yet knowing.

I nodded silently. She hated Fields too, but there was nothing she could do about it. We were all caught just as she said. We couldn't escape him. He held all the cards.

Spit's leering voice grated in my ear. "Did yuh lay 'er, Danny?"

My eyes jumped to his face. The saliva was running crazily from the corner of his mouth, giving him a wickedly obscene expression. It was almost as if in the shadows behind him I could see Maxie Fields hanging over his shoulder. I grabbed his shirt and pulled him toward me. "What if I did?" I asked harshly, remembering what she had said: "What I have to give you, Danny, is something he could never buy—no matter how much he was willing to pay."

"What if I did?" I repeated angrily. It was none of his affair.

Spit struggled in my grasp. "Nothin', Danny, nothin'." His frightened eyes stared up at me. "Le' me go!"

I stared at him coldly. "What for?" I asked, my grip still tight in his shirt.

"I'm yer friend, Danny," Spit gasped, his collar suddenly

tight around his neck and choking him where I held it. "Didn' I bring yuh to Fields? Put yuh in a way to make some dough?"

I laughed. That was rich. My friend? I laughed again and let go of his shirt.

He stepped back, staring at me nervously. "Jeeze, Danny," he wheezed hoarsely. "Fer a minute I t'ought yuh was gonna slug me."

I laughed again. About that he was right. My fist sank into his soft belly clear up to my wrist. He doubled over and began to sink to his knees. I looked down at him contemptuously. "I was," I said.

He stared up at me, his eyes blurred with stupid confusion. His voice was hoarse. "What's wrong wit' yuh, Danny? I was on'y doin' you a favor."

I slapped him across the face with my open hand, knocking him on his side. "I don't want any favors," I snapped harshly.

He sprawled flat at my feet for a moment; then his hand reached for the doorknob and he began to pull himself to his feet. The expression in his eyes had changed to raw hatred. His free hand fumbled beneath his shirt.

I waited until the switch knife was free in his hand, then I hit him again, low in the groin, and the knife clattered to the sidewalk. He fell forward, retching violently.

I watched the pool of vomit spread around his face. There was cold satisfaction coursing in me. Maybe I had no chance against Maxie Fields, but there was somewhere along the line I could level.

His face turned up to me. "I'll get yuh for this, Danny," he swore in a low, husky voice. "God help me, I'll get yuh for this!"

I laughed again. "I wouldn't try that, Spit," I said, bending over him and pushing him back into his vomit. "Your boss might not like it."

I turned my back and left him lying in the mess in the doorway.

I paused in my hallway and looked at my watch. It was almost two thirty. I began to climb the stairs. A light was coming from under our kitchen door when I reached the landing. I hoped Papa wasn't up. I'd had enough for one night.

I put my key in the door and opened it. Mamma's face

looked out at me. I smiled at her. "You didn't have to wait up for me, Ma," I said, closing the door behind me.

She got out of her chair and came toward me, her eyes searching my face. "Are you all right, Danny?" she asked anxiously.

"Sure, he's all right." Papa's voice came from the other doorway. "That's Dynamite Danny Fisher. Nothing can hurt him. It says so here in the morning paper." His hand waved the paper at us. "A new name they got for him," he continued sarcastically, "in honor of breaking a boy's jaw in two places with one punch in tonight's fight."

I stared at him in surprise. "It's in the paper already?"

Papa waved the paper again. "What did you think? It would be a secret? What were you doing all night, celebrating with your shiksa?"

I didn't answer him. There was no use in talking to him any more. He could never understand that it was an accident.

Mamma's hand was on my shoulder. Her face was lined and worried. "It said in the paper you took a terrible beating in the first two rounds."

I squeezed her hand gently. "It wasn't so bad, Mamma. I'm okay now."

"But that boy's not!" Papa burst out. "Now you'll stop maybe? Or you'll go on until you kill somebody?"

"Don't be a fool, Papa," I snapped. "It was an accident. Those things happen sometimes. I didn't mean it!"

"Accident, hah!" Papa shouted disbelievingly. "How can it be an accident when the main purpose is to beat up the other boy? Baloney!" He turned to Mamma. "Some day we'll have in our house a murderer, and then he'll tell us that's an accident, too!"

The harsh monotony of his continual shouting ripped apart my nerves. "Leave me alone!" I shouted hysterically. "Leave me alone, I tell yuh!" I sank into a chair and covered my face with my hands.

I felt Mamma's hands grip my shoulders. Her voice came from over my head, filled with quiet strength. "Harry, go in to bed," she told him.

"You're doing wrong, coddling him," he warned ominously. "Some day he'll kill somebody and you'll be to blame as much as him!"

"So I'll be to blame," she answered quietly without hesitation. "He's our son and whatever he is or will be, we'll have to take the blame."

"You will, not me," Papa retorted angrily. "I made up my mind. He gives up this fighting or I'm through. One more fight and he don't have to come home. I won't have any murderers sleeping under my roof!"

His footsteps stamped down the hall to the bedroom. There was a moment's silence, then Mamma spoke gently to me. "Danny, I got some fresh-made chicken soup. I'll warm it up for you." Her hands were stroking my hair.

I raised my head and looked at her. Her eyes were filled with a sorrowing sympathy. "I'm not hungry." I felt dull and numb.

"Take some," she insisted. "It'll do you good." She turned the light on under the pot.

Maybe Papa was right, but if we hadn't been so hard up for dough, it might never have happened. There was nothing else to do now.

Mamma put the plate of soup in front of me. "Eat," she said, slipping into the chair next to me.

I tasted the soup. It was good and I could feel it warm away the numbness in me. I smiled gratefully at her, and she smiled back.

The warm soup was making me drowsy. I could feel the weariness creeping through me, the ache returning to my back and sides. I picked up the paper idly from the table where Papa had dropped it and began to turn the pages to the sports section. Some pieces of white notepaper fell from it. I looked at them curiously. There were figures scrawled in pencil all over them.

"What's this?" I asked, holding them toward Mamma.

She took them from me. "Nothing," she said. "Your father was just trying to figure out something."

"What?"

"A friend of his has a store he wants Papa to buy, and Papa was trying to figure out where he could get the money for it." She looked at the sheets of paper in her hand. "But there's no use," she continued, a note of hopelessness creeping into her voice. "He can't get the money. He's got enough stock that he put away at Uncle David's the night he closed up the other store, but he can't raise enough cash for a down payment. We might as well forget it."

I was awake again. Maybe if I could get the money he wouldn't think I was so bad. "How much does he need?" I asked.

Mamma got to her feet and took the empty plate from in front of me. She went to the sink and began to wash it. "Five hundred dollars," she said tonelessly over her shoulder, "but it might as well be five million. We can't get it."

I stared at her back. Her shoulders were drooping tiredly. There was an air of futility and resignation about her. The fight had gone, the only thing left was the concern of existing from day to day.

Five hundred dollars. Fields should be good for that—easy. He had told me himself that he had booked over four grand on the fight. I looked up suddenly. Mamma was speaking.

It was almost as if she were speaking to herself, though she had turned around and her eyes were on my face. "It was nice even to think about, Blondie. Then maybe things would be again like they were. But it's no use."

I got to my feet. My mind was made up. "I'm tired, Ma. I'm going to bed."

She came toward me and took my hand. "You'll listen to your father, Danny," she said gently, her eyes pleading with me. "You'll give up this fighting business. He means what he said. He swore it all night."

I wanted to tell her what had happened, but I couldn't. She wouldn't understand. There was only one answer I could give her now. "I can't, Mamma."

"For my sake, then, Blondie," she begged. "Please. In June you'll graduate school, then you'll get a job and everything will work out."

I shook my head. I looked down at the sheets of notepaper with the figures on them that Mamma had left on the table. That wasn't the answer. We both knew it. "I can't quit now, Mamma. I gotta do it."

As I started from the room, her hand caught at my arm and pulled me toward her. She pressed her hands to the side of my face and looked into my eyes. Fear was mirrored in her face. "But you might be hurt, Danny. Like that boy tonight."

I smiled reassuringly at her and caught her head to my chest. "Don't worry, Mamma," I said, pressing my lips to her head. "I'll be all right. Nothing will happen to me."

Chapter Fifteen

I PAUSED in front of the store for a moment, peering through the window. My reflection peered back at me, my hair gleaming with a bluish tinge from the glass that made it almost white. The store was empty, only one man behind the small cages. I walked in.

The man looked up at me. "What d'yuh want, kid?" he asked in a surly voice.

"I want to see Mr. Fields," I replied.

"Beat it, kid," the man snapped. "Fields ain't got no time for punks."

I stared at him coldly. "He'll see me," I said levelly. "I'm Danny Fisher."

I could see his eyes widen slightly. "The fighter?" he asked, a note of respect coming into his voice.

I nodded. The man picked up a phone and spoke into it quickly. People were beginning to recognize my name. I liked that. It meant I wasn't a nobody any more. But it wouldn't last. After the next fight I'd be just another name again, another guy who tried and didn't make it. I'd be forgotten.

He put down the phone and gestured at the door in the back. "Fields said for you to go right up."

I turned silently and went through the door. The horse room was empty. It was still morning, too early for the players to be out. I went through it and up the stairway, stopped in front of Fields's door, and knocked. The door swung open and Ronnie stood there. Her eyes widened and she stepped back.

"Come in," she said.

I brushed past her into the room. It was empty and I turned back to her. "Where is he, Ronnie?" I asked.

"Shaving. He'll be out in a minute." She came toward me quickly. "Spit was up here this morning," she whispered, her face close to mine. "He told Maxie what you did. Maxie was boiling."

I smiled. "He'll get over it, Ronnie."

Her hand caught at mine. "Last night you called me Sarah. I thought you weren't coming back."

"That was last night," I said in a low voice. "I changed my mind."

Her eyes dipped into mine. "Danny," she asked breathlessly, "did you come back on account of me?"

I closed my memory. "Yeah, Ronnie," I said flatly, shaking off her hand. "For you—and money."

"You'll get both," Fields's voice boomed from the doorway. I turned toward him as he came into the room. "I said you were a smart boy, Danny. I knew you'd be back."

He was wearing a lounge robe of pure red silk. It was tied around his big middle with a contrasting blue cord, and yellow pajama trousers stuck out beneath it. His blue jowls were shiny from the soap, and a big cigar was already clenched between his teeth. He looked as I always thought Maxie Fields would look.

"I hear you pay good, Mr. Fields," I said quietly. "I came back to see if what I heard was true."

He dropped into a chair in front of me and looked up into my face. He was smiling, but his eyes hadn't changed; they remained crafty. "You did a job on Spit," he said softly, ignoring my statement. "I don't like my boys handled that way."

I kept my face impassive. "Spit used to be my friend," I said slowly. "We did a couple of jobs together. But he broke the contract when he spied on me. I don't like that from a friend."

"He was doing what I told him," Fields said gently.

"That's okay with me—now," I said, my voice as gentle as his. "But not before, when he was supposed to be my friend."

The room was silent except for the sound of Fields sucking on his cigar. I stared into his eyes, wondering what was going on behind them. He was no fool, I knew that. I knew he had understood what I had said. But I didn't know whether he would buy it.

At last he took a match from his pocket, struck it, and held it to his cigar. "Ronnie, get me some orange juice," he said between puffs.

Slowly she started from the room. "And get some for Danny too," he called after her. "That won't break his training."

When the door closed behind her, he turned to me, chuckling. "She treat you right?" he asked.

I allowed myself the flicker of a smile to hide the surge of relief coursing through me. "Good enough."

Fields laughed aloud. "I told her I'd beat hell outta her if she didn't. She knows her business."

I dropped into the chair opposite him. I had kissed her in this chair last night. And she had kissed me and told me things. I had believed her, too. Suddenly I wanted to get it over with. "How much?" I asked.

Fields put on a look of pretended innocence. "How much for what?"

"For throwin' the fight," I said bluntly.

Fields chuckled again. "Bright boy," he rasped. "You catch on quick."

"Sure," I said caustically, growing more sure of myself. "Mr. Fields don't waste time unless there's a buck in it for him. I can do worse than follow him. What's in it for me?"

Ronnie came back into the room with a glass of orange juice in each hand. Silently she handed one to each of us. I tasted it. It was good. It had the taste that only freshly squeezed oranges could have. It had been a long time since I'd had orange juice. Oranges were pretty expensive. I drained my glass.

Fields was sipping his juice slowly, his eyes watching me appraisingly. Finally he spoke. "What do yuh say to five C's?"

I shook my head. I was on home grounds. I knew a bargain when I saw one. "You'll have to do better than that."

He finished his juice and leaned forward in his seat. "What do you think it's worth?"

"A grand," I said swiftly. That would leave him with a clean three according to his own words.

He waved his cigar at me. "Seven fifty. And the doll here."

"Talk money," I smiled. "I already had the doll. She's too rich for my blood."

"Seven fifty's a lot of dough," Fields grumbled.

"Not enough," I told him. "It's gotta look good. That means I gotta take a helluva beating to make three grand for you."

He got to his feet suddenly, came over to my chair, and looked down at me. His hand clapped down on my shoulder heavily. "Okay, Danny," he boomed. "A grand it is. You get the dough right after the fight."

I shook my head. "Uh-uh. Half before an' half after."

He laughed aloud and turned to Ronnie. "I told yuh the kid was sharp." He turned back to me. "Deal. Pick it up the afternoon before the fight. You can come aroun' the day after for the rest."

I rose to my feet slowly, keeping my eyes veiled and cautious. I didn't want him to know how good I felt. "You got yourself a boy, Mr. Fields," I said, starting for the door. "I'll be seein' yuh."

"Danny." Ronnie's voice turned me around. "You'll be coming back?"

My gaze swung from her to Fields and then back to her. "Sure, I'll be coming back," I said carefully. "For the dough!"

Fields's laughter boomed in the room. "The kid also makes with the fast answer."

Her face flushed angrily and she took a quick threatening step toward me, her hand raised to slap me. I caught her arm in midair and held it tight. For a second we stood staring into each other's eyes.

My voice was low, it carried only to her ears. "Let it go, Sarah," I said. "We can't afford dreams."

I released my grip and her arm fell slowly to her side. There was something in her eyes that almost seemed like tears, but I wasn't sure, for she turned her back on me and walked over to Fields. "You're right, Max," she said, her back to me. "He is a bright kid. Too bright."

I closed the door behind me and started down the stairway. Someone was coming up and I stood aside to let him pass. It was Spit.

His eyes were startled as he recognized me. Instinctively his hand shot to his pocket and came out with a switch knife.

I smiled slowly, watching carefully. "I'd stash the shiv if I were you, Spit," I said softly. "The boss might not like it."

He glanced quickly up at Fields's door, then back at me. Indecision showed on his face. I didn't take my eyes from him. Suddenly Fields's voice bellowed out into the hallway: "Goddammit! Spit, where the hell are you?"

Quickly the knife disappeared back into Spit's pocket. "Comin', boss," he called out, and hurried up the stairs.

I watched him enter Fields's apartment before I continued

down the stairway. It was a bright, clear day and I decided to run over to Nellie's house. It was early and there might be just enough time for me to see her before she left for work

And the way I felt, seeing her could do me nothing but good.

Chapter Sixteen

I AWOKE that morning to the drone of my father's voice. I lay sleepily on the bed, vaguely trying to puzzle out his words. Suddenly I was wide awake. Today was the day. Tomorrow it would be over and I would go back to normal. Back to being a nobody.

I swung my feet over the side of the bed, found my slippers, and stood up, stretching. Maybe it was better so. The old man should be happy then. He would have his dough and I would be through fighting. Then maybe things would be quiet around here. This last week between fights had been hell; Papa had picked on me all the time.

I tied my bathrobe around me and went into the bathroom. I looked in the mirror and fingered my face. No sense in shaving today, it would only leave my skin too tender and easy to cut. I was willing to lose, but I didn't want to bleed to death into the bargain.

I brushed my teeth, washed my face, and combed my hair. I decided to leave the shower till later this afternoon when I was down at the gym. They had hot water down there. As I went back to my room, the sound of Papa's voice followed me through the hall. I dressed and went to the kitchen.

Papa's voice died away as I came into the room. He looked up at me coldly over the rim of his coffee cup.

Mamma hurried over to me. "Sit down and have some coffee."

Silently I sat down at the table opposite Papa. After tonight he would have nothing to bitch about, I thought. "Hi, Mimi," I said as she came into the room. Things were so bad I was even talking to her.

Her smile was warm and genuine. "Hi ya, Champ," she jested. "You going to win tonight?"

Papa's fist slammed down on the table. "Goddammit!" he shouted. "Has everybody in this house gone crazy? I don't want to hear no more fight talk, I tell you!"

Mimi turned a stubborn face toward him. "He's my brother," she said quietly. "I'll say what I want to him."

I could see Papa's jaw fall. I think it was the first time in her life that Mimi had ever spoken back to him. He sputtered for breath as Mamma's hand fell restrainingly on his shoulder.

"No arguments this morning, Harry," she said firmly. "Please, no arguments."

"B-but you heard what she said?" Papa seemed confused.

"Harry!" Mamma's voice was sharp and nervous. "Let's eat our breakfast in peace."

A tense silence fell across the room, broken only by the clinking sound of the dishes as they moved to and from the table. I ate quickly and silently; then I pushed my chair back from the table and stood up. "Well," I said, looking down at them, "I gotta go to the gym."

No one spoke. I forced a smile to my face. "Anybody here gonna wish me luck?" I asked. I knew it wouldn't make any difference, but it would be a nice thing to take with me.

Mimi grabbed at my hand, reached up, and kissed me. "Good luck, Danny," she said.

I smiled gratefully at her, then turned to Papa. His head was bent over his plate. He didn't look at me.

I turned to Mamma. Her eyes were wide and anxious. "You'll be careful, Danny?"

I nodded silently. A lump came into my throat as I looked at her. Suddenly I could see all the changes the last few years had wrought in her. She pulled my face down to her and kissed my cheek. She was crying.

I fished in my pocket. "I got two tickets for you," I said, holding them toward her.

Papa's voice rasped at me. "We don't want them!" He stared angrily at me. "Take them back!"

I still held the tickets in my hand. "I got them for you," I said.

"You heard me! We don't want them!"

I glanced at Mamma and she shook her head slightly. Slowly I returned the tickets to my pocket and started for the door.

"Danny!" Papa's voice called me back.

I spun around hopefully. I was sure he'd changed his mind. My hand was already in my pocket taking out the tickets again. Then I saw his face and knew nothing had changed. It was white and grim, and his eyes stared hollowly at me.

"You still going to fight tonight?"

I nodded.

"After what I told you?"

"I got to, Pa," I said flatly.

His voice was cold and empty. "Give me your key, Danny." He held his hand out to me.

I stared at him for a moment, then at Mamma. Automatically she turned to Papa. "Harry, not now."

Papa's voice quavered hollowly. "I told him if he fought again he would not come back here. I meant it."

"But, Harry," Mamma pleaded, "he's only a child."

Papa's voice burst into rage. It filled the small kitchen like thunder in a summer storm. "He's man enough to kill somebody! He's old enough to decide what he wants! I took enough trying to make something for him. I'm not going to take any more!" He looked at me. "You got one more chance!"

I stared at him for one blazing moment. All I kept thinking was that he was my father, that I had sprung from him, from his blood, and now he didn't care. Almost with surprise I saw the key fly from my fingers and ring crazily on the table in front of him. I stared at its shining silver brightness for a second and then turned and went out the door.

I stood in front of Fields's desk as he counted out the money and dropped it on the desk. There was no smile on his lips now; the eyes, almost hidden in their rolls of fat, were crafty and cold. He pushed at the money with a pudgy finger. "There it is, kid," he said in his husky voice. "Pick it up."

I looked down at it: five crisp new one-hundred-dollar bills. I picked it up. It felt good in my hands. Papa would sing a different song when I showed him this. I folded it and stuck it in my pocket. "Thanks," I said grudgingly.

He smiled. "Don't thank me, Danny," he said quietly. "And don't cross me."

I looked at him in surprise. "I wouldn't do that," I answered quickly.

"I don't think you would either," Fields said, gesturing with his hand, "but Spit thought you might."

I looked at Spit, who was leaning against the wall, cleaning his nails with his switch knife. He met my gaze. His eyes were cold and wary.

"What ever gave him the idea he could think?" I asked Fields sarcastically.

Fields laughed loudly. His chair creaked as he got out of it. He came around the desk to me and clapped a heavy hand on my shoulder. "Bright boy," he said, geniality back in his voice. "Just don't forget that's my dough you're wearin'."

"I won't forget, Mr. Fields," I said, starting for the door.

"There's one more thing I don't want yuh to forget, Danny," he called after me.

From the doorway he looked immensely gross and powerful, standing there in front of his desk. This was the Maxie Fields I had heard about.

"What's that?" I asked.

His eyes seemed to open suddenly, revealing colorless agate irises and beady pupils. "I'll be watchin' yuh," he replied, his voice heavy and menacing.

I opened the door to the gymnasium and a sudden silence swept across the big room. Before that there had been plenty of noise, but now it was dead quiet in the East Side Boys Club.

Mr. Spritzer was standing in the corner of the room. His face turned slowly toward me. I walked across to him, conscious of every eye on me. I wished they wouldn't look at me like that, as if they were proud of me. There was five hundred dollars in my pocket that gave them nothing to be proud of.

"I—I'm here, Mr. Spritzer," I said nervously. By this time I was sure that everyone in the room had seen through me.

A bright smile flashed across his face. "Hello, Champ!"

That seemed like a signal for bedlam to break loose. Everyone in the gym crowded around me. They were all shouting at once, trying to attract my attention. I tried to smile at them, but I couldn't. My face seemed frozen into a strange sort of mask.

Then Spritzer's arm was through mine and he was clearing a path through the milling boys, leading me toward his office.

"Later, fellers, later!" he was shouting above the others. "Save your yelling till after the fight!"

Numbly I let him lead me into his office.

Chapter Seventeen

THE HOARSE shouting of the crowd came down to the dressing-room and beat against my ears. It was a heavy monotonous sea of sound, a cry as old as time. People screamed like this in the jungle when two animals fought; they screamed like this in the Colosseum on Caesar's holidays. Five thousand years hadn't changed them.

I turned my head on the table so that my arms covered my ears and deadened the sound, but I couldn't keep it out altogether. It was there, only fainter now, just below the range of hearing, but it would come back the minute I turned my head.

A buzzer sounded sharply in the room. I felt Spritzer's hand on my back. "That's us, kid."

I sat up and swung my feet off the table. There was a lump of lead in my stomach. I swallowed hard.

"Nervous, kid?" Spritzer was smiling.

I nodded my head.

"It'll pass," he said confidently: "Every fighter gets it first time in the Garden. There's something about the place."

I wondered what he would say if he knew. It wasn't the place that threw me; it was the fight I was going to throw. We came out of the dressing-room and stood on the edge of a ramp, from which I looked out into the Garden. It was a sea of anonymous faces awaiting decision on the bout just ended. Sam was somewhere out there, Fields too. And Nellie, even she had come. Only my father and mother—they had not come.

The roar of the crowd grew louder as the verdict was announced. "Come on, Danny," Spritzer said. We started down the ramp to the white flood of light that was the ring.

I could hear them yelling. Some of them were even calling my name. I followed Spitzer stolidly, my head down, my face framed by the big white towel like blinkers on a horse. I could hear Zep's excited breathing near me. His voice rose above the roar of the crowd. "Look, Danny!" he said excitedly. "There's Nellie!"

I raised my head and saw her smiling at me, a tremulously sweet and anxious smile, and then she was lost in a sea of other faces.

I was at the ring now and climbing through the ropes. The bright white lights burned into my eyes after the dimness of the ramp. I blinked rapidly. The announcer called my name and I moved out into the center of the ring. I heard his voice, but I wasn't listening to him; I knew his little speech by heart.

"Break clean when I tell you. . . . Go on to the nearest neutral corner in event of a knockdown. . . . Back to your corner an' come out fightin', an' may the best man win."

Ha ha! That was a joke. May the best man win! I slipped out of my robe. That lump in my belly was the five hundred bucks in my pocket.

Spritzer's voice was in my ear. "Stop worryin', kid," he was saying. "The worst that kin happen is that you lose this one."

I looked up at him in surprise. He was more right than he knew. My biggest worry was somebody's clipping the five C's from my trousers back there in the dressing-room. The fight wasn't anything to worry about, I had already picked the winner.

I looked across the ring curiously. When I was out there in the center of the ring listening to the referee, I hadn't looked at the kid I was going to fight. He was staring at me with a tight nervous look on his face. I smiled at him. He didn't have a thing to be nervous about if he only knew it. He was Tony Gardella, an Italian kid fighting out of the Bronx.

The bell sounded. I moved out to the center of the ring feeling curiously lightfooted and sure of myself. Knowing that I was going to lose this fight gave me a confidence I could win it that I never really felt before. I had stopped worrying about what might happen since I already knew the answer.

I jabbed with my left to feel the kid out, wondering if he really had it. He was slow in countering and automatically I threw a fast right under his guard. The kid staggered on his feet. Instinctively I moved in for the kill. The crowd was roaring in my ears. I had him and I knew it. Then I remembered: I couldn't finish it. I was supposed to lose. I let him slip into a clinch and tie me up. I faked some light punches to Gardella's back and kidneys. As I felt his strength returning, I shoved him away, and kept him away for the rest of the round. I couldn't take any chances on hurting him.

The bell sounded and I came back to my corner. Spritzer was boiling, he was shouting at me: "Yuh had 'im, why didn't yuh follow him up?"

"I couldn't get set," I answered quickly. I would have to be more careful or he would get wise.

"Shut up!" he snarled. "Save yer breath!"

When the bell sounded, Gardella came out of his corner cautiously. I lowered my guard slightly and waited for him to come in. He hung back carefully, staying just out of range. I stared at him in amazement. How in hell did he expect to win this fight? By my knocking myself out? I moved toward him. Maybe I could lead him into it. He backed away. It was getting harder to lose this fight than to win it.

The crowd was booing by the time we went back to our corners. I sat down on the little stool, my head down, my eyes fixed on the canvas.

Spritzer was yelling again. "Rush him. Don't give him time to get away. Yuh hurt him. That's why he was bicyclin'."

At the bell I came out of my corner quickly and was more than halfway across the ring when I met him. He was throwing punches wildly. He, too, had orders to fight. I blocked a few of them by reflex. How this kid ever got to the finals I would never know; he was easy. It was a shame to let a joker like this win, but I had to. I had made a deal. Purposely I dragged my guard for a moment. His punches tore past my arm. There was a strange sweet pain in them, a kind of reward. It was as if I were two people and one of them was glad the other was taking a licking.

It was time for me to counter. I had to make it look good. I shot a wide whistling right. It was blocked easily and I was jarred by a blow in the stomach. The kid smiled confidently at me. That burned me. He had no right to feel like that. I'd give him a few shots to teach him a little respect. I stabbed with my left and tried to follow through with a right uppercut, but he got away from it easily.

I was getting sore. I followed his dancing figure. Blows were stinging me but I shrugged them off. I was going to give this baby one shot to let him know who was boss; then he could have the Goddam fight.

There was a sudden blinding explosion in my face and I felt myself go down to my knees. I tried to get up, but my legs weren't working. I shook my head savagely and caught the referee's count. Seven! I could feel the strength returning to my legs. Eight! I could get up now, my head was clear again. I knew I could. Nine! But what for? I was going to lose any way. I might as well stay down for the count.

But I was on my feet when the referee's hand started going up. What the devil did I do that for? I should have stayed down. He stepped back and Gardella came rushing at me. The bell rang and I quickly stepped aside and went back to my corner.

I slumped onto the stool. I wished Spritzer, yelling in my ear, would shut up. There was no use in it. Suddenly his words were tearing into my gut: "What d'yuh wanna be, Danny? A bum all yer life? A nobody? You kin take this boy. Shake the lead out and take 'im!"

I raised my head and stared across the ring. Gardella was grinning confidently. Me a bum, a nobody? That was just what would happen. I would be like everybody else on the East Side, nameless, faceless, another guy lost in the shuffle.

I was on my feet at the bell and moved out into the ring. Gardella came rushing at me, wide open. He had thrown all caution to the winds. I almost laughed to myself. He thought it was in the bag. To hell with you, Gardella! To hell with Fields! He could have his five hundred back and go screw himself!

I felt the jarring pain shoot up through my arm almost to my elbow. That one had steam on it. One more. If you thought the last one hurt, you son of a bitch, wait'll you feel this one.

I blocked his feeble blow almost lazily and brought my hand up in a right uppercut. My fist seemed to move jerkily in the blur of light. The kid suddenly slumped against me and I stepped back.

He was falling. I was watching him fall. It was almost in slow motion. He sprawled out at my feet. For a second I stared down at him, then I dropped my hands and jacked up my shorts and swaggered to a corner. I was in no hurry, I had all the time in the world. The kid was through fighting for the night.

The referee gestured toward me and I danced back toward him. He held up my arm. The crowd was yelling for me as I went back to my corner grinning. Champion! I was as high as a kite. The feeling stayed with me all the way down to the dress-room. I was on a jag, walking on air.

Abruptly it was all gone, the elation running out of me like air out of a pricked balloon. Leaning against the wall outside the dressing-room was a familiar figure. The roar of the crowd faded as I stared at him.

It was Spit. He was smiling at me with a peculiar smile. He had been cleaning his nails with a switch knife. Now he lifted it, still smiling, and gestured at me. I could feel the flesh on my throat crawl. Then he disappeared into the crowd. Quickly I looked around to see if anyone had noticed. No one had seen him. They were all talking. I let myself be carried along in their flow.

Sam was in the dressing-room, his face wreathed in a smile. His hand grabbed at mine. "I knew you had it, kid! I knew it! Way back that first time in school!"

I stared at him dumbly, I couldn't speak. The only thing I wanted was to get away from here. Fast.

Moving Day
MAY 17, 1934

GOOD NIGHT, Champ." Zep was smiling as he left us in the dimly lit hallway and trudged up the stairs. We watched him disappear around the turn of the first landing.

We turned and looked at each other. She smiled up at me and put her arms around my neck. "First time tonight we've been alone," she whispered reproachfully, "and you haven't even kissed me yet."

I bent my head to kiss her, but as our lips met, there was a creaking sound from the staircase overhead. I drew back and stood there listening tensely.

"Danny, is something wrong?" Her voice was filled with concern.

I looked down at her. Her eyes were watching me closely. I forced a smile to my lips. "No, Nellie."

"Then what are you so jumpy about?" she asked, her arms pulling my face down to her. "Aren't you ever going to kiss me?"

"I'm still excited," I answered lamely. I couldn't tell her what was on my mind, I couldn't tell anybody.

"Too excited to kiss me?" she teased, smiling.

I tried to match her smile, but I couldn't, so I kissed her instead. I pressed my mouth to her, hard. I could feel her lips crush beneath mine. She cried in gentle pain.

"What do you think now?" I asked.

Her hands were fingering her bruised lips. "You hurt me," she accused.

I laughed wildly. "That isn't all I'll do to you!" I promised, pulling her close to me again. I pressed my mouth against her throat, along the nape of her neck, my arms crushing her against me.

"I love you, Danny!" she cried against my ear.

"I love you," I whispered back, still holding her. I felt her relax in my arms, her body close to me. Our lips met again and there was a flame in her kiss that went racing through me.

"Nellie!" I cried hoarsely, spinning her around in my grasp. Her back pressed into my waist and my arms were crossed over her breasts. I pressed my lips against her shoulder where the neck of her blouse had fallen from it.

Her face turned toward me. Her hand stroked the side of my cheek. Her voice was very low. "Danny," she murmured, "my legs are so weak I can hardly stand."

I fumbled with her blouse, and her breasts were warm in my fingers. She sighed deeply and sagged back against me. We stood like that for what seemed a long time.

At last she moved in my arms and turned her face toward me in the dimness. Her eyes were tender and loving. "My back hurts," she said in a weak apologetic voice.

I loosened my hold on her and she turned to face me, her hands holding mine to her breasts. She smiled up at me happily. "Feel better now?"

I nodded. It was true. For a little while I had forgotten about everything else.

She kissed me happily and took my hands from her blouse. Her face was flushed and warm, her dark eyes dancing, her lips curved in a gentle smile. "Now maybe you'll be able to go home and get some sleep?" she asked. "You've been so nervous all night."

I nodded again. She was right, I had been jumpy and on edge all evening. In the restaurant where Sam had taken us all for dinner I had started at every footstep. I could hardly eat. I didn't think anyone had noticed. I seized her hand and kissed its palm. "No matter what happens, Nellie," I said quickly, "don't forget I love you."

"And I love you no matter what happens," she replied earnestly. She held her face up to me to be kissed. "Good night, Danny."

I kissed her. "Good night, honey." I watched her vanish up the stairway, then I went out into the street.

I had walked only a few steps up the block when the sensation that I was being watched came over me. I stopped and looked back. The street was deserted. I started on again, but the curious feeling persisted. I paused at the street lamp on the

corner to look at my watch. It was after two in the morning.
Suddenly I thought I saw a movement in the shadows behind me.
I spun around and my heart began to pound. I was poised for
flight.

Out of the shadows came a small gray cat, and I almost
laughed in relief. Next thing I knew, I'd be seeing ghosts. I went
on again.

The lights of Delancey Street loomed in front of me. I
stepped into the crowd, basking in their nearness. Nothing
could happen to me here. Slowly I moved along with them and
gradually began to feel better.

On the next corner a newsboy was yelling: "Mawnin' papers!
Gloves winners!" I dropped two pennies in his hand, picked up
a paper, and turned to the back page, where the sports news was.
I looked closely at the fight pictures there. Mine was in the upper
right-hand corner. The camera had caught me as I was standing
over Gardella, sprawled at my feet. A thrill of pride ran
through me. Champion! Nothing could ever take that away
from me. I wondered if any of all the people passing by recognized me, if they knew that I, Danny Fisher, was standing
there, smack in the middle of them.

My smile vanished suddenly. I was looking directly into the
eyes of one who had recognized me: Spit. He was leaning
against the window of the Paramount Cafeteria, smiling at me.
The paper slipped from my nerveless fingers into the gutter. I
had been right all along: they had been watching me, waiting to
get me alone.

Spit was nodding to a man standing near the curb. I recognized him too. He was known to the neighborhood as the
Collector. Fields used him to go after people who refused to
pay up. After he got through with them they were generally
glad to square accounts. If they were able.

I turned quickly into the crowd, fighting an impulse to run. I
was safe as long as I could stay with them. When I looked back
over my shoulder, Spit and the Collector were sauntering casually behind me, just like two ordinary men coming from a late
movie. Though they seemed to be paying no attention to me, I
knew their eyes were on me every second.

I turned up Clinton Street, where the crowd was thinner, but
I was still safe. The next block would be the bad one. It was
usually almost empty at this hour of the morning. If I could
make it, I'd be just around the corner from my house.

I peered over the crowd in front of me, and my heart sank. The next block was completely empty. My steps slowed as I toyed with the idea of turning back toward Delancey Street.

A backward glance chased the thought from my mind. They were too close behind me. They would block me off. The only way I could go was straight ahead. My mind churned desperately. I was almost at the corner. A picture of that block ran through my mind. About three quarters of the way up it there was a small alley running between two houses. It was just wide enough to allow one person through at a time. If I could reach it before them, I had a chance. An outside chance, but it was the only one.

At the corner the traffic light was changing as a big trailer truck started to make its turn directly in front of me. I darted out into the street in front of it. The brakes squealed behind me as I reached the other curb, but I didn't look back. Spit was shouting at the truck, which had cut them off. I was almost halfway to the alley before I dared cast a nervous look over my shoulder.

Spit and the Collector had just reached the sidewalk and were running after me. Fear gave an added spurt to my legs. I almost ran past the alleyway in the darkness. Sharply I cut into it, my shoulder slamming against one side of the building. I bounced off the brick and fled deeper into the shadows.

It was dark in here, so dark I couldn't see where I was going. I moved more slowly now, one hand feeling along the wall beside me to guide my way. The alley ran the full length of two buildings, almost forty feet from the street, and ended in a blank wall. My hand suddenly touched the wall in front of me. I stopped, my fingers exploring it. There should be a small ledge a few feet up here. There was. Quietly I climbed up on it and turned, facing the street. I reached out in front of me, seeking a steel bar that I knew ran between the two buildings.

My eyes were getting used to the dark and I found the bar in the dim reflected glow coming from the street. My fingers grasped it firmly and I crouched there, waiting. My eyes strained through the darkness. Only one of them at a time could come after me here. My heart was bursting inside my chest. I tried to breathe quietly.

There was a murmur of voices at the end of the narrow alleyway. I tried to make out the words, but I couldn't tell one voice from another. Then they were silent and I heard footsteps scuffling slowly along the alleyway toward me.

The light from the street framed the shadow of a man. He was moving cautiously into the dark, his hand groping along the wall as mine had done. I could see another shadow up near the entrance. Good. One was waiting in the street. I wondered which of them was coming after me.

I didn't have to wonder for long. A voice hissed huskily in the dark at me. "We know yer in there, Fisher. Come with us tuh see the boss an' yuh got a chance!"

I drew in my breath sharply. It was the Collector. I didn't answer. I knew the kind of chance they would give me. He was about halfway down the alley toward me now.

The Collector spoke again, about ten feet from me now. "Yuh hear me, Fisher? Come out an' yuh got a chance!" The light behind him illumined his bulky frame. I drew myself up tensely, my hand gripping the steel bar. He was about six feet away from me. Five feet. Four. He couldn't see me hidden in the dark, but I could see him.

Three feet. Two. Now!

My feet flew off the ledge, my hands holding the bar in a tight grip. I vaulted through the air, my feet aimed at his head. Too late he sensed the sudden danger. He tried to move side-ways, but there wasn't room. My heavy shoes caught him flush on the chin and face. There was a dull thud and something gave way beneath my heels. The Collector dropped to the ground.

Hanging from the bar in the air over him, I looked down trying to see him in the darkness. He was a crumpled shadow on the ground. He moaned a sighing little sound. I let go of the bar and dropped beside him. There was a stirring movement against my leg and I lashed out viciously with my foot. His head made a queer crunching sound as it snapped into the wall beside him, and then there was silence.

My fingers flew rapidly over his face. He lay there quietly, not moving. He was out.

I looked toward the entrance. Spit was still standing there in an attitude of listening. His body was framed against the light as he tried to see back into the darkness. His voice floated back to me. "Did yuh get 'im?"

I grunted as if in assent. I had to get him back in here if I wanted to get out whole. It was my only chance. I crouched low against the ground.

Spit's voice came at me again. He was moving slowly into the alley. "Hol' 'im. I wanna put my mark on the bitchin' double-crosser!"

A glint of light flashed along the wall near his hand. It was his switch knife. I crouched still lower and inched forward, holding my breath. A few more steps.

I came out of the dark ground, my fist aiming at Spit's chin. His head jerked back quickly, warned by an instinct of danger, and my fist grazed the side of his face.

Against the street light his knife flashed down at me. Desperately I lunged and caught it. He was struggling in my grasp, his free hand scratching at my eyes. A searing pain ran up my arm as Spit twisted the blade of the knife gripped in my palm. My hand jerked in reflex and I lost my grip. There was a burning pain in my side as Spit's hand flashed downward.

I gasped in sudden shock and grabbed at the knife hand. I caught it and held on tightly. Spit began twisting the knife again and the nerves in my arm screamed in agony, but I didn't dare let go. His free hand was clawing at my throat. In the dark I snapped a punch at his face. There was a sharp pain in my knuckles as they smashed against his teeth, but it was a welcome pain. I brought my knee sharply into his groin between his legs. He gasped and began to double up.

I bent his knife arm around behind him, straightening him up. I had his back against the wall, my shoulder pressing hard into his throat. With my free hand I threw punch after punch into his face. At last he slumped against me.

I let go of Spit's arm and stepped back, my breath rattling through my throat as he slid crazily to the ground. He sprawled out at my feet, lying on his stomach. I leaned over him, searching for the knife.

I found it, its point two inches into his side. It must have happened when I held him against the wall. There was no emotion left in me. I was neither glad nor sorry. It was him or me.

I straightened up and slowly walked out of the alley. I wondered if Spit was dead. Somehow I didn't care. It didn't matter. Nothing really mattered if only I could get home and into bed. Then everything would be all right. In the morning I would wake up and find it had been nothing but a dream.

I stood in the hallway outside my door, searching my pockets for my key. It wasn't there. Nothing was there except the five hundred-dollar bills and a stub of a pencil. Wearily I tried to remember what I had done with it.

It came back to me suddenly. I had thrown it on the table in front of Papa that morning. We'd had an argument. Now I couldn't even remember what the argument was about. There was light coming from beneath the door. Somebody was still up. They would let me in. I knocked softly.

I heard a chair scuffle inside the room, then footsteps approached the other side of the door. "Who's there?" a voice cautiously asked. It was my father's voice.

A lump had formed in my throat when I first missed the key. Now I almost cried in relief. "It's me, Papa," I said. "Let me in." Everything would be all right now.

For a moment there was silence, then Papa's voice came back heavily through the door: "Go away."

Slowly the words penetrated my mind. I shook my head to clear it. I was hearing things. My father didn't say that, he couldn't. "It's me, Danny," I repeated. "Let me in."

Papa's voice was stronger now. "I said go away!"

A cold fear was running through me. I banged on the door, leaving bloody imprints from my hand. "Let me in, Papa!" I cried hysterically. "Let me in! I got no place to go!"

I could hear Mamma's voice. She seemed to be pleading with him. Then I heard Papa again. His voice was hoarse and rough and as immutable as time. "No, Mary, I'm through. I meant what I said. This time it's final!"

The sound of her sobbing came through the door, then the click of the light-switch. The light under the door had gone out. The sobbing behind it faded slowly into the house. Then silence.

I stood there a moment in shocked, frightened bewilderment. Then I understood. It was over, all over. Papa had meant what he said.

I slowly went down the stairs, feeling lonely and empty. On the stoop again, the night air was cool on my face.

I sank to the steps and leaned my head against the iron railing. I made no sound, but the tears were rolling down my cheeks. There was a burning sensation in my arm. I rubbed my hand along it. My fingers came away wet and sticky. The palm of my hand was cut and bleeding and my right sleeve was torn open. Through the rip I could see a cut on my arm in the dim light. The blood welled slowly into it, but it didn't matter. It meant nothing to me now, I was so tired. I rested my head against the railing and closed my eyes.

They were closed only a moment when I opened them suddenly. The feeling I'd had earlier that evening came back upon me. Someone was watching me. My eyes felt puffy and swollen as I peered up the street.

An automobile was parked across the way. Its lights were out but the motor was running quietly. They were after me again. Spit and the Collector must have reported back.

Without getting to my feet I rolled over on my belly and crawled back into the hallway. There I huddled for a moment, wondering what to do. Maybe I could sneak out the back and over the roof to the next house and duck them that way.

A feeling of hopelessness came over me. What good would it do? They would keep after me until they found me. They had friends everywhere. There was no place to hide.

My fingers dropped into my pocket. The money was still there. Maybe if I gave it back to them they would let me go. But even as I thought of it, I knew it wouldn't do any good. I had gone too far. I was in too deep.

But the dough was still good for what I'd got it for. The old man could still use it to buy that store. At least Mamma and Mimi would get a break that way. If they caught me with it they would only have everything. Why give them the whole pot?

On the floor near my hand there was a circular. I picked it up and looked at it. "BIG SALE AT BERNER'S DRUGSTORE." I turned it over. The back was blank. I reached in my pocket for the pencil.

The words took shape on the paper, in pencil and blood:

> *Dear Mamma—The money is for the store. Don't let him throw it away again. Love, Danny.*

I folded the dough in the paper, got to my feet, and shoved it in the mailbox. For once I was glad the government had made the landlord put in new mailboxes, because the old ones were broken and anybody could open them. Mamma would find it there tomorrow morning when she came down for the mail.

The car was still standing out in the street, its motor purring. I brushed off my trousers. There was a dull sick feeling in my stomach as I slowly went down the steps. I turned my back on the car deliberately and started walking away. Halfway up the block I heard its gears shift and the sound of its tires rolling away from the curb. Fighting an impulse to run, I glanced back over my shoulder. The car was swerving across the street toward me.

The impulse to run grew stronger. I checked it. To hell with them! I stopped and turned to face the oncoming car. Tears were running freely down my cheeks and a freezing fear had turned my body into ice. I swallowed desperately, trying to choke back the nausea that was rising from my belly.

I moved a few steps back. My fingers felt the cold metal of a lamp-post and I sagged weakly against it. Already I could taste the bitterness of the vomit that was creeping into my mouth, and a million crazy thoughts leapt frantically through my mind.

When did you grow up, Danny Fisher?

There is a time in everyone's life when he has to answer that question. There in the cold black night of morning I found the answer.

I was afraid to die. And there, while that shapeless fear ran through my body, turning my stomach into crawling rebellion, my kidneys into a freezing lump, and my bladder into a leaking, uncontrollable faucet—I suddenly grew up.

I grew up with the knowledge that I was not immortal; that I was made of flesh that would rot and decay into dirt, and blood that would turn black in my veins when I died. Then it was that I knew I would have to face my judgment day. That my mother and father were only the mechanics of my creation and not the trustees of my soul. I was the accident of their creation.

I was alone and in a lonely world of my own. In that world I would die and no one would ever remember my name. Death would descend on me, dirt would cover me, and I would be no more.

My legs had turned to watery jelly, and despite my frantic grip on the lamp-post I sank to my knees on the sidewalk. I shut my eyes tightly, the lids squeezing out the tears from under them, as the car pulled to a stop. I heard its door open and footsteps ringing hollowly on the pavement as they hurried toward me.

I turned my face to the post and buried it in the crook of my arm. I could feel my lower lip turning into blood beneath my teeth. I began to pray. Not for life, but for death. Death to be kind and to come and take from me this terror I could not live with.

There was a soft hand on my arm, a voice was whispering in my ear. "Danny!"

I tried to bury my face deeper in my arms. A cry of fear stifled in my throat. Death's voice was gentle like a woman's, but it was so only to torture me.

The voice was insistent. "Danny!" it repeated. "I've been waiting for you. You got to get away!"

This was not the voice of death. It was a woman's voice filled with warmth and sympathy. It was a voice of life. Slowly, scarcely daring to look, I raised my head.

Her face was white in the glow of the street lamp. "I've come to warn you," she whispered quickly. "Max has got Spit and the Collector out looking for you!"

I stared at her for a moment as the words sank into my mind. Then I couldn't help it. It was Sarah called Ronnie. I began to laugh weakly, hysterically. I was still safe!

She stared at me as if I had suddenly gone mad. Her hands shook my shoulder. "You gotta hide," she whispered insistently. "They're liable to be here any minute!"

I looked up at her, the tears still running down my face. I stopped my laughter and held my hands toward her. "Help me up," I asked her, the words coming huskily from my burning throat. "They won't come."

Her arm was under my shoulder and she was lifting me to my feet. "What do you mean they won't come?" she asked.

I was standing now. Suddenly her hand came out from under me. I sagged against the post as she stared at it "You're bleeding!" she cried.

I nodded. "They caught up with me already."

A frightened look came to her face. "What happened?" she breathed.

"What happened?" I rasped. I began to laugh again. "I don't know what happened. I left them in the alley. I think Spit is dead. Maybe the Collector is too. The whole thing's very funny. They came to kill me and instead I killed them!"

The laughter gurgled in my throat as I leaned my head back against the post and closed my eyes. It was a hell of a joke on Maxie Fields.

Her hand pulled at my arm. I stumbled forward and almost fell. "You gotta get away! Fields will kill you when he finds out!"

I stared at her, still smiling. "Where can I go?" I asked. "There's no place to go. Even my father won't let me in the house."

Her eyes were staring into mine. "No place to go?" she asked.

I shook my head. "No place." I began to slide toward the sidewalk again.

Suddenly her arms were around me and she was dragging me toward the car. I followed her numbly. She opened the door and I stumbled into the back seat. The door closed and she got in behind the wheel. I felt the car begin to move beneath me. I turned my face to the seat and closed my eyes.

Once when I opened them we were on a bridge. It looked like the Manhattan Bridge, but I was too tired to see and closed my eyes again. I turned uncomfortably. I was beginning to get very warm.

She was pulling at my arm again. I woke up. There was a smell of salt air in my nostrils. I stumbled from the car wearily, my eyes trying to focus. We were parked on a dark stret. A few feet from us I could see a boardwalk, and beneath it the sand was white. From beyond the beach I could hear the rolling sound of the ocean. She was leading me toward a small building just beneath the boardwalk. There was a sign on it:

BEN'S PLACE SODA HOT DOGS HAMBURGERS
CANDY

"Where are we?" I asked.

Her eyes flicked at my face. "Coney Island," she answered briefly.

She led me around behind the building to a small bungalow. I was weaving back and forth and she kept an arm around me as she knocked at the door. "Ben! Wake up!" she called softly.

A light flickered on inside the bungalow. There was a tapping sound. Then a voice came through the closed door, a man's voice, heavy and husky from sleep: "Who is it?"

"Sarah," she replied. "Hurry up, Ben, open up!"

The door swung open quickly and the light poured out on us.

A man was standing there, a smile on his face. "Sarah!" he exclaimed. "I didn't expect you back so soon!" The smile left his face as soon as he saw me. "Sarah, what's this?"

"Let us in," she said, helping me over the doorway.

Silently the man stood aside. There was a small cot against the wall and she helped me to it. I sank back on it gratefully. She turned to the man. "Get some hot water," she said quickly.

I stared at her and then at him. As he started to move across the room, there was a tapping sound. From the bottom of his pajama leg protruded a stump of wood. I looked up wonderingly as he turned. One sleeve was pinned to his side. I closed my eyes. I was dreaming. When I opened them again, they were still there, Sarah and the man with one arm and one leg.

"He's hurt, Ben," she said. "We got to get some hot water and clean him up."

I pulled myself to my feet. I was very warm. The room seemed to blur in front of my eyes. The man kept it so warm in here. "I'm all right," I said. "Don't bother. I'm all right."

Suddenly the room began to spin in front of me. They were both standing on their heads. I couldn't figure it out. Maybe I hadn't got out of the alley at all. There was a ray of light way down in the corner.

"Papa! Let me in!" I cried, and pitched headlong into the light. I went through it as easily as fish through water and came out into the darkness on the other side.

All the Days of My Life

THE THIRD BOOK

Chapter One

THE JULY sun was climbing out of the water, its golden-red rays capping the waves with a freshly laundered look as I came out from under the boardwalk. The sand beneath my feet was white and clean. Later in the day it would grow dirty and strewn with litter, but now it was fresh and cool and I liked the feel of it.

The boardwalk was deserted. Two hours from now the first of the crowd would be coming. I took a deep breath of the fresh morning air and trotted down to the water. This was the only time of the day for a swim. You had the whole Atlantic Ocean for yourself.

I dropped the towel from around my shoulders and looked down at myself. There was only a faint white scar line left along my arm where Spit had caught me. The rest was all gone, lost in the almost black tan that covered my body. I was sure lucky.

I knifed into the water and began to swim briskly toward the far pole. The bitter-sweet taste of the salt water was in my mouth and nose. It was brisk and invigorating. The beach seemed far away and small. I turned over on my back and began to float. It was almost as if I were in a world all my own.

It was hard to believe that it was almost two months since the night Sarah had brought me out here. That night had not really happened to me, it had happened to someone else living in my body, a kid with my name. But it was all behind me now. Sarah had christened me with a new name as she dipped the cotton in the warm water and washed away the dirt and crusted blood from my cut arm and side.

Danny White. That was the name she had given me as she introduced me to her brother. I smiled as I thought about it. At first I had been too weak to protest, but when I saw the papers the next day and my name under the Gloves pictures, I had been glad. The less her brother or anyone knew about me, the better off I was.

We had scanned the paper eagerly for word of what happened to Spit and the Collector. There was nothing in it. We had exchanged curious glances, but didn't dare speak until later in the afternoon when Ben went out to get something to eat.

"D'yuh think they found 'em yet?" I had asked.

She shook her head, a worried look on her face "I don't know," she answered. "I'll know more when I go back tonight."

"You're going back?" I asked incredulously.

"I have to," she answered quietly. "If I don't show up, then Maxie'll know something is wrong and come looking for me. It's the only way we have of keeping safe."

I tried to sit up in the small bed, but I was too weak and fell back against the pillow. "I'll get out of here," I muttered. "I'll bring yuh nothin' but trouble."

She looked at me curiously. "Where will you go?"

"I don't know," I answered. "I'll find some place. I can't stay here. Sooner or later they'll get wise. Then you'll get it too."

She leaned forward and her hand stroked my cheek lightly. "You'll stay here, Danny," she said quietly. "You'll stay here and work with Ben. He needs help and can't work the place by himself."

"But what if someone recognizes me?" I asked.

"No one will recognize you," she said surely. "Coney Island is a big place. Over a million and a half people come down here in the summer, and a crowd is the best place for you to hide. They'd never suspect your being down here anyway."

I stared at her. What she had said had made sense. "But what about you?" I asked. "He'll want to know where you were last night. What'll you tell him?"

"Nothing," she said flatly. "The hired help is entitled to a day off. If he asks me what I did, I'll tell him I went to visit my brother. He knows I do that every week."

It was my turn to be curious. "Does your brother know about Maxie?"

She nodded her head, her eyes looking away from me. "He thinks that I'm Maxie's personal secretary. Before that he thinks I worked as a model." She turned back to me, a pleading look in her eyes. "After his accident five years ago and he found out that his arm and leg were gone, he wanted to die. He felt there was no work left for him to do and that he would always be a burden to me. We are all the family we have. That was the year I graduated from high school. I told him not to worry, that I would work and support him until he was well enough to work again. The way he supported me after my father had died. I would go out and get a job."

She turned a mirthless smile toward me. "I was a kid then. I didn't know how much money we would need for medicine and doctors, I didn't know how little they paid stenographers and typists. The fifteen dollars a week couldn't cover even a small part of our expenses. My first job was with a vaudeville booking agent. I learned quickly, and a few weeks later when I went to the boss and asked for a raise, he just laughed at me. I didn't understand him and asked what he was laughing at.

" 'You're a bright kid,' he said, 'but I can't afford to pay you any more.'

" 'But I need more money,' I cried.

"He stood there a moment, then walked around his desk. If you're really that hard up,' he said, 'I can put you in the way of some real sugar.'

" 'How?' I asked; 'I'll do anything. I need the money!'

" 'There's a party going on tonight,' he told me. 'Some friends came into town and they asked me to send up some girls for the evening. They pay twenty bucks.'

"I stared at him. I don't suppose I really knew what he meant, but the twenty dollars was a lot of money, so I went to the party. I had never seen anything like it and was just about to leave when my boss came in and saw me standing stiffly against the wall. He smiled at me understandingly and brought me a drink. It made me feel good and relaxed, so I had a few more. Then I remembered going into a room with him.

"In the morning when I woke up, I was alone in a strange room and had a terrible headache. I staggered blindly out of bed looking for my clothes. They were on a chair with a white note pinned onto them: 'You can come in a little late today,' it read. Beneath the note was a twenty-dollar bill. I was a professional now. I stared at myself in the mirror. There was no change on my face that anyone could see, there was no scarlet letter on my forehead. Nothing had changed but the fact that I had found a way to make twenty dollars when I needed it. And as time wore on, I came to need it very often."

She got to her feet and looked down at me. Her face was impassive, her voice flat and emotionless. "And that is how it was. I worked and paid the doctor's bills and for medicine but it wasn't until I met Maxie Fields at a party and he liked me that I could get enough money together to fix this place up for Ben."

I didn't know what to say. My mouth was dry and I wanted a cigarette. I reached for a pack near the bed. She guessed what I wanted, our hands met on the cigarette package. I held hers and her eyes stared somberly down into mine.

"That's the way it was until the night you stayed because I asked you. Because you didn't want Maxie to think I had failed him, because you didn't want him to hurt me. Never for love, always for money. Never for myself. Always for money. Until that night. Then suddenly I realized what I had traded away. But it was too late. I had already set the price and I couldn't back out of the sale now."

She let go of my hand and held a cigarette toward me. I put it in my mouth and she lit it for me.

"You have to go back, Sarah?" I asked.

"I have to go back," she answered tonelessly. She smiled vaguely at me. "It almost seems funny to hear you call me Sarah. It's been so long since anyone but Ben called me that."

"You got no other name that I can remember," I said.

The somber look vanished from her face. "Danny," she said, a nice look coming into her eyes, "let's keep it like that between us—always. Let's be friends."

I took her hand. "We are friends, Sarah," I said quietly.

Then Ben had come back with a container of hot broth. I had some and dozed off. When I woke up again, she had gone and Ben was sitting looking at me.

"She's gone?" I asked, my eyes looking around the small room.

He nodded. "Her boss, Mr. Fields, expected her back this afternoon. He keeps her pretty busy."

I agreed with him. "He's an important man."

He hesitated a moment, then cleared his throat. "She says you want to work here this summer."

I nodded.

"I can't afford to pay very much," he half apologized. "I don't know yet how we'll make out."

"Let's not worry about the dough," I said. "It ain't what you can pay me that's important. It's what I can repay the both of you that counts."

He had grinned suddenly and held out his hand. "We'll get along, Danny," he had said.

And we had. For almost two months now. Sarah would be down to see us once a week and things began to work out all right. Business had been just fair, but Ben made expenses and was happy with that. I was happy too, because I was out of Fields's reach.

When Sarah had come down the next week, I was already back to normal. Outside the soreness in my arm I could get around all right. The first thing I had asked her when we found a moment alone was about Spit and the Collector. Nothing had appeared in the papers all that week.

They were in the private hospital of some medic that Fields knew. The Collector had a broken jaw from my kick, and Spit had nine stitches taken in his side where his knife had gone into him. Another inch and a half and he would have croaked; it would have reached his heart. In a way I was glad. I wouldn't have wanted a rap like that hanging over me.

Fields had been really burned. He had sworn that he would get me and that when he did I would be sorry. Before that night was over he had had the neighborhood gone through with a fine-tooth comb, looking for me. After a week he was still raging.

Then as the weeks went by, Sarah told me, he spoke less and less about me. Fields was convinced that I had lammed it out of town with the dough. I was happy to let him think so.

Many times I had wanted to ask Sarah if she could find out anything about Nellie and my family, but I didn't dare. I didn't even try to write them because for a long time Fields had kept a watch on them, according to Sarah. I wondered if Papa got the store with the money, if Mimi was working, how Mamma was and if they missed me and were sorry that I was gone. At night I would lie on my small cot and think about them. Sometimes when I closed my eyes I could imagine I was home again and Mamma was cooking supper and the house would be heavy with the odor of chicken soup. Then Papa would come home and a bitterness would rise in me. I would open my eyes and they would be gone.

Then I thought about Nellie. Her face would be clear before me in the night, smiling at me, her dark eyes warm with tenderness and love. I wondered if she understood, if she guessed why I had gone away. I wondered if she remembered what I had told her: "No matter what happens, remember that I love you." She would nod her head at me in the dark and I could almost hear her whispered answer: "I remember, Danny."

Then I would close my eyes tightly and the sound of Ben's snores would lull me to sleep. In the morning the sun would be shining brightly in my eyes when I woke up.

Like it was shining in my eyes now as I floated face-upwards in the water. My body felt lightly buoyant in the water and I paddled gently. The waves slupped easily past me.

"Danny!" The familiar voice came toward me from the beach.

I got a mouthful of water as I spun around toward it. Sarah was standing on the beach waving at me. I waved at her, smiling as I swam back to the shore.

Chapter Two

SHE had found my towel and was dropping her terry-cloth robe beside it by the time I reached her. I grinned at her. "What are you doing down here?" I asked. "We didn't expect you until the day after tomorrow."

"Maxie had to go out of town," she explained. "I have the whole week-end to myself."

I was curious. "What happened?"

She was tucking her hair under a bathing cap. "How do I know?" She shrugged. "It's none of my business. All I care about is that I can spend a week-end down here with you."

The meaning of her words didn't reach me until we were in the water again. She hadn't said anything about Ben. Just me.

I turned my face in the water and looked at her. She wasn't a bad swimmer for a girl. She had a pretty good beat crawl stroke, which moved her through the water easily.

"Did yuh see Ben?" I called to her.

"Yeah," she replied. "He told me you were out here." She stopped swimming and treaded water. "The water is wonderful," she cried. "I'm all out of breath."

I swam over to her and put my arms under her shoulders. "Rest a minute," I said. "You'll get it back."

She weighed nothing in the water. I could feel the firmness of her body as the waves pushed us back and forth. A familiar warmth began to rise in me. Quickly I let her go.

She turned in the water and looked at me. She had felt it too. "Why did you let me go, Danny?" she asked.

"The waves were getting too much for me," I explained awkwardly.

She shook her head. "What's the reason, Danny? Don't kid me."

I stared at her. Her face was small and cute under her yellow cap, her eyes fresh and young as if the water had swept away everything she had ever known, all the hurt, all the knowledge. There was no use trying to hide anything from her. You don't hold out on a friend.

"I'm making it easy on myself," I said frankly.

"How?" she persisted.

I stared at her. "I'm not a machine," I said, "and you're beautiful."

I could see she was pleased. "Nothing else?" she asked.

"What else could there be?" I was puzzled.

She hesitated a moment. "What I am?" she asked slowly.

I shook my head emphatically. "You're my friend," I said. "Nothing else matters."

Her hands were on my arms and she was holding onto me in the water, her eyes scanning my face. "Sure, Danny?"

I nodded. "Sure." I took a deep breath. "I just don't want to louse things up, that's all."

She looked down at the water. "And if you kissed me, you think that might louse things up, is that it, Danny?"

"It might."

Her eyes turned up to mine. "Because you're in love with someone else, Danny?"

I nodded silently.

A curious hurt came into her eyes. "But how do you know if you don't even try, Danny?" she asked. "There are many kinds of love that you may not even know about."

Her lips were moving tremulously. There was a shining moisture in her eyes that hadn't entirely come from the salt water. I pulled her closer to me and kissed her. Her mouth was soft and tasted from the salt and yet was sweet and warm. She closed her eyes when I kissed her and she was limp against me. I looked down into her face.

She turned her head away and looked out into the sea. I bent my head to hear what she was saying, her voice was so low. "I know you can never love me the way you love her, Danny, and that is the way it should be. But there is something for us that we have to give each other. Maybe it's not very much or for a very long time, but for whatever it is or as long as it lasts let's make it important."

I didn't answer. There was nothing to answer.

She turned her face up to me. She looked very young. "Remember what I told you, Danny? It was: 'Never for love, always for money. Never for myself.' For once I want it to be different, for once I want it to be for me. For what I want, not for what I'm paid."

I pressed my mouth gently to her lips. "It will be as you want it to be, Sarah," I said softly. One thing I had already learned: you don't pay off friends by telling them that you haven't got for them what they want from you. And if they are willing to accept a reasonable facsimile for the real thing, you're not fooling them; they're fooling themselves.

Sarah had to find a way to repay herself for many things, and I was it.

She was drying my back with the towel. "I didn't realize it until just now," she said, "but you're almost black and your hair is burned white from the sun. Nobody would recognize you now."

I grinned over my shoulder. "You recognized me."

"I knew where to find you," she said quickly. A puzzled expression crossed her face. "That reminds me. Do you know Sam Gottkin, the concessionaire?"

"Yeah," I answered. "What about him?"

She looked up into my face. "He was down to see Maxie about you the other day"

"What did he want?" I asked quickly.

"He wanted to know where you were. There was an Italian boy with him. Zep, I think his name was. You know him?"

I nodded. "He's my girl's brother. How'd they get to Maxie?"

"They had heard that Maxie was looking all over for you the night of the fight, so they came down to find out why. Sam and Maxie are old friends. Sam said he didn't know you were gone until your sister came up to see him. Why would she do that?"

"I worked for Sam before," I explained quickly. "Besides, Sam was all set to manage me when I turned pro. What did they say?"

"Maxie told them what he knew. That was nothing."

"Did he tell them why he was looking for me?" I asked.

She nodded her head. "Sam flew into a rage at that. He told Maxie that he should have kept his hands off you. He called him all kinds of names."

I looked at her wonderingly. "Maxie took it?"

"Not entirely," she answered. "Maxie felt that Sam should have given him a piece of you since you came out of Maxie's territory. They had a big argument then. Maxie said when he caught up with you, you'd be taken care of. Sam said that he should do nothing until he let him know first, that he had a score of his own to square."

I stared at her. That really did it. There was nobody I could depend on now. "Did Maxie agree to that?" I asked.

"He agreed to it then," she answered, "because afterwards they all sat down and had a few drinks and talked business. Then Sam called your sister and made a date for that night and he left. When he had gone, Maxie stamped up and down the room and swore that if he found you, Sam would never know about it until afterwards."

That was about what I expected from him. He wouldn't act any other way. Her next question really caught me by surprise.

"Is your sister engaged to Sam Gottkin?"

My mouth hung open. "Why do you ask that?" I stammered.

"Because one of the reasons Sam gave Maxie that he didn't want you touched until he saw you was that you are his fiancée's brother, and if anything happened to you it might queer all his plans." Her voice was curious. "Didn't you know that?"

I shook my head slowly. "Uh-uh. I didn't even know they had met." I wondered how that happened. It seemed stranger than anything else I had heard. Sam and Mimi—somehow I couldn't believe that.

A voice called to us from under the boardwalk. Ben was standing there beckoning to us. "Hey!" he shouted. "Aren't you ever coming back to work? What do you think this is—Christmas?"

Chapter Three

I WAS seated below the counter, bagging peanuts. Ben began to swear. I looked up at him, surprised at his vehemence. "Goddam them kids!" he swore.

"What's the matter?" Sarah asked.

He turned to her, his good arm waving at the beach. "A customer was coming over here, but one of them damn kids got to him first. It's a wonder we can make a livin' at all with those kids around."

Sarah's voice was tolerant. "Take it easy," she told him soothingly. "It doesn't help getting all excited over it."

Ben's voice was angry. "But we're shellin' out good dough for this concession, and those kids are ruinin' it. They don't pay nothin' for takin' out boxes of ice cream and peddlin' them on the beach. There oughta be a way of stoppin' them."

"The cops chase them when they see them," Sarah said.

"But most of the time they're too busy watchin' the dames to even bother," Ben replied heatedly.

"All the same," she said, "I wouldn't want to spend a day out in that sun and hot sand peddling a carton of ice cream just to pick up a few bucks."

He stamped away from her voicelessly, his wooden leg dragging along the floor into the back room.

I got to my feet wearily and stretched. "He sounded mad," I said.

Her eyes were troubled. "He has a right to be," she answered. "This place was his big dream and he wants to make a go of it. The way things are going, he'll just clear expenses for the summer. He won't make enough to carry him through the winter. That means he'll have to come to me for money again. He doesn't like that. He's a pretty independent guy."

I didn't answer her and began to stack the peanuts up on the counter. I guess she was right. I knew how he felt. There were four of them out there on the beach right now that I could count. I could hear their hawking cries floating back toward us on the breeze.

"Hot knishes!"

"Dixie cups!"

"Fudgie-wudgies! Popsicles!"

They were mostly youngsters. Seemed like nice kids too. I had spoken to several of them from time to time. Most of them were lucky to earn more than a buck a day, because the dealers they bought their stuff from robbed them. The guy who came along and gave those kids a really square shake could clean up a fortune. There were hundreds of them on the beach.

Suddenly I was excited. What a fool I had been not to see it before! That was the only thing I had learned from Sam up in the country. Sam made a buck from his concessions up there because he cut his boys in for a fair shake. Why couldn't Ben do the same thing down here?

I turned to Sarah. She and Ben were standing at the register looking out on the beach. I tapped him on the shoulder and he turned around "The kids'll work for you same as anyone else," I said.

He looked confused. "What kids? What are you talking about?"

I jerked a thumb at the beach. "The kids out there. Why don't you take them in?"

"Don't be a jerk," he snorted. "I ain't got the time to be chasin' after them to collect what they owe."

"You don't have to chase 'em," I said. "They pay in advance for their stuff."

"Half only," he pointed out. "The rest you have to hustle 'em for. Besides, why should they do business with me? They can get the same thing from anybody."

"There must be a way to get around that," I said. "Supposin' we don't take any dough in advance? What if they left us somethin' for a deposit? Like a watch, or a bike? Then they wouldn't have to lay out any dough an' they'd come to us."

"Forget it," Ben said disgustedly. He picked up a rag and began to wipe the counter. "Besides, we haven't the room to handle them."

Sarah's voice made him look up. "You got all that room in the back that isn't being used," she said. "You could put a cold locker in there."

"But, Sarah," he protested, "where'll we get the time? I just can't go out and get the kids to come in here just because I say so."

"I'll get the kids for you," I said quickly. "I'll get all the kids you want."

She looked up at me, then turned challengingly to her brother. "Well?" she asked.

He hesitated a moment, not answering.

She smiled slowly at him. "What's the matter, Ben?" she asked. "You always said you wanted to make a real buck. This is the first good shot you can get at it. Or don't you like money any more?"

An embarrassed grin began to spread over his face. He turned gratefully toward me. "Okay, Danny," he said, "we'll try it. Sometimes I forget I don't have to do things by myself any more."

I checked my watch. It was almost dusk. Time enough for all the kids who were going to be there to have shown up. For the past hour I had been sitting on a bench watching a steady stream of boys disappear beneath the boardwalk below me.

I lit a cigarette, got up, and went down the stone steps leading to the beach. The hum of conversation came to my ears as I ducked under the boardwalk, and I smiled to myself. I had been right. The quickest way to get to a gang of kids was to find their crap game.

About twenty of them were playing on a strip of concrete just behind the rest rooms. Only a few seemed to be about my age and height, most of them were smaller. I pushed through them to the inner ring of the circle. One of the kids was getting ready to shoot. There was a lot of silver lying on the concrete

around him. Casually I dropped a five-dollar bill on the concrete slab.

"I'll cover every bet," I announced.

All faces turned toward me. I watched them closely. There
was no animosity in them, only curiosity. So far, so good. No
trouble. It was just that a fin was a lot of bucks to these kids.

The boy with the dice in his hand rose to his feet. "Who are
you?" he asked, mild resentment in his voice.

I smiled at him, my cigarette dangling loosely from my lips.
"A sucker for the dice," I replied easily.

He stared at me for a moment, then at the others. Turning
back to me, he said politely: "Pick up yer dough, mister. We
can't go that high."

I knelt and picked up the fin, looking up at him from the
ground. "What's your ceiling?"

"A cuter," he answered.

I stuck my hands in my pocket and came out with a fistful of
change. "Roll 'em," I said. "I'm no snob."

He knelt again and the dice came tumbling from his hand.
They hit the wall sharply and rolled to a stop. "Natural!" he
breathed. His hand reached out and picked up some of the
change before him.

I made a few bets and began to talk to the boy next to me.
"You hustlin' the beach?" I asked.

The boy nodded, his attention on the dice.

"Makin' any dough?" I went on in a friendly voice.

He turned and looked at me. "You jokin'?" he asked.

I shook my head. "I'm not jokin'," I replied seriously. "I
know there's a lot of dough in it an' I was wonderin' whether
you guys got any of it."

"What are you talkin' about?" the boy asked. "All we get is
twenty cents on the buck, an' we're lucky if we come out with
six bits a day."

I stared at him. This was even better than I had thought.
"You guys are bein' taken," I said flatly. "The Rockaways are
payin' forty on the buck, and no advance dough either."

He scoffed at me. "Maybe there they do, but not on the
Island."

"I know a place they do," I said quickly, my eyes on his face.
"And they're lookin' for hustlers too."

He was interested. He watched me, the crap game momen-
tarily forgotten. "Where?" he asked.

"D'yuh think your friends would be interested?" I asked evading a direct answer.

He grinned at me. "Who ain't interested in dough?" He turned from me to the crowd of boys. "Hey, fellas," he called, "this new guy here says he's got a place that pays forty on the dollar and no dough in advance."

That was the end of the crap game as they crowded around me. They were all talking at once.

I held up my hand to quiet them. "If you guys will show up at Ben Dorfman's tomorrow morning, I got twenty-five boxes for yuh to take out." I looked around, counting the heads quickly. There were about twenty of them. "Bring your friends too," I added quickly. I wanted to get all the boxes out. That way, I figured, at least enough boys would show up to put all the boxes in use.

I was only wrong about one thing. The next morning almost fifty boys showed up, and by the end of the week there were one hundred and fifty boys hustling for us.

Chapter Four

THE BATTERED old alarm clock on the shelf read eleven when Ben looked up from the table. The light from the solitary bulb glowing overhead cast weary shadows on his face. He pushed the small amount of change remaining on the table toward his sister. "Here, Sarah," he said in a tired voice, "you count the rest of it. I'm dead."

Silently she began to run the silver through her fingers and he turned to me. "What a week!" he said exhaustedly. "I never been so tired on a Sunday night before. Those kids knock hell outta you."

I smiled. "I told yuh, Pops. I figure we grossed about eight hundred bucks since we started Thursday morning. The full week oughtta be good for twelve hundred. That's four C's clear."

He nodded his head, faintly smiling. "You were right, kid," he admitted. "I gotta hand it to yuh."

Sarah finished rolling the change into small paper wrappers. She stood up. "I never saw so much change in my life," she said.

Ben looked at her meaningfully. She nodded to him and he turned back to me. "Me an' Sarah want you to know we appreciate this, Danny. You done a lot for me, an' from now on you get twenty-five per cent of the hustlers' take."

I stared at him in surprise. A lump came up in my throat. I'd never figured on anything that good. I stared helplessly at them. I couldn't speak.

He spoke quickly. "What's wrong, Danny? Ain't that enough?"

Finally I managed to shake my head and smile. "I—I didn't expect that, Ben. I just don't know how to thank you."

"Don't thank me, kid," he said. "It's Sarah here. She thought it's only fair that you should drag down a piece because if it weren't for you we would have none of it."

Sarah was smiling gently at me from the shadow just beyond the table. "It's only right," she said.

Our eyes met. I didn't speak. There are some things you just can't say, some feelings you just can't find a voice for. I owed her a lot. If it wasn't for what she'd done I might not even be around right now.

Ben's voice interrupted my thoughts. "I wish there was a hot bath in this place. I sure could use one and then a real bed to sleep on instead of this damn old cot."

Sarah looked at him. "Why don't the both of you come down to the hotel with me? We can afford it now. You can get a room and a bath there and spend the night in comfort."

"That's the best idea I heard all night," Ben said enthusiastically. He turned to me. "What do you say, kid?"

I shook my head. The Half Moon Hotel was too big a place. It drew a big crowd from all over the city. I was better off staying back here. "No, Ben," I said quickly, "you go with Sarah. One of us better stay down here to keep an eye on things."

He looked at me doubtfully, then at Sarah. "What do you think?" he asked.

She glanced at me and I shook my head slightly. She caught

on quick. "I think Danny has the right idea," she said slowly. "You come along with me, Ben. Danny will watch the place."

The door closed behind them and then I went back to the cot and stretched out. I lit a cigarette and reached up over the cot and turned the switch. The glow of my cigarette was the only light in the room.

I was tired. I could just feel it now, stealing in weary waves up from my aching legs. I wished I could go with them. The hot bath sounded like home to me. But I couldn't afford the chance. If Sarah stayed down there, maybe someone else who knew me would show up in the hotel too. At least down here I knew I was safe.

I ground my cigarette out on the floor beneath the cot and put my hands behind my head, staring up through the darkness. I could hear sound of footsteps on the boardwalk over the concession. People were always walking up there. It was a monotonous, muffled sort of wooden sound and after a while seemed to keep time with the beating of your heart.

How strange it all was! Even now I found it hard to believe. I'd been away from home almost two months. I wondered if the family ever thought about me. I guessed Mamma did, but I didn't know about the rest of them. Papa would be too stubborn ever to admit to himself that he did.

I turned my face into my arms and closed my eyes. The muffled beat of the boardwalk ran into my body and loosened the tension in me. I dozed.

There was a knock on the door. I bolted upright in the dark and flipped on the light-switch. By the clock it was almost one in the morning.

The knock came on the door again and I got out of bed, rubbing my eyes sleepily as I walked to the door. I hadn't meant to fall asleep. I had just wanted to rest a little while and then go out for a bite.

"Who is it?" I called.

"Sarah," came the answer.

I opened the door and looked out. "What are you doing back here?" I asked in surprise.

Her face was luminous in the glow from the boardwalk. "I couldn't sleep," she answered, "so I went out for a walk and passed here. I wondered whether you were still awake."

I stepped back from the doorway. "I was just grabbing a nap before going out for a bite."

She came into the bungalow and I closed the door behind her. "Did Ben get his bath?" I asked.

She nodded. "And went right to sleep. He's very happy—the happiest I can remember since his accident."

"I'm glad," I said, going back to the cot and sitting down.

She sat in a small chair opposite me. "Got a cigarette?" she asked.

I fished a pack out of my pocket and tossed it to her. She caught it and took one out. "Match?" she asked.

I got up and lit her cigarette for her, then went back and sat down. She smoked silently while I watched her. At last she spoke again. "How old are you, Danny?"

"Eighteen," I said, stretching it a little.

She was silent again, her eyes blue and thoughtful. Her cigarette burned down to her fingers and she tamped it out in a plate on the table next to her. "I've got to go back tomorrow," she said slowly.

I nodded. "I know."

Her lips tightened. "I wish I didn't have to go, but he'll be back."

I watched her silently.

She stood up, almost startling me by the violence of her movement. "I hate him, I hate him," she said bitterly. "I wish I'd never seen him!"

I tried to make a joke out of it. "Me too."

There was a hurt, frightened look on her face. "What do you know about him?" she asked in a harsh voice. "What can you know about him? He's never done to you what he's done to me. He couldn't. You're a man, not a woman. All he can do is hurt or kill you. He can't do to you what he's done to me!"

The quiet sound of her tears filled the small room. I walked over to her slowly, put my arms around her shoulders, and pulled her head down against my chest. My touch brought a fresh paroxysm of tears.

"The things he's done to me, Danny!" she cried, her voice almost muffled against my shirt. "The things he's made me do! Nobody can ever know, nobody would ever believe it. There's a perverted madness in him that you can't see. I'm so frightened to go back, I'm so afraid of him, of what he'll do to me!"

I held her shaking shoulders firmly. "Then don't go back,

Sarah," I said softly. "Ben's doing all right now. You don't have to go back."

Her wide tortured eyes stared up at me. "I must go, Danny," she whispered. "I have to. If I don't, he'll come after me. I can't let him do that. Then Ben will know everything."

There was nothing I could say about that. She was crying again. I brushed my hand over her soft hair and pressed my lips against it. "Some day, Sarah," I said in a low voice, "you won't have to go back."

She turned her face swiftly and her lips pressed against mine. They clung to me with frantic desperation. Her eyes were closed tightly, the last tear hanging perilously on the fringe of her lashes. I held my breath a moment. So many things were wrong. Still, there was so much I owed her, I could never hope to pay her back. With my little finger I brushed the last tear from her eye.

Her mouth opened slightly and I could feel our breaths intermingling. The warm perfume of her came up to my nostrils. She turned her face slightly, her eyes still closed, and a cry escaped her lips. "Danny!"

I pressed my mouth harder against hers and a heat began to rise up in me. It seemed to come in heavy pulsing waves, spreading in a slow circle through my body like the ripples on the surface of water when a stone is thrown into it. Her breasts were firm, the muscles of her thighs were tense and trembling as she clung to me. "Danny!" Her voice was happy in my ear. "Danny, I can't stand on my feet!"

Quietly we moved toward the cot. I knelt beside her as her clothes fell about her, and pressed my lips to the warm soft parts of her. Then we lay together and there was only the closeness of our bodies and the excitement of our flesh.

She was agile, expert, and proficient. And yet with all the knowledge that I knew was in her, there was something about her that made me understand. And for that understanding I loved her.

It was Sarah with whom I shared my cot that night. Not Ronnie.

Chapter Five

I SNAPPED the lock on the ice-cream locker and pulled on it. It gripped tight. Satisfied, I left the back room and went into the concession. Ben was just putting down the shutters. I gave him a hand.

"Christ, what a day!" he swore, the beads of sweat running down his cheeks. "The night isn't goin' to be any better either."

I grinned at him. "I guess not." The crowds up on the boardwalk were moving along slowly, searching vainly for a breath of cool air.

"It ain't goin' to do them much good comin' down here," he said. "When it's hot like this, it's hot all over."

I nodded. There wasn't even a bit of breeze coming in from the water.

Ben snapped his fingers sharply. "That reminds me, Danny," he said quickly. "Mike was looking for you. I think he wants you to help him tonight." Mike ran the Wheel of Chance concession on the boardwalk almost over our place.

"Pete drunk again?" I asked. Pete was Mike's brother. He worked the place with him except when he was on a jag. Several times before, I had given Mike a lift when that happened.

"I don't know," Ben replied. "He didn't say. He only asked for you to come up when you got through."

"Okay," I said. "I'll go up and see what he wants." I left Ben to finish closing and walked up the ramp to the boardwalk. I pushed my way through the crowds toward the concession.

Mike was there alone, a disgusted look on his face as he surveyed the crowd. His face brightened when he saw me. "Too tired to give me a hand tonight, Danny?" he called almost before I could reach him. "Pete didn't show up."

I hesitated. I was tired, but it was so hot I knew I wouldn't

218

get any sleep down in the bungalow. Ben had done the smart thing; as soon as he had seen that the business was doing all right he moved into the Half Moon Hotel, high up where it was cool. So I had the bungalow to myself.

"Okay, Mike," I said, ducking under the counter and coming up behind it. "Wheel or spiel tonight?"

He stabbed at his face with a damp handkerchief. "Spiel, if it's all right with you," he answered. "I been buckin' the crowd both ways all day an' can't take it any more."

I nodded my head and tied a change apron around my waist. I picked up a long wooden pointer from under the counter and turned toward the crowd. Mike nodded and I began the pitch, forcing my voice into the harsh metallic cry that would carry over the hum of the crowd.

I got a great kick out of the spiel. I knew it by heart already and had heard it a thousand times, but each time it was like new. I liked being able to kid the crowd into getting rid of their nickels for no real good reason. In many ways all of living was like that. You put your dough down on something you knew sure as hell would never pay off.

"Try the Wheel of Fortune, folks. Only a nickel an' there's a winnuh evvy time she spins. Yuh can't lose, yuh kin only win. Come an' getcha money down. Try yer luck!"

I spotted a young man walking along with his girl hanging on his arm. He hesitated a moment in front of the concession. I stabbed at him with my long pointer. "Hey there, young feller!" I shouted at him so that everybody within two blocks could hear. "I mean you with the pretty girl! You get a free chance! The boss jus' tol' me any feller with a pretty girl gets a free chance for the girl along with his own! Put yer nickel down an' cover two numbers. Two fer the price of one!"

The young man looked at the girl; then, grinning embarrassedly, he stepped up to the counter and put a nickel down on one of the red numbers. I slipped the nickel off quickly and threw down two blue chips.

"There's a wise young man," I announced to the people beginning to gather round the concession. "He knows a bargain when he sees one. He knows a pretty girl too, an' all you folks can be jus' as wise as he is. Bring yer girl up to the Wheel of Chance an' get two chances fer one!"

A few nickels began to tinkle down on the counter. I had them working. I looked back over my shoulder at Mike. He nodded his dark head approvingly and reached up behind him and spun the wheel. I could see his foot catch the stirrup beneath the counter. I knew who was going to win.

"There she goes, folks!" I cried. "Round an' round she goes, an' where she stops nobody knows. Evvybody wins when the Wheel of Fortune spins." I held the long pointer ready to tap the young man's girl when the wheel stopped spinning.

Along about midnight a breeze came up and the crowd began to thin out as they beat it home for their beds. Mike came down the counter toward me. "Let's wrap it up, kid," he smiled. "There's nothin' left in 'em any more tonight."

I slipped off my change apron and handed it to Mike. He emptied it into a bag without counting the change. He pressed a switch at the wheel, and the lights went out all over the concession. Mike's face was gray and tired in the dim boardwalk lights after we had slotted in the removable doors and locked up.

"What a pisser of a day!" he exclaimed exhaustedly.

"I got some coffee downstairs," I said. "Come on."

A slow smile broke across his face. "Okay, Danny. I kin use a cup of coffee 'fore I go home."

I put the coffee on the stove to warm up while Mike sank in a chair wearily. "That's the third time in two weeks I had to call on you," he said.

I smiled silently. Mike was an all-right guy. You didn't mind helping him out because you knew he would come through if you needed him.

His voice rose slightly. "Some day I'm gonna th'ow that damn brother of mine out on his ass! Every Goddam time he gets next to a bottle he turns into a sponge."

I put two cups on the table and poured the coffee into them. It was black and steaming. I pushed some milk into it. "Here," I said, handing a cup to Mike, "drink this. You'll feel better."

He looked at me shrewdly over the rim of the cup. "I'm through foolin', Danny. This time I mean it. I know I swore it many times, but this time it'll stick." He raised the cup to his lips and sipped the coffee. "Soon's I find me a guy I can trust, he's out."

I drank my coffee silently. I'd heard this story many times already, but Mike had always taken his brother back. I dragged on my cigarette, feeling the smoke sharp and tingling in my nose.

Suddenly Mike brought his open hand down on the table in a sharp slap. "I'm a jerk!" he exclaimed. There was such a funny expression on his face as he looked at me.

"What now?" I asked.

"I'm lookin' fer a guy," he said quickly, "an' all the time here he is under my nose." He leaned forward over the table. "How'd you like to come in with me, kid?"

I looked at him in surprise. I hadn't thought about that. But I couldn't do it. "I'd like it, Mike," I said quickly, "but I can't run out on Ben now."

"The season's only got two weeks to run, Danny," he said. "I can manage that. I mean afterwards when I take the wheel south for the winter. You got any plans for then?"

I shook my head. I hadn't made any plans for the winter. I hadn't thought about it at all. But the summer had gone so quickly I just hadn't had time to think about it.

"Then come with me, kid," Mike urged. "We close down here the week after Labor Day, grab a couple weeks' rest, and catch up with Petersen's Tent Shows on October 2nd in Memphis."

"Sounds good to me," I said hesitantly. Suddenly I was homesick. Until now it had been just like many other summers. At the end of it, I suppose, I thought I would go home. But now I knew it was different. I wasn't going any place.

Mike grinned at me knowingly. "You'll like it down there, kid," he said. "The gash jumps like rabbits all through the South."

I smiled back at him, still hesitant. I'd talk it over with Sarah before I made up my mind. Maybe she had some other plans. "Can I let yuh know in a couple of days, Mike?" I asked. "There are a few things I gotta check first."

I waited until we were alone on the next evening she came down before I told her about it. She listened silently all the time I was talking. When I had finished, she lit a cigarette.

"Then you're not going home after the summer's over?" she asked.

I stared at her in surprise. "Did you think I would?" I asked.

She shook her head. "I didn't really think so," she answered slowly. "And yet I thought you might."

"Even if I could go home an' my father would let me in, how long do you think it would be before Maxie Fields found out I was back?" I asked. "Then how long do you think I would last?"

She nodded in agreement. "I guess you can't go back, then." Her eyes met mine. "But what about your girl?" she asked. "Won't you let her know what you're doing? She must be worried stiff over you."

Funny she should remember that. A peculiar lump came into my throat. "There's nothing I can do about that," I said stiffly. "I can't take any chances on anything leaking out."

A distant look came into her eyes. "I guess you might as well go, then," she said.

I walked over to her. "You sound mad," I said. "Is there anything wrong?"

She didn't look up. "Nothing's wrong," she answered, shaking her head. "You go with Mike. You'll get along. You don't need anybody."

I put my hands on her shoulders, dropped them over her breasts and around her waist. "I need you, Sarah," I said.

She spun around quickly in my grasp and broke away from me. "You don't need anybody, Danny," she snapped. "Not even me." Then she stormed out the door without looking back.

I stared after her, wondering what had got into her, and it wasn't until the next morning that I found out from Ben what it was. She was quitting her job with Maxie Fields, he told me, and they were going out west together to open up a little business.

Chapter Six

I MADE up with Mike to meet him in Memphis on October 2nd. We shook hands on it. He seemed very pleased. "Now my plans are all set," he said, smiling.

Sarah's plans were all set too. She had told Ben to have everything packed and ready to leave the Thursday after Labor Day. She would come down in the car and pick him up that afternoon and they would start out. I didn't have a chance to ask her if she had said anything to Maxie about it, but I knew from the way she spoke that she hadn't.

For some reason or other she kept away from me the few times she came down to the Island. She didn't seem to want to talk to me and I let her alone. I didn't see any sense in getting into an argument with her, and before I knew it the season was over.

Ben had brought everything back to the bungalow from the hotel, and by the time Thursday rolled around he was all packed and ready to go. He was as happy and excited as a kid with an all-day sucker. He could hardly wait until three o'clock, when she was due to pick him up.

"I wish you were going with us, Danny," he called from the front room of the bungalow, where he was seated amid his luggage. "At first Sarah thought you were coming with us. We were disappointed when you told her you were going with Mike."

Then the whole business was suddenly clear in my mind. I was a prize dope. She had meant to ask me to come along with them all the while, but when I had spoken to her about Mike she had changed her mind. I guess she thought that was what I wanted to do.

Before I had a chance to reply there was a knock at the door. I pulled on my trousers hurriedly and buttoned them. I heard Ben's voice as he went to the door. "Sarah must be early."

I heard the door open, then a chill ran through me. "Is Ronnie here?" It was Spit's voice.

My first impulse was to run, but the only way out was through the front door, so I froze against the wall of the room and strained my ears to the door.

Ben's voice sounded confused. "Ronnie? Ronnie who?"

Another heavy voice answered. "Don't crap us, bud. You know who we mean. Fields's girl."

A note of relief came into Ben's voice. "You must mean my sister, Sarah, Mr. Fields's secretary. Come in and wait. She's not here yet."

I heard heavy footsteps come into the bungalow and pressed my eye to the crack in the door. Spit and the Collector were standing in the center of the room. The Collector was laughing.

"Fields's secretary," he haw hawed. "That's a new name for it!"

There was a puzzled look on Ben's face. "Was there something Mr. Fields wanted?" he asked. "I know Sarah wouldn't mind if she had to stay a few extra days to help him out."

The Collector looked at him. "Why?" he asked Ben. "Was she quitting?"

Ben nodded his head. "Didn't Mr. Fields tell you?"

The Collector began to laugh again. "Maxie'll get a big boot outta that. He'll be surprised to find out his babe quit on him."

A strained look came on Ben's face. "What did you say?" he asked tensely.

"You heard me." The Collector's voice was deliberately cruel. "No whore ever powders on Maxie Fields no matter how high their price."

Ben's voice was the scream of a hurt animal. "That's my sister!" he cried, throwing himself at the Collector.

He moved out of the range of my vision and I heard a sharp crash, then a thud as Ben fell to the floor. He began to scream. "Sarah! Sarah! Don't come here!"

I could hear the sound of several sharp slaps and muttered curses, but Ben kept on screaming. I shifted my eyes along the crack until I could see them again.

The Collector had one knee planted on Ben's chest and was slapping him on the face. "Shut up, yuh son of a bitch!" he swore at him.

Ben kept on squirming and screaming. The Collector grabbed at Ben's arm and twisted it backward viciously. "Shut up, yuh one-armed crumb," he threatened, "or I'll rip yuh other arm out of its socket!"

Ben's face went white and he lay back limply and silently on the floor, his frightened eyes staring up at the Collector. I could feel nausea gathering in the pit of my stomach. I never saw such fear in human eyes.

"Maybe yuh better take him in the back room," I heard Spit say. "If the whore sees him, she might start hollering."

The Collector nodded and lumbered to his feet, still holding Ben's arm. "Get up!" he snarled.

Ben awkwardly tried to get to his feet, but couldn't make it. The Collector yanked on his arm and Ben screamed in pain: "I can't get up! I've only got one leg!"

The Collector laughed. He let go of Ben's arm and lifted him under the armpits as you would a baby and put him on his feet. "Boy," he said callously, "you're a real mess." He poked Ben in the back and Ben stumbled toward my door.

I looked around frantically. There was a steel bar near the door that I used to prop the tiny window up on hot nights. I picked it up and, hefting it in my hand, hid behind the door.

The door opened and Ben came stumbling through, the Collector following him. The Collector kicked the door shut behind him without turning around and went after Ben.

I stepped in quietly behind him and swung the bar. There was a dull sound and blood spurted from the Collector's ear where the bar hit him. He tumbled silently to the floor. He never knew what hit him.

"I was wondering where you were," Ben whispered hoarsely.

I looked up from the Collector and met his eyes. "I was here," I whispered, "but I had to wait for a spot." My mouth had a bad taste in it.

He bought my explanation. There was something more important on his mind. "Did you hear what they said about Sarah?" he whispered.

I nodded.

"Is it true?"

I looked at him. There was a pain in his face that nothing physical had put there; this came from the heart. Sarah was his kid sister. He had put her through school after their parents died, and then she had taken care of him when he was hurt.

Suddenly I knew he would believe whatever I told him. For many reasons he had to, but mostly because he wanted to. Maybe some day he would find out what she had done. But not from me.

I shook my head. "No," I said surely. "Maxie Fields is a racket boy with a lot of legit business. Sarah became his secretary, and by the time she found out what he was and wanted out, she already knew too much for him to let her go."

Some of the pain disappeared from his face, but not all of it. "Poor kid," he murmured. "What she went through all because of me." He turned his eyes to mine. "How did you meet her?"

"I got into a jam with this guy and I was hurt. She saved me." It was the first time he had ever asked me what had happened. Until now he had taken her word that I had fallen from her car that night while she was bringing me out to work for him. "She's a very square kid," I said.

His eyes held level with mine and I let him search me for the truth. Slowly his face relaxed and the rest of the pain disappeared from his eyes. "What about that guy outside?" he asked.

"We'll take care of him," I said. I bent down over the Collector. He was breathing heavily as I flipped open his jacket and pulled his gun from the shoulder holster. I straightened up, hefting it cautiously in my hand. I didn't want any accidents to happen.

Ben was staring at the gun. "That explains a lot of things," he said wonderingly. "That's why she had to get away in such a hurry. That's why she couldn't wait for me to get ready but would pick me up on the way out. That's why she always had to run right back to work. She didn't want me to know."

"Yeah," I nodded. "That's it."

The sound of an automobile stopping outside reached our ears. We turned and looked at each other. I waved Ben back to the cot and stepped behind the door. We both stood very still.

I heard the front door open. Spit's voice was very calm. "Hi yuh, Babe. Maxie sent us after you as soon as he saw yer clothes was gone."

I could almost hear her sharp intake of breath. Then she screamed: "Ben! What have you done with Ben?"

Spit's voice was anxious and reassuring. "He's okay, Ronnie. The Collector's got him in the back room just to keep him out of trouble."

I heard her quick footsteps on the floor, then the door opened. She flew into the room. "Ben! Ben!" she cried. "Are you all right?"

Ben stood up. He was smiling at her. Spit was following her into the room. I stepped in behind him and pressed the gun into his spine.

"Stand quiet, Spit," I said slowly. "I'm very nervous. I never worked one of these things before!"

I'll say this much for him. Somewhere through the summer Spit had grown up too. He'd picked up savvy. He didn't turn his head. Matter of fact, he didn't move at all. His voice was careful, yet curious. "Danny?"

I prodded him with the gun. "Over against the wall, Spit," I said. "Till your nose touches."

He stepped cautiously over the Collector. "Up to your old tricks, huh, Danny?" he asked. "First Maxie's money, then Maxie's broad."

I reversed the gun in my hand and swiped him across the face. He staggered a little and I pushed him with my hand. He landed against the wall with a thump. I shoved the gun into his back again and pulled his knife out of its sheath.

"Maxie ain't gonna like this, Danny." Spit's voice was threatening. "You got away with it once. He ain't gonna like your hurting his boys again."

I laughed. "His boys'll like it even less if they're dead," I said coldly. "Or has Maxie got a direct phone in hell too?"

He shut up and stood against the wall. I turned slightly and looked back.

Ben's arm was around Sarah. She was crying wildly against his chest. "Don't cry, honey," he said. "You'll never have to work for that man again."

Her crying stopped suddenly and she looked questioningly at me. "Does he know, Danny?" she asked in a hushed frightened voice. "Did they—"

"I told him what kind of a man you were secretary to, Sarah," I interrupted her quickly. "I told him how he wouldn't let you quit because you knew too much about his business."

"I know all about him now, Sarah," Ben said. "Why didn't you tell me before? We would have found a way out together."

She was looking at me gratefully now. I smiled at her. She

turned back to her brother. "I was afraid of him, Ben. I didn't dare."

Ben's voice was reassuring. "Well, you don't have to worry now. We'll just turn these guys over to the police and be on our way."

Fear had come back into her voice. "We can't do that, Ben!"

My voice joined hers. "They'll only hold you up and you'd never get started," I said. "You better get going. I'll turn them in after you've gone."

"Will that be all right?" Ben hesitated.

"Sure it will," I said quickly. "Now hurry. Get your stuff into the car."

Spit's voice came muffled from against the wall. "I can't stand this way much longer, Danny. Can I turn around?"

"Sure," I said, reaching for a piece of wire lying on a shelf. "In just a minute."

I pulled his hands behind him and looped the wire around them. I jerked it tight and turned him around. His eyes were flashing at me.

"Sit down, Spit. Make yourself comfortable," I said, hitting him flush on the jaw and tumbling him onto the cot.

He sat up sputtering, but he didn't say a word. I looked over my shoulder. Almost all Ben's luggage was gone. Just one small piece remained.

Ben picked it up and looked at me hesitantly. "Sure you'll be all right, Danny?"

I grinned at him. "I'll be fine, Ben. Now get outta here."

He came toward me and his hand brushed my shoulder. "So long, kid," he said. "Thanks for everything."

"Thank you, Ben," I said. "So long."

He turned and walked out the door as Sarah came in. She came up to me, her eyes looking into mine. There was a tense curious look in them.

"Sure you don't want to come with us?" she asked through stiff lips.

I managed a smile. "Can't now," I answered. "I'm a little busy."

She tried a smile at my joke, but she couldn't make it. She half turned away, then looked back at me. "Danny!" she cried, and ran back into my arms.

"Better go, Sarah," I said somberly. "This way you can leave the whole thing behind you. There'll be nothing to remind you and make you remember."

She nodded her head and looked up at me. I could see the tears standing in her eyes. She kissed me quickly on the cheek and walked back to the door. " 'Bye, Danny. Good luck," she said, and she was gone before I could answer her.

I turned back to Spit. He was watching me.

"We looked every place but here, Danny," he said. "But we should have guessed it. Ronnie was out that night too. I remember now."

There was something different about him. I hadn't noticed it at first, but I did now. He'd had something done to his mouth. His lip wasn't split any more and he didn't spray saliva all over when he spoke.

He saw that I had noticed it. His eyes lighted up. "I forgot to thank you, Danny, but you didn't give me a chance. When you slugged me that night you split my lip again and the doctor had to do a plastic job on me, and while he was at it, he fixed the whole thing."

I grinned. "Don't mention it, Spit." I raised my fist threateningly. "Any time."

He shrank back on the cot. "What are you going to do now?" His voice was frightened.

I pulled down another piece of wire. "Stretch out on your belly," I said. "You'll see."

Reluctantly he stretched out on the narrow cot. Quickly I caught his ankles together with the wire and pulled his feet up behind him and ran the wire through his hands, binding them together. I straightened up and looked down at him. He ought to be good for a long time like this.

He lay there quietly and I bent over the Collector. The blood had stopped welling from his ear and he was breathing easier. I flipped open an eye and looked at it. It was dull and glazed. He would keep too.

I picked up the few things I owned and put them in the small valise I had bought, with Spit watching me all the while from the cot.

"You won't get away this time, Danny," he said.

I walked back to the cot and looked down at him. I raised the gun thoughtfully and watched the fear grow in his eyes. "How do yuh know?" I asked.

He didn't answer. Just stared at the gun with big frightened eyes. After a moment I smiled and dropped it into my pocket. A look of relief came into his face.

"It seems to me we met like this before," I said. "Last May, wasn't it?"

He nodded his head. He was too scared to talk.

"Do you love me as much in September as you did in May?" I laughed.

He didn't answer.

I bent over him and slapped his face with my open hand. "If you're as smart as I think you are, Spit," I said, picking up my bag and walking to the door, "you'll be careful not to run into me again." I opened the door. "You might not always be this lucky. They don't fix holes in your head like they do on your lip."

I shut the door behind me and walked through the front room and out of the bungalow. I snapped the padlock on the front door and jammed it tight. I walked up the ramp to the boardwalk and into the novelty store, where I left the key for the renting agent.

The small gray-haired woman who worked the store with her husband took it from me. "Going already, Danny?" she asked, smiling through her steel-rimmed spectacles. "Everything all right?"

"Sure, Mrs. Bernstein," I said with a smile. "Everything's all right now."

Chapter Seven

THE SOUTHBOUND bus was on the ferry leaving the dock as I looked back through the window at the lights of New York. They were sparkling crazily. It had begun to rain.

That was okay with me. It was just the way I felt. I had left something behind me. I didn't know what, but whatever it was, the rain would wash it all away and it was lost. Someday I would come back. Maybe things would be different then.

I settled back into the seat and opened a morning paper. It wasn't until we were rolling through the flatlands of the New Jersey countryside that I saw the item in one of the broadway columns. And, even seeing it there in the cold black type, I found it hard to believe.

SAM GOTTKIN, top concession and hatcheck king and former light heavy contender under the name of Sammy Gordon, was married yesterday to Miriam (Mimi) Fisher, sister of Danny Fisher, Gloves champion. After a honeymoon in Bermuda they will take up residence in a new penthouse on Central Park South that he had specially redecorated for his bride.

Automatically my hand went to the signal bell to stop the bus. My fingers rested there a moment, and then I took my hand away. It would do no good to go back. There wasn't anything I could change.

I sank back slowly in my seat and read the item again. Loneliness stole into me. Mimi and Sam. I wondered how it had happened. How they met. And what became of that guy in her office she was so crazy about? I closed my eyes wearily. It didn't matter now. Nothing that happened would matter any more. Not to me. As far as they were concerned, I was gone as if I never was there.

The tattoo of the rain beat against the bus window and dulled my mind. I dozed fitfully. Pictures of Sam and Mimi kept flashing before me. But they were never together. Whenever one of them would come into focus, the other would disappear. I fell asleep before I could get them to stay together long enough for me to wish them happiness.

I WASN'T THERE WHEN—

She was sitting in front of the dressing-table, crying uncontrollably. Large tears were running down her cheeks, leaving long purple streaks of mascara. Her hands held a helpless handkerchief against her mouth.

Papa turned nervously. "What is she crying about?" he asked Mamma. "It's her wedding. What has she got to cry about?"

Mamma looked at him disgustedly. She took his arm and pushed him out the door into the small marriage chapel. "Go, mingle with the guests," she said firmly. "She'll be all right in time for the ceremony."

She closed the door in his protesting face and snapped the lock. Her face was calm and understanding as she waited for the paroxysm of tears to pass. She didn't have to wait long. At last Mimi stopped weeping and sat small and shrunken in her chair. She stared at the handkerchief her fingers were twisting and turning nervously.

"You don't love him," Mamma said quietly.

Mimi's head snapped up. Her eyes met Mamma's for a moment and then she looked down again. "I love him," she answered in a small, tired voice.

"You don't have to marry him if you don't love him." Mamma spoke as if she hadn't heard a word Mimi uttered.

Mimi's eyes were calm now. She looked at Mamma unwinkingly. Her voice was quietly emotionless. "I'm all right now, Mother. I was just being a child."

Mamma's face was serious. "You think maybe because you're getting married you're grown up? Don't forget I still had to sign your wedding license to give my permission."

Mimi turned and looked in the dressing-table mirror. She got out of her chair quickly and walked to the washbasin in the corner.

Mamma put her hand out and stopped her. "All your life, Miriam," she said softly, "you'll have to live with him. All your life you'll have to live with the way you'll feel. All—"

"Mamma!" A desperate note of hysteria in Mimi's voice halted Mamma's words. "Don't talk like that! It's too late now!"

"It's not too late, Miriam," Mamma persisted. "You can still change your mind."

Mimi shook her head. Her face set into determined lines. "It's too late, Mamma," she said firmly. "It was already too late the first time I went to see him when I wanted to find out where Danny had gone. What am I going to do now? Give him back all the money he spent trying to find Danny for us? Give him back the five thousand dollars he loaned Papa for the store? Give back all the clothes he bought me and the ring, and say I'm sorry, that it was all a mistake?"

The pain in Mamma's eyes grew deeper. "Better that," she said quietly, "than you should be unhappy. Don't let Papa and me do to you what we did to Danny." Her eyes began to fill with tears.

Mimi caught Mamma to her. "Don't blame yourself for anything that happened," she said swiftly. "It was all Papa's fault."

"No, I could have stopped him," Mamma insisted. "That's why I'm talking to you. The same mistake I should not make again."

Mimi's face was determined. "There's no mistake, Mamma," she said surely, as if she knew all the answers. "Sam loves me. If I don't love him as much as he loves me now, that will come in time. He's good and kind and generous. Everything will work out all right."

Mamma looked into her face questioningly.

Impulsively Mimi bent and brushed her lips across Mamma's brow. "Don't worry, Mamma," she said softly. "I know what I'm doing. This is what I want."

She sat up in the bed, her body tense with anticipated fear. She could hear him brushing his teeth noisily in the bathroom. The sound of the running water stopped abruptly. She heard the click of the light-switch, lay down quickly in the darkness of the bed, and curled her body into a small huddled mass.

She heard him walking around his side of the bed in the darkness and felt the bed sagging beneath the weight of his body. She lay there quietly, her body stiff and suddenly chill, her teeth almost chattering.

There was a moment's silence, then his hand slowly touched her shoulder. She clenched her teeth tightly. Then she heard him whisper: "Mimi."

She forced herself to answer. "Yes, Sam."

"Mimi, turn around." His whisper was a pleading sound in the darkness.

Her voice was low and carefully controlled. "Please, Sam, not tonight. It hurts."

His voice was gentle and understanding. "We won't try again tonight. I just want to hold your head against my chest. I don't want you to be afraid of me. I love you, baby."

Her eyes were suddenly wet with tears. She turned around swiftly and placed her head against his breast. Her voice was very small. "Do you, Sam? Could you really love me after all I did to you?"

She felt his breath against her hair. "Sure, baby. You didn't do nothin'. All nice girls feel like that the first time."

She relaxed slowly in his arms. She lifted her face to him and kissed him lightly on the lips, much as a little girl would kiss her father. "Thanks, Sam," she whispered gratefully. She was silent a moment, then her voice came slowly through her lips. "I'll try again if you want to, Sam."

"Would yuh, honey?" He sounded pleased and happy.

"Yes, Sam," she answered in a low voice.

She shut her eyes tightly and could feel his hands stroke her hair. His lips pressed against her cheek lightly and moved to her neck. George used to do that. Angrily she pushed the flow of thought from her. Why did she have to think of that at this moment? It wasn't fair to Sam. He wasn't responsible for what had happened. It was her fault. She had wanted it this way from the very beginning when she and Nellie had gone to see him.

Contritely she raised her hand and stroked his cheek. His face was smooth. He had just shaved before coming to bed. His lips pressed to her lips. They were warm and gentle. She kissed him back.

She stiffened in momentary fright as she felt his hand, cool, light, under her nightgown. His touch was quiet, soothing; and slowly she relaxed, letting her body go limp and unresisting. His heart was pounding against her.

She began to feel warm and tingling. She used to feel like that before. . . . What was she thinking? . . . This was good and she was glad she could feel like that now.

His lips were against her bosom. She felt content and her hands held his head still as she kissed his forehead. She shut her eyes and thought of George. It would have been like this with him. It would have been easier with him. She wasn't afraid of him as she had been with. . . .

His voice was an anxious whisper in the night. "Are you all right, honey?"

She nodded her head fiercely, not trusting herself to speak.

Sam was lying quietly beside her, his hand soothing on her flushed cheek. There was secret pride in his voice as he whispered: "See, darling, it wasn't anything to be afraid of, was it?"

She hid her face against his breast. "No," she whispered. But in her heart she knew she was lying. She would always have to lie to him. She would always be afraid. It wasn't his face that came before her eyes at the shattering moment of orgasm. "Oh, God," she prayed silently, "will I have to go through life like this? Always afraid?"

The answering voice was in her mind. It was rich and heavy, and its words were from the marriage ceremony: "Repeat after me, my child. 'I, Miriam, take thee, Samuel, to be my lawful wedded husband, for richer, for poorer, in sickness and in health, to love, to honor, to cherish, until death do us part.' "

He was sleeping, his breath coming deeply and contentedly. She looked at his calm face in the darkness. He was happy now. Better so.

She moved back to her pillow and closed her eyes. She had gone to him to find me, and now she would spend the rest of her days and nights beside him. But he would never know the failure. It wasn't his to know. Only she would know that she had cheated him and would cheat him in all the frenzied moments of their life together.

Chapter Eight

I STOOD in the center of the deserted midway with the rain pouring down over me. I pulled the collar of my slicker up around my neck so that it was snug under the brim of my soft slouch hat, and dragged at my cigarette. I looked up at the sky. This rain wasn't going to stop. I stared down the midway. The wet walls of the gray and tan tents flapped cheerlessly in the rain-swept wind.

Two years of this. It had been a long time. I'd put a large piece of time into these canvas-covered walls. There had been days so hot that the heat came baking you until you felt you were standing in an oven in some crazy part of hell, and nights so cold that the marrow in your bones seemed to freeze like the ice on a lake in winter.

Two years of this. Of the crowds pushing through the midway, gawking, their mouths filled with cotton candy, hot dogs, and ice cream. Of crowds with their eyes wary, looking upon you as they would on a vagrant, eager to purchase your wares, resentful that you were selling them.

Two years of not being at home, of not knowing what happened. Nellie. Mamma and Papa. Mimi. Sam. The names still hurt. Every time I thought I was used to it, the same lonely feeling would come back. It was buried deep, but it was always there.

And now I was almost home. Almost, but not quite. Philadelphia. I could get a train at the Market Street Station and in a little while get off at Penn Station. It was easy when I thought about it. Only an hour and ten minutes away from home.

But things were always simple when I thought about them. They were never as simple when I started to do them. All the memories of what had happened come pouring back into me. And I am angry again. Resentful at my enforced exile. Afraid of what would happen if I were to return.

And yet I want to go home. I always want to go home. There are ties that bind me to those who are there, even when they do not want me to return. Ties that I cannot spell into words, but are emotions in me. Today I am only one hour and ten minutes away from these things. The day after tomorrow, when the tents move southward again on their annual path, I will be six hours away, a week later twenty hours away, and in a month it will be a journey of many days and I may not travel it in all my lifetime.

I look up to the sky again. The rain clouds are low and steady, the wind brushes its wetness into my face, my cigarette is sodden between my lips. The rain will spend the night on the midway.

I let the cigarette fall from my mouth and it sputters in a puddle at my feet. I could almost hear the angry hiss of its tiny fire as it vainly fights away the water. I think I am like that cigarette and I am fighting for my life against the quickly rushing rain. I cannot breathe, the air is heavy in my lungs. I must go home. I must, I must. I must see Nellie again. And Mamma and Mimi. And Papa too, whether he wants to see me or not. Even though I know I cannot stay, even if I must come back to the midway tomorrow. It may be a long time before I can go home again. I am tired of being lonely.

The inevitable card game was in progress as I came through the tent flap. The players' eyes glanced at me briefly as I swung my hat against my trousers, shaking the water from it; then they looked back at their cards.

The feeble light from the oil lamp flickered on their faces as I walked around the table. I stopped behind Mike and looked down at the cards in his hand, smiling to myself. He would never get rich trying to fill a three-card straight.

"It's gonna rain all night," I said.

"Yeah," Mike answered absently. He was concentrating on his cards.

The dealer's voice came across the table. "How many?"

Mike's voice was low. "Two."

The cards flickered across the table to him. He picked them up quickly and looked at them. A sigh of disgust crossed his lips. "I'm out," he said, dropping the cards on the table and turning to look up at me.

There was a quick showing of cards and the dealer took the pot. "Want a hand, Danny?" he asked genially.

"No, thanks." I shook my head. "You guys got enough of my dough." I looked down at Mike. "How about the night off?" I asked.

Mike grinned. "Get a dame lined up for me too and we'll both take the night off."

"Not this night, Mike. I want to run up to New York. We're not goin' to do anythin' tonight."

The dealer scoffed at me. "Playin' hard to get, Danny? Yuh better look out for these Phillie chippies. Ever' one of them has a brother on the force."

Mike's eyes turned serious. "What yuh want to go up there for?"

I had never told him very much, but he was a bright guy. He must have guessed something had gone wrong back there. But he never asked any questions and he wasn't going to get any answers now. "A vacation," I said quietly, meeting his eyes.

Mike looked down at the table. The cards were coming toward him again. He picked them up, turning each one over cautiously in his fingers. Six. Nine. Seven. Eight. Ace. All black and curly. His fingers tightened on them. I could see he had forgotten about me.

"What d'yuh say, Mike?" I prodded him.

He didn't look up from the table. "Okay," he said absently.

"But be back by eleven in the morning. The papers say it's gonna clear up and we're gettin' outta here."

The rain was still beating against the windows of the train as the tired conductor came through. He tapped me on the shoulder. "Tickets, please." I gave him the ticket silently. "Bad night," he said, shaking his head. He punched my ticket and handed it back to me.

"Yeah," I answered, watching him move away. But I didn't really agree with him; I was going home. I looked at my wristwatch. New York was only fifty-five minutes away.

Chapter Nine

IT WAS drizzling when I came up the subway steps, but the crowd on Delancey Street was as large as ever. Rain didn't bother them, they had nowhere else to go. It was always good to walk along Delancey Street and look in the shop windows and think about what you might buy if you had the money.

I lit a cigarette as I waited for the traffic light to change and let me cross the street. The store windows hadn't changed; they would never change. The haberdasheries still had their fire sales; the cakes and bread in Ratner's window were just as they were the last time I had been there; the hot-dog stand on the corner of Essex was just as crowded.

The traffic halted in front of me and I crossed the street. Things hadn't changed a bit. The same beggars were selling their pencils, the same whores were casing the crowds with weary disillusioned eyes. But I had changed. I knew that when one of the whores jostled me and whispered something as I passed. I looked after her, smiling. Two years ago it wouldn't have been like that. I was a kid then.

I continued down the street toward the five and ten. Nellie would be there, I was sure of it. I don't know why, but somehow I knew she would be there. The clock in the Paramount window told me it was five minutes to nine. Another five minutes and the store would close and she would be out. Suddenly I was anxious to see her. I wondered if she had changed too. Maybe she had forgotten me, maybe she had another fellow. Two years was a long time for a girl to wait, especially when she had no word. And I had never written.

I was at the store entrance. I stopped and looked in. There weren't many people in the store, but a nervous reluctance kept me from crossing the threshold. Maybe she didn't want to see me. I stood there, hesitating a moment, then I retraced my steps to the corner.

I stood under the street light—the same street light where I had always waited for her. I leaned my back against the lamp-post and smoked my cigarette, oblivious of the rain falling about me. If I closed my eyes and listened only to the night sounds in the street, it would be as if I had never been away.

The lights in the five-and-ten window went out suddenly and I straightened up. I threw my cigarette into the gutter and watched the store entrance. It should only be a few minutes now. A few minutes. I could feel a faint pulse ticking in my temples; my mouth was dry. A group of girls came chattering from the darkened store. I watched them avidly as they walked past me, still talking. She wasn't with them.

My gaze went past them to the door again. More girls were coming out. My fingers drummed nervously against my leg. She wasn't with them either. I looked at my wristwatch quickly. Almost five past nine. She had to come out soon.

I wiped my face with my handkerchief. Despite the cool chill in the air, I was sweating. I stuffed the handkerchief back in my pocket and watched the door. Girls were still coming out. I scanned each face quickly and my eyes would leap to the next. She still wasn't with them. They were coming out more slowly now, two together or singly. They came out into the street, glanced quickly up at the sky, and then hurried toward home.

I looked at my watch again. Almost twenty after. Disappointment began to course through me. I half turned, about to go away. It had been silly of me to think she would still be there. It was probably silly of me to believe that the two years hadn't mattered. Still, I couldn't walk away like that. I turned back and waited for the store to empty completely.

More of the lights in the store were going out. Another few minutes and the manager would come out and the store would

be closed. I took a cigarette from my pocket and struck a
match, but the wind blew it out before I could get it to my
cigarette. I struck another one, this time cupping it in my hand
and turning my back to shield it from the breeze. The sound of
more girls' voices came to my ears, and among them I heard
another voice. I froze there, holding my breath. It was her
voice. I knew it. "Good night, Molly."

I stared at her. She was turned away from me as she spoke to
another girl, who was starting to walk in another direction. The
cigarette hung warm in my lips as I looked at her. In the dim
light of the street lamp it seemed as if she hadn't changed at all.
The same sweet mouth, soft white skin, rounded cheek, and
wide brown eyes she always had. And her hair—there was
never hair like hers, so black it was almost blue in the reflected
light. I took a step toward her and then stopped. I was afraid to
move, afraid to speak. I stood there helplessly, looking at
her.

The other girl had walked away, and she was starting to open
an umbrella. It was a gay red plaid umbrella, and as she lifted it
over her head, her eyes followed it upward, she saw me. Automatically she finished opening the umbrella; there was a
stunned unbelieving expression on her face. She took a tenta-
tive, hesitating step toward me and then stopped.

"Danny?" Her voice was a husky whispered question.

I was staring into her eyes. I could feel my lips move as I
tried to speak, but no words came out. The cigarette tumbled
from my mouth scattering tiny sparks against my clothing as it
fell toward the ground.

"Danny! Danny!" she was screaming as she ran across the
few feet separating us. The umbrella lay open and forgotten in
the doorway behind her.

She was in my arms now, kissing and crying and repeating
my name all at once. Her lips were warm, then cold, then warm
again. I could feel her tears against my cheek, her body shiver-
ing beneath her tiny short coat.

There was a mist before my eyes that was not rain as I looked
down at her. I closed them for a moment. I said her name:
"Nellie."

Her fingers were on my cheek and I bent my face toward her
and kissed her. Our lips clung together and melted away all the

time that had come between us. It was as if nothing had ever happened. This was all that mattered—being together again.

Her eyes were searching my face. "Danny, Danny," she whispered brokenly, "why did you do it? Not a word, not a word in all this time."

I looked at her dumbly. There was no answer in me. Only now I knew how wrong I'd been in what I had done. When I could speak, my voice was hoarse and shaking. "I couldn't help it, baby, I had to."

She was crying. The sobs in her came painfully to my ears. "We tried to find you, Danny, we tried so hard to find you. It was as if the world had swallowed you up. I almost died."

I held her very close to me. I brushed my lips through her hair. It was all that I remembered. Soft and sweet-smelling and fine to touch. A peace I had not known for a long time came into me.

Her face was hidden against my breast and her voice came muffled to my ears. "I couldn't stand it again, Danny."

Then everything suddenly became very simple. I knew how it had to be, how it should be. "You won't have to, baby. From now on, we'll be together. Always."

Her face was white and childlike and trusting as she looked up at me. "Honest, Danny?"

For the first time that day I could smile. "Honest, Nellie," I answered. "D'yuh think I came back just for a visit?" It was all straight in my mind. What I wanted, all I wanted. I didn't know I was going to quit Mike when I stood there, back on the midway with the rain falling on me, but I knew it now. I would see Mike and explain it to him. He would understand. I had come home to stay.

"From now on, Nellie," I said gently, "whatever I do, we do—together."

Chapter Ten

THE SAME old sign was still in the window:

CHOW MEIN 30¢ CHOP SUEY

The same old Chinese ushered us to our seats and handed us a tired fly-dirtied menu.

Her eyes were bright and shining. "You remembered."

I smiled at her.

Her hand reached across the table toward me. "We came here the first time, remember? The first day I met you."

I clasped her hand and turned it palm upward. I studied it with a pretended concentration. "There's a tall dark man about to come into your life," I said, imitating the carny fortune-teller's heavy voice.

She laughed and squeezed my hand. "Wrong color hair." Her eyes were suddenly serious. "Danny."

I could feel the laughter fade from me as I looked at her. She was going right inside me. "Yes, Nellie."

"I hope I'm not dreaming," she said quickly. "I hope I'm not upstairs in my bed dreaming, because I'll wake up in the morning and my eyes will be red and my sister will tell me I was crying in my sleep."

I raised her hand and kissed it quickly. "That ought to prove you're awake."

Her eyes were soft and swimming. "If I'm dreaming, I never want to wake up. I just want to sleep and dream." Her voice was husky.

I was able to smile now. "You're awake."

Her hand gripped mine tightly. "I love you, Danny. I loved you the minute I saw you, I guess. Sitting at the counter with a chocolate soda." Her eyes were earnest and searching again. "I

242

never went out with another fella. All the time you were away."

A strong guilt was in me. I couldn't meet her eyes. "Aw, go on," I said uncomfortably.

Her hand turned in mine. "Honest, Danny," she insisted. "Mamma wanted me to, but I didn't. Somehow I knew you would come back. I just knew it. Even before that girl came from Maxie Fields and told me."

I stared at her in surprise. "Girl?" I asked. "What girl?"

"Miss Dorfman," she answered quickly. "Don't you remember her? She and her brother came into the store a few days after Labor Day and said they had spoken to you and that you were all right and sent your love. They were very nice to do that on their way through New York. She said you had got into some trouble with Fields, but that you would be back as soon as things straightened out."

Suddenly I felt better. Sarah was okay. There were some people who were on the level. She had tried to help. Maybe if it wasn't for Sarah, Nellie wouldn't be here now. This way there was someone missing me, someone loving me, someone waiting for me. I wasn't altogether alone.

Her eyes were watching me earnestly. "Is it true what they said, Danny—that you took money from Fields to throw the fight that night?"

I didn't answer her question. Something else was more important. "They said?" I asked. "Who?"

"Mimi came to see me when she was looking for you. This was about a week after you'd disappeared. Zep and I took her up to Mr. Gottkin, and that's what Fields had told him." She was still watching my face. "Is it true what he said, Danny?"

I nodded slowly.

Her hand still held mine. There was a hurt echo in her voice. "Why did you do it, Danny? Why didn't you tell me?"

"There was nothing else I could do," I said in a low voice. "I needed the dough. I wanted Papa to buy a store with it, and Fields had the squeeze on me anyway. Then I couldn't lose the fight—even if I tried."

"But your father locked you out that night, Mimi told me," she said. "Why didn't you come to my house and say something?"

I stared at her. Nothing I could say to her could make

anything right. I had screwed up everything. "I had to get out. Fields would have been after me."

She closed her eyes wearily. "It's all so terrible, I still can hardly believe it. Two years of not knowing what happened to you, of not knowing who to believe, what to believe."

The pain on her face made me squirm inside. "Maybe it would have been better if I hadn't come back," I said bitterly. "Then you could have forgotten about me and everything would be all right."

Her eyes were looking inside me again. "Don't say that, Danny, don't ever say that again. I don't care what has happened or what you've done so long as you don't go 'way again."

I held onto her hand tightly as the waiter took our order. This was the way I thought it should be. And it was.

I pushed the plate away from in front of me and held a match to her cigarette, then to my own. She leaned back in her chair, letting the smoke blow idly through her lips.

"You got thin," she said.

I grinned at her. "Uh-uh." I denied it. "I weigh ten pounds more now than I did two years ago."

Her gaze was thoughtful. "Maybe you do," she conceded, "but you look thinner. Your face was rounder before—more boyish."

"Maybe it's because I'm not a kid any more."

She leaned forward quickly. "Yes, that's what it is," she said in a slightly surprised voice. "You were a boy when you went away. Now you're grown up."

"Isn't that what's supposed to happen?" I asked. "Nobody stays the same forever. You've grown up too."

Her fingers reached out and touched my face slightly. They rested a moment on the corners of my mouth, then swept gently along the ridge of my nose and across my chin. "Yes, you've changed," she said reflectively. "Your mouth is firmer, your chin is stronger. What did your folks say when they saw you?"

I kept my face blank of expression to screen the hurt of her question. "I haven't seen them," I answered.

"You haven't seen them?" Her voice was wondering. "Why, Danny?"

"I don't know whether I want to," I said flatly. "I don't think they want to see me. Not after all that happened. Not after I was thrown out."

Her hand gripped mine. "In some ways you're still a baby, Danny," she said gently. "I should think they would want to see you."

"Do you?" I asked bitterly, and yet inside me I was glad she had said that.

"I know Mimi would," she said confidently, "and your mother." She smiled up at me. "Do you know that Mimi met Mr. Gottkin when we went up there and they got married? And that Mimi has a little son?"

More surprises. "I knew they were married," I said quickly, "I saw it in the papers; but I didn't know about the baby. When did that happen?"

"Last year," Nellie said. "And now she is going to have another."

"How do you know so much about her?" I asked curiously.

"We call each other every few weeks," she said. "In case either of us heard about you."

I wondered at that. In some ways I felt good; that meant Mimi missed me too. "I couldn't believe it when I read she had married Sam," I said.

"He's been very good to her," Nellie said quickly. "He's done a lot for your folks too. He's helped your father out in business."

I drew a deep breath. That was one thing that had bothered me. During the last few years I had become certain that my father needed someone to help him. Now, at least, Sam would see to it that everything would be okay. I wondered what Sam thought about me, whether he was sore at me for what I did. I guessed he was and I couldn't really blame him.

"Are you going up to see them?" she asked.

I shook my head. "No."

"But, Danny, you should," she said quickly. "After all, they are your family."

I smiled mirthlessly. "That's not what my father said."

"What difference does that make?" she asked. "I know they don't like me and what they think about me, but if I were in your place, I would go to see them."

"I'm not going!" I said flatly. "I came home to you, not to them."

Chapter Eleven

WE HUDDLED together in the doorway, our lips pressed together in a fierce, burning intensity. There were hungers in me at this time of parting that left me no peace. Suddenly she was crying. Quiet, heart-wracking sobs that shook her body.

Gently I turned her face toward me. "What's the matter, honey?"

Her arms went frantically around my neck, pulling my face close to her cheek. "Oh, Danny, I'm so frightened! I don't want you to go away again. You'll never come back!"

"Baby, baby," I whispered, holding her close and trying to make her understand, "I'm not going away this time. It's just good night. I'll be back."

Her voice was an anguished cry against my ear. "You won't, Danny! I just know you won't!"

I could feel her tears against my cheek. I kissed her. "Don't cry, Nellie," I begged her. "Please."

Her voice was more wild, more frightened than before. "Don't go away, Danny, don't leave me again. If you do, I'll die!"

"I won't leave you, Nellie," I promised. I held her still against me until her outburst of tears had subsided.

Her face was hidden against my chest and I had to strain my ears to hear what she was saying. "If there was only some place we could go, some place we would be together, so I could just sit and look at you and say to myself: 'He's back, he's back!' "

She raised her head and looked up at me. In the darkness her eyes were deep and shining. "I don't want to go home tonight and sleep with my sister and wake up in the morning and find out it was only a dream. I want to go with you and hold onto your hand so that the early light of morning doesn't take you away from me."

"I'll be back in the morning," I said softly. "I love you."

"No, you won't," she retorted desperately. "If I let you go this time, you'll never come back. Something will happen and you won't come back." The tears began to fill her eyes again. "You said that last time, Danny. Remember what you said? 'No matter what happens, remember I love you.' And then you didn't come back. But I remembered and remembered." The tears were flooding down her cheeks. Her arms held me desperately. Her voice was heavy with a pain I could not know. "I can't do it again, Danny, I can't. I'd die this time. I can't let you go."

I tried to smile, to make a joke out of the way she felt. "We can't stay in this doorway all night, honey."

"Then find a place we can stay, Danny," she said, her eyes flashing up at me suddenly. "Find a place we can stay, where I can sit and talk and hold your hand until tomorrow comes and I believe that this is no dream."

I didn't like the look on the face of the tired desk clerk in the lobby of the run-down hotel when we walked in. I liked it less when after I had signed the register: "Daniel Fisher and Wife," the man looked up at me, saying with a faint smile: "Two dollars, please, in advance."

I put the money on the counter and asked him for the room keys. I could feel Nellie's hand on my arm as she stood slightly behind me.

The clerk picked up the two bills and held them in his hand. He looked down at the floor near my feet. "No luggage?" he asked.

"No luggage," I replied quickly. "We didn't expect to stay in town tonight."

The clerk's eyes filled with a knowing look. "I'm sorry, sir," he said in a politely impolite voice, "but in that case the room will cost five dollars. Hotel rules, you know."

I fought down an impulse to slug him. Not because he was hijacking me for three bucks that the hotel management would never see, but for that look in his eyes. He must have read in my face something of how I felt, because he shifted his gaze and looked down at the counter. With a quick glance at Nellie, I put three more dollars beside the register.

The clerk picked up the money. "Thank you, sir," he said, pushing a room key across the counter. "That's room 402, sir.

Take the self-service elevator down at the end of the hall to the fourth floor. You'll find it, second door from the elevator."

I locked the door and turned back to the room. An embarrassed silence descended upon us as we studied it. It was a small room. A washbasin stood in one corner opposite a closet door; there was a tiny dresser with a mirror to match against the wall next to it. Against the opposite wall was a small double bed. One chair stood next to the bed, and a leather-covered two-cushioned seat was placed in front of a narrow window.

Awkwardly I walked around the leather chair and looked out the window. "It's still rainin'," I said.

"Yes," she agreed in a small voice as if she were afraid it could be heard beyond the thin walls. She was watching me nervously.

I took off my hat and slicker. "I'll bed down on the club chair here," I said, walking to the closet. "You stretch out on the bed and try to get some sleep. It'll be morning soon."

I hung my coat and jacket in the closet. Quickly I slipped off my tie and draped it over one of the hangers. When I turned back to the room, she was still standing there looking at me. Her coat was still on. I smiled at her. "Don't be frightened."

"I'm not—any more," she answered softly. She crossed the room and stood in front of me. "I'm not afraid of anything when you're near me."

I kissed her lightly on the forehead. "Then take off your coat and lie down. You need the rest."

Silently she hung her coat in the closet while I sat down on the chair and slipped out of my shoes. I leaned back crossways on the couch and put my feet over one side and watched her. She was a funny kid—afraid to let me go, yet afraid to stay in the same room with me.

"Comfortable?" she asked me as she walked past the couch.

I nodded. "Yeah."

I heard her footsteps behind me. There was a faint click and the room slipped into darkness. I heard her walk to the far side of the bed. There was a faint rustle of clothing, then the sound. of her shoes dropping to the floor.

I looked through the darkness, but she was only a faint white shadow on the other side of the room, sinking softly onto the bed. There was the sound of bedsprings protesting at her weight, and then the only sound in the room was the sound of our breathing.

I placed my arms behind my head and tried to fit myself into the small couch. My legs, draped over the side of the chair, began to ache. I tried to shift them quietly, but my trousers made a slithering sound across the leather.

Her voice almost startled me. "Danny."

"Yes," I answered quietly.

"Are you awake?"

"Uh huh."

"Can't you sleep?"

I shifted position again. "I can sleep all right."

There was silence for a moment; then her voice came out of the darkness again. It was very low, I could hardly hear her. "Danny, you forgot something."

"What?"

"You didn't kiss me good-night," she whispered plaintively.

I was on my knees at the side of the bed. The sheet rustled as she sat up to meet me. Her lips were soft and warm against mine. Her arms were tight around my neck, and the sweet warmth of her body came up to me through the night.

My arms tightened around her, her heart was pounding against my chest. The small cold snap of her brassiere was in my hand and I pressed my fingers against it. I felt the brassiere suddenly loose in my fingers and her breasts were free against me. I bent my head quickly and pressed my lips to them.

Her hands held my head tightly and her voice was soft against my ear. "Hold me, Danny, hold me. Never let me go."

There was a choking in my throat. "I'll never let you go, darling."

Her voice was filled with wonder. "I love you to touch me, Danny. I love the feel of you close to me. I fill with a sweet pain for the nearness of you."

I raised my head to look at her in the darkness. There was a curious inconsolable pain inside me too, a longing that I'd never known before, a strain of emotion in me that was stronger than all the physical drives my body had ever known. I tried to speak, to tell her that I loved her, but I couldn't. My voice was lost in a muscular constriction of my throat.

Her fingers explored my face in the darkness. "Danny, your cheeks—Why, Danny, you're crying!"

The tears seemed to loosen the cords that knotted my voice. "Yes, I'm crying," I answered, almost defiantly.

I could hear her draw a deep breath, then her arms tightened around my neck, drawing my face down to the pillow on which she lay. Her lips pressed lightly against my eyelids. Her voice was very low and there was a warmth and sympathy in it that no human ever had for me before. "Don't cry, darling, don't cry," she whispered "I can't bear to see you unhappy."

Chapter Twelve

THE SUN pouring through the window reached my eyes. I turned in the bed to avoid the light, and my outstretched hand hit something soft in the bed. My eyes opened quickly.

She was lying on her side, her head resting on one hand, her eyes fixed on me. She smiled.

I stared at her for one unbelieving second, then my lips curved to match her smile. The night came back to me and an incredible warmth coursed through my body. "It's morning," I said.

She nodded and her hair cascaded down around her hand, framing her oval face in its blue-black softness. Her eyes went to the window, then back to my face. "It's morning," she agreed solemnly.

"You look even beautifuller in the morning," I said.

Her face flushed. "You look beautiful when you sleep," she replied in a low voice. "I was watching you. You look like a little boy then."

I sat up in the bed in mock anger, the sheet falling from me, leaving me naked to the waist. "You mean I don't look good when I'm awake?" I asked fiercely.

She laughed. Her fingers traced a pattern on my ribs. "You're skinny," she said. "Every bone on you sticks out. I'll have to fatten you up."

I grabbed her shoulders and pulled her face close to mine.

"You can start right now," I said, kissing her. "Mmmmmh. I'm so hungry I could eat you."

Her hands framed my face. "Danny," she asked in a low voice, her eyes searching mine earnestly, "do you love me?"

I turned my head quickly and nipped at her hand. "Course I love you." I was laughing.

Her hands twisted my face back to her. Her eyes were very serious. "Danny," she said sharply, "say it like you mean it. Like you said last night."

I stopped laughing "I love you, Nellie," I said soberly.

She closed her eyes. "Say it again, Danny," she whispered. "I love to hear you say it."

My lips came down on her throat. They moved slowly down to her shoulder, my face pushing away the sheet that covered her body. I cupped her breasts lightly in my fingers, then covered them with my face. "I love you, Nellie," I whispered, resting against her bosom.

She sighed slowly, the breath escaping her lips reluctantly, her eyes still closed. I could feel her body stirring beneath my touch, striving to be closer to me. Her voice was rich and filled with happiness. "I want you, Danny. God help me, I can never get enough of you."

We were passing the open doors of the church when she stopped suddenly and looked up at me. "Danny, come inside with me."

I looked at the church, then back to her questioningly. Her eyes pleaded with me silently. "Okay," I said.

She took my hand and I followed her into the church. In the dimness she turned toward me, her voice trembling. "Danny, you're not angry with me?"

I squeezed her hand reassuringly. "What for?" I asked.

A grateful smile crossed her lips. "I wouldn't feel right if I didn't come here first."

I watched her walk down the aisle and kneel before the altar. She clasped her hands in front of her and inclined her head, closing her eyes. She remained so for a little while, then rose to her feet and came back to me. There was a radiant smile on her face.

I held out my hand to her and she took it. Slowly we walked out of the church and down the steps to the street. We walked along silently for a moment, then she turned and looked up at me.

"I feel better now," she admitted shyly.

"I'm glad," I said.

"I—I just had to go in, Danny," she explained. "I wouldn't have felt right if I didn't."

I whistled a cab to a stop in front of us. "Good," I said slowly. "I wouldn't want a bride who didn't feel right."

I opened the door and helped her in, then got in beside her. The driver's face looked back inquiringly at me. "City Hall, please," I told him.

There were several other couples in the small waiting-room outside the door marked: "MARRIAGE CHAPEL," in frosted black letters on opaque glass. They were all as nervous as we were.

I looked at my watch again. Ten o'clock. Time for the chapel to open. I smiled at Nellie. Somehow it wasn't as bad in here as it had been outside where we got the license. I guess it was because out there we had so many questions to answer. But we lied just a little and got the license with less trouble than we had expected.

The door opened and everyone in the room started nervously. A thin-lipped, gray-haired woman came into the room and looked around importantly. She consulted a list in her hand and then glanced around the room again. "Mr. Fisher and Miss Petito will please come in," she announced.

I rose to my feet and turned to Nellie, holding out my hand. I could feel the eyes of the other couples on us. Nellie's hand was trembling in mine. I squeezed it reassuringly.

The woman nodded her head and we followed her into the chapel. She closed the door behind us and led us down to a podium. "Have you the license with you, young man?" she asked in a dry matter-of-fact voice.

"Yes, ma'am," I answered quickly, giving it to her.

She glanced at it briefly. A man came silently into the room through another door and stepped up on the podium. She handed the license to him without a word.

He looked down at us. "Don't be nervous"—he smiled slightly at his own joke—"it'll all be over in a minute."

We both tried to smile with him, but I don't suppose we made it. We were too nervous.

"Did you bring any witnesses with you?" he asked.

I shook my head. I could feel my face flush.

He smiled again. "Well, no matter." He turned to the woman. "Miss Schwartz, will you ask Mr. Simpson to step in for a minute?"

"Yes, Mr. Kyle." The gray-haired woman went out the door.

Mr. Kyle looked down at the license in his hand. "You're Daniel Fisher?" he asked of me.

"Yes, sir," I said.

"Age?" he asked.

"Twenty-three," I answered quickly, hoping he would not question my word. "Like it says there."

He shot me a brief suspicious glance. "I can read," he said succinctly. He looked at Nellie. "Eleanora Petito?"

She nodded silently and he continued to read the license in front of him. The door opened again and he looked up. The gray-haired woman had returned with a small birdlike man in a single-breasted suit.

Mr. Kyle looked down at us, smiling. "We're ready to begin now," he said, pushing the paper toward us. "If you will just sign this where I indicate—"

Nellie signed first in a nervous tiny hand. Then it was my turn, and after me the witnesses and finally Mr. Kyle. He blotted the ink dry on his signature and looked down at us importantly.

"Will you please join hands," he instructed us.

Nellie placed her hand in mine. It wasn't trembling now. I could feel faint beads of moisture gathering on my forehead.

I was glad the ceremony was fast. It seemed as if it were over almost before it had begun. The only words I could remember were the last few. I don't think the whole thing took more than two minutes.

"Do you, Eleanora Petito, take this man, Daniel Fisher, to be your lawful wedded husband?"

Her eyes were fixed on me. "I do," she answered in a solemn hushed voice.

He turned to me. "And do you, Daniel Fisher, take this woman to be your lawful wedded wife?"

I was watching her. Her eyes were soft and luminous, there were faint tears in the corners of them. "I—I do," I stammered huskily.

"Then by the authority vested in me by the City of New York, I hereby pronounce you man and wife." His voice rasped dryly at my ears. "You may kiss the bride, young man, and pay the clerk two dollars on the way out."

We kissed awkwardly and turned and hurried toward the door. His voice, drier than it had ever been during the ceremony, called us back. We turned around, startled.

He was smiling. His hand held a sheet of paper toward us. "Don't you think you ought to take your marriage certificate with you?" he asked.

I could feel my face flushing heavily as I went back and took the certificate from his outstretched hand. "Thank you, sir," I said quickly. I hurried back to Nellie and we went out the door.

The couples we had left in the waiting-room looked up at us. Some of them smiled. We smiled in return and almost ran out of the building.

We stood on the steps of City Hall and looked at each other. It was the same world we had left a few minutes ago, but it was changed now. We were married.

Nellie put her hand through my arm. "First we'll go down and tell my folks," she said proudly.

"Okay," I said.

"Then we'll go and tell your family," she added.

I looked at her in surprise. "What for?" I asked. "It's none of their business. Besides, they don't give a damn."

A firm resolution glowed in her eyes. "But I do. And I want them to know."

"But they don't care about us. I don't have to tell 'em nothin'," I protested.

She squeezed my arm, smiling. "Look, Danny Fisher, we're not going to start our marriage with a quarrel, are we?"

I smiled down at her. Her face was flushed and her eyes were happy and sparkling. "N-no," I answered.

"Then we'll tell them," she said definitely, starting down the steps.

"Okay, so we'll tell them," I agreed, walking beside her. "I'll even go on the radio and tell the whole world if you want me to."

She laughed happily and looked up at me. "Say, do you think that's a bad idea?"

Chapter Thirteen

THE DOORMAN reached out his hand and stopped us, an inquiring look on his face.

"Mr. Gottkin's apartment, please," I told him.

He nodded his head politely. "Mr. Gordon's apartment is C21. That's on the twenty-first floor."

We walked past him to the elevator and the door swung shut. The elevator man faced the front of the car stolidly. I looked at Nellie. "What's this 'Gordon' business?" I whispered.

"He changed his name legally last year," she whispered back.

I nodded my head. Logical. I guess he thought Gottkin might be good enough for Brooklyn, but in these fancy apartments on Central Park South, Gordon was more in keeping.

I looked at my watch. It was a few minutes after nine. After we had left Nellie's folks, we had gone out to dinner and then up to my folks' house. They lived in a nice place up in Washington Heights now, but nothing near as good as this. The doorman up there had told us that they usually had dinner at their daughter's house on Friday nights, so we came back downtown again.

I wondered what they would be like. A vague restlessness stirred inside me. Nellie's family hadn't been too bad.

Nellie's father had opened the door. His swarthy face looked angrily out at her. A flood of Italian poured from his lips, and in the middle of it she interrupted him with a few words in the same tongue.

Abruptly his speech came to a halt and he looked at me. I stared back at him. I couldn't tell what he was thinking because his face was still flushed from his anger. Then he silently stepped aside and let us into the apartment.

Nellie's mother descended upon us with loud shrieks. She encased Nellie in her arms and burst into tears. I stood awk-

255

wardly by the door, watching them. Nellie began to cry too. Her father and I just stood there helplessly looking at each other.

Suddenly there was a shout from the next room. "Danny!" Zeb was running toward me, a broad grin on his face, his hand outstretched. Then Nellie's kid sister came into the room and began to cry too. After a while things began to quiet down and her father reluctantly brought out a bottle of wine and they all joined in a toast to our health.

By the time the bottle was almost empty we were all on fairly good terms. I couldn't imagine they were tremendously pleased at what we had done, but they recognized and seemed to want to make the best of it. Mamma Petito even helped Nellie pack her few things so that we could go back to the hotel and wanted us to stay for supper. We begged off, saying we had to go uptown to my folks because we hadn't seen them yet.

The elevator stopped and the doors opened. The elevator operator stuck his head out the door and said: "Fourth door across the hall."

The small nameplate under the bell read: "SAM GORDON." I pressed the buzzer and somewhere in the apartment I could hear chimes ringing. "Real fancy," I murmured, looking at Nellie.

She seemed pale in the dim light of the hallway. She nodded her head silently as we waited for someone to answer the door. I took her hand. Her palms were moist.

The door opened and a small colored woman dressed in a maid's uniform looked out at us

"Mrs. Gott—er, Mrs. Gordon in?" I asked.

The Negress looked at me impassively. "Who shall I say is calling, sir?" she asked in a low, pleasant voice.

"Her brother," I said.

The maid's eyes widened slightly and she stepped aside. "Will you wait here for a moment?" she asked.

We stood in the foyer and looked around the room while the maid disappeared into the apartment. The foyer was as big as all of Nellie's apartment. We could hear the quiet murmur of voices coming from another room. Suddenly there was silence and we could hear the maid's voice.

"There's a young gen'mun an' a lady to see you, Miz Gordon."

I recognized Mimi's voice. "Did they say who they were?" She sounded puzzled.

The maid's voice was stolid. "Yes'm. He say he your brother an'—"

She never finished the sentence. "It's Danny!" I heard Mimi scream. "It's Danny!" Then she was standing in the foyer looking at us.

We stood there for a moment. At first glance I didn't think she had changed, but then as we drew closer I could see that she had. Her eyes were darker than ever and there were faint bluish circles beneath them as if she didn't sleep too well. Maybe it was because she was pregnant again and her belly pushed forward in front of her, I didn't know, but there were tight small lines in the corner of her mouth that I had never noticed before.

Then her arms were pulling my face down to her and she was kissing me. "Danny," she whispered. "I'm so glad to see you." There were tears standing in the corners of her eyes.

I smiled at her. I was glad to see her too. Funny, but I hadn't known how much I'd missed her. When I had been home we fought all the time, but that was forgotten now.

She grabbed my hand excitedly and pulled me toward the other room. "Mamma and Papa are here," she said.

I cast a frantic glance over my shoulder toward Nellie. She smiled slightly at me and nodded her head; she was following us. I let Mimi lead me into the other room.

We were standing on a few steps that led down into a living-room. Mamma and Papa were sitting on a couch with its back toward us but they were turned partly around, looking at me. Mamma held one hand clutched against her bosom, her eyes almost closed. Papa's face wore a look of dull, guarded surprise, punctuated by a long cigar that hung motionless from his lips. Sam was standing facing them, holding a long drink in his hand, his back resting against a large imitation fireplace. A curious light was glowing in his eyes.

Mimi led me around the couch in front of Mamma and let go of my hand. She was staring up into my eyes as if she were trying to read in them all that had happened since we last saw each other.

"Hello, Mamma," I said quietly

Her hand touched the front of my coat and dropped along

my sleeve until she found my hand. Her eyes began to fill. She pulled me down to her, her lips pressing against my hands. "My Blondie," she whispered brokenly, "my baby."

I stood there looking at her bent head. Her hair was all gray now. This was the moment I had been afraid of. I hadn't been afraid of how they would receive me; it was really how I would feel about them. Curious how calm I was, how detached I felt. It was almost as if I were watching this from a seat in the movies. I wasn't really a part of it. It was another guy named Danny Fisher, and he had gone away two years ago and never really come back.

That was what happened. The years and the loneliness had driven a wedge between us that no surge of emotion on either side could ever heal in me. A reluctant sorrow came over me. What great thing had been lost to us, what closeness we would never know again!

I bent and kissed the top of her head. "I'm sorry, Mamma," I said. But no one really knew what I was sorry for.

I straightened up and looked for Papa. He had walked to the far end of the room and was standing there looking at me. There was a frightened, lonely look in his eyes. Slowly I withdrew my hand from Mamma and walked toward him. The only sound in the room besides that of my footsteps was that of Mamma's weeping. I held out my hand toward my father. "Hello, Papa."

His eyes wavered for a moment, then he took my hand. "Hello, Danny." His voice was shaking but reserved.

"How've you been, Papa?" I asked.

"All right, Danny," he replied shortly.

Then we ran out of words and a subtle tension began to creep into the room. I nodded to Sam. He nodded back, but didn't speak. The others stared at me silently.

Disappointment gathered in me. This was about how I thought it would be. It didn't really make any difference whether I had come back or not. Despite myself I could feel bitterness creep into my voice.

"It's been two years," I said, my eyes going slowly from face to face. "Aren't any of you going to ask what I did those two years? How I feel?"

Mamma was still weeping softly, but no one answered. Slowly I turned back to my father. I looked at him coldly. "Aren't you going to ask? Or doesn't it really matter?"

Papa didn't answer.

It was Mimi that came to me, Mimi who took my arm and said softly: "Of course it matters. It's just that we're so surprised we don't know what to say."

I was still watching Papa. I could feel an icy calm descend on me. I had been right: something had gone from us that night the door had been closed to me. It was gone and not all that the years might bring could ever bring it back. I had wanted to see them and not wanted to. Now it didn't seem important—only that I stood among them feeling like a stranger.

Mimi tried to lead me away from Papa. "Come," she was saying, "sit down and tell us what you did. We all missed you."

I looked past her across the room. Nellie was standing in the entrance, forgotten by the others, watching us with wide, pain-filled eyes. Somehow I knew that it was not her pain she felt, but mine. I smiled slowly at her and looked down at Mimi. "I can't stay," I said gently. I didn't want to hurt her; at least she had been trying. "I've got to be going. I got things to do."

"But you can't go now, Danny," Mimi protested. The tears came into her eyes again. "You just came back."

My gaze went across the room to Nellie. "I've not come back," I said quietly, "not really. I only tried."

"But, Danny—" Mimi was crying against my shoulder. I knew how she felt, what she was crying for, but it was no use. It was something that could never be again.

I put my arm around her shaking shoulder and walked back across the room with her. "Stop it, Mimi," I whispered. "You're only making it worse." I left her at the couch and went to Nellie. I took her hand and turned back to face them. "The only reason I came tonight," I said in a low voice, "was because of my wife. She thought we should tell you that we were married this morning."

I saw the expressions that appeared on their faces—my mother's pain, the grim knowing look in Papa's eyes. I writhed inside. "She was the only one that really wanted me back," I said quickly.

I waited a moment for them to speak, but they were silent. Nellie's family hadn't liked our marriage any more than mine, but at least they had acted like human beings. My family had nothing to say, no words of happiness for us. Nothing.

The pain inside me went away rapidly, leaving behind it a cold numb feeling. I kissed Mamma's cheek. She was weeping. I kissed Mimi and stopped in front of my father. His face was bitter and masklike. I passed him without a word or a gesture.

I squirmed restlessly in the bed. I was conscious that I had been crying in my sleep, but now I was awake and my eyes were dry. I tried to lie quietly so that I wouldn't disturb her.

We had undressed in silence in the small hotel room. At last I asked, smiling wryly: "You knew all the time why I didn't want to see them, didn't you?"

She nodded silently.

"And yet you made me go." My voice was almost bitter.

Her hands were on my shoulder, her eyes on mine. "You had to go, Danny," she said earnestly. "Otherwise it might have been between us all our lives. You had to find out for yourself."

I turned away from her, my shoulders heavy and sagging. "Well, I found out all right."

She came after me, her hand clutching my arm. "Now it's over and you can forget."

"Forget?" I began to laugh. There were some things she didn't know. "How can you forget? All the things we had together—the hopes, the fears, the good and the bad. It's easy for you to say forget, but how can I? Can I cut their blood out of me, let it run into the sink and down the drain and out of my life forever? Good or bad, how can I forget? Can you forget your own parents? Does right or wrong mean more than the flesh that ties you together?"

Her voice was pleading. "No, Danny, you don't understand. That's not what you forget. That's what you remember. It's the hurt that you must forget, the hurt that will turn you into something you're not. The hurt that will make you hard and bitter and angry like you are now!"

I didn't understand her. "How can I forget that?" I asked helplessly. "It's all part of it."

"It's not, Danny," she cried, pressing herself against me and kissing my lips. "It's something else altogether. I'll make you forget the hurt. I'll make you remember only the good."

My eyes widened. "How can anyone do that?"

"I can and will," she whispered, looking up at me, her eyes deep and earnest. "I have so much love for you, my husband, that you will never need for affection from anyone."

Then I understood. I caught her hands and pressed their open palms to my lips gratefully. She had made me a promise and I knew that it would be kept. I knew that in the times to come, good or bad, I would find my comfort in her, my strength in her; that no matter what might happen, I would never be alone again.

Moving Day

THE WOODEN steps creaked comfortably under our feet as we climbed the stairway. It was a friendly sound, as if these old stairs had given welcome to many a newly married couple like ourselves. I liked the sound.

The valises I carried were light and I didn't mind their weight. Not that they weighed very much anyway; there wasn't much we had to bring along in the way of clothing. Later when I got a job and made some dough we could get ourselves a few things. Right now all the dough we could scrape together went into furnishing our new apartment.

She stopped in front of a door on the fourth floor and looked over her shoulder at me, smiling. She held a key in her hand.

I smiled back at her. "Open the door, baby, it's ours."

She put the key in the lock and turned it. The door swung open slowly, but she stood in the doorway, an expectant look on her face. I dropped the valises, bent forward, and scooped her up. I felt her arms around my neck as I crossed the threshold. On the other side I looked down into her face. She kissed me. Her lips were soft and trembling, she was light in my arms.

"God bless our happy home, Danny Fisher," she whispered.

I stood there holding her and looking into the apartment. It wasn't a big place. They don't come so big for twenty-five a month. Three rooms and bath. Everything painted white. You don't get colors for that kind of dough. But it was clean. And it had steam heat and hot water and room enough to do a lot of living.

Room enough for us to shoot nine hundred bucks of furniture: a couch and some chairs for the parlor; a big double bed and a dresser with a mirror for the bedroom; a kitchen set and some dishes, pots and pans. It was a lot of dough, but it was worth it even if it left us with next to nothing in the bank. At least we wouldn't have to worry about some collector moving in behind us.

I put her down.

"Bring the bags into the bedroom," she told me.

"Yes, ma'am," I said snappily, picking up the valises and following her. Casually I dropped them on the bed. They sank softly into the mattress.

"Danny, take those dirty bags off the bed!'" she exclaimed sharply. "This isn't a hotel, this is ours!"

I laughed aloud as I looked at her. Give a woman a place of her own and the first thing she'll do is take charge. But she was right. I put the bags on the floor and sat down on the bed. "C'mere," I said, bouncing up and down on the mattress.

She looked at me suspiciously. "What for?"

"I wanna show yuh somethin'," I said, continuing to bounce on the mattress.

She took a hesitant step toward me and then stopped. I reached out a hand and pulled her toward me quickly. She fell against me and I rolled flat on the bed, her weight on top of me.

"Danny, what's got into you?" She was laughing.

I kissed her.

She pulled her face away, still laughing. "Danny!" she protested.

I pushed at the mattress with my hand. "Listen," I told her, "no squeaks. Just like the salesman said."

"Danny Fisher, you're crazy!" Her teeth were very white when she smiled.

I pulled her down on me again. "Crazy about you," I said.

"Oh, Danny," she whispered, "Danny, I love you."

My lips were against her throat. Her skin was smooth, like the satin on a dress in a Fifth Avenue window. "I love you, baby."

She was looking into my eyes. There was an expression on her face that turned my insides into mush. She could always do that—just by looking at me. "Danny, you won't be sorry," she said earnestly.

"Sorry about what?"

"That you married me," she said seriously. "I'll be a good wife to you."

I caught her face in my hands. "It's the other way round, baby. I hope you won't be sorry you married me."

I could feel her tears against my fingers. "Oh, Danny," she said very softly, "I'll never be sorry."

The doorbell rang just when we had finished hanging the curtains. "I'll get it," I said walking to the door and opening it.

Nellie's mother and a priest stood there. Mrs. Petito had a small shopping-bag in her hand. She smiled at me. "Hello, Danny."

"Hello, Mamma Petito," I said. "Come in."

She hesitated a moment, embarrassed. "I brought Father Brennan with me."

I turned to the priest and put out my hand. "Please come in, Father," I said quietly.

A look of relief crossed my mother-in-law's face as the priest took my hand. His grip was firm and friendly. "Hello, Danny," he said in a professionally hearty voice. "I'm glad to meet you."

Nellie's voice came from the bedroom. "Who is it, Danny?"

"Your mother and Father Brennan are here," I called back to her.

She appeared quickly in the doorway, her face slightly flushed. She ran to her mother and kissed her, then turned to the priest and put out her hand. "I'm glad you could come, Father," she said.

He pushed her hand aside in a friendly manner. "Come now, my child," he said, smiling, "sure and ye have a better greeting for an old friend and admirer than that." He placed both hands on her shoulders and gave her a resounding kiss on the cheek.

Mrs. Petito looked at me doubtfully and placed the shopping-bag down on the floor. "I bring some things for the house," she said.

Nellie opened the bag excitedly and looked in it. She spoke excitedly in Italian, and her mother answered her. Then Nellie turned to me and explained: "Mamma brought some food to the house so that we should never be hungry."

I turned to Mrs. Petito. People may be different, but their basic concerns are the same. I remembered when we moved to the house in Brooklyn my mother had brought some salt and a loaf of bread to the house for the very same reason. "Thank you, Mamma," I said gratefully.

Her hand patted my cheek. "You're welcome, my son," she said. "I only wish we could do more."

Nellie looked at them. "How about some coffee?" she asked. "Danny will run down and get some cake and we'll have a little party."

Mamma Petito shook her head. "I gotta go home an' cook supper. Father Brennan, he come along to wish Nellie luck."

Nellie turned to the priest smiling. "Thank you, Father. I'm so glad you could come. I was afraid you might—"

The priest interrupted her. "Oh no, Nellie, nothing like that. Of course I'm disappointed that you didn't let me marry you, but this is the next best thing."

A look of doubt crossed her face. "But I thought because of him we couldn't get married in church."

The priest turned to me, smiling affably. "Would you object to being married in the true church, son?" he asked.

Nellie answered before I could. "That's not a fair question, Father," she said quickly. "Neither of us spoke about it before."

He looked at her. The smile was gone from his face now. "You realize of course, my child, that while your marriage is recognized by the church, it is not sanctioned by it."

Nellie's face was pale. "I know that, Father," she answered in a low voice.

"Have you ever thought about children?" he continued. "What religious benefits they might receive but will be deprived of?"

This time I answered. "If I understand rightly, Father, the church will not discriminate against children because of the faith of their parents."

He looked at me. "Does that mean you are willing to allow your children to be brought up within the church?"

"It means, Father," I said simply, "that my children will be free to believe in what they choose. Their faith or lack of it will be a matter of their own election, and until such time as they are old enough to decide for themselves, I am perfectly willing to allow them to attend their mother's church."

Nellie came over to me and took my hand. "I think it's a little early to be talking about things like that. After all, we've only been married a short while."

The priest looked at us. "As a Catholic, Nellie, you are fully aware of your responsibilities. Therefore it is always best to decide things like this beforehand so that no unhappiness may result."

Nellie's face was white. She spoke through motionless lips. "I appreciate your concern and your visit, Father. Please feel sure that we will do what is right for both of us, and feel free to visit us again when you're in the neighborhood."

I could have kissed her for that. In the nicest way possible she had told him to go peddle his papers somewhere else.

He knew it too, but not a sign crossed his face. "A priest's life," he sighed, "is sometimes filled with many difficult decisions. He is only a human being in the last analysis, and like all people can only pray for divine guidance in his actions. I hope and pray, my child, that my visit with you will have a good and proper effect."

"We are grateful for your prayers, Father," my wife replied politely, her hand still in mine.

I followed Father Brennan slowly to the door, where he put out his hand. "Glad to have met you, my son," he said, but there was no enthusiasm in his voice. I'm sure he thought I was the devil's child from the way he shook my hand this time.

The door closed behind him, and Nellie spoke to her mother rapidly and angrily in Italian. Her mother raised her hand in protest and answered in a stumbling fashion. Tears came to her eyes. As the argument grew hot and heavy, I stood there dumbly, not knowing what they were saying. Then as quickly as it had begun, it was over and Nellie's mother clasped her arms about her daughter and kissed her.

Nellie turned to me apologetically. "My mother is sorry she brought him here. She meant well and hopes you are not insulted."

I looked at her mother for a moment; then I smiled. "Don't be sorry, Mamma Petito," I said slowly. "I know that you meant everything for the best."

Then Mamma Petito's arms were around me and she was kissing my cheek. "You're a good boy, Danny," she said stumblingly. "All I ask is that you take good care of my Nellie."

"I will, Mamma," I promised, looking at Nellie. "You can be sure that I will."

After her mother had gone we finished straightening up the apartment. It was still early afternoon. I sat down in the parlor and turned on the radio. Soft music filled the room. It was the right kind of music to start a new day: Frankie Carle's *Sunrise Serenade.*

Nellie came into the parlor and stood next to me. "What would you like for dinner?" she asked seriously.

"You mean you can cook too?" I asked mischievously.

A reproving look crossed her face. "Don't be silly, Danny," she said quickly. "What would you like?"

"What do you want to cook for?" I asked. "We'll eat out tonight and celebrate."

"Uh-uh." She shook her head. "It's too expensive. It's time we started watching our money until you get a job. After that we can eat out if you like."

I looked at her with a new respect. It had been growing on me all day that she was a lot more grown up than I had given her credit for being. I got to my feet and turned off the radio. "Make whatever you like and surprise me," I said. "I'll take a run uptown to the agencies and see if there's anything doing."

The bright sunlight blinded me for a moment as I came out of the hallway, and I stood in front of the house for a moment. Then I started toward the subway station. A shadow fell across my path and stood in front of me. Without looking up, I started to walk around it. A hand fell on my arm and a familiar voice came to my ears.

"Now that you're back and settled down, Danny, the boss feels you owe him a visit." I didn't have to look up to know who it was. I had been expecting him ever since I had returned. I knew they would never forget.

Spit was standing there, a slight smile on his lips but none in his eyes. He looked very neat, too, in his dark expensive-appearing tailored suit and freshly laundered shirt. He had so much clothing on that for a moment I almost didn't believe it was him.

"I'm in a hurry," I said, trying to step around him again.

His hand tightened on my arm. His other hand moved slightly in his jacket pocket. I could see the dull outline of the gun he held there. "You're not in that much of a hurry, Danny, are you?" he asked.

I shook my head. "No, I'm not," I agreed.

He gestured toward the curb. A car was standing there, its motor running "Get in," he said sharply.

I opened the door and climbed into the back seat. The Collector was sitting there. "Hello, Danny," he said quietly, and hit me in the stomach.

The pain tore through my guts and I doubled up and fell forward on the floor of the car. I heard the door behind me close quickly and the car started off.

Spit's voice seemed to float in the air over me. "Cut out the rough stuff The boss'll be sore."

The Collector's voice was sullen. "I owed the son of a bitch that."

Spit grabbed my collar and pulled me onto the seat beside him. "Don't say anything to the boss about this or next time yuh'll get worse."

I nodded my head and swallowed the vomit that threatened to rise in my throat. A few minutes passed before I was feeling good enough to realize what he had said. "Next time"—that meant, for some reason I didn't know, that I was off the hook. I wondered what had happened. I knew Maxie Fields was not the forgiving type.

The auto swung to a stop in front of his store. Spit got out of the car in front of me, the Collector behind. Together we walked into the narrow hallway beside the store and up the stairs to Fields's apartment. Spit knocked at the door.

"Who is it?" Fields's voice roared through it.

"It's me, boss," Spit answered quickly. "I got Danny Fisher with me."

"Bring him in," Fields shouted.

Spit opened the door, pushed me through it, and followed me into the room My stomach still hurt, but I was beginning to feel better At least I could stand up straight now.

Maxie Fields stood like a huge Gargantua behind his desk. His eyes glittered at me. "So you couldn't stay away?" he said heavily, coming around his desk toward me.

I didn't answer—just watched him coming toward me. I wasn't afraid of him this time. Spit had tipped me off without knowing it. I saw Maxie's open hand flying at my face and instinctively ducked away from it.

A sharp stabbing pain in my kidneys straightened me up. Spit, standing behind me, had jabbed me with the butt end of his knife. This time I caught Maxie's swing flush on the cheek. I rocked on my feet unsteadily, but didn't speak. Talking wouldn't do any good and it might only make things worse.

Fields grinned at me viciously. "You're not the only one who couldn't stay away." He turned and bellowed into the other room: "Ronnie, bring me a drink. An old friend of yours has come to pay us a visit."

I turned to the other door, my ears ringing. Sarah was standing there, her wide eyes fixed on mine, a drink in her hand. For a second we stared at each other, then her eyes fell and she walked slowly across the room to Fields. Silently she handed him the drink.

He was smiling maliciously at her. "Ain't you gonna say hello to your old friend?"

She turned to me, her eyes dull and vacant. "Hello, Danny."

"Hello, Sarah," I answered.

Fields looked at me, the drink still in his hand. "Just like old times, isn't it, Kid?" He took a sip of the drink and almost emptied the glass. "Nothing has changed, has it?"

I was watching Sarah's face. It was still and impassive, with no flicker of expression. "Nothing has changed," I answered quietly.

"Ronnie couldn't stay away from her sweetie. She came back all by herself, didn't she?" Fields asked.

I thought I saw a moment's fire in her eyes, but it passed too quickly to be sure. "Yes, Max," she said dully, like an automaton.

Fields pulled her close to him. "Ronnie can't live without her Max, can she?"

This time I could see her lips trembling. "No, Max."

He shoved her away angrily. "Get in the other room," he roared.

Without looking at me, she walked toward the door, paused for a moment in the doorway, then went right on through without looking back.

Fields turned to me. "No one gets away from Maxie Fields," he boasted.

I looked at him. He didn't have to tell me that; he had convinced me. I wondered what he'd done to bring her back. I wondered if anything had happened to Ben.

He went behind his desk and sat down heavily, his

fat-covered eyes staring at me. "Remember that, Danny. Nobody ever gets away from Maxie Fields."

"I'll remember," I said.

He was breathing heavily as he stared at me. After a moment he raised his glass to his lips and finished the drink. "Okay," he said, putting the tumbler down on the desk in front of him, "you can go now."

I stood there unbelieving, not daring to move, wondering what was up his sleeve now. It was too easy. He wasn't going to let me off that easy—not Maxie Fields.

"You heard me!" he roared in sudden anger. "Get out and stay out of my way. The next time yuh won't be so lucky. I might not be feelin' so good!"

I stood there, not moving. I was afraid to turn around.

The telephone on his desk began to ring and he picked it up. "Yeah," he barked into it. There was a crackle of a voice, and a subtle change came across his face. "Hello, Sam," he said cordially. The voice in the phone began to crackle again and he covered the mouthpiece with his hand.

"Throw him out if he won't go by himself, Spit," he said almost cordially.

I didn't need another invitation. I got out of there in a hurry. It wasn't until I was in the familiar dirty streets again that I began to realize what had happened. I still didn't know why he had let me go, unless—there could be only one reason. Sarah had made a deal with him. That's why she didn't look at me or speak to me. That must be it. It was the only thing I could think of.

I looked at my wristwatch. It was only two thirty; I still had time to run uptown and case the agencies. No use getting back early or Nellie would wonder why I hadn't gone, and I didn't want to tell her about this. She would only worry.

I covered about four agencies, but there was nothing doing. They all told me to come back in the morning. I quit a little after four and started back downtown thinking I'd have to get an early start tomorrow if I wanted a job. There weren't many of them around.

She made chicken cacciatore and spaghetti and we had a bottle of Chianti that her mother had brought. The meal was delicious, but I had to force myself to eat, because my stomach hurt. Still, I packed enough away to make it look good.

"Yuh want help with the dishes?" I asked.

She shook her head. "Go into the parlor and turn on the radio," she said. "I'll only be a few minutes."

I went inside and sank into the club chair by the radio and turned it on. The voice of the Kingfish echoed through the room and I listened delightedly to Andy's efforts to get his friend a job.

That seemed to be everybody's worry then: to get a job. Mine too. Would be good when I got one, though. We could save a few bucks. Maybe when things got a little better and I made a little more dough, we could buy a little house. Out in Brooklyn, maybe in my old neighborhood. I liked it there. The streets were clean and the air was fresh. It wasn't like down here on East Fourth and First Avenue. But this was a better place than most in the neighborhood. The house was clean. It was a four-story, twelve-family affair, and it didn't look as run down as the others. It didn't make for a bad beginning.

I heard Nellie coming into the room and looked up. "All through?"

She nodded. "I told you I wouldn't be long," she said proudly.

I pulled her down to me. She rested her head on my shoulder, her eyes looking up at my face. We sat there quietly. I felt peaceful and happy and content.

"Danny, what're you thinking?"

I smiled down at her. "About how lucky I am," I said. "I got everything I ever wanted."

"Everything, Danny?"

"Just about," I answered, looking into her eyes. "What else is there to want? I got my girl, m' own home. All I need now is a job an' everything'll be rosy."

Her eyes turned serious. "I meant to ask you, Dannny, how did things look? Was there anything?"

I shook my head. "I can't tell yet, baby," I said lightly. "After all, I did go out in the afternoon and was in only a few places. I'll know more when I get out in the mornin'."

A worried look crossed her face. "The paper says that unemployment is at an all-time high."

"The paper," I scoffed, "says anything that'll make a headline."

"But look at all the families on relief! That must mean something."

"Sure it does." I looked down at her confidently. "Those people jus' don't wanna work. You can get a job if you want to bad enough. I want to work. I'll get a job."

"But, Danny," she went on, "not all of them are like that."

"Look, Nellie," I told her. "Only bums'll go on relief. Not me. We'll never have to worry about that."

She was silent for a moment, then her face turned up to me again. "But what if you don't get a job for a while?"

I smiled at her. "We'll manage. We don't have to worry about that. You're still workin'."

"But what if I can't work, if I have to stop?" She blushed slightly and looked away. "What if I become pregnant?"

"You don't have to," I said pointedly. "There are ways to prevent that."

The blush left her face suddenly, leaving it pale and nervous. "Catholics don't believe in it. It's against the religion. It's a sin," she explained, looking down at the floor.

"Then what do they do?" I asked. "Yuh just can't go around pregnant all the time."

"There are certain times that are safe." She didn't meet my eyes.

I began to feel slightly embarrassed. There was much I had to learn. "But what if it happens some other time?" I asked curiously.

She still avoided my eyes. "It doesn't. You don't let it happen."

"That's the bunk," I said strongly. "We'll do what everybody else does." The sound of a sniffle came to my ears. "My God!" I exclaimed. "What are you crying about? I didn't say anything wrong!"

She flung her arms around my neck and pressed her cheek against mine. "I can't do it, Danny!" she cried. "I can't do it. I've done enough wrong things as it is. I can't make it any ___!"

___er close to me. Her body was rigid with a fear I didn't ___nd. Even though she had stood up to him, that visit from the priest had loused things up for sure. "Okay, Nellie, okay," I said soothingly. "We'll do it your way."

Her tears turned into a radiant smile. "Oh, Danny," she exclaimed, kissing me with quick little kisses all over my face, "you're so good to me! I love you!"

"I love you too, baby," I said, smiling down at her, "but is it safe?"

All the Days of My Life
THE FOURTH BOOK

Chapter One

SHE walked past the cosmetic counter, down along the fountain to my station, and climbed up on a stool. She squirmed there for a moment, getting her seat right so that her lungs showed over the counter. Out of the corner of my eye I could see Jack, the boss, watching her. I didn't blame him a bit. She had a healthy pair of lungs.

I finished mopping my face with the cold towel before I picked her up. It was one of those hot, muggy nights you hit in New York in October when the last piece of summer fights its losing battle. I leaned over the counter and smiled at her.

"Yes, miss?" I asked, checking the clock on the wall behind her.

"A short Coke with lime, Danny." Her eyes, as she smiled back, were as heavy and sultry as if she were taking me to bed.

"Comin' right up," I replied, sexing her right back. Without turning around, I reached behind me and took a glass from the shelf. Her smile grew deeper and warmer.

I held the glass under the spigot and goosed the pump. The brown syrup spurted forth and I pushed the glass under the seltzer spigot, pushing the handle back with the heel of my hand. While the glass filled, I squeezed an eighth of a lime into it, jacked it with a spoon, then cut off the seltzer.

She had an unlit cigarette in her mouth when I put the Coke down in front of her. I beat her to the match. Its dancing light flickered in her eyes as I held it for her. "Thanks, Danny." She glowed at me.

"Nothin'," I said, tapping out a straw for her.

She took the straw daintily from my fingers and stirred it slowly in the glass. "They ought to have places on the subway

274

where you can get a Coke if you're thirsty on a night like this," she said before sipping her drink.

I grinned at her. "I wouldn' like that a' tall," I said, stretching the South in my speech. All soda jerks were supposed to be from the South. "Then I'd never get to see yuh."

She gave me an appreciative smile and pushed her lungs out a little farther. I gave them the expected, appreciative double-O before I walked up the front of the counter to Jack. It was all part of the game. The kids that sat in front of your counter expected it. It was their way of getting hunk for the way they lived. Romance at a soda fountain. Real cheap for a nickel Coke.

"After one o'clock, Jack," I said. "Clean up now?"

From the register Jack looked up at the clock. He nodded his head, his eyes going back to the girl. "Yeah, Danny," he said, grinning. "It must be that blond hair and blue eyes that gets 'em."

I waved my hand modestly. "Nuts," I answered. "It's my clean-cut red-blooded American look."

He shook his head. "I don' know what it is, but four outta five heads that come in here pass me up to set down at your station. An' the come-ons yuh get! Man, I'd be eatin' muh heart out all the time."

I grinned at him. "Don' be jealous, Jack. I may attract the dames, but you got all the dough."

"Honest, Danny?" he queried. "Yuh never bother with 'em at all?"

"You know me, Jack. A married man with a kid's got no time to fool aroun', an' besides not havin' the time I ain't got the dough." I checked the broad in the mirror behind the counter. She smiled at me and I smiled back. "On top o' that yuh keep away from these chicks. They all hold C.T.U. cards an' if yuh make a move they holler."

He grinned again and looked down at the register. "I don' believe a word yuh're saying," he said in a friendly voice. "But it's okay to start cleanin' up now."

I walked back down the counter and punched out a ticket for the girl. I dropped it on the counter in front of her just as she finished her drink. "Thank you, miss."

I pocketed the nickel she left for me as she clambered down

off the stool, and turned back to the fountain. It was one fifteen but I didn't need the clock to tell me that. I was tired. My legs were weary and my back ached from the steady seven hours and fifteen minutes I had been on my feet that night since six p.m. But what the hell, I told myself as I began to pull the pumps, it was a job, and jobs weren't too easy to get this fall of 1939, even if a war was going on in Europe. I ought to know, I'd been looking long enough.

Almost three years to be exact. Sure I got some jobs, but they didn't stick. Something always happened and then I'd be hitting the streets again. It wasn't so bad while Nellie was working. We could manage then. But when Vickie came along, things were a little different. We ran head-first into something that time and economics stacked up against us.

I remembered the day Nellie came home from work and told me she was going to have a baby. There must have been a funny look on my face because she put out her hand and touched my arm.

"Danny, you don't look pleased?" she asked, a hurt deep in her dark eyes.

"I'm pleased all right," I said shortly.

She drew closer to me. "Then what's the matter?"

"I was wonderin' what we're gonna use for dough."

"You'll get a job," she said. "Things can't keep up like this forever."

I turned away and lit a cigarette. "That's what I keep tellin' myself," I said.

She turned me back to her. The hurt on her face went deeper than just her eyes. "You're not happy that we're having a baby," she said accusingly.

"Why shouldn't I be happy?" I asked, letting the smoke out through my nose. "I'm dancing in the streets. It's great. We'll be lucky if we don't wind up livin' there, the way things are going. I never been so happy in my life."

Her eyes fell from mine. "I couldn't help it, Danny," she whispered apologetically. "I—it just happened."

"Sure, it just happened," I said sarcastically. "There's a dozen ways to keep things like that from happenin', but my wife don't believe in 'em. She's gotta believe in some crackpot idea about rhythm. She's gotta—"

"Danny!"

I stopped talking and looked at her. Her eyes had filled with tears. I dragged at my cigarette silently.

Through her tears she asked plaintively: "Danny, don't you want a baby?"

The pain in her voice ran all the way through me and wound up in my heart. I pulled her to me roughly. "I'm sorry, Nellie," I said quickly. "Of course I want a baby. It's just that I'm worried. Babies cost dough, and that we ain't got."

She smiled tremblingly through her tears. "Babies don't ask for much," she whispered. "All they need is love."

But it hadn't been quite that easy. They needed a few bucks too. I remembered how, when the last buck we had saved ran out, we had gone downtown to the relief office and applied for help. The way the clerk had looked at us—at me, then at Nellie with the child big in her—as if to ask what right did we have to bear children when we couldn't take care of ourselves. There had been the endless questionnaires to fill out, and the investigators had come to the house at all hours. The endless probing until there was no part of our lives that remained private, that could be called our own.

I remembered when the investigator had brought us the first check. She was a fat woman wearing an old fur coat. "This is for food and other necessities of life," she had said as I took the check from her.

I had nodded without meeting her eyes.

"If we hear," she continued in a flat warning tone, "that you have spent any part of this on whisky or gambling or any purpose for which it is not intended, we will immediately stop further checks."

I could feel my face flaming, but I didn't look at her. I couldn't. The way I felt, I would never be able to look at anyone again.

That was before Vickie was born. The first time I saw her was when the nurse in the city hospital let me peek through the glass-paneled doors. Vickie, my daughter, my baby. Little and pink and blonde, like me. I thought I would swell up and bust. I knew than that I had done nothing to be ashamed of, nothing wrong. It was worth any humiliation, any pain, just to stand there and look at her.

Then the nurse had let me go in and see Nellie. She was in a small ward on the fourth floor of the hospital, with seven other patients in the room besides her. She watched me walk up to the bed, her dark eyes wide and steady. I didn't say anything. I didn't know what to say. I bent over her bed and kissed her lips, my hand pressing down on her arm.

As she looked up at me, I could see a thin blue vein pulsing in her throat. She seemed very tired. "It's a girl," she said.

I nodded.

"But she's got your hair," Nellie added quickly.

"And your eyes and your face," I said quickly. "I saw her. She's a beauty."

Then Nellie smiled. "You're not disappointed?" she asked in a small voice.

I shook my head violently. "She's just what I wanted," I said emphatically. "Another you."

The nurse came by. "You'd better be going now, Mr. Fisher," she said.

I kissed Nellie again and left the small ward. I had gone home and spent a restless night in the lonely apartment. Early in the morning I went out looking for a job.

As usual there had been nothing. Finally, frantic with fear that I wouldn't be able to support my child, I decided to see if Sam would help me. I remembered how I stood in the street in front of the Empire State Building, in which he had his office, for almost an hour mustering up my nerve. Then I went inside and rode the elevator up to his office.

The receptionist wouldn't let me go into the office. He didn't want to see me. I went downstairs to a public telephone and called him. His voice was gruff when he answered. His first words sent a chill through me and I slammed the receiver back on the hook with a sick feeling in my stomach as his words still echoed in my ear. "What's the matter, kid? Yuh lookin' for another handout?" It wasn't until then that I realized that all the doors had closed behind me. There was no one I could really turn to. I had made my bed.

Nellie came home with the baby and the whole summer had almost gone by before I found anything. That was just a few weeks ago, and the job didn't even pay enough to live on. It had been night work and I was so desperate for something to do that I grabbed at it. Clerk at a soda fountain, six bucks a week and tips. If I could keep it a secret from the relief people, we'd be able to get along and the few extra bucks would be a great help. The seventy-two dollars a month they doled out didn't go very far.

I flushed down the last pump and looked up at the clock. Half past two. I pulled off my apron and tucked it away beneath the counter where I could find it tomorrow night. If I hurried to the subway I could be home by three o'clock. That way at least I could get a few hours' sleep before the relief investigator came in the morning with the check. She usually got to the house by seven o'clock.

Chapter Two

I COULD hardly keep my eyes open as I sat at the table and listened to Miss Snyder's nasally monotonous voice. Miss Snyder was the relief investigator in charge of our case. She was one of those people who are expert at everything. Right now she was giving Nellie instructions on how to prepare a meat sauce for spaghetti without meat.

"I think that's wonderful, don't you, Danny?"

Nellie's voice snapped my eyes open. "What?" I stammered. "Yeah. Sure."

"You weren't even listening, Mr. Fisher," Miss Snyder said, coldly reproving me.

"Oh, I was, Miss Snyder," I said quickly. "I heard every word you said."

She looked at me sharply through her thin steel-rimmed glasses. "You seem very tired, Mr. Fisher," she said suspiciously. "Were you up late last night?"

I was wide awake now. "No, Miss Snyder." I hastened to relieve her suspicions. "I went to bed early, but I couldn't sleep. I was very restless."

She turned back to Nellie. I could see that I didn't impress her. "And how is the baby, Mrs. Fisher?" she asked gurglingly.

"Would you like to see her, Miss Snyder?" Nellie was on her feet already. I smiled to myself. Nellie knew how to handle her. Miss Snyder was a spinster and a sucker for babies. From now

on I could fall asleep and snore at the table and she wouldn't
know I was there.

I waited until Miss Snyder left; then I stumbled blindly back
into bed. I didn't even bother pulling off my trousers before I
was asleep. I awoke with the feeling I was alone in the house. I
turned my head to look at the clock on the table next to the
bed. It was noon. A small white paper propped up against the
clock stared at me. It was from Nellie.

*Went down to cash the check, pay the bills, and do some
shopping. Took Vickie with me so that you could get some
sleep. There is coffee on the stove. Will be back by three.*

I dropped the note back on the night table and rolled out of
bed, stood up, and stretched. The bones in my shoulders
snapped gratefully. I headed for the bathroom and stared at
myself in the mirror as I spread the shaving soap over my face.
I looked weary and older. The skin over my cheekbones seemed
taut and dry, there were faint crinkles in the corners of my
eyes. I took a deep breath and began to work the lather into my
skin. I felt better when my face was completely covered with
fluffy whiteness.

The key rattled in the lock just as I finished shaving. I put
down the razor and went to the door. Nellie was standing there,
Vickie in one arm, a bag of groceries in the other. I took the
baby from her and walked back to the kitchen. Nellie followed
me with the groceries.

"I paid up the butcher and the grocer," she said, putting the
bag down on the table, "and I've got six dollars left over after
the rent, gas, and electricity is taken out."

"Good," I said. Vickie seemed curiously quiet. Usually when
I held her she would squirm restlessly and playfully. "What's the
matter with Vickie?"

Nellie glanced at her. "I don't know," she answered, a worried look crossing her face. "She's been like that all morning. In
the store she began to cry. That's why I'm home so early."

I held Vickie up in the air at arm's length over my head.
"What's with my baby girl?" I crooned, jouncing her lightly,
waiting for her to gurgle happily as she always did when I held
her like that.

Instead she began to cry. Her loud wails filled the room. I

turned bewildered toward Nellie. I never knew what to do when the baby cried, my fingers all turned thumbs.

"Let me put her to bed," Nellie said practically, taking her from me. "Maybe she'll feel better after her nap."

I sat down at the table and had me a cup of coffee while Nellie put her to sleep. I looked through the paper idly. There was an article there about the relief bureau checking up on some people who were suspected of holding out on them. I showed it to Nellie when she came back into the kitchen.

She looked at me doubtfully. "Do you think Miss Snyder suspects anything?"

I shrugged my shoulders. "I don't see how she can. I'm always home whenever she comes up."

"Maybe some of the neighbors might have noticed and said something to her."

"They wouldn't do that. They've enough troubles of their own."

"Still, she acted peculiar this morning. As if she knew something."

"Forget it," I said, more confidently than I felt. "She knows from nothin'."

Vickie began to cry again. Suddenly in the midst of her crying she began to cough, a heavy mucousy cough. Nellie and I looked at each other for a moment, then she turned and hurried into the bedroom. I followed her.

By the time I reached her, Nellie was holding the baby in her arms and patting her back lightly. The coughing stopped. Nellie looked at me with wide, frightened eyes. "She's so warm, Danny."

I touched a light palm gently to Vickie's forehead. It felt warm and damp to my hand. "Maybe she's got a little fever."

"She was coughing last night," Nellie said. "Maybe she caught my cold."

I hadn't thought about that. Nellie had been fighting a cold for over a week now. "Let's get the doctor," I said.

The baby began to cry again. We stared at each other helplessly. Nellie looked down at the baby, then up at me. "Maybe we better," she agreed. "The medical card is on the kitchen shelf. Call him right away on the phone in the hall downstairs."

The doctor turned from the baby and beckoned to Nellie.

"Let me have a look at you while your husband puts the baby back in the crib," he said.

Hesitantly Nellie asked: "Is she all right?"

Out of the corner of my eye I could see the doctor nodding as I placed Vickie in the crib. "She has a cold that seems to have centered in her throat. I'll give you something for it." He held a tongue depressor in his hand. "Open your mouth and say: 'Ah.' "

Nellie opened her mouth and he put the wooden stick against her tongue. She gagged and began to cough. He withdrew the depressor quickly and waited for her coughing spell to pass, then reached into his bag for his thermometer.

"Well?" she asked.

He smiled at her. "Stop worrying, Mrs. Fisher," he said. "Let's see if you have any fever." He put the thermometer in her mouth, took out a small prescription pad, and began to write on it.

Just as I finished covering Vickie, he asked me: "Do you have your assignment number?"

"It's in the kitchen, doc," I said quickly. "I'll get it."

When I came back into the room, the doctor was studying the thermometer he had taken from Nellie's mouth. "You have a little fever too, Mrs. Fisher," he said. "Did you know that?"

Nellie shook her head.

"You better get into bed and stay there a few days," he told her.

"But, doctor," she protested, "you haven't told us what's the matter with Vickie."

He looked at her impatiently. "The same thing is the matter with both of you. You both have a sore throat and a cold. I'll give you a couple of prescriptions, one for you and one for her. Follow the directions and you'll both be okay."

"Do you think she caught it from me?" Nellie asked worriedly.

The doctor was writing again. "I don't know who caught it from who, but just get these filled and keep warm and I'll stop by tomorrow to have a look at you." He held out the two prescriptions and turned to me. "Do you have the number?"

Silently I gave him the small white card that the relief people had issued to me. It was an authorization card to call for medical help at their expense.

The doctor's pen scratched quickly in his notebook. I could see that we had already received all the time he would give us for the two dollars per visit he got from welfare. He finished writing and handed the card and a slip of paper to me. "Give this to your investigator when you see him," he said brusquely, picking up his bag.

I looked at the paper in my hand. It was a Welfare Department medical-call form. "Yes, doctor," I said.

He was already at the door. "Now do as I say," he said warningly over his shoulder before he stepped out. "Keep in bed and take the medicine as directed on the bottle. I'll be back tomorrow."

The door snapped shut behind him and Nellie looked at me. I stared back at her for a second, anger filling my gorge. I crumpled the piece of paper viciously in my hand. "The son of a bitch!" I swore heatedly. "Lookin' for a buck, that's all. Too busy to even talk to yuh because you're on relief! I bet he don't talk to other patients like that!"

Nellie began to cough. "Well, there's nothing we can do about it," she managed to gasp. "At least he comes. Lots of 'em won't bother when they find out who pays the bill."

I was still angry. "He doesn't have to act like we were dirt!"

She walked back to the bed and slumped into it. "You ought to know by now how people are, Danny," she said wearily.

The patience in her face made me ashamed of my outburst. She was right. If I didn't know the score by now, I would never know it. I hurried over to her and took her hand. "Give me the prescriptions," I said. "I'll run 'em down to the drugstore an' get them filled. I think I'll stay home tonight."

She shook her head. "No, Danny," she told me, "just get them filled. Then you can go to work. We need the money."

"But the doctor said for you to stay in bed," I protested.

She smiled wanly at me. "They always say that, but who ever heard of staying in bed with a lousy little cold? You go to work. We'll be all right until you get home."

Chapter Three

I RAN up the stairs and stopped in front of my door. I could hear Nellie coughing as I slipped the key into the lock. A shaft of light coming from the bedroom struck my eyes. I shut the door quickly and hurried to the bedroom. "Nellie, are you up?" I called.

I stopped in the doorway. Nellie was just straightening up over the baby's crib. "Danny!" she cried.

I crossed the room with one long stride. "What's the matter?"

She grabbed hold of my jacket. "You've got to do something!" She was coughing and trying to speak all at the same time. "Vickie's burning up!"

I looked down into the crib, my hand reaching for the baby's forehead. It was hot to my touch. I looked at Nellie.

"She has a hundred and three!" Her voice was trembling.

I was staring at Nellie's eyes. They were dark, feverish pools. I tried to keep my voice calm. "Don't get panicky," I said quickly. "Babies often have fever that high. You look like you've got some yourself."

"Don't worry about me," she said, a note of hysteria creeping into her voice. "We have to do something for Vickie!"

I gripped her shoulders harshly. "Nellie!" I whipped my voice into her ears. "Take it easy! I'll run down to the hall phone and call the doctor. I'll be back in a minute."

She was crying now, the tears running down her face. "Yes, Danny, yes." She turned and straightened the covers over Vickie. "Hurry, Danny, she's on fire!"

The spinning dial on the telephone made a loud ratchety sound in the night-ridden hallway. I heard a click and then the telephone at the other end of the wire began to ring. It rang for several seconds before the receiver was picked up. A man's sleepy voice answered: "Yes?"

"Is this Dr. Addams?" I asked.

"This is Dr. Addams speaking," the voice replied.

"Doc, this is Danny Fisher," I said quickly. "You were over to see my kid today."

His voice sounded slightly annoyed. "Yes, Mr. Fisher. I know."

"I think you better come over right away, doctor. The baby's temperature is up to a hundred and three and she's burnin' up!"

His voice came slowly through the telephone. "Is she sleeping?"

"Yeah, doc," I answered. "But I don't like her looks; she's all red an' sweatin' somethin' fierce. My wife is too. Her fever must be way up."

There was a moment's hesitation before the doctor spoke again. "Did they take the medicine as I prescribed?"

"Yes, doc."

"Then stop worrying, Mr. Fisher." The doctor's voice carried a professionally impersonal reassurance that had no conviction for me. "It's quite customary for a fever to go up at night in the case of a severe cold. Give them both something warm to drink and cover them well. They'll be better by morning and I'll come by then."

"But, doc—" I protested.

"Just do as I say, Mr. Fisher." The doctor's voice came through with firm finality, followed by a click.

I stared at the dead receiver in my hand, suddenly realizing he had hung up on me. Viciously I slammed it back on the hook.

Nellie's eyes were wide as I came back into the apartment. "Is he coming?" she asked anxiously.

"Nope," I said as casually as I could. I didn't want her to worry any more than she had to. "He said it was nothin'. It happens all the time. He said to give you both somethin' warm to drink an' cover you well."

"Danny, do you think it's all right?" Her voice was nervous.

I smiled down at her with a confidence I did not feel. "Sure, it's okay. He's a doctor, ain't he? He must know what he's talkin' about." I led her gently toward the bed. "Now you lie down an' I'll make you some hot tea. You're not feelin' so good yourself an' everything looks worse than it really is."

Reluctantly she got into bed. "Make Vickie a bottle first," she said.

"Sure, Nellie, sure," I said. "Now cover up an' keep warm."

Carefully I carried the cup of tea into the bedroom and sat down on the edge of the bed. "Come on now," I said gently, "drink this. You'll feel better."

She took the cup from my outstretched hand and slowly lifted it to her lips. I could see the warmth go through her. "This is good," she said.

I smiled at her "Of course it's good. Look who made it. Danny of the Waldorf."

She smiled faintly back at me as she held the cup to her lips again. See how Vickie is," she told me.

I bent over the crib. The baby was sleeping quietly. "She's sleepin' like a charm," I said.

Nellie emptied the cup and handed it back to me, then lay back against the pillow, her black hair spreading over the white pillowcase.

"Baby," I said in a wondering voice, "I almos' forgot how good you look."

She smiled up at me sleepily. I could see she was very tired. "Working nights seems to do something for your eyesight, Danny," she aid, rying to joke. "It even makes you see better."

I switched off the light. "Go to sleep, baby," I said, bending over the bed and pressing my lips to her temple. "Things'll be all right now."

I went back into the kitchen and rinsed out the cup. I sat down in a chair by the table and was lighting a cigarette when the sound of the baby's whimper caught my ear. I tossed the butt into the sink and hurried into the bedroom. Vickie was coughing tiny rasping coughs deep in her chest. Quickly I picked her up in her blanket and patted her little back lightly until the coughing had stopped.

Nellie was sleeping a sleep of complete and utter exhaustion. I was glad that Vickie hadn't awakened her. I touched my fingers to the baby's face. It was still warm and feverish. Vickie's head slipped toward my shoulder. She was sleeping again. Gently I put her back in the crib and covered her. "Papa'll be back in a minute," I whispered to her.

I hurried back into the kitchen and ran water over the glowing butt in the sink. Then I turned out the light and went back into the bedroom in the dark. I placed a chair next to the crib and sat down in it, then reached over the side of the crib and felt for Vickie's fingers. Instinctively her tiny hand curled around my index finger. I sat there quietly, not daring to move for fear of disturbing her rest.

Outside the window the moonlight was bright and the night itself seemed new, as if it were another world. I felt Vickie move and I turned to look down into the crib. She was sleeping on her side. In the darkness I could see her curled up into a little ball around my hand. My daughter, I thought proudly. It took a scare like this to make me realize how precious she was to me. There were so many things about her I took for granted—the way she bubbled after she ate, the way her bright blue eyes followed me when I came into the room, the cute little wrinkles on the soles of her feet.

"I'll make it up to you for havin' to live like this, Vickie baby," I promised her. My husky whisper in the darkness startled me.

I looked nervously at the bed, but Nellie was still sleeping. I turned back to the crib, and this time I was careful that my moving lips made no sound. "Get well, Vickie baby," I whispered. "Get well and strong for your daddy. There's a whole world outside, and he wants you to share it with him. There's the sun an' the moon an' the stars an' lots of other wonderful things for your eyes to see, your ears to hear, your nose to smell. Grow big an' strong so that we can walk down the street together, so we can hold each other by the hand and feel our blood thumpin' in each other's heart. I'll buy you lots o' things, Vickie—dolls an' toys an' dresses. Anything you want, I'll get for you. I'll work hard, twenty-four hours a day, to make you happy. You're my baby an' I love you."

I felt her move again and peered down through the darkness at her. What a fool I had been all this time not to have known how rich she had made me! I looked up at the ceiling over her crib.

"Please, God," I prayed for the first time since I had been a kid myself, "please, God, make her well."

The silence of the room was broken by the sound of Nellie coughing in her sleep. I heard her move restlessly in the bed. I got out of my chair and looked at her. The blankets had fallen away from her body. I covered her again and went back to the chair and sat down.

The night seemed long and still, and gradually I began to doze, my hand dangling over the side into the crib. Several times I tried to force my eyes to remain open, but they resisted all my efforts, they were so heavy and so weary.

There was a distant small sound of coughing in my ears and the gray-white light of dawn was beating against my eyelids. My eyes opened suddenly and I was staring into the crib.

Vickie was coughing violently. Frantically I picked her up, trying to pat her back. She couldn't seem to stop coughing. Her eyes were squeezed tightly shut and tiny drops of moisture stood out on her forehead in the morning light. Suddenly she seemed to grow rigid in my arms, her little body stretching taut, her face turning a sick bluish color.

Desperately I forced her tiny mouth open with my lips. As hard as I could, I blew my breath into her, the fear and knowledge of what was happening constricting my heart.

Again and again I tried to make my breath her breath, my life her life, even long after I knew that there was nothing I could ever do for her again.

I stood there silently in the room, holding her still body against my breast, feeling the chill of the morning enter into her. This was my daughter. I could feel the salty edge of tears coming into my eyes.

"Danny!" Nellie's frightened voice cried from the bed.

Slowly I turned to look at her. I stared at her for a long and knowing moment and a thousand things were said and never spoken. She knew. Somehow she had known all along. This was what she had been afraid of. Her arms reached out toward Vickie.

Slowly I walked toward the bed, holding out our child to her.

Chapter Four

THE WOODEN steps creaked beneath our feet as we slowly climbed the stairs. It was a familiar sound, one that our ears had become accustomed to hearing for a long time, but there was no joy in it now. A little more than three years had passed since we first had climbed that stairway.

We were happy then. We were young and our lives were bright before us. We were laughing and excited. Somewhere in the back of my mind I remembered how I had carried her across the threshold. But even as I remembered, the memory faded and grew dim. It had been so long ago and we were young no longer.

I watched her back, stiff and straight, as she went up the stairway a step before me. She had been strong. Always she had been strong. There had been no tears, no screaming protestations of her grief. Only the hurt in her dark eyes, the twisted pain of her mouth, told me of her feelings.

She paused on our landing, swaying slightly as she turned toward our door. I reached for her quickly, afraid she might fall. Her hand found mine and gripped it tight.

We did not speak as we walked hand in hand to our door and stopped in front of it. With my free hand I reached in my pocket for my key. It wasn't there and I had to take my other hand from her in order to search the pockets on the other side. When the key was in my hand, I still did not place it in the lock, reluctant to open the door. She did not look at me. Her gaze was rigid on the floor in front of her.

I put the key in the lock, and the door swung open at my touch. I looked back at her in surprise. "I guess I didn't lock it," I said.

Her eyes were still fixed on the floor in front of her. Her voice was so low I could hardly hear her answer. "It doesn't matter," she said. "We have nothing more to lose."

I guided her through the door and closed it behind us. We stood there awkwardly in the tiny foyer, afraid to look at each other, afraid even to speak. We had no words in us.

At last I broke the silence. "Let me have your coat, darling," I said. "I'll hang it up."

She slipped out of her coat and let me take it from her hands. I put it in the closet, then hung mine next to it. When I turned back to her, she was still standing there, rigid.

I took her arm again. "Come inside and sit down. I'll get you a cup of coffee."

She shook her head. Her voice was dull and tired. "I don't want anything."

"Better sit down anyway," I urged.

She let me lead her into the parlor and seat her on the couch. I sat beside her and lit a cigarette. Her eyes were fixed straight ahead, blank and unseeing though she seemed to be staring out the window. There was quiet in the room, a thick, deep, unfamiliar quiet. I found myself listening to it, listening for the familiar sounds my daughter had made in the house, little sounds of no consequence that at times had seemed so annoying.

I closed my eyes for a moment. They were beginning to burn and smart from the long hours of the day. This was a day to forget, to hide away and bury in some secret corner of your mind so that you didn't remember the empty aching loss that had come into you. Forget the solemn, quiet sounds of Mass, the tiny white coffin gleaming in the soft yellow light of the candles on the altar. Forget the metallic sounds of the shovels biting into the earth, the rain of dirt and stone pouring down on the little box of wood. Forget, forget, forget.

But how can you forget? How can you forget the kindness of your neighbors, their sympathy and gentleness? You knocked at their doors and wept in their kitchens. You had no money and your child would lie in a pauper's grave if it were not for them. Five dolalrs here, two dollars there, ten dollars, six dollars. Seventy in all. To pay for a coffin, for a Mass, for a grave, for a resting-place for a part of you that was no more. Seventy dollars torn from the poverty of their own lives to lighten some way the bitterness in your own.

You want to forget, but a day like this you can't forget. Some day it will be buried deep, but it will not be forgotten. Just as she will not be forgotten.

Strange, but you are reluctant to say her name, even to yourself, and in place of it you say "she." I shook my head to clear it. There was a numbing fog aching in my ears. "Say her name!" I commanded myself desperately. "Say it!"

I drew a deep breath. My lungs were bursting. "Vickie!" Its sound exploded silently in my ears. But it was a triumphant sound. "Vickie!" Again her name was glowing in my mind. It was a glad name, a glorious name for living.

But not any more. Despair crept over me. From now on, it would be nothing. Only "she" would remain, and somehow I knew it.

I took a last drag at the cigarette and put it out. "Don't you think you'd better lie down?" I asked.

Slowly Nellie turned her face to me. "I'm not tired," she replied.

I took her hand. It was cold as ice. "Yuh better lie down," I repeated gently.

Her eyes flew swiftly to the bedroom door, then back to me. There was a lonely look in them. "Danny, I can't go in there. Her crib, her toys—" Her voice trailed away.

I knew exactly how she felt. My voice was shaking when I spoke again. "It's all over now, baby," I whispered. "Yuh gotta keep on goin', yuh gotta keep on livin'."

Her hands were gripping mine fiercely. There was a wild look of hysteria spilling into her eyes. "Why, Danny, why?" she cried.

I had to answer her though I had no idea what to say. "Because yuh gotta," I replied weakly. "Because that's the way she would have wanted it."

Her fingernails were tearing into my palms. "She was a baby, Danny! My baby!" Her voice broke suddenly and she cried for the first time since it had happened. "She was my baby and she wanted only one thing: to live! And I doomed her, I failed her!" Her hands covered her face and she was weeping bitterly.

Clumsily I put my arms around her shoulders and pulled her to me. I tried to make my voice as comforting as I could. "It wasn't your fault, Nellie. It wasn't anybody's fault. It was in God's hands."

Her eyes were black with misery and they gleamed dully against the pallor of her skin. She shook her head slowly. "No, Danny," she said in a hopeless tone, "it was my fault—my fault from the very beginning. I did a sinful thing and let her become a part of it. She paid for my sin, not me. I should have known better than to think that I knew better than God."

Her eyes as she looked up at me were flaming with a fanaticism I had never seen before. "I have sinned and lived in sin," she continued dully. "I have never asked God's blessing for my marriage. I was willing to settle for man's word. How could I have expected His blessing for my child? Father Brennan told me that in the very beginning."

"Father Brennan said nothing like that!" I said desperately. "In church today he said that God would make her welcome." I held her face up to me with my hands. "We loved each other, we still love each other. That's all that God asks."

She looked at me with sad eyes, and her hand touched mine lightly. "Poor Danny," she whispered softly. "You just can't understand."

I stared back at her. She was right; I didn't understand. Love was a thing between people, and if it was real, it was a blessed thing. "I love you," I said.

She smiled slowly through her tears, got to her feet, and looked down pityingly at me. "Poor Danny," she said again in that soft whisper. "You think that your love is all you need and can't see that it is not enough for Him."

I kissed her hand. "It always has been enough for us."

There was a distant look in her eyes. She nodded her head slightly. "That's what has been wrong about it, Danny," she said in a faraway voice. "I, too, thought that it would be enough for us, but now I know it isn't." I could feel her hand brushing lightly across my head. "We have to live with God too, not only with ourselves."

She went into the bedroom and closed the door behind her. I could hear the creak of the bed as she lay down on it, and then there was silence. I lit another cigarette and turned to the window. It had begun to rain. A day to forget. The silence began to creep into my bones.

Chapter Five

A CURIOUS numbness had crawled into my body, bringing with it a strange half-awake, half-asleep feeling. It was almost as if my body had fallen asleep while my mind remained awake and I had lost all sense of time. Only thoughts were with me. Half-formed and indistinct remnants of memories slipped through my mind while my body remained coldly aloof from the pain that came with them.

That was why I didn't hear the buzzer the first time it sounded. That is, I heard the sound, but didn't recognize it. The second time it rang, it was more strident, more demanding. Dully I wondered who was ringing the doorbell.

It rang again, this time piercing my consciousness. I jumped from my chair. I remember looking at my watch as I walked to the door and being surprised that it was only three o'clock. It seemed as if a year had passed since morning.

I opened the door. A strange man was standing there. "What do you want?" I asked. This was a hell of a time to be bothered by peddlers.

The stranger took his wallet from his pocket and flipped it open in front of me. He held it so that I could read the badge pinned to it: "N.Y.C. Dept. of Welfare. Investigator." "Mr. Fisher?" he asked.

I nodded.

"I'm John Morgan of the Welfare Department," he said quietly. "May I see you for a moment? I have some questions that I have to ask you."

I stared at him. This was no time for me to be answering questions. "Can't you make it some other time, Mr. Morgan?" I asked.

He shook his head. "I have to ask them now," he replied, an unpleasant tone coming into his voice. "Miss Snyder has come across some information regarding your case that must be verified. It would be for your own good to answer my questions now."

I looked at him suspiciously. "Where is she?" I asked.

A definite note of hostility had come into his voice now. "That is none of your concern, Mr. Fisher," he snapped. "All I want you to do is answer a few questions."

I began to resent this guy. A Department of Welfare badge didn't make him God. I planted my feet firmly in the doorway. I wasn't going to let him in. "Okay," I said coldly, "I'll answer your questions."

He looked around uncomfortably for a moment; then, apparently deciding I wasn't going to let him into the apartment, took out a small notebook and flipped it open. He glanced at it briefly, then at me. "You buried your daughter this morning?"

I nodded silently. The words coming from his lips, the way he spoke them, coldly and impersonally, hurt. It was profane.

He made scratches in his little book. All these investigators were the same. Give them a little notebook and automatically they begin to make scratches in it. If you ever took their little book away from them they wouldn't be able to talk. "Undertaker's services including casket were forty dollars, cemetery fees were twenty dollars, total sixty dollars for the funeral. Is that right?"

"No," I answered bitterly. "Yuh left out somethin'."

His eyes were sharp. "What?"

"We gave ten bucks to the Ascension Church for a special Mass," I said coldly. "The whole thing came to seventy dollars."

His pencil made scratching sounds in the notebook. He looked up again. "Where did you get the money, Mr. Fisher?"

"None of your Goddam business!" I snapped.

A faint smile appeared on his lips. "It is our business, Mr. Fisher," he replied snidely. "You see, you're on relief. You're supposed to be destitute. That means you have no money, that's why we help you. Suddenly you have seventy dollars. We have a right to know where you got it."

I looked down at the floor. That's where the buggers had you. You had to answer their questions or they'd cut you off. Still I couldn't bring myself to tell him where I got the dough. That was something personal between Vickie and us. Nobody else had to know where we got the money to bury our own child. I didn't answer him.

"Maybe you got the money from working nights without reporting it to us?" he suggested smoothly, a note of triumph in his voice. "You weren't holding out on us, were you, Mr. Fisher?"

My gaze came up from the floor and fastened on his face. How could they have found out about that? "What's that got to do with it?" I asked quickly.

He was smiling again. He seemed very proud of himself. "We have ways of finding out things," he said mysteriously. "It doesn't pay to fool us. You know, Mr. Fisher, you can go to jail for something like that. It constitutes fraud against the City of New York."

My temper wore thin. I'd had enough misery for one day. "Since when does a guy go to jail if he wants to work?" I burst out angrily. "What in hell are you trying to pull anyway?"

"Nothing, Mr. Fisher, nothing," he said smoothly. "I'm just trying to get at the truth, that's all."

"The truth is that three people can't live on seventy-two bucks a month and a supplementary diet of dried prunes and seed potatoes!" I had raised my voice and it echoed in the narrow hallway. "Yuh gotta try to grab an extra buck or yuh starve!"

"Then you admit you had a job nights while pretending to us that you were totally unemployed?" he asked calmly.

"I admit nothing!" shouted.

"Yet you had seventy dollars with which to bury your child," he stated triumphantly.

"Yes, I buried the kid!" I could feel knots in my throat choking me. "That was all I could do for her. If I had any dough do you think I would have waited for your friggin' doctor to come? If I had any dough I would have called another doctor. Maybe then she would be here now!"

His eyes surveyed me coldly. I didn't know a human being could have so little feeling. "Then you were working nights?" he asked again.

Suddenly all the pain and bitterness and heartache welled up through my guts and I grabbed him by the tie and pulled his face close to mine. "Yes, I was workin' nights!" I snarled at him.

His face turned white and wriggled in my grip. "Let me go,

Mr. Fisher," he gasped. "Violence isn't going to do you any good. You're in enough trouble already!"

He didn't know how right he was. A little more wouldn't make any difference now. I hit him flush on the face and he fell back against the wall on the other side of the narrow hallway. I could see a smear of blood coming to his nose as I went after him.

His eyes were frightened and he scrambled quickly along the wall to the stairway. I stood there and watched him run. At the head of the stairs he turned and looked back at me. His voice was almost hysterical. "You'll pay for this!" he screamed back at me. "You'll get thrown off relief. You'll starve! I'll see to that!"

I stepped toward him threateningly. He began to hurry down the steps. I leaned over the railing. "If yuh come back, yuh little bastard," I shouted down at him, "I'll kill yuh! Stay the hell away from me!"

He disappeared down the next landing and I went back into the apartment. I was beginning to feel sick. There was a peculiar shame in me as if I had defiled this day. I shouldn't have acted like that. Any other day all right maybe, not today.

Nellie was standing in the bedroom door. "Who was it, Danny?"

I tried to calm my voice. "Some monkey from Welfare," I said. "A wise guy. I sent him away."

"What did he want?"

She'd had enough for one day, there was no use in making it worse. "Nothin' special," I said evasively. "He just wanted to ask some questions, that's all. Go back to bed and rest, baby."

Her voice was dull and hopeless. "They know about the night job, don't they?"

I stared at her. She had heard. "Why don't you try an' get some sleep, baby?" I ducked her question.

Her eyes were fixed on mine. "Don't lie to me, Danny. It was true what I said, wasn't it?"

"What if it is?" I admitted. "It ain't important now. We'll make out on the job. The boss promised me a full trick soon."

She stood staring at me. I could see the tears welling into her eyes again. I crossed the room quickly and took her hand.

"Nothing goes right for us, Danny," she said hopelessly, not even on a day like this. Trouble, always trouble."

"It's all over now, baby," I said, holding her hand. "From now on things'll go better."

She looked up at me, her eyes dead in her face. "It will never be any different, Danny," she said futilely. "We're jinxed. I've brought you nothing but hard luck."

I twisted her face around to me. "Nellie, yuh gotta forget that idea!" I pressed my lips to her cheek. "Yuh can't go on livin' thinkin' that nothin's gonna be okay. "Yuh gotta hope for better!"

Her gaze met mine levelly. "What is there to hope for?" she asked quietly. "How do you know you even have a job now? You haven't even called up there in four days."

"I'm not worried about that," I said, my heart sinking into my stomach. It was true. I had forgotten all about calling the store. "Jack will understand when I explain to him."

She looked up at me doubtingly. Some of her doubt seeped into me. But as it turned out both of us were right.

Chapter Six

JACK looked up at me as I walked into the store. There was no welcome in his eyes. I looked down the counter. Another man was working my station.

"Hello, Jack," I said quietly.

"Hello, Danny," he replied without enthusiasm.

I waited for him to ask me where I'd been, but he didn't speak. I could see he was angry, so I spoke first. "Something happened, Jack," I explained. "I couldn't come in."

His eyes reflected his anger. "Yuh couldn't even call in five days either, I suppose?" he asked sarcastically.

I met his gaze. "I'm sorry about that, Jack," I said apologetically. "I know I should have called, but I was so upset I forgot all about it."

"Crap!" he exploded. "For two nights I broke my back here waitin' for you to show up an' you don't even have time to call up!"

I looked down at the counter. "I couldn't help it, Jack," I said. "Something happened an' I couldn't call."

"Not even once in five days?" he said unbelievingly. "The world would have to come to an end before I'd pull a stunt like that."

I still didn't look at him. "I had trouble, Jack," I said quietly. "My ba—my daughter died."

There was a moment's silence before he spoke again. "You're not kiddin' me, Danny?" he asked.

I looked up at his face. "You don't kid with things like that," I answered.

His eyes fell. "I'm sorry, Danny. Honestly sorry."

I looked down the counter. The new man was watching out of the corner of his eyes, trying to give the impression that he wasn't interested in what we were saying, but I knew the look. He was worrying about his job. I'd had it too many times myself not to recognize it.

I looked at Jack. "I see you got a new man."

He nodded uncomfortably. He didn't speak.

I tried to make my voice sound casual, but it's hard when what you're saying is the difference between eating and not eating. "Yuh got any room for me?"

He was silent for a moment before he answered. I could see his eyes shift down the counter to the new man, then back. The new man immediately was busy cleaning the grill. "Not right now, Danny," he said gently. "I'm sorry."

I partly turned toward the door so that he couldn't see the tears I felt right behind my eyes. "That's all right, Jack," I said. "I understand."

There was a deep note of sympathy in his voice that I was grateful for. "Maybe something'll turn up soon," he said quickly. "I'll call yuh." A moment passed. "If you'd only called, Danny—"

"If a lot of things, Jack," I interrupted him, "but I didn't. Thanks anyway." I walked out of the store.

In the street outside the store I looked at my watch. It was after six o'clock. I wondered how I could tell Nellie, especially after what had happened this afternoon. The whole day had been miserable.

I decided to walk home. It was a long walk but a nickel is a lot of dough when you haven't got a job. From Dyckman Street to East Fourth took me almost three hours. I didn't mind it. It was that much more time I wouldn't have to tell Nellie.

It was nine o'clock by the time I reached home. The night had turned cool, but my shirt was damp with perspiration as I began to climb the stairs. I stood in the hallway hesitantly before opening the door. What could I tell her? I let it swing wide before I stepped in. There was a light in the parlor, but the apartment was quiet. "Nellie," I called, turning to hang my jacket in the small closet.

There was a sound of footsteps and I heard a man's voice: "That's him!"

I spun around. Nellie and two men were standing in the parlor entrance. Her face was pale and drawn. I took a quick step toward her before I recognized the man standing next to her. It was the Welfare investigator I had chased this afternoon.

There was a white bandage across the bridge of his nose and one eye was purple and swollen. "That's him!" he repeated.

The other man stepped toward me. He held a badge in his hand—a police badge. "Daniel Fisher?"

I nodded.

"Mr. Morgan has preferred charges against you of assault and battery," he said quietly. "I'll have to take you in."

I could feel my muscles tense. This was all I needed to make a perfect day: the cops. Then I looked at Nellie and all the tension seeped out of me.

"May I talk with my wife for a moment?" I asked the detective.

His eyes appraised me for a moment, then he nodded. "Sure," he said gently. "We'll wait outside in the hall for you." He took Morgan's arm and pushed him out into the hall before him, looking back at me before closing the door. "Don't be long, son." I nodded gratefully and the door swung closed.

Nellie hadn't said a word, her eyes were searching my face. At last she drew a deep breath. "No job?"

I didn't answer.

She stared at me for a moment more and then she was in my arms, sobbing violently against my shoulder. "Danny, Danny," she cried in a helpless voice, "what'll we do?"

I stroked her hair gently. I didn't know what to say. I didn't
know what we could do. The walls were closing in on us.

She looked up into my face. "What do you think they'll do to
you?" she asked.

I shrugged my shoulders. "I don't know," I answered. I was
so tired I didn't really care. If it weren't for her I wouldn't give
a damn for anything any more. "They'll probably book me and
let me go until a hearing is arranged."

"But supposing they hold you?" she cried.

I tried a smile. "They won't," I answered, more surely than I
felt. "It's not important enough. I'll be back in a few hours."

"But that Mr. Morgan, he was terrible. He said they were
going to put you in jail."

"That louse!" I said quickly. "There's a lot of things he don't
know. When they hear what has happened they'll let me out.
Don't worry."

She hid her face against my shoulder. "Nothing's turning out
right, Danny," she despaired. "All I've brought you is bad luck.
You should never have come back."

I turned up her face and kissed her. "If I hadn't come back,
baby," I whispered, "I would have missed the only thing in the
world that was important to me. It's not your fault, it's nobody's fault. We just didn't get the breaks."

There was a knock at the door. "I'll be out in a minute," I
called. I looked down at Nellie again. "Lie down for a while," I
said. "I'll be back in a few hours."

She looked at me doubtfully. "Sure?"

"Sure," I answered, taking my jacket from the closet. "I'll be
back before you know it."

Morgan's face glared at me triumphantly as we walked
through the streets. "I told you I'd be back," he sneered.

I didn't answer him.

The detective between us growled at him: "Shut up, Morgan. The lad's got enough trouble without you opening up your
yap."

I glanced at the cop out of the corner of my eye. I could see
he didn't like Morgan. He was one of those warm Irishmen
with tender eyes. I wondered how a guy like that could ever
become a cop.

We had walked almost two blocks before I spoke. "What do
they usually do in a thing like this?" I asked the detective.

His face turned toward me, its ruddy glow shining in the light of the street lamps. "They book yuh on charges against a hearing."

"Then they let you go until the hearing, is that right?" I asked.

The cop's eyes were sympathetic. "If yuh got the bail they do."

The surprise showed in my voice. "Bail?" I exclaimed. "How much bail?"

The cop's eyes were still gentle. "Five hundred dollars usually."

"But what if you haven't got the dough?" I asked. "What do they do then?"

Morgan answered before the cop could. "They put you in jail until the hearing," he said viciously.

I broke stride and looked at the cop. "But they can't do that!" I exclaimed. "My wife is sick. She's gone through a lot today. I can't leave her alone tonight."

The detective took my arm. "I'm sorry, son," he said gently, "but I can't help that. All I'm supposed to do is bring you in."

"But Nellie—my wife"—I could hardly speak—"I can't leave her alone. She's not well."

The cop's voice was still soft. "Don't get excited, son. You'd better just come along."

I could feel his grip tightening on my arm. I began to walk again. I had read in the papers that sometimes hearings took weeks to be arranged. Visions of myself sitting in the pokey until the hearing crept into my mind. I began to seethe. I looked at Morgan.

He was walking on the other side of the cop, a smug, satisfied look on his face. The bastard. If it weren't for him everything might have been better. Things had been bad enough, but he made them worse.

I had to do something, I didn't know what. I just couldn't let them lock me up until they were good and ready to give me a hearing. I couldn't leave Nellie alone that long. There was no telling what she might do.

We stepped out in the gutter just as the light changed. Automobiles whizzed by us as we paused in the center of the street. I felt the cop's hand fall from my arm and instinctively I jumped forward. I heard a muttered curse behind me, then a scream as a driver threw on his brakes. I didn't turn back to see what had happened, I kept running.

There was a shout: "Stop! Stop!" Then another voice took up the cry. I recognized the shrill-pitched tones of Morgan. He was screaming too.

A shrill blast of a police whistle reached my ears. But by that time I had reached the far corner and I looked back over my shoulder as I sped around it.

Morgan was lying stretched out in the gutter, and the policeman was standing over him, looking at me. The cop was waving his hand at me. I could see the glint of metal shining in his hand. He was still shouting for me to stop, but his hand was telling me to go.

I grabbed a deep chunk of air and went around the corner.

Chapter Seven

I WENT the long way around and back to my house. I had to see Nellie and explain to her. I had to tell her what I'd done. I had to tell her not to worry. But by the time I reached the corner I could see the white top of a police patrol car parked in front of my door. I stood stock-still on the corner staring at it, and for the first time I realized what I had done. The cops were after me now. I didn't dare show up home. I had only made things worse.

I crossed the street and went up the block slowly. There was a heavy, sunken feeling of despair in my gut. I felt sick. I had loused things up for sure. I looked at my watch. It was a few minutes after ten. I had been a fool. There was nothing to do now but go back and give myself up. If I kept on running, there would be no end to it. I would never be able to go back.

I started back for the house. Might as well get it over with. Then I remembered. The whole thing had started when I found out I would need bail in order to get out. I still had no bail.

I stopped again and thought. I would have to get the dough some place. Nellie's folks didn't have that kind of money even if they were willing to help me out. The only person I knew that could put his hands on that much dough was Sam.

I remembered the last time I spoke to him. Funny how things worked out. It had been the day after Vickie was born. He had thought I had come looking for a handout then, and I had sworn to myself that I would never go to him for anything after that. But I was in real trouble now. There was nothing else for me to do. It was either go to him or to the pokey. And I had done enough for them to lock me up and throw away the key. I had to ask him.

I went into the candy store on the corner and thumbed quickly through the telephone directory. I tried his home telephone. From the phone booth in the store I could see the police car across the street in front of my house. The cop sitting inside it was sneaking a smoke.

A woman's voice answered: "Hello."

"Is Mr. or Mrs. Gordon there?" I asked quickly, my eyes glued on the patrol car.

"Miz Gordon is away in the country," the voice replied. "Mistuh Gordon is still down at his office."

"May I have the number please?" I asked. "I must get in touch with him right away."

"Sure, the voice replied. "Just a minute, I'll get it for you."

I copied the number down and put up the receiver while I searched my pockets for another coin. I might as well have been looking for a gold mine for all the good it did me. I had just spent my last nickel.

I looked out at the patrol car. The cop had got out of it and was walking up the block toward me. I made up my mind quickly and ducked out of the candy store and around the corner before he got near enough to recognize me.

Sam's office was uptown in the Empire State Building. I began to walk quickly. With a break I could get there in little more than half an hour. I hoped he would still be there.

His name was in the directory on the Thirty-fourth Street side: "Sam Gordon Enterprises Inc., Concessions." Twenty-second floor. I went over to the white sign that read: "Night Elevators." A watchman was standing there with a registry book on a small stand. He stopped me. "Where you going, mister?" he asked suspiciously.

"Twenty-second floor," I answered quickly. "I got an appointment with Mr. Gordon there."

He looked at the register. "Okay," he said. "Mr. Gordon is still up there. He hasn't signed out since he returned from dinner. Sign here." He held a pencil toward me.

I took it and scrawled my name where he indicated. I looked up the page. About four lines above mine I saw Sam's familiar scribble. Next to his name was a circle with the numeral 2 in it.

I looked at the night watchman. "Is there anyone with Mr. Gordon?"

A faint flicker of a smile appeared on the man's face. "His secretary came back with him."

I nodded without replying. His smile had told me enough. If I knew anything, Sam's secretary would be a good-looking head, and Sam hadn't changed a bit.

I stepped out of the elevator and walked down the hall toward Sam's office. His name was spelled out in impressive gold lettering across two large glass doors. I could see clear through into the reception room. A single light glowed there. The doors were unlocked.

There was a door near the receptionist's desk in the lavishly furnished waiting-room. I opened it and found myself in a large general office. There were about twenty desks scattered through the room. On the far side of the room there was another door. I walked toward it.

Again the gold letters spelling out his name gleamed faintly at me in the dim light. I put my hand lightly on the knob and turned it. The door swung gently open. The office was dark. I put my hand out and found the light-switch on the right-hand wall. I pressed it and light poured into the room. There was a muttered curse as I blinked my eyes in the light. I heard a faint, frightened woman's cry. Then my eyes adjusted and I stood looking down at the couch. Sam was rising to his feet, his face glaring at me; the girl was trying to cover her nakedness with inadequate hands.

I stared at her and then turned to Sam with a knowing smile. His face was flushed, almost purple, as he struggled into his trousers. I didn't speak, just backed out of the door, pulling it closed after me. I sat down in a chair just outside his office, lit a cigarette, and waited for him to come out. I had been right. Sam hadn't changed a bit.

I had been waiting for almost fifteen minutes before the door opened again. I looked up expectantly.

I was disappointed. It wasn't Sam who came out, it was the girl. From the way she looked, it was hard to believe that just a few minutes ago I had caught her rocking the cradle. She looked down at me. "Mr. Gordon will see you now," she said formally.

I got to my feet. "Thank you," I deadpanned, and went into his office. I could hear the clatter of a typewriter begin as I closed the door behind me.

Sam was sitting behind his desk. "Yuh find yuh get better work from 'em if yuh relax 'em first?" I smiled.

He ignored my attempt at humor while he held a match to a cigar clamped in his teeth. The light flickered coldly in his eyes. At last he put the match down and stared at me. "What d'yuh want?" he barked.

I could feel a respect for him growing in me. This guy really had it. He was tough. Not one word about my walking in on him. There was no use playing games with him. I walked up to his desk and looked down at him. "I need help," I said simply. "I'm in trouble."

The pupils of his eyes were hard and black. "Why come to me?" he asked.

"I got nobody else," I said quietly.

He put the cigar down gently on an ashtray and stood up behind his desk. His voice was low, but it filled the office. "Blow, bum," he said flatly. "You ain't gettin' no handouts from me."

"I ain't lookin' for a handout," I said desperately. "I'm in trouble and I need help." I stood there stubbornly, staring at him. He wasn't going to chase me this time.

He walked menacingly around the desk toward me. "Get out!" he snarled.

"For God's sake, Sam, listen to me," I pleaded. "Everything's gone wrong! The cops are after me an'—"

His voice cut me off as if I hadn't spoken. "Yuh're no good!" he snapped, his flushed and angry face close to mine. "Yuh never been any good, yuh'll never be any good! I done enough fer you. Get out before I throw you out!" He raised his fist.

I went cold and hard inside. There was only one language this guy understood. "I wouldn't try that if I were you, Sam," I said coldly, watching his hands. "You ain't in condition."

"I'll show yuh who's in condition!" he growled, swinging at me.

I picked off his blow with my forearm. "Remember your own lesson, Sam?" I taunted. "Snap—don't swing like a balley dancer!" I moved away from him without trying to return his blow.

He came after me, both arms swinging. But he was heavy on his feet and I kept away from him easily. One thing I could say in favor of my diet: I never got a chance to roll up the fat around my gut like he did. For a few minutes he kept up the chase. There was only the puffing sound of his breath breaking the silence of the office. At last he sank exhaustedly into his chair, breathing heavily.

I stood on the other side of his desk and looked at him. His face was flushed with the exertion, and perspiration was running down his heavy jowls. "Now will yuh listen to me, Sam?" I asked.

He picked up his cigar and stuck it in his mouth He didn't look at me. "Go away," he said in a low, disgusted voice.

"I ain't goin' no place," I said. "Yuh're gonna help me."

"I had enough of you," he said, looking up at me wearily. "Ever since you were a kid you been putting it over on me. Up in the country with Ceil, then in the Gloves that time you made a deal with Maxie Fields. How many times you think I'm gonna bite?"

He had a memory like an elephant. He didn't forget anything. "This ain't gonna cost you no dough," I said. "All I need is a little help an' a job till I can straighten things out."

He shook his head. "I ain't got no job for you. You ain't trained for nothin'."

"I can still fight," I said.

"Uh-uh," he answered. "Yuh're too old to start in that. You been away too long. Yuh'll never make a nickel as a pro."

There was no arguing about that. Twenty-three was too old, especially after a six-year layoff. "Then how about a job here?" I asked. "You got a big place."

"No," he answered flatly.

"Not even if I promise never to tell Mimi what I seen here tonight?" I asked shrewdly.

I knew from the expression on his face I had scored. "She wouldn't like that," I followed up quickly.

—

He sat there silently chewing on his cigar. I watched him patiently. This was the kind of language he could understand. I was through begging, through groveling, through asking for anything. There was only one way to get along in this world: that was to take what you wanted. That was the way he operated in everything, and if it was good enough for him, it was good enough for me.

His eyes were veiled and blank as he looked at me. "Still the same snot-nosed punk who thinks the world owes him a living, eh, Danny?" he asked coldly.

I shook my head. "Not the same, Sam," I answered bitterly. "This is a new Danny Fisher yuh're lookin' at. I been through too much to ever be the same. I put in a year an' a half on relief, crawlin' on my belly in order to have enough to eat. This afternoon I socked a Welfare agent because he wanted to know where I got the dough to bury my child an' he came after me with the cops. My wife is home sick an' wonderin' where I am. I'm not the same any more, Sam, I'll never be the—"

There was a shocked sound in his voice. "What happened, Danny?"

"You heard me," I answered, staring at him coldly. "I'll never be the same. Now do you help me or do I tell Mimi what I saw?"

His gaze dropped to his desk and he stared at it for a moment. Then he spoke without looking up. "Okay, kid," he said in a peculiarly gentle voice. "Yuh got me."

Chapter Eight

AS SOON as I had pushed my way through the glass doors, the receptionist looked at me and smiled. "Good morning, Danny," she said, shifting the wad of gum to a corner of her mouth. "The boss is lookin' for you."

"Thanks, baby." I smiled back at her.

I went through the other door into the large office. Everybody was at work already. The quiet hum of business came to my ears. I walked through the office to my desk, in a corner of the room near a window. I sat down behind it and began looking through some papers stacked neatly in the incoming basket on the desk.

I had been seated only a few minutes when a shadow fell across my desk. I looked up.

"Danny—" Kate started to say.

I held up an interrupting hand. "I know, baby," I said quickly. "The boss wants to see me."

She nodded her head.

"Well, I'm here," I told her.

"Then what're you waitin' for?" she snapped sarcastically. "An engraved invitation?" She turned on her heel and huffily went back to her desk.

Kate was an all-right kid even if I liked to tease her. I guess she wasn't the first secretary that had ever been jumped by the boss, and she wasn't going to be the last. But she had been edgy with me ever since the first time we met.

I smiled to myself as I thought about it. It was over three and a half years ago. A lot of things had happened in that time. A war was on. A lot of guys had gone away. I had been lucky, though. When the draft board got to me they found something I never knew I had: punctured eardrums. I was out—4 F, a highly personalized kind of abbreviation of the four freedoms.

I shuffled through the papers on my desk again and found the one I wanted. As I got to my feet the phone on my desk rang and I picked it up.

It was Nellie, calling from the war plant on Long Island where she worked. "I forgot to tell you to take the laundry down to the Chink's," she said.

"I remembered, honey," I said. She left early in the morning—six o'clock, before I woke. "How are things going out there?" I asked.

"Hot, Danny," she answered. "It's over ninety in the plant."

"Why don't yuh quit that dump?" I asked. "We don't need the dough now. I'm makin' out all right."

Her voice was patient but firm. We had been through this thing many times already. "What else have I got to do?" she asked. "Stay home all day an' go nuts? I'm better off out of the house. At least I keep busy this way."

I knew better than to argue with her. Since Vickie had died, she had changed. I don't know in just what way, but she had become more silent. Some of the starlight had gone out of her eyes.

"We eatin' out tonight or home?" I asked.

"Out," she answered. "We're almost out of this month's meat points."

"Okay," I said. "I'll pick you up at the house at six."

I grinned at Kate as I opened Sam's door. She made a face at me and bent down over her typewriter, her fingers flying. I smiled to myself as I went in the door. I think Kate liked me despite everything.

Sam looked up from his desk. "So you finally got here," he growled.

I wasn't worried about what he said. I knew that in the few years I had been here, I had learned enough to carry my weight. This was a tricky business, but it was for me. It was made up of the kind of intangibles that only a few guys could turn into money. Guys like Sam and me. And Sam knew it too. "If it wasn't for the air conditioning I wouldn't have come in at all," I said, dropping into a chair in front of his desk. "You don't know how lucky you are."

Sam's face flushed. He didn't look good like that, he was packing too much weight. He had two double chins. He looked just like the Central Park South papa of three boys that he was. "Mimi says for me to ask you an' Nellie up for dinner tonight," he said.

"Okay," I said. "Was that what all the fire was about?"

He shook his head. "No," he said shortly. "I want yuh to come off that slot-machine grab."

I stared at him. "What for?" I asked. "I thought you were hot for it."

"I changed my mind," he said gruffly. "The upkeep on them machines is murder. When they go, they go, that's all there is to it. Yuh can't get replacement parts or nothin' on account a' the war."

"Is that the reason, Sam," I asked, "or is it because I hear Maxie Fields is interested in them too?"

He flushed again. I wondered whether Sam was developing a high blood-pressure. He was at the dangerous age now. "I don't give a damn about Maxie Fields!" he said. "It's just that I don't glom that racket. Give me a nice clean concession in a hotel or a night club. Checking, souvenirs, photographs—something with people running it. I can understand people, I can run 'em. But I can't figger machines."

"But I just spent a week casin' this setup," I protested. "For fifteen grand it's a steal."

"So let Maxie steal it, then," he snapped. "I ain't interested. I ain't goin' for no kick I can't savvy. Fifteen G's is too much spec."

I leaned forward. I thought Sam was missing a good thing. This was the first time I had ever really disagreed with him. "You're missin' the boat, Sam," I said earnestly. "I been all through the setup, an' what they can do with these machines is real sky stuff. Postwar they'll be sellin' everything in those machines from hot coffee to condoms."

"So let 'em," he said definitely. I could see that his mind had been made up. "Right now all they're good for is cigarettes and Coca-Cola and I ain't buyin'." He riffled through some papers on his desk. "I got somethin' else for yuh to look at. The concessions at the Trask in Atlantic City are on the block. I want yuh to run down there an' have a look-see."

I stared at him for a moment. "You mean it about them vending machines?" I asked.

"You heard me," he said angrily. "Sure I mean it. Now forget it an'—"

"I like it, Sam," I said softly, the beginnings of an idea growing in my mind.

His gaze was sharp and penetrating. "So you like it," he said sarcastically. "But it's my dough an' I say no dice. So be a good boy an' stop hokkin' me. Now, I—"

I interrupted him again. "I'd like to buy in, Sam," I said.

He let out a deep breath. "Yuh got the dough?" he asked shrewdly.

I met his eyes across the desk. He knew as well as I that I didn't have the dough. "Yuh know I can't raise that kind'a money on the big seventy-five per you pay me."

He grinned happily. He felt he was going to score. I knew the look. "But what about yer expense account on out-of-town trips? Yuh ever look at 'em? Yuh don't think I know you grab a few bucks there?"

I grinned back at him. "You're right about that, Sam," I admitted. "It's a few bucks, though. You never send me out with enough to make a real take."

"Then where yuh gonna get the dough?" Sam shot at me.

I thought for a minute. "I got about fifteen hundred dollars in our savings account. The bank ought to give me half the deal on a chattel mortgage. The rest I can get from you."

Sam was on his feet. "From me?" he roared angrily. "What kinda stupe yuh think I am? What chance I got to collect from you?"

I looked at him calmly. "Yuh got my word."

He sneered. "I sank five grand once't on your word. Yuh think I'm a sucker for that again?"

I could feel my eyes grow cold. "That was a kid you bought, Sam. That wasn't me, that was your grab outta a hat for glory. I never saw any of it. The only payoff in it for me would have been a punchin' around."

His face was red. "Well, I ain't buyin'," he said flatly, sitting down behind his desk again.

My mind was made up. "But I am," I said, "an' you're comin' in after me."

"What makes yuh think so?" he asked.

I looked at him shrewdly. "Remember how I got my job here?" I asked. "I thought I was somethin'. Since then I been around. You're the original college coxs'n. I never really knew how good you were until I ran into a certain little blonde dancer yuh got stashed in a hotel across town."

I thought he'd burst a blood vessel. His face turned a heavy purplish color. "How d'yuh know about her?" he managed to ask.

"I get around, Sam," I smiled. "I'm a big boy now."

He cleared his throat embarrassedly. His fingers picked up a pencil and toyed with it. "Yuh know how those things are, kid," he said awkwardly, not looking at me. "I'm nuts about your sister, but she's got a screwy idea that every time I come near her she's knocked up. A guy's gotta let off steam some place."

"I'm not criticizing you, Sam," I said tolerantly. "Maybe I'm even a little envious. But I don't think Mimi could appreciate that. She's an awful proud girl, you know."

Sam stared at me, then relaxed in his seat. The rancor had gone from his voice. "Ain't it enough, kid, I come through for yuh when yuh're in trouble an' got no place else to go? Ain't it enough I keep yuh out of the can, go your bail, an' square the rap against yuh, then give yuh a job to boot. Ain't yuh satisfied?"

I got out of the chair and leaned across his desk. I meant every word I said. "I owe you more'n I owe anybody in the world, Sam. Believe me, I'm very grateful for everything you done. I don't like havin' to put the boot to yuh, anymore'n you do. But there's more'n just a job to livin' in this world. A guy's gotta have a buck he can call his own. Yuh never get that on a job, Sam. There's only one way yuh can get it. That's go after the big buck for yourself. You found that out, the first year up in the country, an' you did all right by yourself. Now I want a crack at it. Sure, I'm satisfied, but now I want a chance at the big buck myself."

He looked up into my eyes for a long moment; then a smile slowly spread across his face. He knew when he was licked. But it didn't keep him from making one more try. "Supposin' Fields tries to cut in on yuh?"

"He won't," I said confidently. "I found that out while I was checkin' around for you. It's not big enough for him."

He leaned back in his chair and took out his checkbook. "Okay, Danny," he said in a quiet voice. "How much do yuh need?"

"Six grand," I answered.

"For how long?"

"A year postwar," I said quickly. "I'm not takin' any chances."

"Christ, this war may go on for ten years!" he exploded. I was smiling. "If it does, then you'll be out your dough. I figger these machines'll hold up another three years. Then I ought to be able to get new ones."

Sam was figuring. "Usual rates, Danny?" he asked shrewdly.

Usual rates in this business were usury—generally six for five. "Take it a little easy, Sam," I said. "After all, it's in the family."

"Ten percent per annum on an undated note," he said quickly.

I nodded. "Fair enough, Sam." I grinned at him. "Now yuh want me to run down to Atlantic City for yuh?"

"Hell, no!" he swore, his pen already making scratching noises in his checkbook. "Kill your own swindle sheet. You're in business for yourself!"

Chapter Nine

I CAME out of Sam's office and sat down at my desk. I looked down at the check in my hand. I still couldn't believe I had done it. The thought had never entered my mind until I had gone in there. I spread the check on the desk and smoothed it down. The writing on it stared up at me: six thousand dollars. I had the strangest impulse to grab the dough and run. I had never had that much money in my life.

A temptation came over me to take the check back to Sam and return it to him. Tell him I'd changed my mind and wanted my job back. I was crazy even to think I could get away with a project as big as this. Sam was a pretty sharp apple. If he couldn't see a buck in it, maybe he was right. I had learned enough about the way he did business to realize he was generally right. Guys don't build a business as Sam had done out of nothing but hot air. Who was I to say he was wrong?

I was suddenly tired. I closed my eyes wearily. What had got into me anyway? Why the big ideas? I was making a living. I was content. A few years ago I would have given my eyeteeth for a spot like this. Now it wasn't good enough. I searched my mind for the answer. It was there somewhere, it had to be. Hidden away in some secret corner just out of reach, like a very familiar word curiously lost to your tongue. There had to be a reason. I couldn't believe it had happened just because I'd found out that Sam didn't want it.

I went over the deal again in my mind. Maybe there was something about it that had caught me. It had all started a few weeks ago when Sam sent me out to look over this vending-machine business. Until then I had covered nothing but the concessions Sam dealt in.

The first day I had come to work for him he had called me into his office. It was the first time I had realized that he had really built himself into a big business. He waited until the door had closed behind me before he spoke. From behind his desk his eyes were cold and challenging. His tone of voice was one I had never heard him use before, it was clipped and businesslike. "If you think you're gettin' a free ride here, Danny, you can get off now."

I didn't answer.

"If you think you got the job because you put something over on me, forget it," he continued in the same tone. "I'm payin' yuh thirty bucks a week because I expect you to work thirty bucks' worth." He stared at me for a moment as if he expected me to answer him. When I didn't he went on:

"You're not gettin' any favors because you're Mimi's brother either, so you can forget that too. You'll do your work or get out. There's no other way with me—nothing else counts. I don't care what you think you got on me if you don't do your job, I'll tie a can to yuh before yuh know what's happenin'!" He glared up at me. "Unnerstan'?"

I almost smiled at the familiar word. It was always a favorite of his. "I coppish," I answered. "That's the way I want it. I'm tired of favors and handouts."

He nodded his head heavily. "Good," he said. "Then we unnerstan' each other. Now get outside an' go to work."

He got busy at his desk and I was dismissed. As I went outside, his secretary's face flushed. I smiled at her and went back to my desk, which was at the front of the room then, with the other receipt clerks. My job was to record the business reported by each of the concessions and keep a perpetual check on their inventory.

I didn't see very much of Sam after that. He treated me exactly like the other employees, no better and no worse. I was in that job over a year when the first peacetime draft grabbed one of the checkers. I was promoted to his job. It paid forty-five a week and carried a car along with it. It was my job to visit the concessions and see how things were going, to see whether the company was getting a fair shake. A certain amount of holdout couldn't be avoided in a business as vague and nebulous as this, but we tried to keep it at a fair minimum.

I got pretty good at the work. It got so that I could walk into a place, hang around a little while, and instinctively I would know how we were making out. I learned what the margin was for us, what we had to do to break even. It didn't take long for

Sam to catch on that I knew the business. He began to give me appraising assignments. He would send me into a joint before he took it on and I would case it for him. I spent as much time there as I needed, then I went back to the office and gave Sam the nut. I was generally within a few bucks.

I got a couple of raises and then he began to use me exclusively on appraising. I felt good about that for many reasons, mainly because we both knew I was carrying my weight. There were no favors granted on either side. I was the only person outside of himself whose word he would accept about a concession. Until then he had always appraised the new places himself.

I never thought about doing anything other than my work until Sam sent me out on the vending-machine assignment. Something about that business caught me the minute I walked into Mr. Christenson's place. It wasn't the dough either. Sam had many deals I had recommended to him that involved much more and much less money. It was just the idea in it. I could just see these machines scattered all over the city, in the best locations—restaurants, terminals, airports, every place where people stopped, congregated, went to in order to kill some time. Tremendous metal machines that stood there impersonally with their hands in everybody's pockets, appealing to everybody's tastes, to everybody's needs. Thirsty? Have a Coke. Chewing-gum, candy, cigarettes.

Maybe it was the way Mr. Chistenson had put it. I could see from the way he acted that the man didn't really want to sell. But what could the guy do when his medic told him he had a bum ticker and he had to blow the setup or croak?

How Sam heard about it I never found out; but when I got out there and saw that it ran with only a five-man crew and that the take was three grand a week, it appealed to me. It appealed to me even more when I had gone through the complete business.

Christenson had one hundred and forty-one cigarette vendors working and ninety-two Coke squirters. There were fourteen machines in the shop for which he couldn't get replacement parts, but if they were working they could bring in another three hundred bucks a week. On top of that, forty per cent of the locations were bad, but Christenson was too sick to scout up new spots for them. Relocating these machines could bring the gross up to four grand a week easy.

Christenson figured his net at about ten per cent of the gross, or about three hundred a week clear. I figured that if all the things I had thought of were done we could bring the net up to at least fifteen percent. That would mean six hundred a week on a gross of four grand. That was nice pickings. That was why I recommended the deal to Sam.

He could work a setup like that off the back of his hand, and with his connections he could probably get hold of more machines. That was the first time I had thought about it in personal terms. I had thought that if Sam didn't want to bother with it, I could make a deal to run the outfit for him. Then I went down to the manufacturers of the machines to inquire about replacements and parts. Of course there was nothing available now, they were all too busy with war work; but one of them had rolled out a booklet showing their poswar models.

My eyes had opened wide. This was a field we couldn't afford to miss. There were more real pickpockets in this booklet than at Coney Island on a crowded day. Machines that roasted a hot dog and delivered it in a toasted roll with a napkin rolled around it; machines that sold hot coffee in a disposable cardboard cup; sandwiches—anything you could think of. There was even a machine that sold you an insurance policy at the airport before you made your trip. They had figured out everything but where the locations for them would be.

Opportunity was lying around in the gutter like a two-dollar whore. It wasn't that Christenson's outfit was such a great money-maker now, for it would be just as good if it wasn't making a cent. It was the in it had on the postwar market, the edge that every business was looking for. An outfit like that could sneak around on the q.t. now while everybody was busy with other things and lock up every choice location in the country. Then it would really be big business.

But Sam was just like everybody else. He was doing good; he didn't want to strain his milk. Why go spec when the dough was pouring in like the Johnstown flood?

I looked at the check in my hand. I still hadn't answered my question. What made me want to do it? I knew now that it wasn't the business alone, it was something else. But it wasn't until I got home that night and saw Nellie that I found the answer.

I came into the apartment quietly, wondering how she would

take the news. I hoped she wouldn't be worried, but she was funny about things like that. She made a big thing about working and saving money; and a job was the only way she could see to do it.

Several times when I had wanted to move out of the apartment, she had refused. "Why spend the money for rent?" she had argued. "We're comfortable here."

"But, honey," I had said, "for more dough we can be more comfortable somewhere else."

"No," she had said, "we might as well hold onto it while it's coming in. Nobody can ever tell when it's gonna stop. Then we'll need every penny we ever could keep our hands on."

I stopped talking about it after a while. I could understand what she was afraid of and she had good reason for it. All we had ever known was poverty. What right did we have to expect things would ever change? It was a depression philosophy that left its roots in so deep that nothing could ever tear it out.

I closed the door quietly behind me. "Nellie," I called softly. Sometimes she was napping when I came home. She worked all day on big hot plastic molding presses and it drained her energy.

There was no answer, so I tiptoed toward the bedroom. Halfway through the parlor I saw her, curled up in a corner of the couch, all dressed to go out for dinner and fast asleep. I moved silently to her.

An outstretched hand hung alongside the couch, dangling toward the floor; her other hand was hugged tightly against her bosom. There was something clutched in it. I looked closely. It was a picture of Vickie, the one we had taken up on the roof during the short summer of her life. Nellie had held her while I snapped the shutter on the borrowed camera. I remembered how anxiously we waited for the pictures to come back to the corner drugstore where we had left them for developing, how carefully we clung to the few pennies necessary to pay the cost of printing them. Nellie had been holding the baby up in the air. The baby had been gurgling down at her and she had been smiling happily up at Vickie. I could feel a lump in my throat, Nellie looked so much like a kid herself in that picture.

I looked down at Nellie's face. Her eyes were closed and she was breathing lightly and evenly. Her long black lashes curled over the soft white of her skin. Faint lines in her makeup ran down from her eyes. She had been crying. She had been looking at the picture and crying. Suddenly I knew the answer I had been seeking. All at once I knew the answer to a lot of things.

I knew why we'd never had another child, why Nellie was so afraid to spend an extra penny, why she wouldn't let us move from here, She was afraid. She blamed herself for what had happened to Vickie and she didn't want it to happen again— neither the fear nor the poverty nor the heartbreak.

And I knew why I wanted the big buck, why I had to take the chance. It was either live in the shadow of the fear all our lives or, once and for all, break free of it and have all the things we wanted. That was the whole of it. We had to be free of the fear so that we could think of tomorrow, a tomorrow we had been afraid to look into because it looked so much like yesterday.

Now we would be able to think of ourselves again. Like other people, we could want things again, feel things again, hope things again. That was it.

You just don't die, no matter what happens; you don't quit. You go on living. That's what it is: you go on living. It's not a thing you can turn on and off like the water in a faucet, not as long as inside you the blood is running, the heart is beating, the mind is hoping. That was it. You go on living.

Lightly I took the photograph from her relaxed fingers, put it in my pocket, and sat down in the chair opposite to wait for her to wake up so that I could tell her what I had just learned.

Chapter Ten

I SAT there awkwardly in Mimi's living-room and looked at my father. I wished that she had left well enough alone. It was one of the big things n her life to reconcile us some day, but there was no use in it. Too many things had happened between us, we had drifted too far apart. Now we sat in the same room like strangers and made small talk, each of us extremely aware that the other was near and yet never addressing ourselves to each other.

Nellie and Mamma had gone with Mimi to the children's room to watch them going to bed, and Sam, Papa, and I were left in the living-room before dinner. The only talk was when Sam spoke to either of us. Then we would answer monosyllabically, stiffly, as if we were afraid our words would lead to further conversation.

At last Sam ran out of things to say that might interest both of us and retired into the awkward silence himself. He picked up the paper and turned to the sports section. For a few seconds the only sound in the room was the rustle of the newspaper.

I had been looking out the window across the Park. It was almost dusk and the lights in the buildings were just going on, flashing like yellow topazes on purple velvet.

"Danny, you remember that kid you fought in the Gloves finals—Joey Passo?"

I turned to Sam. I remembered very well. "That was the semifinals, Sam," I corrected him. "He was the kid that almost took me. He was good."

Sam nodded his head. "That's right. I knew you had fought him, though. It says here he's just signed for a crack at the light heavy championship in the fall."

I was aware of my father's eyes on me. "I hope the kid makes it," I said. "He's a good, gutsy kid and he needs the dough."

"You could have made it," Sam said without looking up from the paper. "You were good. You were the best prospect I ever seen."

I shook my head. "Uh-uh. It was too tough a racket for me."

Sam looked up from the paper. "The only thing wrong with you was that you didn't have the killer instinct. A few more fights and you might have got the idea."

My father spoke before I could answer. "A business where a man must be a killer is not a business I should want for my son."

Both Sam and I stared at him in surprise. It was the first time we could recall that he had injected himself into a conversation between us.

Papa's face flushed. "It's a dirty business where a man has to be a killer to be successful."

Sam and I exchanged knowing looks and Sam turned to him. "That's only an expression that fighters use, Dad," he explained. "It means that when you have a man in trouble, you know enough to finish him off quickly."

"An excuse in words is just an excuse," Papa insisted stubbornly. "If it's just words, why is it all the time I read in the papers about fighters getting killed?"

"They're accidents, Dad," Sam said. "You read about people getting killed every day in automobile accidents. That doesn't make everybody who drives a car a killer."

Papa shook his head. "A different thing."

It was Sam's turn to be stubborn. "It's not a different thing, Dad," he continued. "Prize fighting is a highly skilled sport. There are very few people who have all the skills necessary for it. The mental and physical co-ordination plus the will to win. All these things basically are God-given talents, and when you see someone who has them all, you're seeing a very unusual person. Your son, Danny, was one of those people."

He turned and looked at me a moment before he spoke again. There was a respectful affection deep in his eyes. "Danny was one of those people, Dad, who come along once in a lifetime." He was speaking softly, almost as if to himself. "When I first saw him he was a tall gangling kid, big for his age, who got into a fight in school. Before that he was just one of the kids I had in the class, but after that he was something special. He had the God-given talents."

Papa grunted. "The devil's talents, I say."

Sam's eyes flashed. "You're wrong about that, Dad, like you've been wrong about many things. Just as everybody is wrong sometimes. When you know how few people there are really in this world whose arms and legs move exactly and as quickly as their brain commands, you'll know what I mean."

Papa got to his feet. "I don't want to hear about it," he said with finality. "I'm not interested. To me, fighting is a murderer's business."

Sam was getting angry. "If that was the way you felt," he snapped sarcastically, "why was it all right for Mimi to marry me? I was a fighter."

Papa looked down at him. "You weren't a fighter then," he answered.

"But I would have been if I hadn't broken my kneecap," Sam retorted heatedly.

Papa shrugged his shoulders. "Mimi wanted you. It wasn't my business to tell her what to do. She could marry who she liked, it wasn't my place to interfere."

Sam's face was flushed. By now he was thoroughly angry.

"When was it your place to interfere, Dad? When it suited you? That wasn't the way you acted when Danny—"

"Knock it off, Sam," I said quickly, interrupting him. This was between my father and me; there was no point in his getting into the quarrel too.

Sam turned belligerently toward me. "Why should I knock it off?" he demanded. "I got a part in this too. I went for a barrel of dough in that fiasco." He looked stubbornly at Papa. "Everything was okay as long as the kid did what you said, but it was no good when he wouldn't listen to you. Still, you never turned down the dough he brought home for the fights. That five hundred he left for you the night you locked him out cost me five grand and almost cost the kid his life. You didn't know that, did you?"

Papa's face was pale. He looked at me almost shamefacedly. "A son has the right to listen to what his father tells him," he maintained.

"The right, yes," Sam said, "but not the obligation to do what he says. I won't ever feel like that about my kids no matter what they do, right or wrong. They didn't ask me to bring them into the world. And if I wanted them, I have to help them whether I agree or not."

Papa waved his hand excitedly. "I don't want to hear about it," he said. "We'll see what you do."

"You'll never see me close the door on my sons," Sam snapped.

Papa stared at him for a moment, his face turning very white. Then he stalked silently out of the room.

I looked at Sam. His face was still flushed. "What did you do that for?" I asked. "You're only wasting your breath."

Sam made a gesture of disgust. "I was gettin' tired of listenin' to the old man. He's so right about everything. I was getting tired of his cracks about you and what he expected from you and the disappointment you were to him."

"So what're you gettin' sore about?" I asked. "It's got nothin' to do with you. It's me he's talkin' about."

"He knows by now that I wanted you to be a fighter," Sam said, "an' it's his way of gettin' even with me because you listened to me instead of him. Some day I'm gonna make him realize that he's been wrong about a lot of things."

I stared at Sam, then turned away and lit a cigarette. "You'll never do that, Sam," I said to him over my shoulder. "You'll never get him to change his mind about anything. Take my word for it. I ought to know. After all, he's my father."

Chapter Eleven

I LOOKED at my watch as I walked through the small repair room. The mechanic was adjusting one of the cigarette machines. He grinned at me.

"I'll have this working in a couple of hours, Mr. Fisher."

"Take your time," I told him. "There's no use in sending it out again."

An understanding look crossed the man's face. "Nothing coming in?"

I shook my head. "Not a cigarette in a carload." I continued on through the room silently.

And that was putting it mildly. For almost six months now cigarettes had been harder to get than money, and crowds lined up wherever the word got out that there were cigarettes to be had. If I hadn't been smart and guessed something like this was coming, I'd have been out of business by now. But I had guessed right and with the help of a few men who were not averse to making an extra buck I had been able to stock up on them. The way I figured it, I couldn't lose no matter what happened. I could always push the butts out through the machines. But the shortage had come and now I was one of the few guys in the business with stock. It was my turn to make a buck.

I stuck my head in the small room at the back of the shop that served as the office. "Did Sam Gordon call back yet?" I asked the girl sitting there.

She shook her head. "No, Mr. Fisher."

"Well, call me when he does," I said, and walked back into the shop. Sam would call back, I knew he would. He had to whether he wanted to or not. I felt satisfied with myself. If this shortage lasted for a little while longer I would make a bundle of dough. Then I could really set myself up after the war. I ought to be able to raise enough money out of this operation to grab up all the best locations in the city.

I went back to the repair room and watched the mechanic. There was a paper lying on the bench behind him and I picked it up. "How's the war goin'?" I asked casually, flipping the pages.

"Pretty rough," the mechanic answered. "Them Nazis are hard to knock off."

"We'll get 'em," I said, not really thinking about it. I was too busy trying to figure out if Sam would go for the price I had in mind. I took a deep breath. He had to; otherwise he'd have nothing to sell in his concessions.

I glanced at the headlines. The Germans were retreating through France, and Patton's Third Army was hot on their tail. "We'll get 'em," I repeated.

"I sure hope so, Mr. Fisher," the mechanic replied in the tone of voice that an employee uses toward his boss.

I leaned my back comfortably against the work bench and kept turning the pages. A small headline caught my eyes: "Local OPA Says No Cigarette Shortage." I grinned as I read down the column. An awful lot of people were smoking clinchers if there was no shortage.

The paper quoted the OPA as saying that the whole blame rested on the hoarders. Some unscrupulous people were piling them up in warehouses to supply a black market instead of letting them flow into normal channels of supply.

I almost laughed aloud. I wondered what they'd do if they had the same chance to grab a buck that I did. Let them go into normal channels? Like hell they would. They would do just what I did: buy them in, stock them up, and sell them for the most you can get. A guy doesn't get a break like this very often, and I wasn't going to be fool enough to shove them out where I had to sell them at the regular price when I could get double the money or better.

"It's okay now, Mr. Fisher," the mechanic called to me.

"All right, Gus," I said. "If yuh got nothin' else to do, you knock off for the day."

"Thanks, Mr. Fisher." The man grinned at me gratefully. He turned to the machine. "Too bad we can't get enough cigarettes to keep it working, though," he said.

"Yeah." I smiled back at him. "It's too bad. But maybe we're worried over nothin'. The OPA says there's no cigarette shortage."

The man nodded. "I read that," he answered vehemently. "It's them lousy hoarders. They're keepin' honest men like us from makin' a livin'."

I agreed with him. He was absolutely right. I watched him climb out of his jumper, wondering what he'd say if he knew about the butts I had socked away. He'd probably holler copper. He was that kind of an honest shnook. I felt glad I had enough brains to store them in private warehouses away from the shop. That way nobody knew what I had.

I heard the girl's voice. "Mr. Gordon returning your call."

"I'm on my way." I dropped the paper on the bench and hurried back to the office. I picked up the phone. The girl was straightening some papers on her desk, not paying any attention to me.

"Hello, Sam," I said into the telephone.

"What's the black market on butts today, Danny?" he asked.

I grinned into the phone. "Easy, Sam, easy. You know how sensitive I am. You're hurting my feelings."

"Nothin' can hurt your feelings," Sam snapped sharply, "excep' losin' a buck!"

"Is that a way for my only brother-in-law to talk?" I kidded him. "Specially when I'm tryin' to do him a favor?"

"Nuts! I know you," Sam replied in a friendly voice. "What are you gettin' for 'em today?"

"It all depends," I said evasively. "How much do you need?"

"Five thousand cartons," Sam answered.

I whistled. "That's a lot of smoke," I said. "I think you can dig it for three and a half per."

"Three and a half dollars a carton?" Sam's voice almost split the receiver.

"What are yuh bitchin' about?" I asked easily. "Your girls get a half a buck a throw or better." I knew what I was talking about. I hadn't worked those years for him for nothing. Those pretty little half-dressed babes walking around in night clubs with a cigarette tray sticking out in front of them and an almost bare fanny behind knew how to milk the suckers for a buck.

"Three and a quarter," Sam bargained. "Gimme a break. After all, if it wasn't for me you wouldn't be in that racket."

"Three and a half," I insisted. "I think the world of you, Sam, and I still owe yuh six grand, but a cuter is cuter." That was true. I hadn't repaid Sam yet because the dough that came through I was sinking in location setups.

"Danny," Sam pleaded.

"Where do you want 'em shipped?" I asked, ignoring the sound in his voice. I knew he could afford the price. Sam was making dough as he'd never made it before.

There was a moment's silence; then his voice came wearily through the phone. "The usual place."

"C.O.D."

"Yeah," Sam answered without enthusiasm. "And I hope the OPA gets yuh, yuh bastard. Good-by."

I put the phone down, smiling. That was a fast ten grand. They only cost me a buck and a half a carton. I reached into my desk and took out my little book. I studied it carefully. I had made a list of all the locations I wanted to clinch. This dough would come in handy. I was almost all through the book now. Soon I could start making arrangements to get in my machine orders.

I looked up at the calendar. It was near the end of May. A few more days and I would be twenty-seven years old. Time was running away from me; I was getting old.

I looked at the book again. I'd better start getting in the machine orders now if I wanted to be sure of a favored position on the list when the manufacturers began shipment. The whole thing wouldn't be worth a damn if I couldn't get those machines.

Chapter Twelve

I CAME into the apartment smiling. Nellie was bending over the stove, peering into a pot. She turned her face toward me, without straightening up, and I kissed her cheek.

"What's for dinner, baby?" I asked gaily.

"Pot roast," she answered, "with stewed white onions."

I put my head over her shoulder and sniffed at the odors coming up from the pot. "Man, that smells good!" I grinned. "How'd yuh manage it?"

"It's so close to the end of the month that the butcher took some of next month's points," she explained.

"I don't know how you do it," I said in an admiring voice. "Work out at that stinkin' plant all day, then come home an' cook a meal like that."

"So many compliments!" she kidded me. "You must be looking for something."

I shook my head. "Uh-uh. I mean it. We don't need the dough. Why don't you quit?"

"I've been thinking about it," she said, half-seriously, "but the boys are depending on us. Now more than ever."

"And I'm depending on you," I said quickly. "The boys aren't. But how'll I manage if you wear yourself out?"

"Don't be silly, Danny," she said.

"I'm not being silly. I just love pot roast with stewed little white onions."

She pushed me toward the bathroom. "Go in and wash up," she said, laughing happily. "Supper's almost ready."

I went toward the bathroom smiling. It was good to see her so happy. It had been a long time since I had seen her looking as content as that.

"Yuh want some help with the dishes?" I asked, without looking up from the evening paper.

"You pick the right time to ask," she answered dryly. "I'm all through already."

I grunted and settled back in the easy chair and turned to the sports pages. The Yankees looked like a pennant bet even this early in the season.

She came into the parlor and sank on the couch opposite me. "How'd it go today?" she asked in a tired voice.

I couldn't keep the satisfaction out of my voice. "I hooked Sam for five thousand cartons. That's a clean ten grand."

A worried look appeared on her face. "Danny," she said quietly, "I'm scared. What if they catch you?"

I shrugged my shoulders. "Stop worryin'. They ain't gonna."

"But, Danny," she protested, "I saw in the paper that—"

"The papers are full of crap," I interrupted her. "They're just fishing. Besides, what can they do to me? It ain't against the law to sell cigarettes."

The worried look remained on her face. "The money isn't worth it," she said soberly. "Nothing's worth it. It's getting so I can't sleep nights any more."

I dropped the paper and looked at her. "You'd like it better if I was like the rest of the shnooks? We had enough of that, remember? You liked being without enough dough to eat? Not me. I've had enough of it."

Her eyes met mine levelly. "I don't care about that," she said quietly. "All I want is for you to stay out of trouble."

"Don't worry about me, Nellie," I said confidently, picking up the paper again. "I'll be okay. Before this is over, baby, you'll be wearin' minks and diamonds."

"I can live without them," she said, her eyes still troubled. "All I want is for you to be around." She drew a deep breath and I could see her hands clench into tight little fists. "After all, I wouldn't like having to tell Junior that his father is in jail."

The paper slipped out of my fingers to the floor. "What did you say?" I asked incredulously.

She smiled at me calmly, with the secret pride of a woman who carries a child under her heart lurking in her eyes. "You heard me," she said matter-of-factly. "We're going to have a baby."

I was out of my chair in a second, standing excitedly over her. "W-why didn't yuh say something?" I sputtered.

Her brown eyes sparkled with amusement. "I wanted to make sure first," she answered.

I dropped to my knees beside her. "You been to the doctor already?" I asked, taking her hand.

She nodded. "This morning, on the way to work."

I pulled her toward me gently and kissed her cheek. "An' yuh went in anyway? At least you could have called me up and told me."

"Don't be silly." She laughed. "You wouldn't have been able to work."

"An' I been sittin' here like a damn fool lettin' you knock yourself out," I reproached myself. I looked at her. "When are we expectin'?"

"In about seven months," she replied. "Around the end of November."

I sank on the couch beside her. I felt good. I had been right

about many things. Somehow I had known that as soon as
Nellie felt secure we would have another child. I sighed contentedly.

"Happy, Danny?" she asked.

I nodded my head, remembering the last time we had been
through this. Things were different now. It was a lot better this
way. "Now we can get out of here," I said.

"What for?" she asked. "This place is all right."

"This ain't the right neighborhood to bring up a kid if you
can afford somethin' better," I said confidently. "Let's find a
place where there's some air and sunshine."

She leaned back on the couch. "A place like that is so expensive, Danny," she protested mildly. "You know they're hard to
get, and you have to pay under the table for any kind of an
apartment now."

"Who said anything about an apartment?" I asked. "I want
to buy a house!"

"A house!" It was her turn to be surprised. "That's out
altogether. Too much money. I'd rather make do here and hold
onto the money."

"To hell with that!" I said defiantly. "What am I makin' the
dough for, if not for you—and the kid?"

Chapter Thirteen

THE STEAMING August sun straddled my neck and shoulders, squeezing the last drop of perspiration out of me as I got
into the car and switched on the ignition. I pressed down on the
starter. The engine sputtered and gasped. I pulled the choke
and hit the starter again. The engine coughed and began to turn
over slowly; then it sputtered and died.

I looked at the dashboard. The ammeter needle was flicker-
ing over on "discharge." I stepped on the starter again. No use;
the battery had gone. Resignedly I turned off the ignition and
got out of the car. I stood staring at the automobile as if it had

betrayed me. I cursed silently. I had promised Nellie I would be home early too.

I checked my watch. Four thirty. By the time I could get the battery recharged or replaced I'd have lost an hour and Nellie would be mad as hell. I locked the car and started for the subway. The nearest station was six blocks away and I was sweating bullets by the time I reached it. I dropped my nickel into the turnstile and went down to the platform.

As soon as I reached the platform I was thirsty. I looked for a news-stand. Some of them sold cold Cokes. One would go real good the way I felt now. There was a stand down at the far end of the platform, and I covered almost half the distance to it before I noticed it was closed. I stopped, disgusted. Nothing had gone right this afternoon. First the car conked out on me, now I couldn't even get a drink. The thirst came back stronger than ever, renewed by frustration.

I fished in my pocket for a penny and threw it into a chewing-gum machine. Maybe a stick of gum would help until I could get a drink.

A train roared into the station and I boarded it, idly glancing at my fellow passengers. Their faces gleamed eerily at me in the yellow light, shining with sweat from the damp heat. After a while I began to get bored. I wished I had thought to buy a newspaper. All the faces were the same in the subway, dull and tired and blank. They were all probably as hot and thirsty as I, and just as uncomfortable.

I began to read the signs strung out on the side of the train just over my head. The first one to catch my eye was a Coca-Cola ad. There was the usual picture of the usual wholesome, pretty girl smiling. She looked fresh and cool, and behind her was the usual pale blue-green cake of ice. In her hand she held a bottle of Coca-Cola, and beneath it were the usual words: "THE PAUSE THAT REFRESHES."

My mouth watered. The chewing-gum was suddenly dry and tasteless. That was a hell of a thing to see when you were dying of thirst. Teased hell out of you.

The train had stopped again and I looked out the window. A man was dropping a coin into a chewing-gum machine. His face was red and flushed with the heat and I could hear the coin tinkling into the box as the man pulled the handle.

The doors began to close and I looked up at the Coke sign

again. To hell with the gum machines, I thought wearily; what they could use on the subway was a few of my cold-drink squirters. They would really do a business. Then it hit me. I remembered something a girl had once said when I worked at a soda fountain. I remembered the girl too. She had a healthy pair of lungs and I recalled the way she pushed them over the counter at me. "They ought to have places on the subway where you can get a Coke if you're thirsty," she had said.

I stared up at the sign bewilderedly. Talk about shnooks, I could take the prize! It had been here under my nose all the time and I hadn't seen it! The best location in the world: the New York subways. All I had to do was make a deal with the city and I was on Easy Street. I wouldn't have to do another lick of work all my life.

The people in the train all looked hot and thirsty. In my mind's eye I could picture them dropping nickels into my Coke dispensers. Hell, it wasn't only cold drinks; in the winter I could serve them hot coffee.

I began to feel excited. I couldn't afford to fall asleep over this thing. This was the baby I had been looking for, the location to beat all locations. I was glad my car had stalled. It took something like that to wake a guy up. If you really wanted to grab a buck you had to get down where the people were. Where they were was where the dough was. Woolworth had the right idea: grab the nickels and dimes. If you could do that, you were set. And the nickels and dimes on the subways added up to more dough than there was in all the department stores on Fifth Avenue.

I pressed the buzzer impatiently. I looked at Nellie standing in the dull white glow of the hall light. I pressed the buzzer again and smiled at her. I liked the way she looked. Her slightly swollen frame made her look even more attractive.

"I still don't see why you had to come running up here to see Sam," she said in an annoyed voice. "You could have done it tomorrow."

I looked at her understandingly. It was hot and she was uncomfortable. Even more so than usual. "Maybe I could," I answered quickly, "but if I got the idea, it's better'n even money that somebody else got it too. An' this can't keep, we gotta—" I stopped talking as the door opened.

Mimi was standing there. A look of surprise crossed her face as she saw us. "Danny! Nellie! We didn't expect you." She smiled and stepped back to let us in.

I was in the foyer already. "I came up to see Sam on a deal," I explained, looking for him in the living-room. "Is he home?"

Sam's voice bellowing from inside the apartment gave me my answer. "Who is it, Mimi?"

"Danny and Nellie," Mimi called back. "Danny wants to see you." She turned back to us. "Go on in," she invited us. "Sam will be down in a minute."

We followed her into the living-room. "How are you feeling?" she asked Nellie sympathetically.

"Wonderful," Nellie replied happily. "If the doctor hadn't told me I was pregnant I never would have believed it, I feel so good."

"You're lucky," Mimi said. "I'm always sick as a dog." Her voice lowered to the confidential tone that women use when they discuss their pregnancies.

"What's Sam doing?" I asked, interrupting her impatiently. I had heard about Mimi's pregnancies a thousand times since Nellie had told them the news.

"He's taking a shower," Mimi replied. "He can't take this heat, he's such a big man, you know."

I nodded and started for the stairway of the duplex apartment. "You kids go ahead and yak," I called back over my shoulder. "I can talk to Sam while he's showering."

Sam was standing in front of the mirror, a towel wrapped around his waist, combing his hair when I walked in on him. "What do you want?" he asked grumpily.

"How'd yuh like to make a million bucks?" I asked enthusiastically.

He glanced at me in the mirror. It was a suspicious look. "Not interested," he answered quickly. "Every time you come to me with an idea, it costs me money."

"Stop making with the funny cracks," I said. "I really got it this time. Yuh want to hear it or not?"

He put down the comb and turned to me wearily. "All right," he said. "So tell me. I'm gonna hear it anyway."

I grinned. "Did you ever try to buy a Coke in the subway?" I asked.

He looked bewildered. "What the hell are yuh talking

about?" he asked. "You know I ain't been in the subway for years. That's for the peasants."

I dropped the cover on the toilet seat and sat down. "That's just it, Sam," I said softly. "Yuh oughtta get down there with the peasants sometimes or yuh might forget where yuh come from."

Sam was annoyed. "I ain't heard your million-dollar idea yet," he snapped.

"You heard it, Sam," I said, "but the trouble is you been away from the peasants for so long you weren't listening. I might've missed it too if my car hadn't broke down today."

"So I been away from the peasants so long," Sam said disgustedly. "So stop crappin' an tell me or get outta here an' let me dress."

I lit a cigarette and blew a gust of smoke toward him. "Remember way back, Sam," I said quietly, "remember when you were one of the six million peasants in this town who don't live on Central Park South an' you were comin' home from work? You were hot and tired and thirsty, an' when you got on the subway you realized it. You were dyin' for a drink, but when you looked aroun', there ain't none an' you gotta wait till you get off." I paused to catch my breath.

"What're you tryin' to do? Win the Accademy Award for the best performance of the year?" Sam asked caustically before I could continue.

I could feel my face flush. I hadn't realized I had been so dramatic. "You don't see it yet?" I asked. I couldn't see how he'd missed it.

He shook his head. "I don't see it," he said flatly. "I'm the Central Park type. I'm stupid. I'm not one of those smart peasants."

"Would you buy a drink if there were one of my Coke machines on the platform?" I asked quickly.

He had started to rub his face again with a towel. Now he lowered it and stared at me. There was a gleam of interest in his eyes. "Say that again, Danny," he said carefully. "And tell me slow. Now I'm listenin'!"

Chapter Fourteen

IT WAS the big deal all right. Even Sam had to say that. He went for it whole hog. We formed a separate company just to handle it. He would put up the dough and take care of the arrangements, I would run the business. And there were a lot of arrangements to be made, more than I had ever thought possible. I had been so busy since I got into it that I brought Zep in with me to handle the regular business while I devoted myself to the new company.

Coke machines on the subway. Who would think such a simple thing would take so much time and effort? But there were so many people you had to see—city officials, Board of Transportation officials, engineers, Department of Health people. Approval had to come from so many places that at times I had been bewildered. And as if that weren't bad enough, when we had everything lined up, there were still the politicians.

You had to have connections for a job like this. That was why I had gone to Sam in the first place. Sam had the connections, but even there we had run into a snag: Mario Lombardi, a quiet little man who hired a press agent to keep his name out of the papers, not in them. But his name got into the papers anyway. You couldn't keep a man like that a secret. He had too much power. I found out that nothing really big could be done in the city of New York unless Mario Lombardi okayed it. That was in spite of all the honest intentions of the city government.

And there was only one way Sam knew to get to Mario Lombardi. Through Maxie Fields. I wished there had been another way to reach him—any way but through Maxie Fields. But Sam assured me there wasn't, otherwise he would prefer it himself. So we had spoken to Maxie and now we were sitting in the living-room office of Mario Lombardi's upper Park Avenue apartment and it looked as if we were going to take in two new partners at any moment.

I leaned back in the chair, the smoke curling upward from my cigarette. I looked skeptically at Lombardi, seated behind his desk. "So we cut you in, Mr. Lombardi," I said casually. "What guarantee we got that after the war the deal we make will stand up? After all, politics in this town is a tricky business. One time you're in, next time you're out."

Lombardi tapped the ashes from his cigar delicately into a tray, the big diamond in his pinky ring flashing at me. He returned my gaze steadily. "Mario Lombardi don't make promises he can't keep, Danny," he answered quietly. "I don't care who's running the city when the war is over. It's my town and I'll still be callin' the shots."

"That's right, Danny." Maxie Fields's booming voice had a fawning quality in it that made me sick. "You don't clear nothin' in this town unless Mario okays it."

I looked at Maxie coldly. I still didn't like him. There was something about him that rubbed me the wrong way.

Sam's face was inscrutable, but his head nodded impassively.

It was okay with Sam, so I turned back to Lombardi. The small, dark man, dapper in his conservative gray suit, seemed more interested in his fingernails than in our conversation. I sighed lightly. This was as far as we could go; the rest was up to fate. I had already been to see every two-bit politico and they all had told me that Lombardi was the only man big enough to swing a deal like this. So we took in partners.

"Okay, Mario," I said finally. You never call a partner by his last name. "It's a deal. You get ten per cent of the profits."

Lombardi stood up and held out his hand to me. "You won't regret it, Danny," he said. "Any time you want anything, you come an' see me."

I took his hand. "Anything?" I asked smiling.

Lombardo nodded, his teeth startling white in his swarthy face. "That's what I said."

"Then get me an apartment," I said quickly. "My wife is knockin' herself out lookin' for one an' she's six months gone already." Nellie still wouldn't let me part with the dough for a house.

Lombardi's smile turned into a wry grin. He shrugged his shoulder expressively and glanced about the room, a touch of embarrassed humor lurking deep in his dark eyes. "Medium OPA approved rentals?" he asked.

I nodded. "About seventy-five to a hundred bucks a month."

The wry grin broadened on his face. He held up his hands expressively. "Ask me something easy like that, Danny, an' I'm stuck," he admitted. "This morning I spoke to a guy an' got an okay for a judge; I spoke to some other people an' fixed up a buildin' deal; I went to lunch with the Mayor an' earlier this afternoon I arranged a million-dollar loan, but you gotta come along an' ask me somethin' easy which I can't do. Tell your wife to stop beatin' her brains out, Danny. Go out an' buy a house."

"Goin' past my place, Danny?" Fields asked heavily as we stepped out into the street.

I nodded and turned to Sam. "I'll see you tomorrow?"

"Sure," Sam replied as he got into his yellow Cadillac convertible. "In the morning."

We watched Sam drive off, then turned and walked to my car. I was silent. I was figuring. Ten per cent for Lombardi and five per cent for Maxie Fields for the fix. Fields's voice cut into my thoughts.

"That Sam is a bright guy," he said, squeezing his massive bulk into the seat beside me.

I stared at him in surprise. It was the first time I had ever known Fields to say a nice word for anybody. "Yeah," I answered, throwing the car into gear and moving out into traffic.

"He's got himself a hell of a business," Maxie continued blandly. "Growin' all the time too."

I wondered what he was getting at. I confined myself to a cryptic answer. "He works." I said. "He works all the time."

"That he does," Fields agreed readily. Too readily. "I understand you're pretty hep to that racket too. You worked in very close with him."

I glanced at him out of the corner of my eye. Maxie's face was smooth; he was looking out the car window. "Yeah," I answered.

"If somethin' happened to him, I guess you'd have to take over on account of your sister," Maxie continued.

For a moment I was too surprised to even think. "Why yes," I stammered, "I—I suppose I would have to."

We stopped for a traffic light and I could feel Maxie's eyes on my face, watching me closely. "If yuh ever got any ambitions along that line, Danny," he suggested casually, "why don't yuh just talk to me? Maybe I can help you out."

There was a sick feeling in my stomach. I gripped the wheel tightly, my knuckles white against the back of my hands. I managed to keep my voice as casual as his had been. "I'm satisfied with what I got, Maxie. I'm doin' all right."

"Well, the black market in butts won't last forever, kid." His voice was bluff and hearty. "An' the war may not be over for a long time. Just remember what I said in case you should change your mind."

The rest of the ride downtown passed in silence. I couldn't wait for him to get out of the car. It was bad enough I had to do business with him; I couldn't stand having him around me any more than was absolutely necessary.

As I let myself into the apartment quietly, I could hear the hum of an electric fan coming from the bedroom and tiptoed toward it. Through the open door I could see a figure on the bed.

Nellie was sleeping, her head resting on one arm, the gentle breeze from the fan stirring the sheet over her. I watched her for a moment, then turned and silently began to leave the room.

Her voice called me back. "Danny?"

I turned to her. Her dark eyes were watching me. "I was so tired," she said in a small voice, "I fell asleep."

I sat down beside her on the bed. "I didn't mean to wake you up."

"You didn't wake me," she replied. "I have to make supper anyway. But I spent all day looking for an apartment and didn't find one. Then I felt so weak I just had to take a nap."

I smiled tolerantly at her. "Why don't you quit an' let's buy us a house. Even Mario Lombardi can't get us an apartment."

"But so much money, Danny," she protested, sitting up in the bed.

I leaned toward her. "Stop worrying about money, honey," I said gently. "Lombardi okayed the subway deal for us. We can afford it."

Her eyes searched mine. "Are you sure that's what you really want, Danny?"

I nodded. "All my life I wanted my own house." Even as I said it I realized how true the words were. I had never been so happy as when I was in my own house. "That's what I want," I added.

She drew in a sharp sudden breath and flung her arms around my neck. "Okay, Danny," she breathed against my ear. "If that's what you want, that's what we'll do."

Chapter Fifteen

"THE TREES are all grown now," I thought as I turned the car into the street. Nellie was silently looking out the window. I couldn't tell from her face what she was thinking as I let the car roll slowly up the street.

Almost twenty years had changed many things. The houses on the block had settled into homes. A little older, weather-beaten. Some of them needed repainting badly. But one thing hadn't changed. Despite the individual differences, each house looked very much like the others.

I pulled the car to a stop at the curb in front of our house, cut the motor, and turned to Nellie. She was still sitting silently, her eyes fixed on the house. I looked at it too.

A warmth swept through me, a strong satisfaction that I had not known for a long time. Now it would really be my house. "The agent said he would be waiting for us inside," I said.

Nellie's eyes were darkly thoughtful. "Danny," she said hesitantly, "maybe we ought to wait a little while longer. Maybe we shouldn't rush into this. Something else might turn up."

"What?" I asked skeptically. "We spent a month and a half lookin' an' we seen nothin' we liked. It's the middle of September now, an' if we want a house to move into by October 1st, we gotta make up our minds."

"We don't have to rush," she said. "We can wait until after the baby comes."

I shook my head. "Uh-uh. I want everything ready." I opened the door. "Let's go."

She got out of the car slowly and stood on the sidewalk. Her hand reached out and touched my arm. There was a deeply worried look in her eyes. She shivered slightly.

I looked at her in quick concern. There was no reason for her to shiver. It was almost hot with the sun beating down on us.

"What's the matter?" I asked. "Don't you feel well?"

She shook her head. "I feel all right."

"Then why the shiver?" I asked. "Are you cold?"

"No," she said in a low voice. "A terrible feeling just came over me. I was frightened."

I smiled at her. "What have you got to be frightened about?"

She turned and looked at the house. "Suddenly I was afraid for you, Danny. I feel something terrible is going to happen."

I laughed aloud at that. "What can happen?" I asked. "We're set now. Nothing can go wrong."

Her grip tightened on my arm. "That house means a lot to you, doesn't it, Danny?" she asked, still looking at it.

"Yeah," I said. "It was supposed to be my house from the very beginning and it never really was. Now it will be."

She turned to me, a sudden knowledge in her face. "And all your life you've been trying to get even."

I didn't understand her. "What do you mean?"

"All the time this is what you wanted. More than anything else," she explained.

I thought for a moment. Maybe she was right. But it couldn't make any difference now. It just happened that my old house was available when we were looking for one. And the way things were, there was no new housing available. Things had a way of working out. That it should be on the market just at that time seemed only right to me.

I turned toward the house without saying anything to her. Her hand pulled at my arm.

"Danny, maybe we shouldn't buy the house," she said earnestly. "Maybe it was intended that you should not live there. I got a feeling that we're tempting fate if you come back to it."

I smiled. Pregnant women were always having hunches and making gloomy predictions. Carrying children seemed to bring with it a spurious foreknowledge. "Don't be foolish, Nellie," I said. "All we're doing is buying a house."

She started for the front door, but I steered her toward the driveway and we walked between the two houses to the garden in the back. It had changed too. When we had lived there, the back yard was bare, but now it was neatly turned and filled with shrubs and bushes and plants. I looked over toward the corner near the fence and remembered the night I had come back with Rexie and buried her there. A big rosebush covered the spot. I wondered if her rest had been disturbed.

"Mr. Fisher!" a voice called.

I turned around. The real-estate agent was coming up the driveway behind us. I waved to him.

"Ready to look at the house now, Mr. Fisher?" he asked.

I nodded my head. I was ready.

The wooden floor creaked comfortably under my feet. It was a welcoming sound. "Hello, Danny Fisher," It seemed to whisper softly. The bright sun at the windows faded as a cloud crossed its face and the room grew dark.

I paused on the threshold of my old room. Nellie and the agent were in another part of the house. I entered the room quietly and closed the door behind me.

Once, long ago, I had done this. I had thrown myself on the floor and pressed my cheek against the cool wood. I was too big to do that now. Some day my son would do it in my stead.

"It's been a long time, Danny," the room seemed to whisper.

It had been a long time. I looked down at the floor. There was no dark spot there where Rexie used to lie. Many scrapings and varnishings had taken it away. The stippled wall had vanished under many layers of paint, the ceiling behind many coats of calcimine. The room seemed smaller than I remembered. Maybe it was because I remembered it when I was very small myself and saw everything in relation to me. I crossed the room and opened one of the windows. Instinctively I looked across the driveway to the next house.

Years ago, there was a girl who had that room. I tried hard to remember her name but I couldn't, I could only remember what she looked like with the electric light shining behind her. I could hear her shadowed voice calling me and I looked at the windows opposite. They were blank and the blinds were drawn.

I turned back into the room. It seemed to move with a sibilant life all its own. "I've missed you, Danny," it whispered. "Have you come home to stay? It's been so lonely without you."

There was a weariness inside me and I leaned back against the windowsill. I'd been lonely too. I'd missed this house more than I had realized. Now I knew what Nellie had meant. There was a promise here that somehow I knew would be kept. It was written everywhere I turned. "I will care for your son, Danny, as I have cared for you. I will help him grow tall and strong, happy and content, wise and understanding. I will love him as I love you, Danny, if you'll come home to stay."

There was a noise outside in the hall and the door opened. Nellie and the agent came into the room. She took one look at my face and hurried to me. Her voice echoed warmly in the empty room. "Danny, are you all right?"

Slowly I came back to her. A deep concern was in her eyes as she looked up at me. "All right?" I echoed her. "Of course I'm all right."

"But your face is pale," she said.

Just then the sun came out from behind the clouds. "It's just the light in here," I laughed, beginning to feel normal.

Her eyes were still on mine. "Sure you're doing right, Danny?" she asked anxiously. "No ghosts to bother you?"

I looked at her in surprise. I didn't believe in ghosts. "No ghosts," I said gently.

The real-estate agent looked at me curiously. "Your wife tells me you used to live here, Mr. Fisher."

I nodded.

He smiled broadly. "Well, in that case I don't have to tell you anything about the house itself. About how well it's made. Recent buildings are nowhere near as well constructed. What do you think, Mrs. Fisher?"

She looked at him for a moment, then turned back to me. "What do you think, Danny?"

I took a deep breath and looked around me. I knew what I was going to say. I had always known. And there were sounds in the house that made me feel as if it knew the answer, too.

"I think we're going to take it," I said. "Could you arrange to have the painters in tomorrow so that we can occupy on the 1st?"

Chapter Sixteen

I GOT to my feet in surprise as Sam walked into my office. This was the first time he had ever come out here. "Sam!" I said, my surprise echoing in my voice. "What's the occasion?"

He looked meaningfully at the girl sitting at the next desk to mine in the small office.

I sent the girl out and turned back to Sam. "What's on your mind?"

Sam slipped into the chair she had vacated. "I'm gettin' a little tired of havin' to call you every week for cigarettes. I want to fix up a steady thing with you."

I smiled in relief. For a moment I had thought that he had come to complain about the orders I had placed for the subway drink dispensers. I had been spending his capital as if it were mine. "You ought to know better'n that, Sam," I said reproachfully. "Nobody can guarantee it. The stuff's hard to get."

"You can get it," he said confidently.

"I wish I could be sure," I said quickly.

"I want two hundred boxes a week," he said, his voice hardening. "You'll see that I get it."

"And what if I don't?" I challenged. I could do it all right, but I wanted to find out what had made Sam so sure of himself.

He took a folded sheet of paper from his pocket and threw it on the desk. "Glom that," he said.

I picked it up and looked at it. It was a copy of my warehouse receipts. That meant he knew where I had stashed every last pack of butts. I turned to him in bewilderment. "Where'd you get that?" I demanded.

He smiled broadly. "I got ways," he answered evasively. "Now do I get them butts?"

"Supposin' I say no anyway?" I asked.

"The OPA would love to have a copy of those receipts." He smiled.

"You wouldn't do that to me, Sam!" My voice was shocked.

He smiled again. "Of course not, Danny," he replied casually. "No more'n you'd tell Mimi about other matters."

I put a hurt, disillusioned look on my face. "I never thought you'd do a thing like that, Sam," I said mournfully, swallowing an impulse to smile.

Sam's face wore a delighted expression of triumph. "You don't like it when the shoe's on the other foot, you little black-mailin' bastard?"

That did it. I couldn't choke back the laughter any more. It echoed loudly in the tiny office.

Sam stared at me in surprise. "What's with you, Danny?" he asked in a gruff voice. "You gone off your rocker?"

I looked at him through the tears that came into my eyes. Finally I caught my breath. "I was just thinkin', brother-in-law," I gasped, "that this is a fine way for a couple of partners to act to each other!"

Then he saw the humor in it and began to laugh too.

After a while I took him out into the shop and showed him around. It seemed to open his eyes a little. He hadn't realized that the thing had turned into such a big proposition. Then when we came back into the office and I showed him the list of locations I had already signed for, I could see a new respect dawning in his eyes.

"You got almost as much here as we got in the subway deal alone," he said in surprise.

"More," I said quickly. "Before I'm through, it'll be twice as big." I offered him a cigarette and lit it for him. "Compliments of the house," I said.

He was still thinking about what he had learned. "Now I know why you're always short of dough," he said.

I nodded. "I been throwin' it back as quick as it came in."

He looked at me through the cloud of smoke coming from his nostrils. "How about puttin' the whole thing together in one package, kid?" he suggested. "It'd make it a lot easier for yuh."

I played cagey. "You throwin' your business in too, Sam?" I countered.

"Uh-uh." He shook his head. "I just mean this. I'll give yuh a fair price for half an' then supply the dough jus' like on the subway deal."

It was my turn to say no. "That was a big one I couldn't handle alone, Sam," I said. "This is mine. I built it a little brick at a time. I'm gonna keep it."

He was silent a moment. I knew that look on his face: he was figuring out an angle. When at last he looked up at me, I could tell from his expression that he had given up. "Okay, Danny," he said genially. "But if you should ever change your mind, say the word. By the way," he asked, turning to leave, "how's the house comin'?"

"Okay. We'll be in it next week, Tuesday, like we figured."

He walked back toward the desk. "You should've seen your old man's face when Mimi told him."

"What'd he say?" I asked. I couldn't conceal my interest.

"At first he didn't believe it, but when Mimi swore that it was the truth, he couldn't speak. Your mother began to cry."

I couldn't understand that. "What was she crying for?"

"She kept saying something to your father about that was what you wanted all the time and he wouldn't believe you. He couldn't speak, he just chewed away on that cigar of his and after a while he went over to the window and looked out. All through dinner he was very quiet, and toward the end of the meal he looked up at Mimi and said a very funny thing." Sam paused for breath and looked at me.

I didn't say anything.

"He said: 'So Danny's going home.' And your mother said: 'That's what he wanted all the time—to come home. And you wouldn't let him.' Then your father said: 'I'm an old man now and for me it doesn't matter any more. My mistakes I'll take with me to my grave. But happy I am that Danny found his way back.' Then they got up and your father said he was tired and they went home."

My cigarette had burned almost to my fingers and I dropped it into an ashtray.

"Y'know, kid," he said softly, "I think the old man is about ready to throw in the towel if you'll go to him."

I breathed deeply and shook my head. "It's more'n that, Sam," I replied. "He's got to square away with Nellie first. There were too many things he said, too many things he did. He's got to level all the way round."

"He will if you give him the chance, Danny."

"He's gotta do that by himself," I said. "I can't do that for him."

"You know how he is, kid," Sam said gently. "He's proud and stubborn and he's old. Only God knows how much time he's got left to—"

"I'm his son, Sam," I interrupted him wearily. "You don't have to tell me anything about him. I know him better'n you. And I'm a lot of things that he is too. I'm proud and stubborn. In a way I'm old too, older'n he is. I gone through a lot of things because of how he acted that made me older. I buried a child, Sam. She died in my arms because we didn't have anyone to turn to for help. Yuh think that can happen 'thout getting older? Yuh think yuh forget a thing like that? You can't," I answered myself. "Yuh can't forget. An' yuh can't forget that it all started when your own father locked his door on you." I shook my head. "He'll have to do it all by himself, like I had to. Then maybe we'll be able to level again and feel right with each other."

I dropped into my chair and lit another cigarette. I was very tired. When all the rush of moving and business died down and Nellie had the baby, we'd go away for a while. We both could use the rest. I couldn't ever remember feeling so tired all the time.

I looked up at Sam again and switched the subject. "Where d'yuh want the butts sent, Sam?"

He stared at me for a second before he answered. "The usual place, Danny."

"They'll be there tomorrow morning," I said.

He was still watching me. After a few moments he said: "Okay, Danny," and walked out the door.

I sat there silently for a while, thinking. Then I got up and went to the door of the little office. "Zep!" I called out into the shop.

He came running in from the workroom. "Yes, Danny?"

Time hadn't stopped for any of us. It was just a short run from the workroom, but Zep was out of breath. "Get on the other phone, Zep, an' try to scout up new warehouse space for us," I said. "We're gonna have to move everything tonight. Sam has all the places spotted."

He nodded quickly, sat down at the telephone, and began dialing. I looked at him fondly. He was okay. He knew enough not to waste any time asking questions; they could keep until after the job was done.

I picked up my phone and called Nellie. I didn't want to tell her I was going to be late again tonight, but there was nothing else I could do. She was approaching the nervous stage of her pregnancy and everything seemed to upset her. But she calmed down a little when I promised her that I would be home early every night after this and that she wouldn't be alone until the baby arrived.

Chapter Seventeen

I PUT down my coffee cup and got up from the table. I carefully skirted several filled cardboard cartons and walked around the table to where she was sitting, and bending, kissed her cheek. "S'long, honey," I said. "I'm off to work."

"Be home early tonight," she said, looking up at me. "I want to finish the packing."

"Stop worryin'," I told her. "We can always do a few things tomorrow before the movers come. They won't be here until eleven."

"I don't like leaving things until the last minute," she answered. "You always forget something and then you're upset. I want everything ready."

It really wasn't very much that we were moving. We were taking none of the furniture with us. We had bought everything new for the house and it was already out there. But women were like that. I remember my mother had been the same way when we had moved.

"Okay, Nellie," I said, walking to the door. "I'll be home early."

Her voice called me back. As I stood in the doorway, she came running to me clumsily and I held my arms out to her. She came running into them and rested her head against my shoulder, trembling. I kicked the door shut with my foot and stroked her hair. "Baby, baby," I whispered, "what's the matter?"

I could scarcely hear her voice, muffled by my jacket. "Danny, I'm frightened. Suddenly I'm frightened."

I held her close to me. The years had taken their toll even from her. I could notice a few tiny gray hairs under my fingers, and the closer the baby came, the more nervous she was. It hadn't been like this with Vickie; she hadn't been so nervous then. "Don't be scared, baby," I whispered. "Everything'll be all right."

She looked up into my face. "You don't understand, Danny," she whispered. "I'm not frightened for myself, I'm frightened for you."

I smiled reassuringly at her. "Don't be nervous, baby. Nothing will happen to me. I'll be all right."

She hid her face against my shoulder again. "Let's not move tomorrow, Danny, let's not move there. Let's find another place. We can wait."

"Don't talk foolish, baby," I said. "You're just nervous and upset. You'll love it, once we move in."

She was crying. "Don't go back there, Danny," she pleaded. "Please don't go back. You can't make things over again, you can't change what was meant to be. I'm afraid for you to go back!"

I put my hand under her chin and turned her face up to me. "Stop crying, Nellie," I said firmly. "It won't do any good. You're just making yourself hysterical over nothing. It's a place to live just like any other place—nothing more and nothing less. So stop trying to make it into something it's not, and try to be sensible."

Slowly she stopped weeping. "Maybe I was wrong," she admitted in a taut, controlled voice, "but I've got such a terrible premonition."

"I remember my mother saying that was one of the symptoms of her pregnancy—premonitions. Everybody has them."

She smiled doubtfully through her tears. I took out a handkerchief and wiped her eyes gently. "Forgive me, Danny," she whispered. "I was just being a woman."

I kissed her mouth. "Forgive you nothing, baby," I said, smiling. "That's the way I want you."

As the men brought in another machine, I walked out of the

office and followed them back to the workroom, where they put it down. Zep and a mechanic were already examining it.

"What's wrong with this one?" I asked.

Zep looked at me. "The usual thing, Danny," he answered. "Somebody got mad because there weren't any cigarettes an' took it out on the machine."

I looked at the machine philosophically. I was getting used to it now. This made the fifteenth machine in two weeks that had come in damaged. That was a curious thing about people, how they could vent their anger on a machine.

I studied it carefully. This one was pretty well shot. I turned to Zep. "Put it in the storeroom," I said casually. "There's no use trying to do anything with it. It'll only be a waste of time."

He nodded and I started back to the office. My secretary was just coming to the door.

"There's a long-distance call from Buffalo for you, Mr. Fisher," she said.

I crinkled my brow trying to think who might be calling me from there. I didn't know anyone up that way. "Who is it?" I asked.

"He wouldn't give me his name," she answered, a puzzled look on her face. "He just insisted on talking to you."

"Okay," I said, my curiosity aroused. "I'll take it. Make out another vandalism claim for the insurance company," I told her as I picked up the phone. "You can get all the dope from Zep."

She nodded her head and went out toward the workroom. I waited until the door closed behind her before I spoke. "Fisher talking," I said.

"Danny, this is Steve Parrish," a voice crackled in the receiver.

There was a good reason for this guy not giving his name. He was a salesman for one of the big cigarette jobbers who specialized for the most part in big black-market deals. He was the first guy I had contacted when I went into the business. "Steve," I said pleasantly, "what're you wastin' your dough on long-distance calls for? Yuh got money to burn?"

Steve's voice took on a confidential tone. "I got a big deal up here," he almost whispered, "and I wanted to check with you before I let it get anywhere else."

I sat down in my chair and lowered my voice to match his. "How many boxes?" I asked.

"A full truckload," his voice answered quickly. "All standards. One thousand boxes. You interested?"

Sure I was interested. Who wouldn't be interested in a thousand boxes of cigarettes when there was hardly that many in the whole town? "What's the deal?" I asked cautiously.

"Two dollars a carton, a C note a box," he answered.

I whistled. That was a lot of dough: one hundred grand. "They hot?" I asked.

Steve laughed metallically. "Don't ask questions, Danny. Stuff like that don't come out of the icebox these days. I only found out about them by accident because these guys have to unload and grab their dough. I thought of you right away."

"All-cash deal?" I aked.

"All cash," he replied flatly. "That's why you're gettin' the two-dollar price. If they had the time they could unload for three and a half."

"Where'm I gonna get that kind of cabbage?" I asked.

There was the faintest note of challenge in his voice. "If it's too big for yuh to handle, Danny, let me know. Sam Gordon's been after me for a long time to throw some stuff his way, but I wouldn't do that. I'm not out to cut your trade an' I know he's one of your customers."

He would know that all right. I had first met him when I was working for Sam. "I didn't say that, Steve," I said quickly. "I was just wonderin' where I could raise that kind of dough. How much time have I got?"

"No time at all, Danny," he replied. "The boys want their dough tonight. Maybe I better give Sam a buzz, he's got the dough."

My watch said one thirty. The banks were still open, but all I could get there was about nineteen grand that I had socked away in a safe-deposit box. All the other money had been plowed back into the business. I stalled for time.

"Can you wait a half-hour so I can do some figurin'?"

"If yuh ain't got the dough, Danny, forget it," he answered. "There's no use humpin' around. I'll call Sam."

I snapped my fingers. I had it. And he had given me the answer without knowing. "Look," I said quickly, "I didn't say I didn't have the dough. I just said I needed a half-hour to get it.

Then I'll call yuh back an' we can make up where to meet. I can hop a plane up there an' you'll have it tonight."

I heard a whispered consultation going on at the other end of the wire; then Steve's voice came back on the phone. "Okay, Danny, the boys say they'll wait a half-hour for your call."

"Good," I said quickly. "Gimme your number an' I'll call you right back." I wrote the number down on a scratch pad and put down the phone.

There was a clean fifty thousand dollars in this for me if I could pull it off, and that kind of dough didn't fall into your lap every day. I picked up the phone again and began to dial. The phone on the other end of the wire was ringing. If Steve hadn't been so quick to suggest finding another customer I wouldn't have had this idea. I owed him never-to-be-spoken thanks.

There was a click. An operator's voice sang through the receiver: "Sam Gordon Enterprises."

"Mame, this is Danny. Put me on the boss's through line."

"Okay, Danny."

I heard another click, another ring, and then Sam's voice: "Hello."

"Sam, this is Danny," I said.

"Yeah, Danny. what's up?"

"If yuh can use six hundred boxes of standards, I got a deal for yuh," I said quickly.

Sam's voice grew cautious. "I can always use 'em, but what's the deal?"

"Three bucks a carton, a hundred an' fifty bucks a box. Cash in advance. Delivery tomorrow," I said.

He hesitated a moment. "Sounds okay," he answered, still cautious. "But that's a lot of the long green. What if you can't make delivery?"

"I'll guarantee the delivery," I said confidently.

"S'posin' somethin' goes wrong?" he asked. "Then I'm out ninety grand."

I thought quickly. Sam's ninety thousand almost carried the deal by itself. I'd have to be a dope if I passed up a shot like that. "Look," I said, "you know the layout here. I got close to sixty grand worth of the stuff stashed away. The business, location options, and orders for new machines are worth another forty G's. I'll bring over the warehouse receipts and an assignment for the business an' you can hold onto that until the stuff is delivered. Then you give it back to me."

"An' if you don't deliver?" he asked carefully.

I laughed shortly. "Then the whole pot is yours. What d'yuh say?"

He hesitated a moment. "I can use the butts okay, an' I'm int'rested in the business, but not for myself. I'm out on my elbow there. I can't run it."

"So you'll give me a job"—I laughed again—"an' I'll run it for yuh."

He still hesitated. "Sure yuh want it that way, kid?" he asked slowly.

Fifty grand's a lot of dough. "You heard me, Sam," I said surely. "I'm willing to take a chance if you are."

He cleared his throat. "Okay then, Danny," he said quietly. "Come on over, the dough'll be waitin' for yuh."

I jammed my fingers on the telephone, jiggled the bar for a second until the dial tone came to my ear, then spun the long-distance operator. I gave her the Buffalo number that Steve had given me. When Steve's voice came on the wire, "I got the dough, Steve," I said quickly. "Where'll I meet yuh?"

"Good, Danny." Steve's voice sounded relieved. "Room 224, Royal Hotel. What time will you get here?"

"I'll be on the first plane I can get on," I replied. "I should be up there no later than seven tonight. Is everything ready?"

"The truck's loaded and ready to roll," he told me. "It'll leave the minute you get here with the dough."

"Okay," I said. "I'll see you tonight." I put down the phone and looked at my watch. It was almost two o'clock. I would have to hurry if I wanted to make the bank.

I went to the door of the small office and called Zep over. "Make arrangements for storage of four hundred boxes," I told him.

His eyes widened. "That's a lot of stuff, Danny. Where you gettin' it?"

In a few words I told him of the deal. He seemed worried. "You're takin' a hell of a chance, Danny," he said. "Too many things can go wrong. Maybe yuh better take me with you."

I shook my head. "Somebody's gotta stay here an' keep an eye on things. I'll be okay. You stay here. I'll call yuh as soon's I hit town with the stuff."

It wasn't until I was at the airport, waiting for the plane, that I remembered I hadn't called Nellie. I hurried to a phone booth and dialed home. She answered.

I spoke quickly before she had a chance to get in a word. "Baby, somethin' came up an' I gotta fly up to Buffalo on business. Don't wait supper for me. I'll be back in the morning."

"But, Danny," she cried, "we're moving tomorrow!"

"Don't worry," I said. "I'll be back in time."

Fear came into her voice. "Don't go, Danny, please don't go. I'm scared."

"There's nothin' to be afraid of," I said. "I'll be back in the morning."

"Then wait, Danny," she pleaded. "Wait until after we move."

"It won't keep, baby," I said hurriedly. "There's fifty grand in it for us an' there's no way of keepin' that kind of cabbage on ice. I ain't lettin' it get away from me!"

She began to weep into the telephone. "I knew something would turn up," she wailed bitterly. "I had a hunch—"

"But, Nellie," I interrupted, "it's fifty grand! Fifty thousand Uncle Sam dollars! We can do a lot with that much dough."

"I don't care!" she sobbed. "Sometimes I wish I never heard of money! Since you went into business, you're not like you used to be."

"When this is over, Nellie, I'll see that everything goes the way you want it," I promised desperately.

"You always say that," she wept accusingly. "But I don't believe you any more. You don't mean it. You'll never change! The minute there's a buck involved, you become an entirely different person. You forget everything else!"

"Don't be a fool!" I said heatedly. "This is a practical world. Without a buck, you're nothin' but crap, like everybody else! Maybe you're willin' to settle for that, but not me!"

I could hear the sharp intake of her breath through the receiver. There was a moment of shocked angry silence, then I heard a click and the phone went dead in my hands. She had hung up on me. I began to swear to myself as I searched my pockets for another nickel with which to call her back. Just then the announcer's voice came through the loudspeaker:

"Flight number fifty-four on runway three. Buffalo flight fifty-four on runway three. Taking off in five minutes."

I looked back at the phone, then up at the clock on the wall.

Quickly I made up my mind and left the phone booth. She'd feel better when I saw her with the dough tomorrow. Fifty grand can cure a lot of hurt feelings.

Chapter Eighteen

I GLANCED around the lobby of the hotel as I walked toward the desk. It was plainly furnished but neat and clean, just the type of hotel that a salesman might stay in. The desk clerk came forward to meet me.

"Do you have a single?" I asked.

"Yes, sir," the clerk answered, spinning the register toward me. "Sign there. With or without bath, sir?"

"Without bath," I said quickly as I scrawled my signature in the register.

"Yes, sir," the clerk said again. He punched a bell on the counter. "That will be three dollars, sir," he said, turning to take a key from the rack behind him.

I put the money on the counter just as a bellboy came up to the desk.

"Show Mr. Fisher to room 419," the clerk said, picking up the money and handing the key to the bellboy.

"Wait a minute," I interrupted. "Can I check an envelope here?"

"Surely, Mr. Fisher," the clerk said smoothly. "I'll put it in the hotel safe for you. Just write your name across the seal." He pushed a brown manila envelope toward me.

I took the envelope with the dough in it and placed it in the envelope that he had given me. I sealed it carefully and wrote my name across it as I had been told. I watched the clerk turn and place it in the safe, wondering what he'd do if he knew there was a hundred grand in that envelope.

He turned the lock. "It will be safe and sound here until you want it, sir," he said to me.

I thanked him and looked at my watch. It was almost seven

o'clock. "I don't think I'll go to my room just yet," I said to the clerk as if an idea had just come to me. "I promised a friend of mine I'd meet him here at seven—Steve Parrish. Is he here yet?"

The clerk looked over his shoulder at the key rack. "He's in, sir," he replied. "Shall I tell him you're here?"

"Please."

He whispered a few words into a telephone, waited a few moments for a reply, then looked up at me. "He says for you to come right up, sir. Room 224."

"Thanks," I said. I was already walking to the back of the lobby where I had noticed the elevator.

The gilt numerals on the door glittered in the dimly lighted hallway. I knocked. I could hear the hum of conversation that had been coming from the room suddenly fade away into silence.

The door opened slowly and Parrish peered out. "Danny!" he said, smiling when he saw me. He stepped back from the door, pulling it open. "You're right on time. Come on in."

There were three other men in there with him. They stared up at me from their seats. I turned to Steve. Steve's face was a little pale and drawn, but he held a fairly steady hand toward me. I shook it.

"I'm glad you were able to make it, Danny," he said.

I nodded my head without answering.

Steve turned to the other men in the room. "Gentlemen," he announced, "this is Danny Fisher." Then, one at a time, he introduced them to me.

One at a time they rose and shook my hand briefly. They didn't try to make any conversation.

"How about a drink, Danny?" Steve held a bottle of whisky in his hand.

"No, thanks, Steve," I replied quickly. "Never drink while I'm workin'."

Steve nodded as he poured himself a drink. "Good policy, Danny," he said, swallowing it. "Approve of it highly."

I looked at him closely. Steve had quite a few drinks in him already. I pulled out a cigarette and lit it. "Ready to get down to business?" I asked.

Steve looked at me. "I guess so," he said hesitantly. "You bring the money?"

I nodded.

One of the men got to his feet quickly. "Let's see the color," he said.

I turned to him and smiled. "You'll see it," I replied, "after I see the stuff."

"You got it on you?" the man asked suspiciously.

"Do I look like that kind of a fool?" I retorted quietly. "Don't worry, though. If the stuff's okay, you'll get your dough. Where you got it?"

"In a garage a few blocks from here," the man replied. "Want to see it?"

"You bet."

The man picked up his hat from a chair. "Well, come on then," he said, starting for the door.

The truck was loaded just as Steve had told me it would be. I stared at the neatly piled cases skeptically. I had a feeling that something was wrong, but I didn't know what it was. Maybe it was because everything was going so smoothly. I turned to the man I had spoken to back in the hotel room. "No offense meant," I said politely, "but this is a lot of dough. I'd like to score the load."

"That'll mean unloading every box and putting it back on the truck again," the man protested.

My eyes met his levelly. "Like I said, it's a lot of dough and I'd like to check."

He looked at the others and then turned back to me, shrugging his shoulders. "It's okay with me, but you won't get out of here until two in the morning."

"I don't mind," I said.

I looked at Steve wearily, then at the others. They were standing in a semicircle around me, their faces flushed and their shirts damp with sweat. "I guess it's okay," I said. But I couldn't understand it. That feeling still hung on. I shrugged nervously; I guess I was catching it from Nellie.

"I told you that right away, Danny," Steve said quickly. "You didn't have to check."

"For a hundred grand," I said flatly, "I check." I turned back to the others. "Who's driving the truck down?" I asked.

One of the men stepped forward. "I am," he answered.

"Okay," I said. "Then hop in the truck and drive me back to the hotel. We'll start from there."

"Now?" the man asked, staring at me.

"Now." I nodded.

"But my helper ain't due to show up till morning," he protested.

"We ain't waitin'," I said. "I'll ride down with you. This stuff's gotta be in New York by tomorrow morning."

The desk clerk turned toward me. "Yes, Mr. Fisher?"

"I had to change my plans," I said. "I'm checkin' out. If you'll give me my envelope—"

"Right away, Mr. Fisher," he answered in a tired voice. He opened the safe, tossed the envelope on the counter in front of me, and watched while I ripped open the hotel envelope and took out the smaller one that I had enclosed. "Everything all right, sir?" he asked with a yawn.

I nodded and put a dollar on the counter for him. "Fine," I said, turning away. His thanks followed me out into the street.

The truck was waiting under a street lamp. The men were standing around it. I climbed into the cab and handed the envelope down to Steve. Steve turned and gave it to the man who had done the talking in the hotel. He ripped it open quickly and peered into it. His fingers riffled the bills as he counted them.

Then he looked up at me and made a half salute toward me. I waved back at him and turned to the driver. "Okay, boy," I said. "Let's hit the road."

I glanced wearily at my watch as we came out of Newburgh. It was a few minutes after ten. I turned my eyes back to the road as my foot went down on the accelerator. Slowly the truck began to pick up speed. The road loomed white and clear before me.

I threw the engine into overdrive and looked at my companion. The man was sleeping with his head resting uncomfortably against the door. I was hungry, I hadn't eaten since yesterday afternoon, but I didn't dare stop. This load was too hot. Besides, if I kept on rolling I could make New York by noon.

The driver's voice cut into my thoughts. "I'll take over now, Danny," he said. "You get yourself some sleep. You look bushed."

"I don't mind driving a little while longer," I said. "This baby handles like a charm."

"All the same, you better knock off for a while," he said. "Your eyes are all red. You may not feel it, but you're tired."

"Okay," I answered, pressing my foot down on the brake pedal. The powerful air brakes hissed as they took hold. Slowly the big truck rolled to a stop. I pulled up the safety brake and moved out from behind the wheel.

He clambered in front of me and got in behind the wheel. "You better get some sleep," he said, lowering the safety brake. "You haven't slept since we left Buffalo an' you been up all night."

"I can sleep when this ride is over," I replied. "I'll feel a lot better then." I put my hands up behind my head and leaned back against the seat.

The truck began to move and the hum of the engine to fill the cab. I tried to take my eyes from the white line that ran monotonously down the road before us, but it fascinated me. There was something about the way it stretched endlessly before us, as far as the eye could see. A little white line running down the middle of the road. Stay on the right side of it and you were safe. Cross it and you were dead. Stay on the right side—the right side—the right side—the . . . right . . . side . . . I could feel my head lolling sleepily against the door. I shook it desperately, trying to keep my eyes open, but there was no use. I was too tired. Reluctantly I let myself slip into slumber.

I awoke with a start. The truck was standing still, its engine silent. Blinking my eyes rapidly, I turned to the driver, sitting next to me. "What's the matter?" I asked sleepily. "Is anything wrong?"

He was looking at me with a sardonic expression. He didn't answer.

A voice came from the other side of me and I snapped around. My eyes widened. I was awake now. A man was standing on the running board of the cab. There was a gun in his hand, and it pointed at my face. "Okay, sleeping beauty," the man was saying. "Rise and shine."

I started to lean forward, my hand reaching for the wrench that lay on the floor beneath my feet.

The man gestured swiftly with the gun. "Keep the hands up where I can see them, Danny boy," he said softly.

Slowly I brought my hands back to my lap. My mind was working furiously. I looked at the driver again. He was sitting absolutely motionless, his eyes fixed steadily on the road before him. Things began to add up. "You in on this?" I asked unsteadily.

The driver didn't answer. Instead the man with the gun spoke again. "What do you think?" he asked sarcastically.

I turned quietly toward him. "I got dough if you let me get this load into New York," I said desperately.

The gunman grinned at me, showing yellow discolored teeth. He spit a stream of tobacco juice toward the road. "We already got your dough," he said flatly. His hand twisted the door open and he stepped down from the running board, his gun still pointing at me. "Get out," he said. "The buggy ride is over."

"Ten grand," I said quickly, staring at him.

He gestured with his gun. "I said come down outta there."

Slowly I clambered down from the seat. The sky loomed dark and ominously gray overhead. It was going to rain. I could feel my anger rising. I had been a sucker. What a fool I had been! I should have known better.

My legs were stiff and weary and I moved awkwardly. I heard footsteps coming from the rear of the truck and turned my head. An automobile was parked directly behind us. They had probably been on my tail ever since we left Buffalo, waiting for a spot like this to jump me. The anger spilled over into my mouth and I could taste the heated bile rising from my belly. What a shnook I had been, shooting the works on a deal like this! I should have had my head examined!

The man coming from behind me called out: "Everything okay there?"

The gunman's eyes shifted from me to the man behind me. Desperately I lunged at him, my fist grazing his jaw as he instinctively jumped to the side. I shot past him and my feet slipped in the dirt on the side of the road. Frantically I tried to keep myself from falling.

A sudden pain exploded against the side of my head and I sprawled face-forward into the dirt. I tried to raise myself on my hands and knees, but there was another burst of pain in the same place and all the strength in my arms and legs ran out of me. The dirt was all around my face and a wave of darkness was rolling heavily toward me. I forced it back with my mind, but it was coming toward me inexorably. I could feel myself sliding into it.

Faintly, as if from a distance, I could hear voices. I tried to make out what they were saying, but some of the words weren't clear. One of the men was saying that Gordon wouldn't like this. Another was laughing sarcastically.

I let myself slide toward the darkness. Then a split second's thought raced through my mind before I gave myself completely up to the darkness. Crossed! Crossed right from the beginning! That was why Steve had kept talking about Sam when he called me. To make me think of him!

Then the thought was gone and I couldn't remember anything. I drew a deep breath and tried to pull myself up through the darkness. But it was no use. It was all around me now.

Moving Day

OCTOBER 3, 1944

THERE were hands poking at my shoulders. I moved slightly, trying to get away from them. My head hurt.

The hands kept poking at me. I tried to curl myself into a small ball. I wished they would go away and leave me alone. Just when I was getting comfortable. I had been cold for a long, long time, but I was just beginning to warm up when the hands started to bother me. I tried to push them away and rolled over on my back.

I felt a sharp stinging smack across my face. The pain of it shot through me and I opened my eyes. There was a man kneeling beside me, his face staring into mine.

"Are you all right, mister?" he asked anxiously.

I moved my head a little to see if there was anyone with him. He was alone. Then I became aware of the rain beating down on me. I began to laugh weakly. Was I all right? I had to laugh. That was funny as hell. I tried to sit up.

A sharp, splitting pain tore through my head and I groaned. I felt his arm tighten around my shoulders to support me.

"What happened, mister?" his frightened voice asked.

"I was jumped. Hitch-hikers," I answered. I couldn't tell him what had really happened. "They stole my car," I added.

His face eased into a smile of relief as he helped me to my feet. "Lucky thing for you I got weak kidneys," he said. "I heard you groaning in the ditch at the side of the road."

I stood there, weaving slightly. I was still shaky, but I could feel the strength seeping back into my body.

"You might have got pneumonia," he said.

"Yeah," I nodded. "I was sure lucky." I looked at my watch to see the time, but it had been smashed. "What time is it?" I asked.

"Five after one," he answered, looking at his watch.

I stared at him in surprise. I had been out more than two hours. My watch had stopped at a quarter to eleven. "I gotta get back to town," I muttered. "We're movin' today and my wife'll be scared stiff. She hasn't heard from me."

The man's hand held my arm, steadying me. "I'm going to New York if that's on your way," he said.

He looked like an angel standing there with the rain pouring down on his halo. "That's the town I mean," I said.

"Come on back to the car then, mister," he said. "I'll get you into town by two thirty."

I followed him back to his small Chevvie and climbed in the front seat beside him. As soon as the door closed behind me, I began to shiver.

He took one look at my blue lips and reached over and turned on the heater. "Lean back and rest," he said considerately. "This'll warm you up and dry your clothes a little. You're soaked."

I leaned my head back against the seat and looked at him with half-closed eyes. He wasn't a young man, I could see the fringes of gray hair peeping out from beneath his hat. "Thanks, mister," I said.

"That's all right, son," he said slowly. "It's what I'd expect any human to do for another."

I closed my eyes wearily. He was wrong. Some humans didn't even have the faintest trace of what he expected them to have. The quiet clicking of the windshield wipers was a very soothing sound. My thoughts began to come slower. Sam wasn't like that. Sam didn't give a damn who you were. Sam thought only about himself.

I was getting too big. Sam didn't like that. After all, I had latched onto this racket right under his nose. He hadn't wanted it then, but that didn't matter. Now he knew what he had missed and he had made up his mind to get the whole thing back. And he had it back. There was nothing I could do about it, either.

Nothing? I began to wonder, anger seeping into me. That was where Sam was wrong. I had worked too hard to give up this easy. I was through being his patsy. He'd pay for this. I'd been a fool to sucker for a setup like this anyhow, but it wasn't over yet. He'd find out. The anger had brought a curious warmth into me and I began to doze.

I felt a hand on my arm and I woke quickly. I looked around. We were just coming onto the West Side Highway.

The man looked at me. "Feeling better?" he asked.

I nodded silently. My headache had gone.

"Where can I drop you?"

I gave him my address. "If it's not out of your way," I added.

"Its okay," he said. "I pass there on my way home."

It was a quarter after three when we pulled up in front of my house. I got out of the car and turned back to the driver. "Thanks again, mister," I said. "I won't ever forget this."

"That's okay, son," he answered. "Like I said—any human being."

Then, before I realized it, he had put the car into gear and drove off. I stared after the car. I had forgotten to even ask his name. Funny world. Someone you know all your life tries to kick your teeth in, and a man you never saw before and will never seen again comes along and saves your life.

I watched the car until it turned the corner out of sight; then I turned and walked into the house. The superintendent was sweeping out the hall. He gaped at me, his mouth open. I guess I did make a hell of a picture. My face was all cut up from the beating I had taken, and my clothes were filthy from the ditch.

"The van's gone already, Mr. Fisher," he told me. "Your wife waited around as long as she could. She was very upset, but your brother-in-law told her to go ahead."

"My brother-in-law was here?" I asked in a husky voice.

He nodded. "He came down when your wife called him. Her brother was here already, but she was still worried about you." He looked up at me curiously. "Your brother-in-law gave me a message for you if you showed up."

"What?" I asked.

"He said for you to see him, he'd be in his office." He smiled slightly. "Your brother-in-law sure is a nice guy all right. He seemed worried about you, too. Mine don't care whether I live or die."

"Thanks," I said succinctly, and left the house. Sam worried about me all right. Ninety grand worth of worry. No, two hundred grand now that he'd taken the whole pot. No wonder he showed up when Nellie called him.

I walked round the corner and grabbed a cab up to his office.

I went past Sam's secretary without waiting for her to announce me. I opened the door and stepped into his office, closing the door behind me.

He was just putting the telephone down when he looked up and saw me. He held it suspended in the air while his eyes swept over me from head to foot. "Where the hell have you been?" he finally roared, putting down the telephone. "I was just gonna put the cops on your tail."

Something in his voice hit me the wrong way; it made the hair on the back of my neck crackle. "What's the matter Sam?" I asked in a husky voice. "Didn't you expect me?"

He got up from behind his desk and came toward me. I could feel his heavy footsteps in the floor beneath my feet. "You give a guy ninety grand an' he don't show when he's supposed to, see what you think?" he said roughly. "I thought you powdered with the dough."

If it wasn't me that was catching the wrong end of the stick, I could almost admire the way he operated. This boy was tough. Right down to his toenails. He played it rough, too, adding insult to injury. He was everything I thought I could be, but now I knew I had a long way to go. I stared at him. He wasn't fooling me any more, though. I'd had enough of that.

"You know I wouldn't do that, Sam," I said softly. "You know me better'n that."

He stared at me for a moment and then turned back to his chair and sat down. His dark eyes glittered. "How would I know?" he demanded. "Ninety grand is a lot of moolah. Maybe you were getting tired of your wife and wanted to blow town. You could have a dozen reasons that I don't know about."

My eyes locked with his and stared him down. "You just don't trust nobody, do you, Sam?" I asked softly.

He looked down at his desk. "I don't make a livin' from trustin' jokers," he answered sullenly. He glanced up at me again, his eyes bright and sharp. "Where are the butts?" he asked.

I shrugged my shoulders. "I don't know," I answered simply. The wrong guy was asking the question. I'd bet he knew the answer.

He sprang to his feet angrily. "What d'yuh mean yuh don't know?" he roared. "What happened?"

I could admire this guy. He didn't miss a trick. He was the greatest. "I was tooken," I answered quietly, studying his face for any flicker of knowledge. "I got hijacked on the way and dumped in a ditch. I'm damn lucky to be alive."

He went right down the line with his act, but I thought I could detect a false note in his anger as he pounded his desk. "I should've known better'n to give yuh ninety grand like that!" he shouted.

I smiled at him bitterly. "What're you yellin' about, Sam?" I asked quietly. "You lost nothin' on the deal. It was me who got cleaned. You got the whole business now."

"Who the hell wanted it?" he roared. "I need it like I need a hole in the head. I got enough troubles. I'd rather have the ninety grand!"

That was the first false note he struck. He was hollering too much for a guy who wasn't hurt. "You sure, Sam?" I asked.

He stared at me, his eyes suddenly cautious. "Sure I'm sure," he said quickly. "Now I'm stuck with the damn thing an' you besides. I gotta have you to run it. I won't know what to worry about first. How much you're gonna be clippin' me for or how the damn thing will do? I'd've been better off doin' business with Maxie Fields instead of a punk like you. At least he's got an organization."

I stared at him for a moment before I answered. The thought kept getting bigger in my mind. That was the second idea that someone had fed me in as many days. But this one was involuntary. "That's an idea, Sam," I said gently. "That's the best idea I've heard all day."

His mouth fell open and he was staring at me as I turned and walked out of his office. I could hear him roaring for me to come back as I walked past his secretary and out the front door. There was an elevator waiting and I got in. The doors closed and we began to drop down.

By the time I hit the street, I was sure I had it figured. Sam thought he had found a way to have his cake and eat it. But he was wrong. I would turn the cake into dirt in his mouth.

The same old sign was on the window: "FIELDS CHECK CASH-ING SERVICE." The same old dirt was on the streets. Nothing had changed. Nothing would ever change down here. I pushed open the door and went in.

A man behind the cage looked up at me. "Yes, sir?" he asked.

"Is Maxie Fields around?" I asked.

The man's expression changed subtly. "Who wants to see him?"

"Danny Fisher," I said harshly. "Tell him I got a hundred grand wrap-up. He'll see me."

He picked up a phone and pressed a buzzer. He whispered into the phone, then looked up at me again. "Through that door," he said, pointing to the back.

"I know the way," I tossed back over my shoulder as I move toward the door. It closed behind me and I was standing in the hallway. I stared up the staircase, then began to climb it slowly.

He was standing in the doorway when I reached the landing. His hard eyes were shining blackly in his round face as he watched me. His body blocked the entrance to the apartment. "What's on yer mind, Danny?" he asked as I drew near him.

I stared back into his eyes. "Yuh still like money, Maxie?"

He nodded his head slowly.

"Then I got a bundle for yuh," I said quickly. "But let's go inside. I can't do business in the hall."

He stepped back into the room and I walked past him. The apartment hadn't changed either. It was still a lush joint. I heard the door close and turned around to face him.

"How about a drink, Maxie?" I asked.

His eyes studied my face; then he turned and roared into the next room: "Ronnie! Bring two setups." Without waiting for a reply he walked around me and sat down behind his desk. He sat down heavily. The only sound in the room was his breathing. After a moment he looked up at me. "What's the deal, Danny?"

I sat down in the chair opposite him. Footsteps came into the room behind me. I looked around.

Ronnie was carrying two glasses in her hands. For a moment she didn't see me, then an expression of surprise crossed her face. Her mouth opened as if she was going to speak, but it snapped shut quickly. Silently she placed the two glasses on the corner of Maxie's desk and started out of the room.

He called her back, his eyes glittering. "You remember our friend Danny, don't you?" hs asked sarcastically.

She looked at him for a moment, then at me. Her eyes were dull and beaten. For a moment something flickered deep inside them, but only for a moment and then it was gone. Her voice was flat and lifeless. "I remember," she said. "Hello, Danny."

The years had changed her little outwardly. She looked much the same. But the spirit had gone, it had vanished and been beaten by the oppression of time. "Hello, Ronnie," I said quietly. I remembered it had been just like this the last time I had been here, but then I hadn't been looking for him, he had been looking for me.

He wasn't content to leave well enough alone. He had to rub it in, he had to make the most of his triumph. "Danny's come back to make a deal with me," he said, a note of power showing in his voice. "Nobody can keep away from Maxie Fields, baby. That's what I always said."

There was no expression in her voice. "Yes, Maxie." She turned and started from the room again, but he called her back.

"Sit down, Ronnie," he said roughly. "Sit down and keep us company."

Obediently she dropped into a chair near him. She sat there stiffly like an automaton, no emotion visible on her face at all.

He turned to me and picked up his drink. "Now, Danny," he said heavily.

I picked up my drink and sipped at it. It tasted good and the liquor warmed my belly. I held up the glass and looked at him through it. "A hundred grand worth of butts," I said simply.

He put his drink down without having touched it and leaned forward. "What about them?" he asked.

"They're all yours," I said quietly, putting my drink down beside his. "If you do me a favor."

He drew in a deep breath. "I know you, Danny," he wheezed hoarsely. "You give ice away in the winter. Besides, where do yuh get this stuff?"

"I got it," I said. "Listen." Step by step I told him the whole story—how I latched onto the butts, how I lost them. When I was finished, I could see he was interested.

"How're you gonna get them back?" he asked.

"I'm taking over Sam's business," I said confidently.

Caution jumped like yellow traffic lights into his eyes. "How do you figger?"

"Simple," I answered. I was cold as ice. "Remember what we talked about the day I drove you down from Lombardi's? Remember what you said?"

Maxie nodded slowly. "I remember." His eyes watched me carefully. "But is anything going to happen to him?" he asked.

I picked up the drink again, shrugging my shoulders. "You tell me."

"No, Danny!" There was a terrifying sound in Ronnie's voice. I turned in surprise to look at her. Her eyes were suddenly alive in her face. "You can't do that! Sam was the only—"

Maxie's voice cut her off. "Shut up, Ronnie!" he roared fiercely.

She turned to him, a frightened expression on her face. "Maxie, you gotta tell him—"

There was a movement from behind me, and Spit was standing at her side. I hadn't even heard him come into the room.

"Get her outta here!" Maxie roared.

Spit reached quickly for her hand, but she evaded his grasp and fled from the room, her hands over her face.

Maxie was breathing heavily when he turned back to me. He waved Spit to the chair she had just left. He stared at me for a moment. There was a greedy ring to his voice when he finally spoke. "How do I know you'll pay off?" he asked. "Yuh don't even know for sure if he's got 'em."

"Let me use your phone for a minute an' we'll know," I answered.

He nodded and I picked up the phone and dialed Sam's warehouse. Good thing I had worked for him; I knew everybody there.

A voice I thought I recognized answered the phone.

"Joe?" I asked.

"Yeah," he answered. "Who is it?"

"Danny Fisher," I said quickly. "I'm checkin' if my truck got in there yet. The big trailer from upstate."

"Sure, Danny," Joe answered. "We're unloadin' it now."

"Okay, Joe. Thanks." I put down the phone and turned to Maxie. He had heard the conversation. "Satisfied?" I asked.

His eyes were shining. I could see the dollar signs in them. "I get the whole load?" he asked.

"You heard me," I answered. "The whole load."

"Fair enough," he wheezed, struggling to his feet. "Spit and the Collector and me will cover the job ourselves. Before the night is over, the whole thing'll be cleaned up."

"Stay away from this guy, boss, he's poison!" Spit's voice was angry. He was on his feet, staring at Maxie.

"What's the matter, Spit?" I asked coldly. "Chicken?"

He turned to me snarling. "I don't trust yuh. I know yuh too good!"

Maxie's voice was heavy with command. "Sit down and shut up, Spit!" he snapped. "I'm runnin' this show!"

Slowly Spit subsided into his chair, his eyes flashing angry lights at me.

Maxie's voice was still heavy, only he was talking to me now. "It's a deal, Danny," he said slowly. "But there's no backin' out now like yuh did before. This time yuh try an' run me aroun' an' yuh're deader'n hell."

In spite of myself I shivered as I got to my feet. At the doorway I turned. Spit was watching me, his eyes filled with hatred. Maxie's were cold, his face without expression. I could see him breathing heavily.

"You make up the bill, Maxie," I said quietly. "I'll pay it!" I closed the door behind me and went down the stairs.

It was a few minutes to six when I paid the cab-driver off in front of my house. As the cab pulled away, I paused on the sidewalk and looked at the house. I felt tired and old and empty. It was good to be coming home again.

Suddenly I realized that I had never thought of any place else as home. None of the other places I had lived meant anything to me. None of them were mine, none of them belonged to me the way this did. Then, as I stood there, I thought of what I had done, and all the satisfaction of coming home drained out of me. Now it didn't seem to matter.

I had gone through too much. I had come a long way. I was not the same person who had left this house so many years ago. I had lost my childish wonder. Life was too grim. You had to fight it all the time or you would be nothing. There was no peace, no friends, no real happiness. This world was a war for survival. You had to kill or be killed.

My footsteps echoed on the cement stoop. It had taken me a long time to wise up. You couldn't feel too much if you wanted to get along. You had to close your heart and lock it against people. No one must touch you, for you were alone on the day you were born and you'd be alone on the day you died.

I put out my hand to open the massive front door, but it swung open before I touched it. "Hello, Danny," the voice said quietly.

There was no surprise in me. I had heard the voice before. It was the voice of the house that had spoken to me the day Nellie and I came to buy it.

"Hello, Papa."

My father took my hand and together we walked into the house as once we had many years ago. For a moment we didn't speak, there was no need for words. Then we stopped in the living-room and looked at each other. There were tears standing in his eyes. It was the first time I had ever seen him weep. His voice was low, but filled with a tremendous pride, and I realized as he spoke that his pride was for me.

"We've all come home again, Danny," he said humbly. "If you can forgive an old man's mistakes, we'll never have to leave what we found here."

I smiled slowly, beginning to understand many things. His voice was the voice of the house. It had never really been my house at all, it had belonged to him. When I had told the house of my love, I was speaking to him, and when the house spoke to me, he was speaking to me. It would never be my house until he gave it to me, no matter how much I paid for it.

I looked around the room. Something had been missing all the time, and now that he was here, the house was warm and alive again. I was glad that he had come. I didn't have to say anything either; he seemed to know just how I felt.

"It was the most wonderful birthday present I ever had, Papa," I said.

Then for the first time he became aware of the way I looked. "My God!" he exclaimed. "Danny, what happened?"

His words snapped me back to the present. "I had an accident, Papa," I replied harshly. "Where's Nellie?"

His face stared up at me. "Mamma's got her to lie down upstairs. She was almost hysterical with worry over you."

There was a sound at the top of the stairs. Nellie was standing there, her white face looking down at me. In the harsh white light of the still unshaded stairway bulbs I must have been a hideous sight. Her lips parted in a half scream. "Danny!"

Her voice was still echoing against the walls as I started up the stairway toward her. She took a small step down toward me, then her eyes turned upward in their sockets and she fainted.

"Nellie!" I shouted, springing to catch her.

But she was falling, tumbling clumsily down half the flight before I could stop her. She was a small huddled heap near the wall and I was on my knees beside her, my hands frantically turning her face toward me. "Nellie!" I screamed at her.

Her face was the white transparency of a bottle of milk, and her eyes were squeezed tight with pain. I could see her bloodless lips whispering in her agony. "Danny, Danny, I was so worried about you."

I turned wildly toward Papa. "There's a doctor in the corner house across the street," I shouted at him. "Get him! Quick!"

I turned back to Nellie, hearing the front door slam. I rested her head against my shoulder. Her eyes were closed and she was very still. She seemed to be hardly breathing.

My mother came down the stairs, a deep world of sympathy and understanding in her eyes. Wordlessly she pressed her hand against my shoulder.

I looked at Nellie again. Why did I have to learn so many things so late? I could see the whole thing now. It was my fault. Nellie had been right. I hugged her head against my breast. It couldn't happen, it mustn't. She was all my world. I shut my eyes tightly and prayed, the tears seeping from beneath my eyelids.

"Please, God. . . . Please . . ."

I paced nervously up and down the small hospital waiting-room. It seemed as if I had been there for days instead of only a few hours. I stuck another cigarette in my mouth and tried to light it. I broke three matches before Zep finally lit one for me and held it to my cigarette.

I looked at him gratefully. I don't know what we would have done without him that day. All day he had stayed with Nellie, calming her and helping her, and now he was here with me. "Thanks, Zep," I muttered.

Exhausted, I dropped into the chair between my father and him. "The doctor's been out an awful long time," I said.

Zep looked at me understandingly. He knew how I felt "Don't worry, Danny," he said, awkwardly patting my shoulder. "She'll be okay. The doctor said she had a chance and I know my sister. She's a scrapper. She'll come through."

That was it. She had a chance. The doctor had said that. She had a chance. I had to keep thinking of that over and over or I would go mad—stark, raving mad. All the way down to the hospital, riding next to her, her cold limp hand in mine, as we roared through the streets in the screaming ambulance, I had to keep thinking that.

She had hurt herself inside. The baby had shifted, the doctor said. There was a pressure inside her and she was torn and bleeding. All inside where you couldn't see it. You could only know it when you looked at her face, white and bloodless.

Quickly and efficiently they had placed her on a small white table and rushed her up to the operating-room. Her eyes were still closed, she couldn't see me. Through her pale lips came a thin small sound of pain. Then she was gone through the white doors and I had to wait.

That was more than two hours ago and I was still waiting. We were still waiting. I looked over at her mother, sitting on a chair by the window, nervously twisting a handkerchief. Her eyes were puffy with tears as she listened silently to my mother trying to console her. She hadn't said anything to me, but I knew that she blamed me for what had happened to Nellie. And in a way she was right. But still, if it hadn't been for Sam none of this would have happened.

There were steps in the corridor outside. Mimi was coming toward me, an anxious look on her face. "Danny, what happened?"

I didn't answer her; my eyes were fixed on Sam, walking behind her. There was a strange uncomfortable look on his face. "What are you doing here?" I shot at him.

"Your father called and told us Nellie had an accident. Mimi was too upset to drive, so I brought her out here," he explained.

I got to my feet slowly. I could feel my legs trembling with rage. My mouth was suddenly dry. "You satisfied now?" I asked harshly. "This the way you wanted it?"

There was a peculiarly shamed look in his eyes. "This wasn't the way I wanted it, Danny," he replied in a low voice.

I stared at him for a moment, then the pent-up anger in me

burst its dam and I stepped forward, my fist flying. I caught him flush on the jaw and he tumbled backward to the floor. The crash echoed through the small room as I started for him again.

Two hands grabbed at my arms. I heard Mimi's voice screaming at me. Desperately I tried to shake my arms loose. I would kill him myself. I was crying. He might as well have admitted the whole thing.

Then I heard the doctor's voice: "Mr. Fisher!"

Sam was forgotten as I turned and grasped the doctor's lapels. "How is she, doc?" I asked huskily. "How is she?"

His face, covered with weary lines, relaxed slightly as he looked at me. "She's resting comfortably, Mr. Fisher," he answered quietly. "She's in considerable pain, but she'll be all right."

I went limp, all the emotion drained out of me. I sank weakly back into a chair and covered my face with my hands. For once my prayers had been heard.

I felt the doctor's hand on my shoulder and looked up at him. "Can I see her, doc?"

"Not just yet." He shook his head, his face was grave. "Mr. Fisher, we have an outside chance to save your son's life if we can find the right type of blood."

I was on my feet again. I didn't understand him. "What d'yuh mean, doc?"

His eyes were on mine. "Your son wasn't badly hurt, maybe because he was premature and therefore small, but he has lost some blood. If we can replace it soon enough, he has a good chance of growing up."

I was pulling at his arm. "Come on, then," I said anxiously. "I got plenty."

He shook his head again. "I'm afraid your blood wouldn't do," he explained. "There was a mild Rh factor involved, and your blood would be incompatible. The type we need is one that only one donor in a thousand might have. I've put out a call for one already. It all depends on what time we can get him here."

A sinking feeling came back into me again. No luck. I slipped back into the chair. The doctor's voice continued his explanation. "The only chance your baby would have had anyway was by a Caesarean section with complete blood replacement."

That was no comfort. My son was alive now and he had a

chance. That was what counted. The despair worked its way into my bones like an ache.

Zep's voice spilled into my ears like the sweetest music. "Maybe my blood will match, doctor."

I looked at him gratefully, then back at the doctor. "Maybe it will, " the doctor said wearily. "Come with me and we'll see." He looked around the room. "If any of you would like to be tested, come along."

We all followed him out of the waiting-room. Mimi was helping Sam to a chair as we stepped out into the corridor. A few steps down we turned into a small laboratory, where a nurse was sitting, reading a newspaper. She got to her feet quickly as we entered.

"Check the blood type of these people right away, nurse," the doctor said.

"Yes, doctor," the nurse replied, already turning to the table behind her.

I watched her prepare the slides and place them near the microscope. When they were all finished, she deftly inserted one under the lens.

"I'll look at it, nurse," the doctor said quickly.

She stepped aside as the doctor bent and peered into the microscope. He shook his head and she slipped the next one into the rack. I held my breath until he had looked at them all. Then he straightened up, shaking his head.

"No, doc?" I asked hopelessly.

He looked around the room. My mother and father, Zep and his mother were watching him intently. He turned back to me. "Sorry, Mr. Fisher," he said sincerely. "No one here will do. I guess we'll just have to wait for the donor to get here."

"But it might be too late," I said weakly. "My son might— might—" It was the first time I had said those words: my son. But I couldn't finish the sentence.

The doctor's hand rested sympathetically on my arm. "We can only hope that he'll get here soon," he said comfortingly. "He might be here any minute."

The door opened and I turned toward it hopefully. Then I felt my heart slipping down into my shoes. It was only Sam.

Awkwardly he pushed his way into the room. There was a large bruise on his jaw, turning black. Mimi followed him. He looked at me with embarrassment for a moment, then turned to the doctor.

"Down at the blood bank, doc," he said in his rough heavy voice, "they told me I got a rare-type blood. Maybe it's the type yuh're lookin' for."

"We'll find out in a minute," the doctor said. He beckoned to the nurse.

I stared at Sam for a second, then walked past him out into the corridor. The laboratory door swung shut behind me. There was no use in hanging around; he could do me no good. All he brought me was trouble. From the first time I saw him.

"Danny! Danny!" Zep's voice echoed excitedly behind me. He was running down the corridor toward me, his dark face alive with excitement. "The doc says Sam's blood is the type!"

I stared at him, not believing my ears.

Half an hour later the doctor came into the waiting-room where we were sitting. There was a smile on his face. He came toward me, holding out his hand. "I guess you'll be passing out cigars after all, Mr. Fisher," he said. "Congratulations!"

I could hardly see his face through the blur in my eyes. "Thank you, doc," I said fervently. "Thank you."

The doctor smiled again. "Don't thank me," he said quickly. "Just thank God and your brother-in-law for being around! It's a miracle for a seven-month premature Rh to get even this far!"

My mother-in-law began to cry happily. Zep was hugging her. Mamma, Papa, and Mimi were crowding around me. Mimi's arms were about my neck, her lips against my cheek. My tears were wet on her face. Nothing else mattered—only the joy of this moment.

I turned to the doctor. "Can I see my wife now, doc?"

He nodded. "But only for a few minutes," he warned. "She's still very weak."

The nurse sitting at the side of the bed rose quickly when I came into the room, and I heard the door close softly behind me. I stared at the bed. Only Nellie's face showed above the white sheets, her bluish-black hair cascading across the pillow behind her. Her eyes were closed. She seemed to be sleeping.

I walked over to the bed and sat down beside her, scarcely daring to breathe for fear of disturbing her. But somehow she knew I was there. Her eyes fluttered open. They were dark brown and gentle. Her lips barely moved. "Danny." She tried to smile.

I put my hand on the sheet where I could see her hand beneath it. "Don't try to talk now, baby," I whispered. "Everything's all right."

"The baby too?" Her voice was faint and doubtful.

I nodded. "He's perfect," I said. "Everything's perfect. Don't worry now. Just rest and get well."

Tears gathered in her eyes. "I almost messed things up, didn't I?" she asked.

I put my face close to her cheek. "You didn't," I said. "It was me. You were right. I shouldn't have gone yesterday."

She tried to shake her head dissentingly, but it was too much effort for her. She closed her eyes wearily. "No," she whispered, "it was my fault. I should have known you would come home if something hadn't kept you. But I kept remembering how I felt the last time you went away and I couldn't bear the thought of living without you. I had such a feeling about you, Danny." The tears rolled down her cheeks silently. "That something terrible was going to happen to you—to us—and I would be alone."

"Forget it, we'll never be alone again," I said earnestly. "No matter what happens now, we'll always have Junior with us."

Her eyes opened and she looked at me. "Did you see him yet, Danny?" she asked almost shyly. "What's he like?"

I had caught a quick glimpse of him when I came upstairs with the doctor. He had stopped in front of the nursery and let me peek into the incubator.

Nellie's eyes were on my face warmly. I could see the faintest tinge of color coming back into her cheeks. I smiled at her.

"He's tiny and he's cute," I said softly. "Just like his Mamma."

An excited chatter was coming from the waiting-room as I returned to it. My hand was seized enthusiastically the moment I stepped in.

"*Mazeltov*, Danny!" my father was saying, a happy smile on his face. Everybody crowded around me, all talking at once.

My mother-in-law seized my other hand and planted a big wet kiss on my cheek. I grinned happily at her. From somewhere my father had obtained a bottle of whisky. Now we were standing in a small semicircle, the liquor in the paper cups making a small sloshing sound. My father made the toast.

"To your son!" he said, looking at me proudly. "May he ever be happy! And to your wife, may she ever take pleasure in him! And to you, may you ever take pride in him—as I do in you!"

The tears were in my eyes and they weren't put there by the whisky. I had waited a long time for my father to say that. Maybe I didn't really deserve it, but I wanted to hear the words anyway.

Papa raised his cup again. He turned to Sam. "And to my other son," he said quietly, "who made an old man see how wrong he'd been and now puts me further in his debt with his blood!"

I was bewildered. "What do you mean, Pa?" I asked.

Papa looked at me. "It was Sam that fought with me and made me realize what I had done. It was he who convinced me of what a fool I had been and made me go to you."

I stared at Sam. His face was flushing. Papa's voice in my ear seemed to be coming from a great distance: "And now he has saved your son's life with his blood. We both owe him a great deal. Me for bringing you back to me, you for giving your son life." Papa seemed to laugh a little. "A great deal," he repeated. "In the old days a man would have to repay in kind. He would have a right to our blood, even to our lives if he should want them."

I moved closer to Sam, a feeling of gratitude rising in me. My father was still talking.

"Now that you have a son, Danny, you will learn the pain of your deeds. Even those little things you think will bother no one will hurt him, and so hurt you. May you never know the pain I have known, the pain of having your child pay for your errors."

Papa was right. Maybe I would never pay for what I did, but my son might. I was still staring at Sam. He was smiling at me. Then I remembered.

Fields was waiting for him somewhere. And I had made the deal. My mind raced madly. There had to be a way to call him off.

I glanced quickly at the clock on the waiting-room wall. It was after ten. I had to reach Maxie now and cry quits. I had to. "I gotta make a call," I said wildly, and ran out of the waiting-room.

There was a telephone booth in the corridor. I ducked into it and dialed Fields's number hurriedly. The phone rang several times before anyone answered. It was a woman's voice.

"Is Maxie Fields there?" I asked harshly.

"He isn't in," the tired voice answered. "Who's calling?"

"Danny Fisher," I said quickly. "Do you know where he is? I've got to find him!"

"Danny!" the voice cried. "Yes, you've got to! This is Ronnie. You can't let him go through with it. Sam was the only friend you ever had! He was the one who made Maxie lay off you when you first came back; Sam swore he'd kill him if he ever laid a hand on you!"

I closed my eyes wearily. "And I thought it was you," I said.

"No," she answered, "he'd never listen to me. I came back because Ben got sick and I needed money for him. But it didn't do any good. He died."

"Sarah, I'm sorry."

I don't know whether she heard me, because the words kept spilling out of her like a flood. She was talking about Sam again—Sam and me. "You can't let him do anything to Sam, Danny. You mustn't! It was Sam who kept him from moving in on your business. He persuaded Lombardi to tell Maxie to lay off because he was taking it over and Maxie couldn't do anything about it. He was furious. You don't know how bad he is. You gotta stop him, Danny!"

"I want to, Sarah," I said fiercely. "Listen to me. Do you have any idea where I can find him?"

"He said something about going out to Brooklyn," she answered. "He said that Sam would probably show up at your new house tonight."

I sagged limply in the booth. That meant he was probably waiting for Sam near my house, and when we came back from the hospital he would be ready for him. I stared stupidly at the telephone. There was only one thing I could do now. That was to get home before anyone else did.

"Okay, Sarah," I said slowly, putting the receiver back on the hook. I left the booth and went back into the waiting-room.

I walked up to Sam and tried to keep my voice as casual as I could. "Can I borrow your car for a few minutes, Sam?" I asked. "I promised Nellie I'd bring a few things from the house for her, an' my car is still at the airport."

"I'll drive yuh over, kid," he offered.

"No, no," I said quickly. "You're still weak from the blood transfusion. Rest here a little while. I'll be back in twenty minutes."

His hand came out of his pocket with a car key. He held it toward me, smiling. "Okay, Champ."

I looked suddenly into his eyes. He hadn't called me that in years. I could see the warmth of his smile reach them.

"Everything okay, Champ?" he asked. Only the two of us knew what his words meant. There was a world of meaning in them.

I took his hand. "Everything's okay, Champ," I answered. His grip tightened on mine and I looked down at our hands. They were clasped together. Funny the way our hands were alike—the same shape, the same kind of fingers. I looked up into his face. His eyes were warm toward me and I loved him. He was everything I ever wanted to be. That had always been the way it was. In everything I did I tried to make myself over into him. I smiled slowly as I began to understand. "Everything's okay, Champ," I repeated. "Thanks, Sam. Thanks for everything." I took the car key from his fingers and started for the door.

My father stopped me. "Drive carefully, Danny," he admonished me. "We don't want anything should happen to you now."

"Nothing will happen. Papa," I answered. "And if it does, there'll be no regrets. I've had about everything there is to be had in life. I'll have no complaints, no kicks coming."

Papa nodded. "Good you should feel like that, Danny," he said solemnly. "But be careful just the same. "You're still excited over your son."

The powerful motor beneath the hood of the canary-colored Caddy convertible hummed as I headed the car toward home. I was glad I had Sam's car. It would make it that much easier for me to find Maxie, because Maxie would be looking for the car. I wasn't worried about him. I would find a way to square him off.

I sped down Linden Boulevard to Kings Highway, then left to Clarendon. At Clarendon I made a right turn and headed toward my street. I glanced in my mirror. A car behind me was blinking its lights. It wanted to pass me. I laughed to myself and pressed my foot down on the accelerator. I was in a hurry too.

The big car responded quickly to my foot and we hurtled through the night. I looked in the mirror again. The other car was creeping up on me. Then I got the idea: Maxie must have tailed Sam out to the hospital.

I eased my foot off the gas and the car slowed down to fifty. Quickly the other car crept up alongside me. I glanced out my window. I had been right. Spit's face was staring at me from the other car. I grinned at him and waved my hand.

Then I saw the chopper resting on the window in Spit's hand. He was raising it slowly.

"Spit!" I yelled at him. "It's me! Danny! The whole thing's off!"

The chopper was still coming up. I yelled at him again: "Spit, yuh crazy bastard! It's me, Danny!"

I saw him hesitate a second. His head turned toward the back seat of his car and I saw his lips move. I stole a quick look back there, but all I could see was the faint glowing of a cigar. Then he turned back to me and the chopper kept coming up. I remembered Maxie's words: "There's no backin' out now. . . ." It was Maxie in the back seat.

There was only one thing left to do. I stepped on the gas as the chopper began to blaze. I felt a sudden pain tearing me away from the wheel. Desperately I fought the wheel, twisting it in my desire to hold onto it.

For a brief second I was blinded; then my vision cleared. The car was rocking crazily on the road in the night. I looked across at Spit. He was grinning at me. I was seized by a terrible anger. A hatred for him and all I had been spilled over into my throat, warm and hot and sticky like blood. He was raising the chopper again.

I looked past his car to the corner. It was my corner, my street. I could see my house standing there, with a light in the window we had forgotten to turn off when we left. I would be safe if I could get home. I would always be safe there. I knew that.

With all my strength I twisted the wheel toward my street. Maxie's car was in the way, but I twisted the wheel just the same. I could see Spit's white face contorted in fright. Sparks blazed from the chopper, but I didn't feel anything. He'd have to get out of my way or I'd run right through him. I could feel the wheels lock, but I didn't care. I was going home.

There was a blaze of light and I could feel the car soaring into the air. I drew a deep breath, bracing myself for the crash, but it never came.

Instead I was a kid on a van moving into a new neighborhood. I could hear the gravel crunching under the wheels. It was daylight, bright daylight, and I couldn't understand it.

Something had gone wrong. Time had run off its track. My mind wrestled crazily with the thought. It couldn't be true. Things like this just didn't happen. I was back at the beginnings of memory.

Then it was gone and I felt the steering wheel shatter. One moment I was looking stupidly at my hands holding onto the remnants of a wheel that was no longer a wheel, and the next moment I was flying crazily into a looming, leering darkness.

Somewhere deep in the silent, noiseless dark, someone was calling my name. It echoed hollowly, metallically, in my mind, the syllables rolling toward me like the waves in the sea.

"Dan—ny Fish—er. Dan—ny Fish—er." Over and over again I could hear the voice calling me. Somehow I knew that I mustn't listen to its siren song. I mustn't listen to its sound. I mustn't even hear it in my mind. Desperately I fought against it. I pushed hard and closed my mind to its echo. A sudden pain rushed through me and I tensed in the excruciating agony.

The pain grew stronger and stronger, and yet it was not a physical thing that I was feeling. It was a vague disembodied pain that floated through me like the air I used to breathe.

The air I used to breathe. Used to breathe. Why did I think that? The pain filtered into me again and permeated my consciousness, and my question was forgotten. I could hear my voice screaming in the distance. Its shout of agony was ringing in my ears. Slowly I slipped back toward the darkness again.

"Dan—ny Fish—er, Dan—ny Fish—er." I could hear the strangely soothing voice again. It was soft and gentle and held within it the promise of rest and peace and relief from agony, and yet I fought against it, with all the strength I had never used against anything before. Again the voice faded from my mind and the pain returned.

How sweet the taste of pain when all else is gone from your body! How you cling longingly to the agony that binds you to the earth! You breathe the pain as if it were the sweetest air, you drink the pain with all the thirsty fibres of your being. You long for the pain that lets you live.

It was roaring sweet and agonizingly pungent inside me. The pain I loved and held so close to me. I could hear my distant voice screaming in protest against it and I was happy in the feeling. Anxiously I reached for it with my hands but could not hold it, for once again it slipped from me and I was plunging into the quiet, restful dark.

The voice was very close to me now. I could feel it in my mind as once before I had felt the pain in my body. "Why do you fight me, Danny Fisher?" it asked reproachfully. "I only come to give you rest."

"I don't want to rest!" I shouted against it. "I want to live!"

"But to live is to suffer, Danny Fisher." The voice was deep and warm and rich and comforting. "Surely you must know that by now."

"Then go away and let me suffer," I screamed. "I want to live. There are so many things I have to do!"

"What is there for you to do?" the voice asked quietly. "Remember what you said a few short minutes ago? The words you spoke to your father: 'There'll be no regrets. I've had about everything there is to be had in life. I'll have no complaints, no kicks coming.' "

"But a man says many things he doesn't mean," I cried desperately. "I've got to live. Nellie said she couldn't go on without me. My son needs me."

The voice was as wise and as tolerant as time. It echoed hollowly through my mind. "You don't really believe that, Danny Fisher, do you?" it asked quietly. "For surely you must know that life does not cease to exist in others for any man."

"Then I want to live for myself," I wept. "To feel the firm soft earth beneath my feet, to taste the sweetness in my wife's body, to take pleasure in the growing of my son."

"But if you live, Danny Fisher," the voice said inexorably, "you will do none of these things. The body you once inhabited is smashed beyond repair. You will not see, you will not feel, you will not taste. You will be but a shell that remains a living organism, a constant burden and agony to those you love."

"But I want to live!" I screamed, fighting against the voice with all my might. Slowly I could feel the pain returning to my being.

I welcomed it as a woman would welcome a long-absent lover. I embraced it and let it enter me. I could feel the sweetly welcome agony flowing through as the blood would flow. Then suddenly there was a moment of pure clean light and I could see again.

I was looking at myself, torn and twisted and shapeless. Hands were reaching toward me, but they stopped, frozen in horror, at the sight of me. This was my body and this was the way people would look at me forevermore.

I could feel the sorrowing tears mingling with the agony that was in me. Was there nothing left of me that might bring joy to someone's heart? I looked closely down at myself. My face was clean. It was calm and still. There was even the remnant of a smile upon my lips. I looked closer.

My eyelids were closed, but I could see behind them. The hollow sockets stared vacantly at me. I turned in horror from myself. The tears were running through my mind, washing away all the strange new hurt.

The pain began to slip from me again as the light grew dim and the dark returned. The voice was once more at the gateway to my mind.

"Now, Danny Fisher," it said sympathetically, "will you let me help you?"

I pushed the tears from my mind. All my life had been a matter of bargain. Now there was time for just one more. "Yes," I whispered, "I will let you help—if only you can make my body whole that my loved ones do not turn from me in horror."

"I can do that," the voice replied quietly.

Somehow I knew that it would be done and there had been no need for me to ask. "Then help me, please," I begged, "and I will be content."

There was a sudden loving warmth around me. "Rest then, Danny Fisher," the voice said softly. "Give yourself up to the quiet, peaceful dark and do not be afraid. It's just like going to sleep."

I reached out confidently toward the dark. It was a friendly, loving kind of dark and in it I found the warmth and love of all I ever knew. It was just like going to sleep.

The dark rolled around me in gentle swirling clouds. The memory of pain was dim and far distant now, and soon even the memory had gone. Now I knew why I had never known peace before.

I was content.

A Stone for Danny Fisher

Y OU *place the stone quickly on the monument and stand
there gravely, your blue eyes wide. Within you there is a
small but creeping doubt. Your father.*

*I have no shape, no rounded image, in your memory. I am
nothing but a word, a picture on the mantelpiece, a sound on
other people's lips. For you have never seen me and I have seen
you but once.*

*Then how can I reach you, my son, how can I make you hear
me when even my voice is an unfamiliar echo in your ears? I
weep, my son, I weep for all the life I gave you that I will not
share. The joys, the sorrows, I will not know with you as my
father has known them with me.*

*For though I gave you life, you have given me even more. In
that short moment that we shared together, I learned many
things. I learned again to love my father, to understand his
feelings, his happiness, his inadequacies. For all the things I
meant to him, in one short moment, you meant to me.*

*I never held you in my arms and pressed you close to my
heart and yet I feel these things. When you are hurt, I feel your
pain; when you sorrow, I share your tears, and when you laugh
there is a joy in me. All the things you are were once part of
me—your blood, your bones, your flesh.*

*You are part of the dream I was that still remains. You are
the proof that once I moved and walked the earth. You are my
legacy to the world, the most precious that I could bestow. All
the values are as naught when compared with you.*

In your time there will be many wonders. The distant corners of the earth will be a moment's journey; the deepest ocean, the highest mountain, perhaps even the stars themselves will be within the reach of your fingers. And yet all these miracles will be as nothing when compared with the miracle of you.

For you are the miracle of my continuing flesh. You are the link that joins me with tomorrow, the link in the chain that spreads from time beginning to time never ending.

And still, there is a strangeness in it all. For you, who stem from the roaring passions of my blood and strength and join me with tomorrow, know nothing of me.

We shared but a moment together, the moment of your awakening, and thus you know me not. "What are you like, my father?" you ask in the silence of your little heart. Close your eyes, my son, and I will try to tell you. Shut the bright green world from your eyes for just a moment and try to hear me.

Now you are still. Your eyes are closed, your face is pale and you are listening. The sound of my voice is the sound of a stranger in your ears, and yet, deep within you, you know who I am.

The lines of my face will never be distinct in your memory, yet you will remember. For some day, in some time, you will speak about me. And in your voice will be a sorrow that we have never known each other. And in that sorrow there will also be a contentment. A contentment that will come from the knowledge that all the things you are stem from me. The things that you will give to your son began with me, and what my father passed on to me, and his father behind him.

Listen to me, my son, and know your father.

Though the memory of man is a temporary thing because his life is but a fleeting moment, there is a quality of immortality in him that is as permanent as the stars.

For I am you and you are me, and the man that began with Adam will live forever on this earth. As I once lived.

Once I breathed the air you breathe and felt the soft give of earth beneath my feet. Once your passions raced in my veins and your sorrows wept through my eyes.

For once I was a man beside you.

I, too, had a charge account at Macy's; a bankbook at the Dime Savings; there are papers lying in some hidden vault with my signature scrawled upon them in now browning and aging ink; a social-security number buried in the mass of statistics in a government file with these strange numerical markings upon it: 052-09-8424.

These things I once had, my son. And for this and for many reasons other than this, my name will not be forgotten. For in these mere written records alone there is evidence of my immortality.

I was not a great man whose history has been recorded for children to study in school. No bells will ring for me, no flags descend upon their mast.

For I was an ordinary man, my son, one of many, with ordinary hopes and ordinary dreams and ordinary fears.

I, too, dreamed of wealth and riches, health and strength. I, too, feared hunger and poverty, war and weakness.

I was the neighbor who lived in the next house. The man standing in the subway on his way to work; who held a match to his cigarette; who walked with his dog.

I was the soldier shaking with fear; the man berating the umpire at the ball game; the citizen in the privacy of the voting booth, happily electing the worthless candidate.

I was the man who lived a thousand times and died a thousand times in all man's six thousand years of record. I was the man who sailed with Noah in his ark, who was the multitude that crossed the sea that Moses held apart, who hung from the cross next to Christ.

I was the ordinary man about whom songs are never written, stories are never told, legends are never remembered.

But I am the man who will live forever in the thousands of years yet to come. For I am the man who will reap the few benefits and pay for the many errors that are created by the great.

And the great are but my servants, for my numbers are legion. For the great lie lonely in their graves beneath their mighty monuments because they are not remembered for themselves but for what they made.

But for me, all who weep for their loved also weep for me. And every time someone mourns, he also mourns for me.

You open your eyes in slow wonder and gaze upon the six stones lying on my grave. Now you know, my son. This was your father. Your mother's arms enfold you, but still you stare *at the stones. Your fingers point to the words written behind them on the monument. Her lips move gently as she reads them to you.*

Listen carefully to them, my son. Are they not true?

To live in the hearts we leave behind is not to die.